THE NIGHTMARA AFFAIR

CALATINI TALES BOOK 2

KATHERINE DOTTERER

KatSpell Press

The Nightmara Affair

Cover by 100 Covers

Edited by Susan Bischoff, Lauralynn Elliott

A KatSpell Press Book

- ISBN 978-1-955614-06-1 (ebook)
- ISBN 978-1-955614-07-8 (trade paperback)

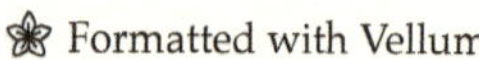 Formatted with Vellum

CONTENTS

ABOUT THE NIGHTMARA AFFAIR

In the kingdom of Calatini, an enchanted ballgown and a magical evening can change everything.

Orphanage matron Kiera didn't expect that sneaking into a masquerade wearing a bespelled ballgown would lead to a magical evening with the king, but for King Devon, it couldn't be more perfect. Kiera is intelligent, compassionate, and strong, everything he longs to find in a wife... and a queen.

And Devon needs a queen now: a generations-old treaty with the nightmara herds is due for renewal, and the matriarchal nightmara deal only with women. Yet when he asks Kiera to marry him, she can't believe he's serious—he's the king and far above her station. So to prove his love and win her heart, Devon convinces Kiera to act as his betrothed to negotiate with the nightmara for the good of the kingdom.

But once the treaty is signed, Kiera is certain their love affair will come to an end. She'll return to her life at the orphanage, and Devon will find a suitable noblewoman to marry. Because surely a king couldn't really marry a poor commoner like Kiera... right?

. . .

The Nightmara Affair is a warm-hearted Cinderella romance with a steel-willed heroine and a noble, kind hero. This rags-to-riches love story is part of the Calatini Tales series of Regency-inspired historical fantasy romance novels and is perfect for T. Kingfisher fans.

CHAPTER 1

"*Y*our majesty?"

Buried in the report on the rare ore unearthed in Magehaven, Devon hummed without glancing at his valet. The mysterious ore was disrupting all magic nearby and was just three days south of the Walle separating Calatini from the kingdoms ruled by magical creatures. Thanks to their longstanding treaty with the horse-like nightmara, Calatini was one of the few human kingdoms other magical creatures traded with, but if the dangerous ore's power spread, it could damage that thriving trade.

Devon grimaced. Almost as much as ending their four-century treaty with the nightmara would. To protect his kingdom, the Nightmara-Calatini Treaty must be renewed when the nightmara queen-heir Moonbud, who was negotiating for the elderly nightmara queen, reached Ormas in a few weeks with her delegation. Yet the treaty's renewal was uncertain because he was the first king without a queen to negotiate with the nightmara. And they would only negotiate with queens—dominant mares led their herds, so they didn't respect kings. But despite pressure from the council, he'd refused to marry for anything less than a grand love like his parents had shared. Now if only he could find the right lady...

Simon coughed. "Although your costume is simple, if you don't change now, you'll be late, your majesty. And they can't start the king's summer masquerade without you."

Devon eyed the clock on the mantel and winced. Engrossed in state affairs, he'd not noticed the late hour. He sighed. Ruling alone was a heavy burden. How had Father managed for twenty-five years after Mother had died? He'd only been king for four years, and sometimes his duties overwhelmed him. Perhaps it helped that Father hadn't needed to find a bride as well.

He sighed again and set down his reports. Not that he'd had success with that so far. And tonight's masquerade, the most exclusive of the season, wouldn't help him find a queen. He'd known all the ladies at court for years, and none were meant to be his queen. His chest squeezing, he rose. "Thanks for the reminder, Simon."

Devon rushed from his study and yanked on the simple tunic and hose Simon handed him. This year he was attending the masquerade as Calator, Calatini's first king. Once dressed, he slid on the silver, melissa torc of an apprentice witch healer like Calator had been before becoming king, but he refused the plain mask the valet offered. Why bother wearing the stifling thing when everyone would recognize him, regardless? Besides, given his uncanny resemblance to his distant ancestor, his costume was better without it.

Then he strode from his quarters with the two royal guards from the door, Stone and his senior guard Millier tonight, shadowing him from a respectful yet watchful distance like always. He headed to the anteroom, which led into the back of the teeming ballroom, to meet the beauteous Lady Annalise Greysnowe as they'd arranged last week.

He'd begun escorting Lady Annalise to court events over three years ago after rescuing her from Herrick Winston, a future baron and despicable fortune hunter. She was a refreshing companion due to her steadfast serenity and disinterest in becoming queen. Not that he'd ever marry her. He couldn't imagine kissing the icy beauty, dubbed Lady Snow by many at court, let alone making love to her. Plus, if he wed her, the centuries-long Greysnowe-Ravenstone feud would erupt like a hydra's many heads severed by an ordinary sword.

When he joined Lady Annalise in the royal anteroom, Devon chuckled at her resplendent costume. 'Twas as fitting as his own. The most beautiful lady in Calatini was dressed as an ethereal yet seductive siren, a magical creature who could enthrall nearly anything, from sailors to the winds.

Her snowy wings and waterfall of white-blonde hair fluttering as she swept a curtsy, Lady Annalise studied him with a cool smile. "Calator, I presume, your majesty?"

Devon shrugged and flashed a wry grin. Although simple, his costume was easy for anyone who'd visited the royal portrait gallery to guess. And most at court had at least once. "I thought it fitting, considering I'm now his age when crowned."

Lady Annalise's cerulean eyes flickered behind her feather mask. "So it is, but unfortunately, it'll encourage my parents' ambitions yet again. As Mother often reminds me, they named me after Calator's queen for a reason."

He almost grimaced as he took her arm. So they had. And the Greysnowes appeared to value Lady Annalise only as a means to best the Ravenstones. Once he'd begun escorting her, they'd spent countless hours attempting to force his courtship and make their daughter queen. If not for pity at her situation, her refreshing company, and not meeting his true queen yet, he'd have ceased escorting Lady Annalise years ago.

Flanked by his guards, Devon swept Lady Annalise into the buzzing ballroom and began greeting his guests. As they circulated, he scanned the ballroom for his best friend and cousin Aragon without success. Odd, Aragon had planned to attend—he'd said he'd be a gargoyle and his wife Selena a naiad. Yet they and Aragon's immediate family weren't there. And as Devon's closest relatives, they'd never missed the king's summer masquerade before. Hopefully, nothing was amiss with Aragon's parents, the Duke and Duchess of Childes, who'd always treated Devon like a beloved nephew rather than the king or a third cousin once removed.

Devon sighed and abandoned finding Aragon. He and Lady Annalise had greeted half the ballroom when the musicians began the first waltz, and he led her onto the floor with his guards observing from the outskirts.

While they glided about the ballroom, Lady Annalise murmured, "Though I'm grateful you've obstructed my parents the past few years, perhaps 'tis time you pursue someone you truly want to marry."

His throat tightening, he shook his head at her. "I would if I could find an available lady I could imagine marrying."

Lady Annalise tsked. "Surely not all the decent ladies at court are taken."

Devon arched a teasing brow as he twirled her in a complicated turn. "No, some are uninterested."

Gliding back into his arms, Lady Annalise shrugged. "'Tis fortunate I am. I'd make an impossible queen. If you wed a Greysnowe, even the *supposedly* genial Lord Ravenstone would explode like a dying firebird. 'Twould be almost as bad as if Alex had killed him at their duel on Summerday last month."

Devon shuddered. Thank the Goddess Lady Annalise had learned of her brother's duel with the enemy count. She'd fetched Devon to halt their duel then saved Lord Ravenstone after her brother had stabbed him near the heart. With remarkable cool, even for Lady Snow, she'd ordered everyone present to fetch a witch healer while she staunched Lord Ravenstone's bleeding.

Lady Annalise nodded toward Lady Blaine dancing with Lord Ravenstone across the ballroom. "You could see if Lady

Blaine would be interested. I believe she's on the hunt for a new husband now that she's completed her year of mourning."

He suppressed a grimace. The sultry countess had lured Aragon's much-older cousin into marrying her when she was just seventeen then devoted herself to remaining fashionable no matter the cost. "Thank you, no. She's attractive, but she'd not make a suitable queen."

As two of his and Aragon's cousins, Pippa and her brother Xavier, romped past, Lady Annalise smiled at the bubbly younger lady. "What about Miss Philippa Hawke? She came out this spring and isn't betrothed."

Devon chuckled and shook his head. "She's a cousin." Plus, Edouard, the new Count of Blaine and Lady Blaine's stepson despite being the same age, had been courting Pippa for the past few months.

Lady Annalise's brows arched until they disappeared behind her feather mask. "A very distant one. 'Twould be nothing if you wished to marry."

He shook his head again. "Perhaps, but being eleven years my junior, Pippa's much too young." And she'd reciprocated Edouard's interest, so doubtless they'd announce a betrothal soon.

Lady Annalise hummed then glanced toward the ladies clustered near the refreshments table. "What about Miss Winston? She's older than me, but not your age. And her slim dowry would mean nothing to you."

Devon eyed Miss Winston beside her mother Lady Winston. He *was* wealthy enough that his bride's dowry was irrelevant. And Miss Winston was pleasant enough. He grimaced. "Except then I'd be related to her brother." The fortune hunter he'd rescued Lady Annalise from, who many other ladies had been rescued from since then.

Lady Annalise quivered a delicate shudder. "No one of sense would want that." She sighed. "Although 'tis most unfair that court avoids poor Miss Winston due to her disgraceful brother and lack of funds."

He inclined his head. "True, but even if I wanted to pursue her, I suspect Miss Winston doesn't care for life at court." Although that and her other impediments wouldn't matter if they loved each other.

Lady Annalise sighed again. "She needs a wealthy country squire to fall in love with her." She pursed her lips. "Since none of my candidates have been satisfactory, your majesty, what kind of lady do you desire as your queen?"

Devon swallowed then drew a deep breath. "Mature and intelligent, yet compassionate and strong." And such a combination was rare.

Lady Annalise arched her brows then glanced over his shoulder toward the entrance and drawled, "What about Miss Keyes?"

He blinked. Wren? The shy lady would loathe being queen, and she loved Aragon's youngest brother, Hawke. "Although Miss Keyes possesses those traits, she belongs to my cousin Hawke, and she despises court events."

Lady Annalise glared at him. "A lady doesn't *belong* to anyone but herself."

Devon swallowed a chuckle. He'd riled the imperturbable Lady Snow. Amazing. He arched his brows. "She does when she gives him her heart." He smiled. "But so too does a gentleman when he gives her his."

Her eyes still narrow, Lady Annalise curtsied as he bowed at the end of their dance. "I *suppose* you could say that."

To distract her, he escorted her to the refreshments table and asked, "What made you suggest Miss Keyes?"

Lady Annalise shrugged as he handed her a flute of sparkling wine. "Nothing in particular."

Devon hummed. Something must have made her think of Wren. Perhaps Hawke had finally arrived. Not that it mattered.

Devon echoed Lady Annalise's shrug, then they began to walk a circuit of the ballroom.

Twirling her flute back and forth before her lips without tasting a sip, Lady Annalise was silent until they reached the entrance to the gardens. She flashed a glittering smile. "I'm sweltering in all these feathers. I must take a turn about the gardens to refresh myself."

He handed their flutes to a nearby servant. Walking in the gardens would be enjoyable. "I'll escort you."

Lady Annalise shook her head. "No, no. Half of court would follow if you leave too. I'll be fine alone." She swept a graceful curtsy then glided into the gardens.

Devon blinked. Lady Annalise was acting even more distant than usual. She must be serious about ending their association. If only he could find the lady meant to be his queen instead.

He sighed then began greeting the guests he'd missed earlier. Halfway through, his eye was ensnared by a mysterious lady in a mermaid costume slipping into the masquerade, and the lively ballroom seemed to still.

Tingling warmth flooded him as he stared at her. The mermaid's lush figure was sheathed in a fitted, blue-green ball-gown sparkling with pearls, shells, and scales. The shade of summer wheat, her dark-blonde curls were also threaded with pearls, moonstones, and shells. If only her shell mask didn't cover her face. Doubtless 'twas as lovely as the rest of her.

His heart stuttering into a new rhythm, Devon swallowed. Goddess, she was perfect. Who was *she*? He'd never felt such instant and visceral attraction.

Still staring at the mysterious mermaid, he fingered the three-stranded, gold bracelet on his left wrist. The powerful protection charm Father had given him on his sixteenth natalday defended him from enchantments, poisons, and unwanted pregnancies. Father had hired the royal witch and ordered her to create it after the only time Father had risked consulting the perilous Mirror of Wisdom. So Devon's attraction couldn't be due to a love spell.

When the mermaid finally met his gaze, he strode toward her as if they were alone in the ballroom. He *must* meet her at once. If her personality matched her beauty, she might be his true queen.

As he approached, the mermaid stilled, and her gaze never left his. But once he halted before her, the mermaid's navy eyes—the color of the moonlit sea, how appropriate—widened, and her sparkling skirt shifted.

To halt her flight, Devon raised his hand with a beseeching smile. "Wait."

CHAPTER 2

The evening of the king's summer masquerade, Kiera swallowed as she approached the palace. Although everyone knew 'twas at the center of Ormas, she'd never visited before. A poor orphanage matron from near the docks had no business at the palace. Yet tonight, she'd *had* to attend the masquerade.

Home to Calatini's kings since the kingdom's founding, the palace was stunning up close. Adorned with elaborate turrets and countless windows, the sprawling white castle glowed in the evening sun like a giant pearl. Nothing like the worn rowhouse orphanage she'd lived in her entire life.

She smoothed her serviceable dress when she finally spotted the servants' entrance. Gulping a bracing breath, she strode toward the humble door flanked by austere guards who eyed everyone with hands on their swords. Hopefully, she resembled one of the many palace maids, so the vigilant guards would let her past. They couldn't possibly recognize every single maid, right?

Her heart pounding in her throat, she lowered her eyes and nodded at the palace guards then bustled through the door as if meant to enter. She swallowed a sigh when they returned her nod without speaking. However, she maintained her brisk pace, so people would assume she'd been assigned an errand. She headed through the servants' areas toward the heart of the palace where the ballroom and the king's summer masquerade should be.

A ballroom she must sneak inside since she'd no invitation to the king's summer masquerade. Only court attended the most exclusive event of the season, and although her best friend Wren was the daughter of a wealthy baronet, Kiera certainly wasn't. Yet when Wren had mentioned the masquerade at luncheon yesterday, Kiera had burned to attend, even though such events rarely interested her.

No doubt her peculiar desire was due to her turbulent dreams the past week. Filled with passion and love and belonging, the dreams had consumed her nights, so every morning she'd woken hungry to experience something new. Although she loved the orphans and would never abandon them, every day at the orphanage was much the same.

This morning the dreams had been so vivid that straight after breakfast she'd visited the witch shop beside the Bedsfords' old miscellany shop. After all, the Bedsford twins claimed the owner of Rhiannon's Veils could magic anything like Rhiannon the founder of human magic. And a spell allowing her to attend the masquerade would be simple for such a powerful witch.

Forcing herself back to the present, Kiera swallowed then glanced around before slipping upstairs to the palace's main floor. Then she continued toward the ballroom until she reached a deserted hall. Glancing around again, she darted into a room and shut the door. She rested against the solid oak until her breath quieted and pulse slowed. Somehow she'd managed to sneak into the heart of the palace without anyone realizing she didn't belong. Now she just must activate her spell to attend the masquerade.

She extracted the shell mask from her pocket. Delicate and opalescent, 'twas worthy of a true court lady and the most beautiful thing she'd ever purchased as well as the most expensive. She'd never expected anything so fine when she'd visited Rhiannon's Veils and blurted to the veiled witch in the empty shop, "I need a spell to transform my dress into a costume fit for the king's summer masquerade."

Black veils concealing her hair and most of her face, the witch had tilted her head. "What do you wish to be?"

Unable to remain still, Kiera had wandered about the dim chamber, and the seashells on the cabinets holding spell ingredients had caught her eye. "A mermaid." She'd adored them as a child. Before she'd learned different creatures couldn't breed, she'd even fantasized her mother had been a mermaid forced to abandon her human child at an orphanage.

When the veiled witch had gathered the seashells, a silver mask, and strings of moonstones and pearls, Kiera had added, "I want the magical costs to be minimal." Since humans didn't generate magic, spells required payment in kind to fuel them, but that cost could be difficult to predict unless the spell was small with circumscribed influence.

The veiled witch had nodded then began murmuring a singsong chant as she fastened the shells and gems to the mask. Once she'd finished, she'd said, "Keep this in the sun until the masquerade to power the spell. If you charge it all day, its power shall last four hours, so use it wisely. To activate the spell, say 'muth-mhara.' The spell pauses if you remove the mask."

Kiera had asked how much then winced and extracted the requested twelve gold from her reticule without protest. 'Twas over half a year's wages near the docks, but she *needed* to attend the masquerade. She'd handed the witch the coins and accepted the shell mask. "And after the spell's power is spent?"

Her bracelets and tiny bells jingling, the veiled witch had pocketed her fee. "Then the mask shall be nothing more than a pretty trinket reminding you of the king's summer masquerade."

Kiera shook off her reverie and glanced at the small clock on the mantel—'twas quarter past the hour. From what Wren had mentioned about balls and masquerades over the years, the masquerade should have just begun, and the unveiling would be at midnight. Leaving while everyone else removed their masks would allow her time to disappear into one of these rooms and dwindle into a pretend maid again. She must hurry if she wanted to use the mask for the full four hours.

She inhaled and set her jaw then donned the shell mask and said, "Muth-mhara." A cool tingling engulfed her, and she glanced down at her serviceable dress, which had transformed into an iridescent blue-green ballgown with a fitted skirt that flared at her knees like a tail. Opalescent pearls, shimmering shells, and glittering scales adorned the fabric. Definitely fit for the king's summer masquerade.

Fingering the exquisite ballgown, Kiera shook her head then blinked at the extra weight. She released her ballgown to touch her head. Her riotous curls were threaded with strings of pearls, moonstones, and shells. Goddess, the veiled witch's magic was truly amazing. Well worth the twelve gold. Her costume would be equal to any worn by true ladies at the masquerade.

She straightened her shoulders then swept from the little room where she'd undergone her transformation. Her pulse quickening, she followed the strains of music until she reached the teeming ballroom. She slipped inside and gaped at the crowd as she skirted along the wall.

The costumes were even more extravagant than her own enchanted ballgown. Desert elf, troll, sultan, roc, fae, shepherdess, firecat, centaur, veiled seer, dragon, and so many more twirled about the ballroom. Although the king's summer masquerade was only held once a year, doubtless the guests would never wear these costumes again. Wren had mentioned court despised appearing poor.

Kiera shook her head as she eyed the guests. If they'd grown up truly poor like she had, they'd never squander their wealth so. They'd save it for something more worthy. The money spent on just one of their extravagant costumes could fund the orphanage for a month at least. Yet experiencing court's splendor was wonderful for one evening. And undeniably something new.

The dancing appeared delightful too. She sighed at the twirling couples. Not that she could risk participating. She'd only performed such dances when Wren included them in one of her plays for the orphanage. Kiera smiled. The orphans adored those ingenious plays because they allowed them to forget, for a short time at least, that their families had either died or abandoned them. But ball scenes in children's plays hardly equaled years with dancing tutors, so her inexpert steps would reveal her an impostor at once.

Her gaze halted on the couple gliding in the center of the ballroom, and she stopped breathing. The white-blonde siren was radiant, almost as much as an actual siren. Yet 'twas the siren's dark-haired partner that entranced Kiera. Although of superior quality, his costume was the simplest in the ballroom—tunic and hose like that worn during Calatini's founding, plus an apprentice healer's silver torc. Unlike the other gentlemen, his strong features weren't hidden by a mask, and he danced with purposeful strides. Considering his simple attire and serious air, the dark-haired gentleman must be a squire up from the country to attend the king's summer masquerade to find a wife.

A masculine drawl interrupted her, "What a *luscious* costume, lady mermaid." A gentleman dressed as a griffin seized her hand and kissed it. "Mr. Winston at your service. Have we met? Surely I'd remember meeting such a lovely lady, yet I don't recognize you."

Kiera stiffened as the gentleman ogled her with cruelty in his cat-like eyes. Nothing like the noble magical creatures renowned for taking lifelong mates and inspiring truth. He was clearly hunting a rich lady like she appeared to be, and he'd not stop at words. She wrenched her hand free. Unlike the true ladies here, she'd been exposed to many dangers growing up, so she could spot a predator with the same ease they spotted a miscut gown.

She shifted away, but gritted a smile. "I believe not being recognized is the point behind a masquerade, sir."

Mr. Winston smirked and slid closer. "No, the point is illicit dalliance, my luscious mermaid." Then he seized her wrist and yanked her to his chest.

Fire flaring through her, Kiera forced herself to remain passive as he drew her into an anteroom. If she defended herself like she normally would in front of the entire ballroom, everyone would realize she was an impostor. Then she'd miss the rest of the masquerade, and it had barely begun.

Yet as soon as she and Mr. Winston were alone in the anteroom, she gouged his eyes behind his mask with her free hand. When he dropped her wrist with a yowl, she thrust her knee between his legs and used his strength to knock him to the floor. Then she kicked him in the groin to ensure he remained down. And finally, she seized a heavy statue of a dancing couple and bashed him on the head, so she'd not encounter him again at the masquerade.

She panted as she smiled at the trounced Mr. Winston. Most unfortunate for the cad that he'd attempted to force an orphan from the streets of Ormas rather than a true lady. Perhaps men like him were why Wren despised court events. Her more sheltered friend hadn't learned to defend herself physically and, as an heiress, was their preferred prey. Not that Wren needed such skills—she never attended court events without Hawke, her childhood best friend who'd do anything to defend her. The pair were obviously in love, yet too scared to admit it.

Kiera shook her head and returned the statue to the mantel. She must cease musing if she was to experience more of the masquerade. But had she torn her enchanted ballgown in the scuffle with Mr. Winston? She smoothed her skirt, yet nothing was damaged. Then she checked her hair, and not a curl was askew. The veiled witch's magic was powerful indeed.

So no one would connect her with the unconscious Mr. Winston, she returned to the hall then circled around to slip inside the ballroom through a different entrance. She scanned the dancers for the squire and the siren, but partners had changed, and neither were dancing. She sighed. He'd never notice her, but she ached to see the dark-haired gentleman again anyway.

Shoving that aside, Kiera glided toward the refreshments table to sample the sparkling wine Wren had mentioned. 'Twas the one thing her shy friend liked about court events, and she'd never have another chance to taste it after tonight. But then an eddy further in the crowd captured her eye.

The dark-haired gentleman had stopped and was watching her with the same peculiar intensity consuming her.

She stilled. He'd noticed her, after all. Her heart surged as he strode straight toward her. She should leave. His scrutiny would shatter her disguise. Yet all she could do was stare at him as he approached.

He soon halted before her, his gaze riveted on her face. Goddess, he was even more handsome up close. His hair was the rich color of dark shokolat truffles, and his eyes were green like the ocean moss sailors sometimes brought back to port. But the expression in his eyes was more entrancing than their shade. Ardent, yet still chivalrous.

Kiera drew a ragged breath, her pulse pounding in her ears. He'd not want her if he knew she was but a poor orphan of unknown parentage. She must flee before he learned the truth. She began to step back.

The dark-haired gentleman raised a beckoning hand and rumbled, "Wait."

CHAPTER 3

When the mysterious mermaid shook her head without a word, Devon stepped closer and offered his hand. Now that they'd met, he mustn't allow her to flee. He must discover if she was the lady meant to be his queen. "Dance with me."

Her navy eyes wide behind her shell mask, the mermaid stilled like a doe before a tygris, the massive feline who ruled the torrid grasslands in the Tsarkan Empire south of Calatini. "I'm afraid my steps are inexpert, my lord."

He blinked at her, his hand still outstretched. Didn't she recognize him? Although he'd not bothered with a crown since his coronation, everyone at court always recognized him as the king. Yet he didn't know her either, so perhaps she was new to court. He'd find out when they danced. "Allow me to lead, and all shall be well."

The mermaid swallowed then licked her lips.

Heat flaring in his veins, Devon clung to his polite smile. He mustn't spook her with his overpowering attraction. "I swear I'm safer than an angel."

Her shells and jewels clinking, the mermaid tilted her head. "Some angels bear flaming swords to smite the unworthy."

He grinned. No angel would ever attack her. "Only the truly wicked, which you clearly aren't."

The mermaid blinked at him as the musicians began the next song.

Devon slid his outstretched hand closer. "Please dance with me. We'll miss the perfect waltz if we don't hurry." He stopped breathing as the mermaid eyed him. Goddess, let her accept.

After a tortuous moment, the mermaid slowly placed her hand in his. Finally.

His pulse surging, he wrapped his fingers about hers and drew her into the center of the ballroom. And although he burned to pull her against him, he was careful to maintain the proper distance as they began dancing. He must allow the mermaid time to become accustomed to his embrace. Besides, all of court was watching.

When she relaxed after several measures, he smiled down at her. "Your steps don't appear inexpert to me." In fact, she was graceful as a nymph dancing beneath the full moon and fit perfectly in his arms.

The mermaid smiled back as they continued twirling about the floor. "'Tis because I'm allowing you to lead, as advised."

Devon chuckled. Her grace was entirely her own, but saying so might fluster her. And now that she was at ease, he must learn more about her to determine if she was his true queen. He used a turn to pull her a shade closer. "Tell me your name, fair mermaid."

Her dark-blonde curls dancing, the mermaid shook her head. "No names tonight, my lord. That spoils the point behind a masquerade."

He grimaced. Plus, if he shared his name now, she'd recognize him as the king, even though tonight was probably her first time at court. And 'twas wonderful being treated like an ordinary gentleman for once. They could share names at the unveiling at midnight. 'Twould allow them to become acquainted first. "Very well, tell me where you're from instead."

The mermaid lowered her gaze. "No, my lord." She sighed. "Although even if I did tell you, you'd not know it."

Devon arched his brows. She must be from an obscure spot in the kingdom, if so. He knew all the towns and major villages in Calatini. As Father had always said, a good king was responsible for the wellbeing of everyone in their kingdom, not just the ones they saw at court. He leaned toward her. "Tell me anyway. I love learning about all parts of Calatini."

Her lips pinching, the mermaid shook her head again.

His stomach tightened. She'd leave if he continued asking, and he'd learned nothing about her yet. Perhaps she'd answer a less revealing question. "Then tell me about your exquisite costume."

The mermaid almost snorted. "My costume is only exquisite because 'tis enchanted."

Devon eyed her elaborate ballgown. Of course it was. Yet his protection charm was dormant, so her enchantment was on herself alone. Was it acting on more than her ballgown? "The most exquisite part of your costume is the enchanting lady inside it."

A blush darkened the mermaid's cheeks as her gaze flew to meet his. "I'm not enchanted, just my costume."

His chest lightening, he grinned and squeezed her hand while they twirled. "Even better." When she blushed more, he chuckled. "Why a mermaid?"

The mermaid looked away, but after a moment, she sighed then murmured, "I never knew my mother, so as a child, I pretended she was a mermaid who fell in love with a human."

Devon echoed her sigh. If only he could kiss the sadness from her lips. But they were at the heart of a crowded ballroom, so he just pulled her another shade closer instead. "I can understand that. My mother died when I was born, but my father often spoke of her before he died, so I never needed to create tales about her. I suppose your father was too devastated to do the same."

Her gaze still averted, the mermaid paled and clutched his hands.

He winced. He'd heightened her grief with his thoughtless comment. To distract her, he leaned forward and drawled, "You've not told me your thoughts on my costume."

The mermaid relaxed then tilted her head and eyed him. "'Tis simple, but it suits you. Who are you supposed to be?"

Devon waggled his brows. "I'm wearing the same apprentice healer's torc, brown tunic, and green hose as in the royal portrait gallery. You must never have visited." Thank the Goddess for that. She'd have recognized him as Calator's descendant if she had.

The mermaid gaped at him. "You're dressed as *Calator*? Did you have to request royal permission for that?"

He flashed a wry grin and swept her in a complicated turn. How could he explain without lying or revealing his identity? "As you said, the costume suits me."

A faint frown twisting her lips, the mermaid stared at him as the music faded. Then she attempted to step back.

However, Devon refused to release her hand or loosen his grasp about her waist. Although attraction still smoldered in his veins, he'd hardly learned anything about her. He required more dances to discover if she was the lady meant to be his queen.

Her frown burgeoning into a scowl, the mermaid slid her free hand from his shoulder to shove his chest. "My lord, release me. Even I recognize dancing the next dance together would be improper."

Devon arched a brow. Her pert protest was adorable. If they were alone, he'd kiss her scowl into a smile. "Consecutive dances are the least of the improprieties that shall occur here tonight. Why else would everyone wear masks?"

The mermaid stilled, but her adorable scowl remained. "You're not wearing a mask."

He shrugged and drew her a step closer. "I don't mind the

scandal if I get to dance with the most beautiful lady at the masquerade." Especially if she would soon be his queen.

Eyeing him, the mermaid pursed her lips. "Are you a rakehell then?"

Devon flashed an impish grin worthy of Hawke, who *had* become a rakehell rather than admitting he loved his best friend Wren. "Not usually, but you inspire me to be."

The mermaid snorted. "I'm not certain that's a compliment."

Tingling warmth suffusing him, he winked at her. "From a man it is."

As another waltz began, the mermaid sighed but settled her hand back on his shoulder. "Very well then, how many dances did you wish?"

Devon grinned as they began twirling about the floor again. "All of them, I think." That might be enough to become acquainted.

The mermaid gaped at him. "*All* of them?"

Aching to kiss her parted lips, he inclined his head. "Yes."

Closing her mouth, the mermaid giggled. "You must be mad to court such scandal for a mermaid you don't know." Her giggles extinguished like a firecat tossed into the sea. "Unless you need it to escape an unwanted betrothal..."

His heart squeezing, Devon smiled at her. She'd not care about that if she wasn't attracted too. "I'm not betrothed." When she opened her mouth, he added, "Or about to be betrothed." Unless he decided to propose to her.

The mermaid blinked then sighed as they swerved around a slower couple. "Am I allowed respite, my lord? I was about to fetch sparkling wine when you intercepted me."

He grinned. He could use some as well. He'd barely tasted the one with Lady Annalise earlier, and that had been ages ago. "We'll fetch some after this dance."

The mermaid poked his chest. "I'll hold you to that."

Devon chuckled and twirled her in a complicated turn that somehow ended with her pressed against him. His body tightened as their touching chests moved in harmony. Savoring her clean lavender scent, he eyed her parted lips then began lowering his head. Goddess, he must kiss her.

She stiffened. Her voice husky, she ordered, "Stop that."

Still hungry, he drew her toward him until her sparkling skirt tangled with his legs. "Stop what?"

"That!" The mermaid braced her hand against his chest. "All of court shall assume the worst."

Devon smiled at her. "About a delectable mermaid? Never." Although court would be wondering if their king had hit his head. He never flirted like this. Yet with her 'twas natural.

The mermaid shoved his chest again.

He sighed and allowed her to withdraw to the proper distance. Although he burned to kiss her, kisses wouldn't help him discover if she was his true queen. They must discuss more substantial matters. So he asked, "Are you excited for the nightmara negotiations in a few weeks?"

Tilting her head, the mermaid shrugged. "I've never thought much about them. The Nightmara-Calatini Treaty hasn't changed much since 'twas first signed four centuries ago."

Devon almost winced. Although his queen must handle the nightmara negotiations, only the royal family and the council cared about renewing the treaty. Everyone else just assumed it would continue. Had she noticed his slip? He must make his question appear idle. He forced a smile. "Have you ever met a nightmara?"

The mermaid blinked. "No, I've not met many magical creatures, but a nightmara would be an interesting one to meet, since unlike most other animal-like magical creatures, they can mentally talk to anyone thanks to their power over dreams and the mind." She paused and hummed. "Although perhaps not— meeting a nightmara might be unsettling since they can read every thought, control dreams, inspire nightmares, or even drive humans mad." She eyed him. "Have *you* ever met one?"

He swallowed to ease his aching throat. Of course, he had,

but he couldn't explain why without revealing he was the king. "Yes, at the coronation four years ago and the last treaty renewal twenty-one years earlier. I was horse mad at four, so the night-mara were fascinating. Imagine, a horse that could talk in your head."

Her eyes gleaming behind her shell mask, the mermaid smiled. "Many children that age adore horses. Even if they've no chance of ever riding one."

His chest warmed as he returned her smile. She sounded both knowing and fond of children. How wonderful. Then the music faded, so he escorted her toward the refreshments table. "Let's fetch that sparkling wine of yours."

After handing her a flute, Devon drew her toward the gardens. "We should stroll outside while we drink." Since they were no longer dancing, court would mob them to flatter him and meet her, so she'd soon learn his identity. Besides, perhaps he could sneak a kiss if they were alone.

Sniffing her sparkling wine, the mermaid allowed him to escort her outside without protest.

At the entrance of the gardens, he glanced back at his still-watching guards and flicked his fingers in the sign for the king's garden retreat. Millier and the other royal guards loathed when he lost them. If he simply left, they'd disrupt the masquerade to find him and alert court to their missing king. Then he'd never get time alone with the mysterious mermaid.

CHAPTER 4

Almost giggling at the bubbles tickling her nose, Kiera sniffed her sparkling wine and allowed the dark-haired gentleman to draw her out into the warm night. Perhaps she shouldn't—they'd just met, after all—but he was so endearingly determined, and she trusted him. Although intense, his eyes held none of the cruelty of Mr. Winston's. Not a predator, simply a decent gentleman intrigued by a mysterious lady.

As intrigued as she was by him. Tingling warmth suffusing her skin, she scrutinized the squire through her lashes while they strode down moonlit garden paths. He allured her like lavender flowers allured the huge bee-like melissae, and she'd never see him again after tonight. Besides, scandal from the king's summer masquerade couldn't follow her to the orphanage. So who cared what court assumed? She must seize her one chance for an evening with such a wonderful gentleman.

A wonderful gentleman in a dreadful rush. Kiera grinned as they raced past the palace's many gorgeous gardens. Their pace would have tangled her legs in her fitted skirt if her ballgown wasn't enchanted. He must be leading them to a specific garden. Hopefully, they reached it before she collapsed, and 'twas worth their haste. She'd spilled half her sparkling wine, and she'd yet to taste it.

The squire finally slowed at a small garden with a stone bench, a burbling naiad fountain, and trellises of fragrant roses.

As he closed the wooden gate behind them, she blinked at the secluded garden. Although lovely, it appeared no different from the others they'd passed. What made this one special? Not that it mattered. She shrugged and inhaled to calm her swift breath. Then she sat and sipped her sparkling wine, giggling when the bubbles tickled her throat.

The dark-haired gentleman slashed her a narrow glance from the gate. "What is it?"

Kiera giggled again as she swallowed another sip. "The sparkling wine tickled. 'Tis delightful." No wonder Wren relished it.

His gaze unreadable in the darkness, the squire eyed her as he settled beside her. "You've not tasted it before?"

She suppressed a wince and set down her nearly empty flute. A true court lady would have tasted sparkling wine many times. Even ones like Wren, who avoided court events. How could she explain without revealing she was an impostor who'd snuck into the king's summer masquerade? She studied his earnest face. And although they'd never meet again, she couldn't outright lie to him. "I've not attended many balls or court events."

The dark-haired gentleman grimaced then drained his flute and set it beside hers. "I often feel I attend too many. 'Tis nice on occasion to escape."

Kiera blinked at him. A country squire attended many court events? Yet she couldn't risk such a personal question, so she winked then nudged him. "To a secluded garden, perhaps?"

The dark-haired gentleman chuckled and nudged her back. "Only when escorting the most exquisite lady I've ever met."

A blush burned her cheeks. The radiant siren he'd danced with earlier was much more exquisite. The enchanted ballgown must be dazzling him like the sun dazzled pegasi. Yet she smiled and leaned toward him. "Thank you, kind lord."

Eyeing her lips, the squire tucked a strand of pearls back into her riotous curls. "So tell me, fair mermaid, what's your favorite color? Blue or green, perhaps?"

Her breath quickening, Kiera swallowed. "No, peach." She waved at the trellis by the gate. "The shade of those roses."

The dark-haired gentleman grinned then bounded to the trellis and plucked a rose. "You must have one then. Mind the thorns."

She blushed again when he bowed and offered her the perfect rose. Warmth flooded her as she cradled it in her palms and inhaled its sweet fragrance. Goddess, so romantic. If only they'd more than tonight. She managed a tremulous smile. "Thank you, my lord. Are you certain the king shan't mind your thievery?"

His gaze on the burbling fountain, the squire dropped beside her again. "A king would never notice one rose missing from many gardens."

She relaxed and almost chuckled. A king who squinted at every rosebush in the palace gardens then inspected guests' pockets for stolen roses would make an excellent character in one of Wren's plays. Kiera twirled the peach rose between her thumb and forefinger. "Likely not, but his gardeners might."

The dark-haired gentleman shrugged. "Then it shall be they who are vexed." He captured her free hand and kissed her palm. "You mentioned children before. Have you any siblings or children of your own?"

Tingling darted from her palm to her chest, and she muttered, "No, although sometimes it feels like I do." She tensed. Why had she allowed his kiss to loosen her tongue? Next, she'd be confessing her true identity as a poor orphanage matron from near the docks.

The squire chuckled as he threaded his fingers through hers. "Raised among a horde of cousins, were you?"

Kiera swallowed and forced a shrug. Being raised at an orphanage was nothing like being raised among family.

The dark-haired gentleman chuckled again and shook his head. "I've no immediate family either. My closest are some third cousins. The summers we spent as boys running wild together in the country were delightful."

She nodded, despite never having left Ormas. Although she almost had the summer she turned twenty. Wren had finally convinced her to visit the Keyes's country estate to celebrate Kiera reaching her majority. Then, Jane, the previous orphanage matron who'd raised her, had died from a fall that spring, so Kiera had assumed Jane's duties instead. Kiera's throat tightened even though Jane had been gone eight years.

When she remained silent, the squire eyed her and caressed her palm with his thumb. "Those summers were the few times I could act as a carefree child. At home, my duties prevented that."

Kiera blinked at him. Although she'd been head girl at the orphanage during much of her youth, even she'd the freedom to act as a carefree child. And at seventeen, she'd rescued Wren and Hawke from the docks, and the twelve-year-olds had rekindled her childhood. But discussing their disparate pasts might expose her, so she merely squeezed his hand.

The dark-haired gentleman coughed and slanted her a side-long glance. "If you could change anything about Calatini, what would it be?"

Kiera tilted her head, her shells and jewels tinkling. A serious question for a masquerade, and her answer wouldn't be that of a true court lady, except perhaps Wren. Could she risk revealing it? She studied the squire, who leaned toward her with his steady gaze fixed on her face—he burned for her answer. So she inhaled then replied, "I'd make basic education mandatory for all children. 'Tis appalling how many of the poor can't read and how they suffer because of that."

His green eyes darkening, the squire scrutinized her without moving for a long moment. Her stomach had begun to twist when he finally beamed. He raised her hand to press another kiss against her palm. "A most worthy goal, one I'd not considered."

She blushed as her pulse surged at his admiration. Of course, he'd not considered education. 'Twas readily available to a wealthy gentleman, but hers was hard-won—most like her had none. But as a shopkeeper's daughter, Jane had known how to read, so she'd insisted all her orphans learn. Then once they'd met, Wren had taught Kiera further studies and proper speech. And when Kiera had become orphanage matron, she and Wren had broadened Jane's education system, and several orphans had earned better livelihoods because of that.

Yet before he could ask why she'd chosen education, she shrugged and smiled at him. "What would you change?"

The dark-haired gentleman hummed. "Over the course of history, humans have never considered long-term consequences, especially around magical creatures. 'Tis what caused the catastrophic Stone Wars and our historic troubles with the nightmara. And as we've seen through our treaty with them, our lives are much richer with magical creatures."

Kiera gaped at him, her heart fluttering. With such a lofty goal, no wonder he'd never considered something like basic education. Yet why would a country squire care about such sweeping matters? Could he be part of the council who advised the king? 'Twould explain why he attended many court events.

The dark-haired gentleman smiled. "But perhaps we can remedy our troubles with magical creatures if we improve our understanding." He kissed her palm again. "And your idea about education would be ideal for that."

Her cheeks warm, she was about to reply when bells tolled in the distance.

Once the bells faded, the squire sighed. "I suppose we should return to the masquerade. 'Tis already half over, and someone might stumble upon us if we remain here much longer." He rose and drew her upright with a heated glance.

"But before we do, may I kiss you? I've been burning to since we met."

Licking her lips, Kiera eyed him. She burned as well, and a single kiss could do no harm since they'd never meet after tonight. She inhaled and tucked the peach rose in her hair. "You may. But just once. And nothing else."

The dark-haired gentleman arched his brows. "How cruel to only offer a sip of your bountiful ocean, my delectable mermaid. May I remove your mask at least?"

She wrested her hand free. If he removed her mask, her enchanted ballgown would vanish, and he'd know she was no lady. "If you mean to impose, I must leave."

Before she could move, the squire grasped her wrist. "I'm sorry. I'll restrict myself to a mere kiss if you like." He drew her into his arms until their bodies molded together then rumbled, "Is this imposing?"

Breathless, Kiera swallowed and shook her head.

The dark-haired gentleman stiffened. Then like a massive roc hunting an olyfaunt, he seized her lips in a fierce kiss.

Heat flooding her, she moaned and threaded her fingers through his dark-brown hair. Goddess, kissing had never been so irresistible. She parted her lips, and he deepened their kiss. Her body throbbing, she shivered as their tongues danced. So much better than dancing in the ballroom.

When he wrenched his head away, she yanked on his hair and mewed. Kisses, she needed more kisses.

The squire rasped, "No, my lady. One kiss, remember?" He gulped a breath then stepped back.

Her knees watery, Kiera wobbled without him. Right, one kiss. She'd not attended the king's summer masquerade to become a wealthy gentleman's mistress. "Thanks for remembering."

The dark-haired gentleman nodded and took her arm. He escorted her back to the ballroom, his pace as rushed as before.

They lurked beside the garden door until the current song ended. Then he swept her to the center of the ballroom.

As they danced, he kept her at the exact proper distance, and neither spoke during the first song. They only exchanged fleeting, hungry glances. But midway through the next song, he spun her in a complicated turn that ended with her pressed against his chest.

Unlike before, Kiera didn't leap back. Instead, she rested her head on the squire's shoulder. She'd only a couple of hours left to enjoy his embrace, and they couldn't go too far in a crowded ballroom. Who cared if court stared?

She and the dark-haired gentleman danced nestled like mated griffins for the rest of the masquerade. If only their evening together could last forever.

When the bells tolled midnight, she didn't rouse until the eleventh ring. Goddess, she must flee. The shell mask's power would end shortly, and she'd be revealed an impostor. Her heart twisting, she shoved his chest. "Goodbye, my lord."

Gaping at her, the squire released her and stumbled backward.

Without a curtsy, Kiera whirled around and darted between the other dancers. By the ballroom door, she careened into the radiant siren then bounced into the doorframe. Her enchanted ballgown caught, but she yanked it free despite the horrible creak of ripping fabric. She must disappear before the dark-haired gentleman recovered his wits and pursued her. Their wonderful evening would be ruined if he saw her as herself.

CHAPTER 5

*A*s the mermaid yanked her sparkling skirt free and fled, Devon thrust through the ballroom full of unveiling guests to catch her. But by the time he reached the door, she'd vanished. All that remained was a scrap of iridescent blue-green fabric snagged in the door.

His heart wrenched. He must find her, so he could reveal his identity and beg her to marry him. The moment she'd revealed her education goal, his visceral attraction had blossomed into steadfast love. Her vision, so akin to his own, had demonstrated compassion, strength, and intelligence. He'd met the lady meant to be his queen. At last.

Millier and Stone sprinting to join him, Devon hurtled from the ballroom to hunt the palace halls for his mermaid. Yet he and his guards found nothing, despite checking every room and asking every servant if they'd seen her. When dawn pinked the sky, he trudged back to the ballroom. The piece of ballgown in the door was his only clue. Since 'twas enchanted, perhaps the royal witch could use it to trace her.

He blinked as he collected the ragged scrap of fabric. It had dwindled to a faded blue. Whatever spell enchanting it had ended. Hopefully, Lady Juliet, the most illustrious witch in Calatini, could still use it. He folded the scrap in his pocketcloth then headed to the royal witch's wing.

At his knock, the door glided open, and the little maid's eyes widened as she bobbed a curtsy. "I'll fetch Lady Juliet, your majesty."

After ordering his guards to remain outside, Devon hastened into the royal witch's immaculate and stylish chambers. Rubbing his heavy eyes, he paced as he waited. He'd succumb to slumber if he stopped moving.

Wrapped in a modish dressing gown, with her hair loose rather than in its usual elaborate coiffure, Lady Juliet whisked into the room. "What brings you by so early, your majesty?"

Weight compressing his chest, he extracted his pocketcloth and unfolded it to reveal the blue scrap. "I met a mysterious mermaid at the masquerade. I must find her. She snagged her enchanted ballgown in her haste to flee. Can you use it to trace her?"

The royal witch hummed and accepted his pocketcloth. Her brow furrowed as she peered at the scrap.

Devon tensed. What could she sense? Please let it lead to his mermaid.

Yet after a long moment, Lady Juliet shook her head then returned his pocketcloth. "Unfortunately not. Only wisps of magic remain in your mermaid's fabric, and using a tracing spell would erase those wisps before my spell found her. You'd be left with nothing more than a scrap of fabric. I'm sorry."

He swallowed as he slipped his pocketcloth back inside his costume. "Thank you for your assistance, Lady Juliet."

His limbs heavy, he plodded to his chambers with his guards. How else could he find his mermaid? She'd avoided revealing many concrete clues. But she must be new to court since he'd never met her and she didn't recognize him. Yet she appeared near his age, so she wasn't new to society. She simply must have lived in the country until recently. No wonder she'd drooped when he'd mentioned his childhood summers with Aragon and his brothers.

Devon sighed. Although he'd few clues, he must find his mermaid. Once he did, she'd accept his proposal, and they'd spend the rest of their lives together. Their rapport and attraction had been too intense for his love to be one-sided. But since he knew so little, the only way to find his mermaid would be to attend a variety of court events.

He grimaced as he and his guards neared the royal wing. Yet with the nightmara delegation arriving soon, he'd be unable to attend many court events. He'd too much to prepare for renewing the treaty, which would be thorny since 'twas the first time a king was negotiating rather than a queen. Although perhaps he might find his mermaid before the nightmara arrived and solve that.

Devon relaxed when he closed his door and his guards remained outside. Alone at last. Not bothering to ring for Simon, he tore off his costume and staggered into bed. He must snatch a few hours' sleep before the council meeting. Thankfully, 'twas scheduled for the afternoon because of the masquerade, rather than the morning like usual. But explaining his intention to find and marry his mermaid would be enjoyable. No doubt the Tsarkan Empire would hear the councilors' screams when he did.

DEVON JOLTED awake when Simon brought a luncheon tray hours later. He groaned and rubbed his eyes. Although he ached for more sleep and his mermaid had pervaded his dreams, he must rise to attend that council meeting. His stomach rumbled at the scent of whitekrab soup, fresh bread, and tea—he was ravenous after dancing all evening, hunting for his vanished mermaid until dawn, and missing breakfast.

He rolled from bed and bolted luncheon. Then he dressed in the clothes Simon handed him before bounding down to the council room with his guards. Time to throw a rock at the melissae hive. Hopefully, he'd not get stung. Although melissae produced healing ambrosia, their stings were deadly. Not unlike the council.

As his guards halted before the door, Devon strode inside the council room and nodded at his twelve councilors, one for each of Calatini's duchies. Nominated by the ducal families every five years, most had served on the council since before he'd become king. Councilors were among the most influential members of court since they served as his advisors and headed government ministries, so most refused to relinquish their position until they were too old or ill to perform their duties. Aragon's father was one of the few who had done so when the latest term had begun. Devon had enjoyed having his best friend on the council for the past two years. He always had an ally, even when he proposed unpopular intentions—like he would today.

He sat at the head of the table with a firm smile. "Afternoon, everyone. Shall we proceed?"

Lord Farson, Aragon's cousin by marriage who served as the Minister of Internal Relations and represented the Golddell duchy containing the Nightmara Plains, sighed with a frown between his brows. "I apologize for continuing to harp on this, your majesty, but your unwed status must be addressed. The nightmara queen-heir and her delegation arrive in under three weeks, and they've always refused to negotiate with kings in the past. We need a queen to negotiate."

Devon's jaw tightened, but he forced himself not to glare at Lord Farson. The baron's concern wasn't misplaced, but he and the other councilors always spoke as if Devon could marry any lady regardless of compatibility or love. And Lord Farson had married for love, so he should understand why Devon refused to settle for less.

The Duchess of Wildewall, the Minister of Justice who'd the misfortune to rule the feuding Greysnowes and Ravenstones, sighed and shook her head. "Lord Greysnowe informed me *again* that his daughter's hand is available. He was riled you neglected her at the masquerade, your majesty."

Devon tapped the table with his finger. Not surprising the ambitious count had mentioned that yet again. "Although I enjoy her company, I'm not marrying Lady Annalise. I don't love her, and she's no interest in becoming queen." He arched a pointed brow at the duchess. "Besides, the Greysnowe-Ravenstone feud would shatter your duchy if I did."

The Duchess of Wildewall grimaced. "I know, but I swore I'd relay Lord Greysnowe's message, so he'd cease pestering me at the masquerade."

The elderly Duke of Osbourne, who'd been the Minister of Intelligence since before Devon's father had become king, laced his fingers then creaked, "Yet you must marry someone, or be betrothed at least, before the nightmara arrive. As Lord Farson said, we need a queen to negotiate the treaty."

Devon narrowed his eyes at the duke. "And as *I've* said, I need a queen I can love. Being king is onerous enough without being tied to a partner chosen for mere expediency." He inhaled then flicked his fingers. "Fortunately, I've met my future queen at last."

None of the councilors, not even Aragon, spoke at Devon's announcement. Instead, they tensed and gaped at him.

To remind them a love spell or other enchantment hadn't created his sudden determination, he fingered the protection charm on his left wrist. "And I'll propose as soon as I find her again. Although that may take time since she left without telling me her name."

The council room remained silent until Lady Morwynne, the Minister of Health and Community, tilted her head and drawled, "I assume by *her*, you mean that mermaid you cavorted with at the masquerade. A queen should know better than to accept every dance with the same partner."

Devon glared at the superior countess. How dare she insult her future queen? His mermaid eclipsed her and every other lady at court. "She only accepted every dance with me because *I* begged her. I couldn't release her after having finally met her."

Before the others could respond, Aragon, who sat at Devon's right hand, slanted him a concerned glance then asked, "But if your lady vanished without revealing her name, how shall you find her before the nightmara arrive?"

Devon set his jaw then shrugged. "I'll use whatever means are necessary. I shan't marry another, not even for the historic Nightmara-Calatini Treaty."

Another terrible hush swept across the council room. Doubtless the councilors feared his means included the Mirror of Wisdom. A faegift Mother had given Father during their courtship, the Mirror of Wisdom could answer any question. Yet the enchanted mirror drew its power from the questioner and could even kill them, like it had Mother. Father had forbidden its use after that and had only risked using it once—before he'd commissioned Devon's protection charm.

Devon met the councilors' silent stares without blinking. Not that he'd risk the Mirror of Wisdom's perilous power. He was the last of the Vireni line, and his family had ruled Calatini since its founding a millennium ago. If he died without an heir, the council would have to elect a new king, and Calatini might be thrown into chaos. So he could only attend court events to find his mermaid.

After a moment, he arched his brows. "But enough about my mermaid." He turned to Lord Islaye, the Minister of Magic who also represented the Magehaven duchy. "Any updates on that mysterious ore found just south of the Walle in Magehaven?"

The studious count sighed and shook his head. "The magical disturbance from the ore appears to be slowly spreading. But my magic marshals have been able to contain the ore so far, even though they're more accustomed to capturing rogue witches. The land rangers Lord Nolan sent to help identify the ore arrived yesterday."

Lord Nolan, the Minister of Natural Resources, nodded.

"Hopefully, between my land rangers and the magic marshals, we'll learn how to handle the mysterious ore soon."

Devon smiled at the bluff baron. "Good." He eyed the rest of the council. "Anything else to discuss?" When no one replied, he continued, "Then that's all for today."

All the councilors except Aragon bowed then left the council room.

Devon relaxed when only he and Aragon remained. Finally, he could discuss his mermaid with his trusted friend.

Aragon eyed him. "So, a mermaid? What's she like?"

Devon sighed with a faint smile. "She's without airs, has a core of strength, and values serving others. When I asked what she'd change about Calatini, she said she'd educate the poor to improve their lives."

Aragon blinked. "Compassionate, astute, and equitable. Impressive."

His chest lightening, Devon grinned at his friend. Of course, a dedicated gentleman like Aragon would be impressed by the mermaid's goal. "Exactly the queen I was seeking. Now I know how you felt when you stumbled upon Selena in that brothel."

Aragon coughed and shifted in his seat. "Hopefully, you don't have to handle a disreputable uncle and his black witch like I did." He clapped Devon's shoulder. "I'm disappointed I didn't meet your mermaid."

Devon arched a teasing brow. "Yes, where were you? You'd said you and Selena would attend the masquerade."

Aragon smiled. "Selena didn't feel well enough."

Devon frowned at him. Why did a gentleman who adored his wife appear pleased she was unwell? "Nothing serious, I trust."

Aragon's smile burst into a proud grin. "Depends on if you consider being with child serious."

Warmth flooding him, Devon squeezed Aragon's shoulder. "Congratulations!"

"Thanks." His grin still brilliant, Aragon inclined his head. "I expect we'll miss most court events in the upcoming months. Selena seems to tire easily."

Devon chuckled. Neither Aragon nor Selena would mind that. Renowned for her intense social rounds, Aragon's mother dragged them to many more court events than they preferred. "Until I met my mermaid, I wished I could skip the masquerade too, so I don't blame you."

"I appreciate the royal pardon." A grimace supplanted Aragon's grin. "Unfortunately, we must attend Kit's water party tonight since Mother and Father have a previous engagement."

Devon echoed his friend's grimace. Although fashionable, Lady Blaine's first event since her husband's death would be painful because she was hunting a new husband. "I've too much work to attend."

Aragon chuckled. "Liar. You simply don't wish to become a quarry in her husband hunt."

Devon flashed a wry grin. True. Besides, a lady fresh from the country wouldn't possess an invitation to such a fashionable event. He'd only time to attend court events that might lead to his mermaid. "With the upcoming nightmara negotiations and having to find my mermaid, I'm busy as a melissa in summer." He rose. "I really must attend those reports I mentioned. You go attend your pregnant wife."

Aragon laughed, and the cousins left the council room together. Aragon headed to the stables, while Devon returned to the royal wing with his guards. He handled his various reports then sorted through his invitations. Given his duties as king, he could only manage one court event each day, so he must pick the one his mermaid would most likely attend.

Over the next two and a half weeks, he managed to attend the court events he'd chosen, but his mermaid didn't. And every night, his dreams of her grew more and more vivid. He'd go mad if he didn't find her soon. During their weekly meetings, he barely avoided snarling at the council when they mentioned choosing another lady to placate the nightmara.

A few hours before the nightmara queen-heir and her delegation would arrive, Devon trudged across the palace grounds to inspect the nightmara stables with his guards following him. Since he'd yet to find his mermaid, he must negotiate with the nightmara himself. And with their negotiations so irregular, everything else must be perfect.

Since the nightmara knew him, Lord Farson would help them get settled when they arrived today. Devon would wait until after tomorrow's council meeting to visit, so they could rest after their lengthy journey. And he'd bring just two advisors, Lord Farson and Aragon, because Calatini's queen traditionally brought only the king and one councilor to advise her during negotiations.

Devon sighed. He'd considered hard before inviting Lord Farson and Aragon earlier this week. The nightmara already trusted the baron, and they'd approve of Aragon's conscientious nature, since they chose their leaders for their worth and abilities, rather than their lineage and wealth. Hopefully, his careful choice in advisors would help the nightmara forgive him for not possessing a queen.

He grimaced. Because he'd be unable to resolve that issue soon. During negotiations with the nightmara, he'd have even less time to attend court events. Goddess, let him find his mermaid before she left Ormas or, worse yet, married another. Perhaps if opening negotiations went well, the nightmara would use their power over dreams and the mind to help him find his mysterious mermaid. Given his lack of success so far, that might be his only hope.

CHAPTER 6

Three days after vanishing from the masquerade, Kiera was still mooning over the peach rose the dark-haired squire had given her. Except when working with the orphans, she stashed it near her. During the day, she hid the teacup containing the peach rose in the top desk drawer, but she kept opening her drawer to admire the perfect rose and remember the squire and their wonderful evening. At night, she placed the teacup on her bedside table and stared at the peach rose as she drifted into vivid dreams about the squire and his irresistible kisses.

Seated behind her desk to review the orphanage's accounts, she sighed and brushed the peach rose's velvety petals. They were wilting on the edges, and its sweet fragrance had faded— perhaps she should visit a witch to preserve it. She grimaced and shut her desk drawer. No, she shouldn't risk using magic for something so foolish. When the peach rose crumbled, she'd still have the shell mask to remind her of the squire. 'Twas hidden in the drawer of her bedside table. Unlike the rose, she'd no compulsion to stash it near her.

After tallying a few lines, Kiera opened her desk drawer to admire the peach rose yet again. 'Twas exquisite. Truly the perfect romantic token. If only she could see the dark-haired squire once more. She stiffened at her impossible yearning. Goddess, she was acting pixie-led. Clever and impish, the tiny magical creatures were renowned for leading humans astray and embroiling them in trouble. She mustn't allow the rose to do the same.

She fingered her throat. Yet she couldn't resist the peach rose's allure. Staring at it soothed the aching restlessness inspired by her turbulent dreams since the week before the masquerade. A restlessness that had only blossomed after meeting the dark-haired squire. Compassionate, unpretentious, and purposeful, he was exactly the kind of gentleman she could love—if he wasn't a wealthy lord far above her station.

Kiera slammed her desk drawer shut when Wren burst into her study. Her lively friend appeared exhausted, thanks to the play she'd stayed up finishing. After scolding Wren, Kiera eyed her blushing friend. Although Wren despised masquerades and wouldn't have attended herself, Hawke surely would have, and he shared everything with her. Perhaps he'd mentioned a squire who danced all night with a mermaid—their unconventional behavior would have inspired gossip. And maybe that gossip included the squire's name. She must encourage Wren to discuss the king's summer masquerade.

Forcing herself to remain relaxed, Kiera asked, "So has Abby forgiven you for not wearing that masquerade costume?"

Wren shrugged. "As much as she ever does."

Kiera drummed her fingers on her knee. Why was Wren acting so reticent? Kiera must be more direct. She managed a chuckle. "Next year you should wear the costume and pretend to attend to stop her fussing. Use tales from Hawke to convince her. What did he say about this year's masquerade?"

Wren shifted in her chair. "Not much."

Kiera almost snorted and arched her brows. "Really? But he usually shares everything with you." And why would Wren refuse to discuss the masquerade?

Wren leapt upright. "I must go. I'll return next week for play rehearsals."

As her friend darted from the study, Kiera frowned after her. Asking about the masquerade had made Wren bolt. Why? Her stomach lurching, she gulped a ragged breath. Had Hawke recognized her dancing with the squire? If Wren knew and didn't approve, she'd refuse to discuss the masquerade to avoid wounding Kiera. But Wren wouldn't care that her poor friend of unknown parentage had snuck into the most exclusive event of the summer. What if the squire had lied about not being married or betrothed?

Her chest tight, she opened her desk drawer to eye the peach rose again. Perhaps she should destroy the blasted thing. It kept distracting her, and who knew what of their wonderful evening was genuine? After all, she'd been disguised as a court lady. Would the squire's disguise be any less a lie?

Kiera reached for the rose, but just before she touched it, she jerked back and slammed the desk drawer shut. No matter how senseless 'twas to keep it, she couldn't destroy the perfect rose the squire had given her. But she'd not take it to a witch to preserve it either. She'd allow it, and her impossible yearning, to crumble to dust over the coming days.

YET AFTER ANOTHER night of passionate dreams about kissing the dark-haired squire, Kiera rushed from the orphanage straight after breakfast to find a witch to preserve the peach rose. Since the spell she sought was a simple one, she didn't return to Rhiannon's Veils. Although the veiled witch could magic anything, Kiera couldn't afford her prices a second time.

Instead, she visited a witch shop selling dried herbs and potions. The tiny shop catered to poor housewives, so its prices would be more affordable. After striding through the tiny shop crammed with herbs, she swallowed and withdrew the wilting rose from her reticule. "Can you preserve this for me?"

The motherly witch behind the counter accepted the rose with ginger care. "Yes, but though it'll look new, it'll be fragile, even more so than an ordinary dried flower."

Kiera frowned and nibbled her lip. Perhaps she should have visited Rhiannon's Veils after all. She eyed the scattered coins in her reticule—she definitely hadn't enough for the veiled witch. Besides, she was already here. She jerked a nod. "Do it."

The witch extended her free hand. "That'll be five bronze or one silver, miss." Once Kiera passed her the coins, the witch dumped them into an apron pocket. "Give me your hand."

Her stomach tense, Kiera narrowed her eyes. What could the witch possibly want? "Why?"

The motherly witch sighed and thrust out her palm. "Because I require your blood for the spell."

Kiera stiffened, keeping her hands by her sides. Blood? The witch could use that to create a magical connection, and such connections could be dangerous. "How much blood?"

Her palm still outstretched, the witch shrugged. "Only a few drops. Just enough for the preservation spell."

Kiera pursed her lips. The motherly witch appeared honest enough, so 'twould be fine as long as all the blood was used in the preservation spell. "Is my blood the only magical cost?"

The witch shrugged again. "The preservation spell usually takes a bit of your energy today, turns a few hairs gray, or causes some wrinkles, but nothin' more than that."

Tilting her head, Kiera hummed. All of those costs sounded minimal, well worth preserving the peach rose. "And nothing after today?" Once the witch nodded, Kiera extended her hand. "Very well."

The motherly witch jabbed Kiera's palm with a lead needle three times. "Keep your palm cupped. Don't lose that blood."

The witch sprinkled three pinches of sand then three pinches of thyme onto Kiera's palm. She crooned a melody and circled a finger over Kiera's palm three times.

Then Kiera gasped as the witch rolled the peach rose across

her palm three times. Goddess, she could feel the energy wicking from her into the rose. How unnerving. She suppressed a shiver.

The motherly witch brushed off her hands and peered into Kiera's face. "No gray hairs or wrinkles. You're most fortunate."

Kiera swallowed but nodded. She lowered her gaze to the peach rose cradled in her palm. It now appeared as fresh as when the dark-haired squire had plucked it. And its sweet fragrance again perfumed the room.

The witch shooed Kiera from her shop. "Remember, take care when handling your rose. A rough touch will make it crumble."

"Thank you," Kiera called from the door. With the peach rose held between her thumb and forefinger, she bustled back to the orphanage. 'Twas truly the most exquisite thing she'd ever seen —even more than her shell mask from the veiled witch.

Peter peered at the rose as he opened the orphanage door. "What's that, Mistress Kiera?"

She forced a shrug. She must appear nonchalant, or the burly porter would quiz her about the rose and the squire forever. Along with Jane, Peter and his wife Mary, the orphanage's cook and Jane's younger sister, had raised Kiera, so both were loving and protective. And they often encouraged her to find a husband and start a family. They weren't as relentless as Hawke's matchmaking mother, but they were bad enough. "Just a rose."

Peter beamed. "Have an admirer? 'Bout time. You're the sweetest girl and will make an excellent wife and mother. I can't wait to tell Mary 'bout your admirer."

Almost wincing, Kiera swallowed. Peter's delight was as bad as expected and unfortunately misplaced. The squire admired a fantasy that didn't exist. He'd not want to marry a poor orphanage matron from near the docks. He'd ask her to become his mistress instead. "'Tis nothing, Peter."

The porter's guffaws followed Kiera as she hurried to her study. Hopefully, Peter and Mary wouldn't ask about the rose later.

· · ·

OVER THE FOLLOWING WEEK, Kiera continued stashing the peach rose near her and admiring it throughout the day. And her passionate dreams about the dark-haired squire kept consuming her nights. If they didn't stop, she'd soon go mad from unrequited desire.

When Wren returned for play rehearsals with Hawke, Kiera grinned as she embraced him. Engrossed by life at court and his various lovers, he'd not visited the orphanage for two years, and 'twas delightful to see him after so long. What had made him return?

She eyed Hawke as she handed him a list of set designers and musicians. He appeared as impish as ever. Her gaze drifted to Wren beside him—her friend appeared even more drawn than she had last week. Something must be wrong. Could they know about Kiera attending the masquerade, and Wren was fretting over it?

Since Wren had refused to discuss the masquerade before, Kiera risked asking Hawke instead. Although she shouldn't, she still burned to learn the squire's name. She smiled at Hawke as he opened her study door to join Wren for tea. "How have things been with you, Hawke? Did you attend the king's summer masquerade two weeks ago?"

Hawke stilled. "Briefly."

Her mouth drying, Kiera sat behind her desk and accepted a teacup from Wren. Had Hawke not seen her? Then he mightn't know the squire's name. "Only briefly? I thought masquerades lasted for hours."

Hawke devoured a sweet biscuit. "They do, but 'twas dull, so I left early."

Still wan, Wren sipped her tea and crumbled the sweet biscuits on her plate. "Hawke has decided to cease attending court events that bore him."

Kiera arched her brows over her steaming teacup. Her friends mustn't realize she'd snuck into the king's summer masquerade. So their unease must be due to their own concerns.

Perhaps Hawke had decided to pursue Wren at last. "Really? Why?"

Hawke shrugged. "I wanted a change, I suppose."

Kiera studied her tea. The hunger to experience something new could be overwhelming indeed. After all, 'twas why she'd attended the king's summer masquerade. "I understand that."

Kiera paused then asked her friends how the first rehearsal went. She watched Wren throughout tea. Something was definitely ailing her. So Kiera urged Hawke to discover what before he and Wren left.

Once they did, Kiera opened her desk drawer to study her peach rose. Perhaps 'twas best she'd not learned the squire's name from her friends. Now she'd no way to find him again. She set her jaw. She'd remain at the orphanage and nurture unwanted children like Jane had nurtured her. 'Twas a worthy purpose, much more than becoming a wealthy gentleman's mistress. She sighed and shut her desk drawer. The king's summer masquerade and the dark-haired squire would soon become nothing more than memories to cheer her during troubling times.

So over the following week, she forced herself to focus on her orphans and the play rehearsals. As usual, the orphans romped through the daily rehearsals and adored chattering about them afterward. Yet she couldn't help admiring the peach rose and remembering the squire whenever she was alone.

In addition to Kiera's preoccupation with her rose, she became more and more concerned by Wren's persistent listlessness. Hawke even had to drag the half-asleep Wren home before tea one afternoon. Yet Wren never confessed what ailed her. So two days before the play, Kiera eyed Wren after another successful rehearsal. Wren still appeared tired, yet at least she was grinning and alert.

Wren tilted her head. "I think we're ready for tomorrow's dress rehearsal. I only hope *something* goes awry then, else it shall during the performance."

Kiera chuckled. Even if it did, the orphans would be adorable as ever when performing. "I doubt that. As usual, you've matters well in hand."

Wren's grin turned wry. "I certainly hope so, considering all the nobles Hawke invited."

Kiera stiffened, her mouth drying. Her worn orphanage wasn't fit for noble guests.

Hawke sipped his tea. "They're just family."

Kiera almost snorted. To *him* they were.

Wren shook her head. "Yes, but your family includes the king." She paused. "He's not attending, is he?"

Kiera stilled. The king here? Such an exalted gentleman would surely disparage her humble orphanage.

Hawke chuckled. "No, Devon, Aragon, and Farson have a meeting with the nightmara delegation that afternoon, remember?"

Her teacup clattering on her desk, Kiera suppressed a shudder. Thank the Goddess the king had that meeting. "You were planning on inviting the king *here*?"

"Why not? He'd enjoy it." Hawke waggled his brows at her. "Just imagine the donations you'd receive if he did."

Donations? Kiera glanced at Wren, who immediately nodded, so he wasn't exaggerating to pacify her. She smiled, her pulse quickening. If the king supported them, others at court would too. "We could afford new clothes for the children, hire better tutors, and send the older ones to trade school." She turned to Hawke. "Invite the king next time."

Yet once Wren and Hawke left, Kiera eyed the meager tea they'd shared. How could her poor orphanage afford to host their noble guests? The orphanage's funds scarcely covered feeding the orphans, let alone wealthy guests accustomed to finer fare.

Thankfully, when she entered the dining hall for the play's dress rehearsal the following day, Hawke drew her aside and said, "I'll provide refreshments for the guests tomorrow."

Tears pricked her eyes as she blinked at him. Of course, he'd recognized 'twould be an issue. "Truly?"

Hawke flashed a crooked grin. "I *was* the one to invite them, after all. 'Tis only fair I feed them too." He winked then joined his musicians.

Kiera beamed as Wren returned with her players and began the dress rehearsal, which the orphans performed with their usual verve. They'd be marvelous tomorrow.

That night, the orphans took hours longer than normal to settle. They were too excited over their noble guests tomorrow. Most had never seen nobility, much less a duke and duchess like Hawke's parents.

Warmth flooding her chest, Kiera gazed at her peach rose on her bedside table as she slipped into bed. The orphans felt like she had just before the king's summer masquerade. Hopefully, they'd have as wonderful a time tomorrow as she'd had with the dark-haired squire. She smiled then blew out her lamp and dreamt of him and his irresistible kisses yet again.

CHAPTER 7

The morning after the nightmara queen-heir and her delegation arrived, Devon strode into the council meeting. Hopefully, 'twould be brief, so he could meet with the nightmara while 'twas still relatively cool. His shoulders tensed. Goddess, let today's negotiations go well. Then he could ask the nightmara to help find his mermaid.

As soon as Devon sat at the head of the table, the Duke of Osbourne creaked, "Since you've no queen, you should bring the entire council to your first meeting with the nightmara queen-heir. Bringing everyone shall demonstrate to the nightmara how important we consider them."

Devon frowned and tapped his fingers on the table. Perhaps, but twelve advisors were a horde compared to the traditional two.

But before Devon could reply, Lord Farson shook his head at the elderly duke. "Such an onslaught shan't impress the nightmara. As shown when Nightwind summoned Queen Sarilee alone to negotiate the first treaty, nightmara prefer small negotiations. Large groups of humans, other than the mara clans, make them uneasy."

Devon's fingers stilled. Originally sent to guard nightmara

from other humans, the mara had been living among the night-mara since the start of the Nightmara-Calatini Treaty and were now practically nightmara themselves. Despite outnumbering the mara by far, the nightmara relied on their dreams to survive, so nightmara herds always traveled with their mara clan. And they were the only humans the nightmara wholeheartedly trusted. He nodded to support the baron. "Yes, so only Lord Farson and Lord Treyvan shall accompany me."

The Duke of Osbourne scowled at Aragon. "Why Lord Trey-van? He's the Minister of Agriculture, and the nightmara don't farm. As the Minister of Intelligence, I'd be better."

Devon arched his brows. True, the duke's spies had probably told him everything about the nightmara, including what they'd discussed over breakfast. Yet his wily nature wouldn't impress the forthright magical creatures, unlike Aragon. "My second advisor may change depending on the issues addressed. But initially, I want an unconnected advisor to provide an impartial read on the nightmara queen-heir and her delegation." Plus, he could rely on his best friend to be truthful with him.

As the elderly duke settled with a grumble, Devon rose and beckoned his chosen advisors. "Come, we don't wish to be late, in addition to having no queen." Besides, if they tarried, the other councilors would simply concoct more objections, like needing a female councilor instead of Aragon, or delays, like the Magehaven ore.

When they and his guards set out across the rapidly warming palace grounds toward the nightmara stables, Devon glanced at Lord Farson. "How did the nightmara's arrival go yesterday?"

Lord Farson shrugged. "Well. They were pleased with the recent improvements you'd made. However, Elise and I didn't remain with them long. We didn't wish for the nightmara to discover your lack of queen from our minds."

Devon inclined his head. Yes, that revelation was best coming from him. Then they could read his honest intentions. "How is your wife?"

A grin brightened the baron's bearded face. "Excited to see the nightmara. When we visited the Flower Herd last autumn to meet the nightmara queen-heir, Elise became close friends with a mara woman, and her friend is part of the delegation." He chuckled. "She'd be visiting today, except Aragon's mother dragooned her into performing a play by Miss Keyes at the duchess's upcoming fete for her first grandchild. So Elise is attending Miss Keyes's play at Waterstreet Orphanage to see what to expect."

Devon coughed to disguise his laugh. Wise of Elise. Performing a play at one of the Duchess of Childes's grandiose affairs would be trying. Thank the Goddess he'd not been dragooned into performing too.

Aragon chuckled. "She'll have fun—watching, at least. Miss Keyes's plays are delightful. Selena is also attending the orphanage play, even though we aren't performing at the fete. *One* benefit to being the guests of honor." He grinned at Devon. "Hawke intended to invite you as well, until I mentioned our meeting with the nightmara delegation. He's determined to find new supporters for Miss Keyes's orphanage."

Devon smiled. Except he'd not be a new supporter. When Hawke and Wren had first convinced their families to donate, he'd had his people investigate the orphanage. Although in a rough neighborhood near the docks, 'twas the best orphanage in Ormas. The staff were conscientious and dedicated to their children. So he'd begun including the orphanage among the places he personally sent anonymous donations to several times a year. Nothing large, since that would cause comment, but enough to help them remain open. "I'd be pleased to support Waterstreet Orphanage."

As they neared the nightmara stables, he grimaced and suppressed a sigh. "And I'd much rather be there watching one of Wren's plays. The nightmara shan't be pleased when they realize I've no queen to negotiate." Hopefully, they'd not "shout" much. If forcible or uncontrolled, the nightmara's mental shouts could drive humans mad or into comas.

Lord Farson rubbed his beard and murmured, "Perhaps the nightmara shan't mind. After all, they're accustomed to dealing with male traders at herdrests." Herdrests were permanent complexes maintained by one nightmara-mara pair, so the nomadic nightmara and mara could occasionally rest inside solid walls and trade with outsiders.

Devon snorted. Renewing a kingdom-wide treaty was nothing like trading for wood to make caravans. And the night-mara had only formed a treaty with Calatini when his ancestor had proclaimed his queen co-ruler. "You sound like you believe that as much as I do."

Lord Farson sighed then rapped on the nightmara stable door. When it creaked open, he gestured toward himself then Devon and Aragon. "The Calatini delegation, here to negotiate."

A black nightmara beside her and her hand resting on the saber at her waist, the mara woman opened the door the rest of the way. Her eyes narrowed as she scrutinized them. "Where's the queen, Lord Farson?"

Lord Farson inclined a small bow. "King Devon shall explain to Lady Moonbud when they meet, Leila."

Leila exchanged a glance with the black nightmara, who must be her partner. Every mara had a nightmara partner, and the pair were rarely apart until their deaths. Together they formed the best cavalry in Damensea, even though nightmara outside of Calatini found being ridden demeaning.

After a moment, Leila turned back to Lord Farson. "I suppose the missing queen is why Elise didn't stay to talk yesterday. I should have realized something was amiss." She jerked her chin. "Follow me."

Devon almost winced. The mara woman's distaste over his missing queen was as bad as he'd feared. How would the night-mara queen-heir react? He traded frowns with Aragon and Lord

Farson before they followed Leila and her partner through the nightmara stables and into the massive paddock.

Spread about the paddock in clusters, fourteen nightmara and twelve mara basked in the summer sun. Each of the thirteen nightmara herds must have sent one mara-nightmara pair, and the two extra nightmara must be the queen-heir and a special advisor.

The nightmara appeared remarkably like dark-colored horses, except more beautiful with an otherworldly air. Plus, obvious intelligence shone in their faces and movements. Even though most had mara partners, none wore saddles—nightmara only endured those when attempting to pass as horses.

Armed with sabers, arrows, or both, the mara appeared little different from other humans, except they moved in harmony with their nightmara partner even when not riding. No doubt 'twas due to the rigorous martial training all mara underwent starting when they were bound to their clan's nightmara herd around age three.

As Devon and the others strode across the paddock, the scattered nightmara and mara ignored them. A few dozed in the sun, a few continued their mostly silent conversations, and a few practiced their special cavalry moves. Yet at the center of them all, like the eye of a mighty storm, stood a dappled midnight mare with a striking presence—the nightmara queen-heir, no doubt.

Leila and her partner led them straight to that midnight mare, and she twirled to face them, more graceful than any dancer, before anyone spoke a word. Her taupe eyes immediately focused on Devon, and her powers pressed against his mind.

Despite the prickles skittering through him, he forced himself to return her stare without flinching and keep his mind open. He'd nothing to gain but her mistrust by keeping secrets, and their negotiations would be thorny enough as it was.

As the nightmara queen-heir's powers receded, Lord Farson

stepped forward with a deep bow. "Lady Moonbud, allow me to introduce King Devon Calator Vireni IV of Calatini. King Devon, Lady Moonbud of the Flower Herd, future queen of the nightmara."

Devon gritted a smile as he and Moonbud inclined their heads at one another. He must start their negotiations by explaining his missing queen, but how?

After a moment, Moonbud craned to look around him. :*Where's your queen, King Devon? Nightrose and Leila tell me you'll explain.*:

His stomach tensing, he sighed but nodded. "I apologize for this break in tradition, but I've no queen to meet you."

Moonbud snorted and tossed her mane. :*No queen? Impossible!*:

As Lord Farson and Aragon flinched behind him, Devon spread his hands in a beseeching gesture. Please let the nightmara queen-heir understand. "Unfortunately, 'tis true. And although irregular, I'd rather negotiate myself than foist a spurious betrothed on you. Can we disregard my lack of queen for the sake of our peoples?"

Moonbud's gaze bored into him as her powers sifted his mind again. :*Your honesty does you credit, your majesty.*:

He suppressed a wince. The nightmara queen-heir sounded as reluctant to negotiate with him as he'd expected. Wonderful. Perhaps 'twould soften if he allowed her to lead. He smiled at her. "Would you care to start?"

Moonbud sighed. :*Very well. Walk beside me.*: She strode toward the fence with Leila and Nightrose trailing her. :*Your lack of queen is most disturbing and demonstrates a flaw in our dealings.*:

Eyeing the nightmara queen-heir, Devon followed her across the paddock with Lord Farson, Aragon, and his guards several steps behind. Although unprecedented, how could his unwed status be considered a flaw in their dealings? "What do you mean?"

Moonbud's midnight tail lashed. :*The Nightmara-Calatini*

Treaty being signed every quarter of a century hampers our communication. We should begin signing the treaty every decade.:

He hummed. Signing the treaty more often wouldn't improve their communication—'twould merely be needless legislation. "We could if you feel it necessary. However, that interval was chosen so each generation of rulers could meet, and that's worked for four centuries."

Moonbud halted beneath an oak along the fence, Leila and Nightrose almost crashing into her. *:We'll return to that later. Allow me to explain my next concern.:* When he nodded, she continued, *:Despite our longstanding treaty, we still continue to suffer poachers.:*

Devon frowned. Nightmara poachers were a serious concern. They stole foals to enslave them as horses with extraordinary strength and intelligence yet smaller appetites. But without the proper training from other nightmara, their powers were uncontrolled at maturity and maimed nearby humans. He crossed his arms behind his back. "Our punishment for nightmara poachers is tantamount to that for murder or kidnapping human citizens."

Moonbud blew a sigh. *:Your punishments are fine. We're more concerned that staying within the Nightmara Plains makes us too easy to capture. Perhaps we should roam all of Calatini instead.:*

As Lord Farson and Aragon exchanged frowns, Devon almost winced. Calatini's southern defense relied on the nightmara and mara. If they abandoned the plains, they'd leave a gaping hole just north of the immense Tsarkan Empire; a hole their southern neighbor would be quick to exploit. Invading nearby kingdoms was how the city of Tsarka had become an empire five centuries ago, and how it had kept growing since then. Yet mentioning the risk of invasion would only nettle the nightmara queen-heir, so he merely asked, "Do you have other concerns?"

Moonbud nodded. *:Yes, one more. As dictated by the treaty, we allow humans of Calatini to join the mara. And although we require their dreams so we don't develop dreamsickness, the number of mara* has grown to almost half of the nightmara on the plains. So many humans living among us has begun to concern us, especially given their loyalty is split between the nightmara and Calatini.:

He stared at her. Since when did the nightmara distrust the mara? "I was unaware the mara's split loyalty troubled them."

Moonbud tossed her mane. :It hasn't yet, but it could if our peoples disagreed on an issue. I think the best solution would be for the mara to renounce their Calatini citizenship.:

Devon tensed. 'Twould be disastrous. His gaze slid to Lord Farson, who'd turned ashen. As the representative of Golddell, he obviously realized that proposal's impact. The nightmara were a sovereign people according to the treaty, so they weren't taxed. However, the mara were, and so were their joint ventures with the nightmara. The mara fully joining the nightmara would beggar Golddell. Yet Devon must remain neutral for now, so he bowed to Moonbud and said, "We'll require time to consider your proposals. Shall we meet again at the end of the week?"

Moonbud inclined her head, then Devon, Aragon, and Lord Farson strode from the paddock with his guards behind them.

Devon forced himself to smile despite his roiling thoughts. Goddess, their opening negotiations had gone much worse than he'd feared. With everything so tangled, he couldn't ask the nightmara to use their power over dreams and the mind to help find his mermaid. Halfway back to the palace, he paused in a deserted water garden. "What's your opinion of Lady Moonbud's proposals?"

Lord Farson frowned. "I was surprised. Lady Moonbud has never voiced such extremist opinions before. I suspect her outrageous proposals are to coerce you to find a queen."

Devon quirked a wry smile. No doubt. If only he'd found his mysterious mermaid before they'd arrived. He glanced at Aragon. "Your thoughts?"

Aragon shook his head. "I agree with Farson. I've not met the nightmara queen-heir until today, but the nightmara have never suggested amendments so disparate from the original treaty." He arched his brows. "How has your hunt for your mermaid gone?"

Weight compressing his chest, Devon sighed and rubbed his forehead. "Not well. With the nightmara arriving, I've not had much time to hunt, and my meager clues led nowhere. 'Tis almost as if she never existed."

Aragon winced and clapped Devon's shoulder. "You'll find her."

Devon sighed again and resumed walking. "Hopefully, *before* I destroy the Nightmara-Calatini Treaty."

He grimaced as they strode to the palace with his guards. The situation with the nightmara was impossible. He required time to attend court events to find his mermaid to appease them. Yet with the nightmara here, he'd no time to attend those events. How was he to find his mermaid before 'twas too late?

CHAPTER 8

The afternoon of the orphanage play, Kiera slipped into her study to snatch a moment alone to settle herself. Although adorable, the orphans' nervous excitement was tumultuous and draining. She strode straight to her desk and opened her drawer concealing the peach rose. As she eyed it, she relaxed with a faint smile. What would the squire make of the play? Would he find her orphans' exuberance endearing too or simply ill-bred?

After a moment, she shook her head and shut the drawer. Not that it mattered, since he'd never meet them. She really must cease mooning over the rose he'd given her. Staring at it only made her impossible yearning worse. Yet how could she stop? She never should have preserved the tempting thing. But she hadn't the will to destroy it.

She sighed then bustled back to the front schoolroom where the orphans not performing waited. On her way, she peeked into the dining hall. Earlier Peter and the older boys had converted it into a theater by moving the trestle tables, setting up the stage, and placing chairs along the back wall for their guests. Now 'twas filled with children swirling about Wren like melissae in a field of summer flowers. Kiera smiled. So adorable.

Since Wren had the players handled, Kiera left without disturbing them and continued to the front schoolroom. Because Wren had arrived, Hawke must be at the orphanage as well. No doubt he was in the kitchen giving Mary the provisions he'd promised. Mary was probably torn between gasps and squeals. Kiera chuckled. If only she were there to see it.

As soon as she entered the front schoolroom, Roger bounded up to her. "How much longer, Mistress Kiera?"

Kiera winked at the wiry boy. Although he'd refused to perform since he'd tripped and knocked over the stage decorations during a performance three years ago, he'd adored watching the plays and spent days talking about them afterward. "Not much longer."

While Roger bounded back to the others, Hawke poked his head into the schoolroom with a crooked grin. "My parents' carriage has arrived. You'll probably want the children settled before my family reaches the dining hall."

She nodded. His family might donate more if the orphans were settled and well-behaved. "Thanks, Hawke." As his head disappeared, she turned to the orphans and grinned. "Did you hear that? Time for the play."

The orphans whooped and burst from the schoolroom then thundered down the hall to the dining hall like a herd of hunting centaurs.

Kiera chuckled as she steered the stragglers to their seats on the floor before the stage. They were so excited they couldn't remain still. And they kept glancing behind them to gape at their guests drifting into the seats along the wall.

Although most of her attention was focused on the orphans, she couldn't resist glancing at their noble guests as well. Would any of them recognize her from the king's summer masquerade? Hopefully not.

When Peter joined her by the orphans, Kiera bustled to the refreshments table. Mary and the children helping her could probably use assistance.

When Kiera began arranging the refreshments, the plump cook beamed at her then sent the children to serve their guests sparkling wine and victuals. "Just look at everythin' that Mr. Hawke brought. I've never seen such fancy food in my life. And he brought treats for the children as well, includin' starpeaches."

Kiera smiled. Most of the orphans adored the sweet, golden-red starpeaches almost as much as cake, which they rarely received. The orphanage could only afford cake for the four festivals of the Goddess and other celebrations.

But before Kiera could reply, Mary glanced toward the back wall where their guests were smiling at the children serving refreshments then said, "Do you recognize any of these fine lords and ladies?"

Her neck prickling, Kiera stopped arranging refreshments to scrutinize their guests like she couldn't do while minding the orphans. She'd met Wren's parents and Hawke's parents and brothers a few times, and some of the others she recognized from Wren's descriptions over the years. As always, their parents sat together, and beside them was a freckled lady who must be Hawke's sister-in-law Selena, although Aragon wasn't with her. Mel was behind his parents, and beside him was a gorgeous lady with sable hair—no doubt Lady Blaine, Wren's childhood rival. The other seven guests must be Hawke's various cousins, although the older couple must be once removed.

Kiera muffled a sigh. Fortunately, all of their guests, except for Lady Blaine, were grinning as they sipped their sparkling wine and waited for the play to start, and none were eyeing Kiera. They were clearly enjoying themselves and didn't recognize her from the masquerade. Thank the Goddess. She turned back to Mary. "I only recognize the ones I've met—Wren's and Hawke's parents and his brother Mel."

Mary tilted her head and slanted Kiera a sidelong glance. "And perhaps a gentleman who adores peach roses?"

Kiera stiffened. Of course, Mary would ask about the squire. She'd mentioned him several times since Peter had seen the rose two weeks ago. So far, Kiera had managed to reveal nothing. She arched her brows at Mary. "How would I know if any of Wren's or Hawke's relatives like peach roses?"

Mary pursed her lips. "You should of invited your admirer, Mistress Kiera. He'd enjoy the play and wooin' you."

Kiera smoothed her serviceable skirt. Although her nicest dress, 'twas a poor shadow compared to their guests' expensive and modish attire. Without her enchanted ballgown, their guests, and the squire, would never see her as their equal. "A true admirer of a poor orphanage matron wouldn't belong among our noble guests." When Mary began to protest, Kiera gritted a smile and continued, "I must go introduce the play before our guests become restless."

She swept onstage to welcome their guests and introduce Wren's play. Then she settled on the floor beside the orphans, rather than returning to the refreshments table and Mary's well-meaning matchmaking. She beamed as the orphans performing the play romped about the stage. They were even more marvelous than usual, probably because of their nervous excitement at performing for noble guests.

When Amaranth's celestial singing echoed through the dining hall, Kiera gaped at the little girl. Goddess, who knew she could sing so beautifully—like a young siren charming the winds? From the strangled gasp behind her, at least one of their guests was as awed as Kiera.

At the end of Amaranth's song, a deafening silence filled the dining hall until the performers began their bows. As she clapped with the others, Kiera rose and slipped across the dining hall. Mary would require additional assistance once the orphans sought refreshments, and she'd be too busy to ask about the squire again.

Mary grinned while handing her a platter of sliced starpeaches. "Another fine play, don't you think?"

Kiera relaxed and inclined her head. The play had driven the squire from Mary's mind. "Very. And the final song was exquisite."

After Wren's and Hawke's bows, the applause and cheering faded, and the orphans mobbed the refreshments tables like a flock of starving sprites about ripe strawberries. And of course, Kiera's line was longest. She chuckled as she distributed the sliced starpeaches. Many of the children immediately returned to the end of the line to receive another slice.

She was well into her second platter when Amaranth reached the front of the line. She beamed at the little girl and offered her a slice of starpeach. "Beautiful singing, Amaranth."

"Thanks, Mistress Kiera!" Amaranth reached for her slice.

Cassandra shoved through the squawking crowd to her younger sister's side. "Come, Amaranth, some of Mr. Hawke's friends want to congratulate you on your singing."

Kiera suppressed a frown at the teenage girl's clipped tone. Something about their guests had upset her. Was it because the girl blamed all nobles for the unknown lord's runaway carriage that had killed her parents? Or was there something more?

Her hand hovering above her slice, Amaranth pouted at her sister. "But I was about to get a starpeach!"

Cassandra snorted and raised her eyes skyward. "Then eat fast. And clean your hands!"

While Amaranth snatched her slice of starpeach, Kiera eyed Cassandra. She was fiercely protective of her much younger sister and never sharp with her, so something was definitely amiss. Kiera leaned toward Cassandra. "Is everything all right?"

Cassandra lifted her chin and bared her teeth in a mendacious grin. "Everything is fine, Mistress Kiera."

Kiera almost snorted as Cassandra whisked Amaranth across the dining hall. Everything was *not* fine. So as she served more starpeaches, she continued watching the sisters. Yet she relaxed when they joined Wren, Hawke, and the older couple she'd noticed earlier. Wren would protect the girls.

The adults and the sisters spoke for a few moments, then

whatever the older couple told them caused Amaranth to bounce like an excited pixie, although Cassandra merely glared. Wren soothed the older girl, and everyone spoke a bit more, then Wren shooed the sisters toward the refreshments table, and they rejoined the line for the starpeaches.

As the final platter of sliced starpeaches dwindled, Kiera eyed the sisters. Although Amaranth bounced and chattered, Cassandra scowled and barely spoke. Goddess, what had the older couple told them?

When they reached the front of the line, Amaranth seized the next-to-last starpeach and darted away. However, her smile tight and mulberry eyes black, Cassandra remained before Kiera and asked, "Could you come with me, Mistress Kiera? Miss Wren wants you to meet the Westons."

Kiera nodded and handed the last slice of starpeach to Roger, who'd already devoured four slices—he adored them as much as the plays. The Westons must be the older couple, and given their name, they weren't Hawke's cousins at all. "Certainly, but why does she want me to meet the Westons?"

Cassandra grunted as they began across the room. "Because we're going to live with them—tonight."

Her chest freezing, Kiera halted to gape at the girl. "What?"

Cassandra shrugged. "*Apparently,* they're our mother's parents."

As she and Cassandra resumed weaving across the dining hall, Kiera eyed the older lady embracing Wren. The sisters resembled the lady, so no doubt she was their grandmother. Yet how had she and her husband not known their granddaughters had been orphaned?

As Kiera and Cassandra approached, Wren patted the older lady's back then exchanged a significant glance with Kiera, asking without words if she required assistance.

Kiera smiled and nodded to show she could handle Cassandra and the Westons alone. Wren should go greet the other guests—doubtless they wanted to praise her delightful play.

Wren extracted herself from Cassandra's grandmother, and Hawke drew her away to their parents just as Kiera and Cassandra reached the Westons.

Her tone too polite to be genuine, Cassandra said, "Lord and Lady Weston, this is Mistress Kiera, matron of Waterstreet Orphanage." Her tone warmed, "Mistress Kiera, this is Lord and Lady Weston."

Before Kiera could speak, Lady Weston embraced her and kissed both her cheeks. "Thank you for caring for our girls."

Kiera blinked as she returned the older lady's embrace. If Lady Weston was so excited, why had she allowed her grand-daughters to live in a poor orphanage for almost two months? She pried herself free with a civil smile. She wrapped an arm about Cassandra's shoulders. "Cassandra and Amaranth are a delight. I've been glad to offer them a home."

Lady Weston's dark eyes shone with tears. "I wish we'd known our Anne had returned to Ormas. We would have recon-ciled and been there for the girls as soon as she was k—" The older lady buried her face in her husband's chest.

His eyes also glistening, Lord Weston patted his wife's back. "There, there. We may not have Anne, but we've her girls now."

Kiera softened. The Westons' estrangement from their daughter explained why Cassandra and Amaranth had come to the orphanage, and their grief was too profound to not be authentic. They'd make loving guardians for the sisters.

Yet a shudder wracked Cassandra's slender body at the mention of her mother.

To soothe the girl, Kiera squeezed her shoulder. Although she clearly mistrusted her newfound grandparents, at least she shared her profound grief with them. Perhaps that would help them connect.

Cassandra remained stiff for a moment then turned into Kiera's embrace.

Her throat aching, Kiera smoothed Cassandra's brown, loose curls. The poor girl had kept her grief contained since shortly after she'd arrived at the orphanage, but meeting her grandparents had torn open her wounds. Hopefully, given time and her grandparents' love, she'd become a carefree young lady again.

To distract Cassandra and the Westons from their grief, Kiera asked, "Lord and Lady Weston, is your home prepared for the Cassandra and Amaranth? Bedrooms and such?"

As Cassandra withdrew from Kiera, Lady Weston lifted her head and wiped her eyes. "Not precisely. We've guest rooms that shall suit Cassandra, but nothing for Amaranth. The nursery has been closed since Anne was small."

Lord Weston nodded. "And we must hire maids for the girls."

A smile trembled on Lady Weston's lips. "We must also purchase new wardrobes. It's been too long since I'd the joy of dressing little girls."

Her hands fisting, Cassandra glared at her grandparents. "Our clothes are fine—Mama made them. And we don't need maids. We can take care of ourselves like Mama and Papa taught us."

Kiera sighed. The poor girl was too heartbroken and defensive to accept help from the grandparents she'd just met. The Westons were in for a difficult time. She tweaked a lock of Cassandra's hair. "No criticism without trying it. Most girls would adore having maids." She turned to the Westons. "'Tis mid-afternoon now. How about you return home and prepare everything? You can return after dinner to collect them."

Lord and Lady Weston exchanged a long glance, obviously reluctant to leave their granddaughters now that they'd found them.

Kiera smiled. Yes, the Westons would definitely make loving guardians for the sisters. How wonderful to meet adults who cared about their orphaned relatives. 'Twas so rare here. "Collecting them after dinner shall give Cassandra and Amaranth time to pack and say goodbye to the others."

Lady Weston sighed. "Very well." She reached out to embrace her granddaughter, but halted when Cassandra stiffened. "We'll see you later, Cassandra."

Lady Weston embraced Kiera again, and Lord Weston bowed, then the Westons strode from the dining hall.

Kiera glanced at the scowling Cassandra. The girl needed time to recover. Keeping her voice light, she asked, "Shall we find Amaranth?"

Her scowl easing, Cassandra pointed across the dining hall. As always, she knew where her sister was. "She's over there with the Bedsford twins."

When Kiera and Cassandra reached them, Amaranth was chattering about her grandparents, and the scampish boys were smiling, but shadows lurked in their tawny eyes. John and Jacob adored Amaranth and would miss her sorely. No doubt their escapades would be worse in the coming weeks.

Kiera extracted Amaranth from the twins then helped the sisters pack. Once that short task was done, they left the baggage by the door for Peter to load into the Westons' carriage later.

At dinner, Kiera told everyone about Cassandra and Amaranth leaving to live with their grandparents. Most of the other orphans congratulated the sisters despite their own yearning to belong to a family. Soon after the bread pudding was devoured, the Westons returned and collected Cassandra and Amaranth.

While lying in bed that night, Kiera studied the peach rose on her bedside table. As a child, she'd shared her orphans' yearning to belong, and sometimes she still did. The dark-haired squire had been the closest she'd come to belonging. Yet despite her passionate dreams about him since they'd met, that sense of belonging was nothing more than a mirage because it had been based on a lie.

CHAPTER 9

As he'd expected, Devon was too busy to attend any court events to find his mysterious mermaid in the days following the nightmara's arrival. Yet every night, his passionate dreams about her grew more vivid, until they felt more real than his waking hours. Goddess, he *must* find his mermaid soon.

The morning of his second meeting with the nightmara, he rubbed his brow as he sipped a cup of kahve at his desk. Hopefully, the bracing brew would help lighten his fatigue due to his restless sleep for the past few weeks. He sighed and leaned back in his chair. Although their opening negotiations had floundered, he must ask Moonbud for time to find his mermaid and possibly the nightmara's help as well. Their power over dreams and the mind would surely succeed.

He drained his kahve. Perhaps Moonbud would agree if he confessed everything. But he couldn't do that with Lord Farson listening, and only bringing Aragon might insult the baron, so he'd not bring any advisors today. He'd tell Aragon and Lord Farson when they arrived shortly.

Devon started when the Duchess of Wildewall knocked on his open study door. The Minister of Justice seeking a private meeting could be troublesome and often involved the

Greysnowe-Ravenstone feud. He forced a smile and rose. "Come in, your grace."

Gliding inside, the duchess shut the door and sat before his desk. "I'm sorry for disturbing you, your majesty, but I've some troubling news you should hear."

He sat and almost winced. What mischief had the Greysnowes or Ravenstones done now? He gestured for her to continue.

The Duchess of Wildewall cocked her head, the frost in her auburn hair shimmering. "Have you found your mermaid yet?"

Devon tensed. Unlike most of the council, the temperate duchess hadn't complained about his mermaid. Did she intend to start now? He narrowed his eyes at her. "No."

The duchess grimaced. "Have you at least made progress?"

"Some." He arched his brows. "What's this about?" His mermaid couldn't be connected to the Greysnowes or Ravenstones.

The Duchess of Wildewall sighed. "At my garden party this morning, Lord Greysnowe accused young Lord Raven-stone of fabricating your mermaid to beguile you from Lady Annalise."

Devon echoed her sigh. Of course, the ambitious count had noticed he'd quit escorting Lady Annalise to events since the masquerade. Now that he'd met his mermaid, he only wanted her and couldn't escort another lady, even one who wanted nothing more than distant friendship.

The duchess continued, "Lord Greysnowe's harsh words would have escalated to blows if Lord Ravenstone weren't so tolerant."

His jaw tightened. "Wonderful. I suppose young Lord Alexander was there, inflaming matters." Lady Annalise's younger brother was a hellion, hence his earlier duel with Lord Ravenstone.

The Duchess of Wildewall shook her head. "No, Lord Alexander hasn't attended any court events since he nearly killed Lord Ravenstone, and he's been quiet about the feud as well."

Devon blinked. Perhaps almost killing someone, even an enemy count, had scared the hellion into sense. For now, at least. Knowing the Greysnowes and Ravenstones, 'twouldn't last long.

The duchess sighed again. "I'd hoped you'd found your mermaid, so I could refute Lord Greysnowe's accusations. He'll continue to harp about it until we prove she's not connected to the Ravenstones."

He suppressed a snort. The count would harp well beyond that—after all, he'd spent his life perpetuating a centuries-old feud. Devon never should have started escorting Lady Annalise, despite her refreshing company. He sighed. "I'll find my mermaid soon. In the meantime, remind Lord Greysnowe that if Lord Ravenstone was responsible for my mermaid, the entire court would have known by the following morning. Neither the Greysnowes nor the Ravenstones can resist crowing when they outwit the other."

The Duchess of Wildewall pursed her lips. "I'll try, but I'm not certain that shall help. Lord Greysnowe is rabid this time."

Devon winced. "If I've time to attend, I'll resume escorting Lady Annalise to court events until I find my mermaid. Perhaps that shall appease Lord Greysnowe." Plus, since Lady Annalise had always been open about her disinterest in becoming queen, she'd doubtless be willing to search among the ladies for his mermaid. He could make himself escort a lady not his mermaid if 'twould help him find her.

The duchess's response was silenced by a rap on the door.

Since it must be Aragon and Lord Farson, Devon called, "Come in."

With Aragon beside him, Lord Farson opened the door and said, "We should leave for the nightmara meeting, your majesty."

The Duchess of Wildewall rose. "I should go."

Devon rose as well with a nod. "Thanks for your information, your grace." And for not complaining about his mermaid, even though his hunt for her was inflaming the Greysnowe-Ravenstone feud and complicating the nightmara negotiations.

Once the duchess glided from the study, Aragon cocked a brow. "Information?"

Devon sighed. No reason not to tell them. All of court would know by evening. "Yes, the Greysnowes are accusing the Ravenstones of concocting my mermaid to distract me from Lady Annalise."

Aragon snorted as Lord Farson raised his eyes skyward.

Devon sighed again. "I know. Ridiculous." He paused then said, "As for today's meeting with the nightmara, after some consideration, I've decided to attend alone." How could he explain without appearing suspicious?

Lord Farson frowned. "Is that wise?"

Devon rubbed his chin. Perhaps the nightmara's wariness would excuse him. "I want to foster rapport with Lady Moonbud. Maybe I'll have better success if we return to private meetings like the first treaty." He shook his head. "And no decisions on the treaty shall be made today."

Aragon eyed him. Clearly, he knew there was more to Devon's decision than that, but he'd not ask unless they were alone. Instead, he nodded and said, "We'll leave then. I, for one, shall be glad to return to my pregnant wife."

Lord Farson sighed. "If only Elise were pregnant as well. She's begun to talk about visiting a healer specializing in fertility. I'm not looking forward to that."

Devon grimaced as Aragon and Lord Farson left. Depending on the issue, fertility spells could have a high magical cost. Goddess willing, Lord Farson and his wife wouldn't need to resort to one.

He strode from his study, the two guards from his door following him. He forced himself to smile as he crossed the sweltering palace grounds to the nightmara stables. Seeing their king troubled would alarm court.

At his knock, Leila opened the stable door. She tsked and

whirled, her brown ponytail almost slapping his face. He coughed to disguise a chuckle. The mara woman definitely didn't like kings.

Devon bounded after Leila and Nightrose through the stables and into the paddock. Hopefully, he could convince Moonbud to feel differently. Their negotiations depended on that. And so did his plea for more time and help finding his mermaid.

As before, Moonbud stood at the heart of the nightmara, but today she was conversing with a nightmara stallion as black as Nightrose. Siblings, perhaps? When Devon reached them, Moonbud cocked her head. :*Where are your advisors, King Devon?*:

He swallowed and inclined a half bow. Goddess, let this succeed. "I thought we could discuss matters alone today, Lady Moonbud."

Moonbud glanced at his guards. :*Alone?*:

Devon flashed a wry smile. To the royal guards, this was alone. But Moonbud was right; they should be truly alone for his requests. "My guards can return to the stables." He glanced at the two black nightmara and Leila. "And so can yours."

Moonbud nickered. :*Very well.*: She eyed her companions, and they trotted away with the grumbling royal guards. Her midnight coat gleaming in the summer sun, she began toward the fence. :*I suppose you've special requests you wish to remain private.*:

He gulped a breath and clasped his hands behind his back as he paced beside her. "I do. As I'm sure you know, frank words can be difficult before bystanders."

Moonbud nodded. :*Which is no doubt why Nightwind approached Sarilee queen-to-queen for the first treaty.*:

Devon almost laughed. Approached? Kidnapped, more like. However, he merely nodded then said, "I'm aware you want to deal with a queen as well."

Moonbud tossed her mane with a snort. :*Then why are you unwed still?*:

He winced. Of course she'd ask that. "I always thought I'd

time to find a wife, but somehow I never did." He shook his head. "I didn't wish to wed just to have a queen."

Moonbud's gaze drifted to the black stallion by the stables. :*I suppose I'd not appreciate being forced to mate for the sake of a treaty.*:

Devon scrutinized her face. The stallion must be the other unpartnered nightmara, but was he her mate or still courting her? Yet prying wouldn't endear him to the nightmara queen-heir, so he only said, "I'm also my father's son—he adored my mother, and even though she died at my birth, thanks to using the Mirror of Wisdom, he kept her alive in his heart until he joined her. I want a grand love like that."

Moonbud turned back to him. :*A true mate.*: Her taupe eyes bored into his. :*And you **never** found such?*:

Not until the masquerade. Tingling warmth flooding him, he halted beneath the oak along the fence. "I did. Four weeks ago, I met my mermaid." Goddess, how he missed her.

Moonbud stilled and studied him askance. :*Your true mate couldn't be a mermaid. Humans and merfolk can't breed.*:

Devon chuckled. She must know about the masquerade from when she'd read his mind before, so his declaration must have startled her into forgetting. "No, she was a human lady dressed as a mermaid at my summer masquerade. But she refused to share her name before she vanished."

Moonbud relaxed with a sigh. :*Yes, of course...*:

He eyed the nightmara queen-heir. "I've been attempting to find her, but with your visit, I've not had enough time to search." He swallowed. "Which brings me to my requests." Please let her agree.

Moonbud's ears pricked forward. :*Which are?*:

Devon forced a shrug. "First, I need time to find my mermaid." He arched his brows at the nightmara queen-heir. "Unless you accept me as negotiator."

Moonbud snorted. :*Queen Nightsnow and the other dominant mares shan't be happy if I allow a stallion to negotiate a treaty of such import, but I can't delay the treaty forever.*:

Devon spread his hands in a beseeching gesture. "Give me a month to find her." Surely 'twould be enough.

Moonbud's powers pressed against his mind. :*Very well, but I want weekly meetings to discuss your progress.*: When he nodded, she continued, :*And what's your other request?*:

He returned her fierce stare without flinching, so she could read his sincerity. "Could you and your delegation use your powers to help find her? I've had no success so far."

Moonbud glanced away and flicked her tail. :*Perhaps. I'll confer with the others, but I can't promise we can find her.*:

Devon bowed, energy surging through his chest. "An attempt is all I can ask. Thank you, Lady Moonbud."

He strode from the paddock with his guards joining him at the stables. Now that he'd more time, he *must* start attending court events again to find his mermaid. He'd go through his invitations then send a note to Lady Annalise to check if she'd accompany him.

While sorting through his invitations, Devon blinked at the letter from Hawke requesting a private ride. Aragon's youngest brother had never done that before. Hawke must want a favor, perhaps about the arachne silk, the latest find he was promoting at court.

Devon smiled and wrote back, asking to meet Hawke after luncheon the following day. On their ride, he almost laughed when his cousin said he was also hunting a vanished masquerade lady. Finally, someone who truly understood his hunger to find his mermaid. Yet unlike his mermaid, Hawke's dryad had left behind a strong spell from a Rhiannon descendant, the most powerful of all witches. So Devon arranged an appointment for Hawke with the royal witch to further his hunt. Plus, if Hawke found his dryad, the powerful witch she'd patronized could help Devon find his mermaid.

Devon attended various court events with Lady Annalise over the next several evenings, but he never found his mermaid.

And his passionate dreams about her were as vivid as ever. Goddess, would he ever find her?

Although he'd nothing to report, he met with Moonbud the morning of the Duchess of Childes's fete for Aragon and Selena's child. His pulse quickening, he glanced at the nightmara queen-heir as they walked along the paddock fence. "Unfortunately, I've still had no luck finding my mermaid. You?"

Moonbud snorted and tossed her mane. :*Your ma—mermaid is most strong-willed, King Devon. She's somehow resisting our powers.*:

Even though his ribs tightened, Devon almost chuckled. Moonbud sounded both impressed and affronted by his mermaid's resistance. "I'm not surprised. My mermaid is extraordinary, and her strength is one of the reasons I love her."

Moonbud snorted again. :*She'll make an excellent queen—if we can ever find her.*:

He nodded then returned to the palace. That evening, he attended the fete with Lady Annalise, and they hunted for his mermaid without success yet again. Beside Wren's delightful play performed by Aragon's family, the most interesting sight at the fete was Hawke lusting after Wren and not realizing it. So when his lovelorn cousin asked him to check on her, Devon and Lady Annalise headed out to the balcony, arriving in time to rescue Wren from Winston—like he had Lady Annalise three years ago. One day, the fortune-hunting cad would go too far, and someone would murder him.

After telling Hawke about Winston, Devon coughed a laugh when his cousin snatched Wren's tea and bolted across the ballroom to find her. How long until Hawke recognized he loved Wren and abandoned his hunt for his vanished dryad? Devon sighed as he scrutinized the ladies at the fete once more, but without Lady Annalise's help since she'd slipped away again. Unlike his cousin, he loved his mermaid, so he'd not quit until he found her, no matter how long his hunt.

CHAPTER 10

$\mathcal{I}$n the days following the play, Kiera's waking hours were consumed by the orphans. It always took them a few days to become accustomed to their usual afternoon lessons instead of play rehearsals, and Wren hadn't visited to settle them with hints about the next one, probably because of the play for the duchess's fete. Plus, the Bedsford twins had misbehaved more since Amaranth left, and their escapades grew more extreme every day. The twelve-year-olds needed something more than the orphanage's basic schooling to distract them—they'd soon become impossible to handle.

Considering how busy she was, Kiera should have swiftly succumbed to deep sleep when she fell into bed, but passionate dreams about the dark-haired squire still consumed her nights. The dreams became so vivid she could taste his kiss on her lips when she woke, and every morning she ached as if she'd not slept. Yet she couldn't help mooning over the peach rose and keeping it near her. 'Twas a sweet reminder of their wonderful evening and her sense of belonging in his arms.

Almost a week after the play, she started awake in the middle of the night from an impossibly lifelike dream where the squire had knelt before her and begged her to marry him. Goddess, if only that could happen. But the most he'd ask a poor orphanage matron was to become his mistress.

As she flailed about her bed to escape her tangled covers, a crash shattered the silence.

Kiera froze, her chest tight. Please let it not be... She lit the lamp on her bedside table with trembling hands.

The perfect, peach rose the squire had given her was crumbled into powder amid the broken teacup.

She swallowed a sob. Just like her dreams would if the squire saw her as herself.

Kiera slid from bed despite the tears burning her throat. Careful of stray shards, she disposed of the mess. Perhaps 'twas beneficial. Doubtless her preoccupation with the peach rose had inspired her restless dreams, and without it, she could cease remembering the masquerade and focus on her real life.

She crawled back into bed but barely slept the rest of the night. And when she did, that impossible dream about the squire proposing returned. Despite the headache behind her eyes, she forced herself to rise at her normal time. At breakfast, she gulped several cups of kahve, which she seldom drank, to help wake her.

Shoving everything from her mind but the orphans, Kiera remained collected until the Bedsford twins made a mounted fish dance and sing during luncheon. The cavorting fish terrified the little ones to tears. Once she and Mary soothed the crying children, Kiera hauled the twins to her study and scolded them, but they were unrepentant. Yes, they definitely needed something to distract them, but what?

As the twins burst from her study, she sank into her chair and rubbed her forehead. Goddess, she was exhausted. If only she could take a nap. But she'd too much to do.

Then Wren slipped into Kiera's study with a tea tray. Her friend was wan again and appeared even more exhausted than Kiera, which Wren blamed on visiting witch shops to help Hawke hunt for a mysterious dryad he'd met at the king's summer masquerade. Kiera gaped at Wren. Hawke was seriously pursuing another lady? But he and Wren had been in love for as long as she'd known them. Poor Wren.

Her throat tightening for her friend, Kiera tsked and picked up her teacup. To distract Wren from Hawke, she drawled, "I can't help but wonder what else you failed to mention about the king's summer masquerade." Like a mermaid and a squire dancing together the entire evening.

Wren shrugged. "The only other masquerade gossip I know involves the king, but I didn't hear about it until recently."

Kiera arched her brows as she sipped her tea. Despite being unwed, gossip about King Devon was rare. Everyone in Calatini knew their noble king was too dutiful to court scandal. "Oh?"

Wren nodded. "Like Hawke, King Devon was enthralled by a mysterious lady who vanished, although in his case, 'twas a mermaid."

Kiera choked mid-swallow. A mermaid? The extravagant costumes from the masquerade flashed before her eyes. She'd been the only mermaid there that night. But the dark-haired squire *couldn't* be the king! He'd not worn a crown, and he was too unpretentious, and his arms couldn't have felt so right. Yet him being the king would explain his assured air of purpose as well as his Calator costume and lofty goals for Calatini. Dear Goddess. She managed to croak, "Really?"

Wren blinked at her. "Are you well?"

Kiera dredged up a weak smile. No, but how could she explain? Not even Wren would approve of a poor orphan of unknown parentage dancing all night with the king. "'Tis nothing. Swallowed wrong."

Wren winced. "According to Hawke's family, the king's obsession with his mermaid is damaging the talks with the nightmara herds."

Kiera gaped at her. Obsession? Despite their intense attraction, a king couldn't be obsessed with *her*. Surely he'd met true ladies much more worthy of his regard. Yet obsession fit her preoccupation with the peach rose and her passionate dreams about him over the past month.

Her stomach clenched. But how could she have damaged the nightmara negotiations? She'd nothing to do with the legendary Nightmara-Calatini Treaty. "Why?"

Wren shrugged. "Nightmara are matriarchal, and he needs a wife, or at least a betrothed, to negotiate with them. Until the masquerade, everyone assumed he'd offer for Lady Annalise Greysnowe, but now he only wants his mermaid."

Nausea swamping her, Kiera dropped her teacup. How could this have happened? Succumbing to her hunger to experience something new had tangled the king's life as well as her own. "Oh dear."

Her hazel eyes dark, Wren frowned at Kiera. "Are you *certain* you're well?"

Kiera rubbed her forehead. She needed a plausible excuse to distract her clever friend from realizing the truth. "No, I'm afraid this tea made me ill for some reason." Would that be enough?

Still frowning, Wren rose. "Do you need me to fetch someone?" When Kiera shook her head, Wren continued, "Then I'll see you later."

Once Wren drifted from the study, Kiera tottered to the door and locked it. She required time alone to recover from the devastating news Wren had shared. She staggered back to her desk and collapsed into her chair then gulped her tea. If only 'twere the strongest spiritwine.

Goddess, no wonder the dark-haired squire had been so perfect—he was actually the king! His confidence and determination had been fostered since birth, and the Vireni kings were known for their compassion and dedication since their founder Calator, an erstwhile apprentice healer. And those traits, rather than his strong features, had attracted her like gold apples attracted firebirds. Yet since he was the king, their irresistible attraction was even more impossible.

She rubbed her aching chest. And being the king explained

why he'd not bothered with a mask. Surely everyone at court recognized him no matter what he wore. He must have realized she was a stranger to court. Had he not revealed his true identity because her ignorance amused him? She crumbled the half-eaten sweet biscuit on her plate. No, considering King Devon's serious and chivalrous demeanor, he'd never torment a lady so. He must simply have enjoyed not being recognized.

Kiera leapt upright and began pacing about the study. Yet why had a king known for his dutiful nature courted scandal by dancing with a mysterious lady all night? Especially when court assumed he was about to offer for another lady, doubtless that radiant siren he'd danced with first. He'd claimed he wasn't almost betrothed, so perhaps he'd sought to escape the siren for some reason. Dancing all night with another lady would certainly accomplish that.

She wet her lips. But why was King Devon still hunting for a mysterious lady who'd vanished like a ghost at dawn? Despite their attraction, their wonderful night was nothing more than a dalliance. If it had been more, he would have revealed his true identity.

Kiera gasped, her heart freezing. Although she'd requested a small spell, what if the shell mask had been more than a disguise? Could it have caused King Devon's erratic behavior? She pressed a hand against her roiling stomach. She must visit the veiled witch to make sure.

She bolted to her room and snatched the shell mask from inside her bedside table. As she stuffed it in her reticule, her eye caught on the basket containing the crumbled rose, and she almost cackled. It had been a portent.

After telling Mary and Peter she'd an errand, Kiera rushed to Rhiannon's Veils despite the blazing summer sun. She flung open the witch shop's weathered red door. Her nose itching at the pervasive incense, she strode through the empty witch shop. "Madam witch!"

The glass beads over the back door jangling, the veiled witch burst into the witch shop then glared at her.

Kiera yanked the shell mask from her reticule and waved it at the veiled witch. "Tell me this couldn't have inspired obsession." Please, Goddess.

The veiled witch relaxed, and a chuckle undulated her black veils. "I'd wondered if you were the king's mermaid."

Kiera scowled and waved the mask again. This was too momentous to chuckle about. "Tell me!"

The veiled witch's exotically lined eyes narrowed. "The king's obsession, as you call it, is no magic of mine."

A chill skittering across her skin, Kiera lowered the shell mask. "So 'tis magic then."

Tilting her head, the veiled witch hummed and scrutinized Kiera. "Not exactly. Your aura appears unchanged by magic. Although there's still that peculiar shimmer about you." She paused and arched her brows. "Tell me, how have your dreams been lately?"

Kiera tensed as tingling warmth flooded her. Consumed by the king and his irresistible kisses. "Vivid and ardent."

The veiled witch flicked her fingers, jingling bracelets and tiny bells. "Not surprising. I'd follow those dreams if I were you. They speak your deepest truth."

Kiera snorted and crossed her arms. The king kneeling at her feet as he had in this morning's dream echoed through her. Her heart squeezed. "No, they speak of impossible fantasies. Ones that can *never* come true."

The veiled witch purred a chuckle. "Sometimes never is impossible." With that, she sashayed through the glass beads and disappeared.

Kiera gaped after her. Had the veiled witch just hinted King Devon would marry a poor orphan of unknown parentage? She shook herself. No, of course not. The veiled witch was just maintaining her cryptic air. But *why* did she think her dreams were significant? She'd said they weren't magic.

Kiera swallowed then whirled and strode back to the orphanage. Unable to disguise her distress, she told Mary and Peter she was ill then retired early. Although exhausted, she only succumbed to slumber after hours of staring at the ceiling, and her dreams were still about the king.

DURING THE DAYS THAT FOLLOWED, Kiera focused on her orphans and buried all thoughts of King Devon except when alone. Yet her busy days didn't prevent the dreams. Every night, the king begged her to marry him and removed her shell mask once she accepted. But she always jerked awake before he reacted to her enchanted ballgown disappearing to reveal her true identity. Even asleep, she knew 'twas an impossible fantasy. If only the dreams would stop so she could get some decent sleep.

So Kiera was still weary when Wren finally returned a week later, appearing worse than before, as if the entire world was crushing her. Had she somehow discovered Kiera's secret? Yet Kiera relaxed once Wren admitted she was Hawke's dryad and now carried his child. She'd disguised herself with a spell from the veiled witch, a powerful Rhiannon descendant. No wonder the veiled witch could magic anything.

Soon after, Hawke burst into the study to find Wren. After whispered words of encouragement, Kiera shooed them home to settle matters.

A few days later, while Kiera was reviewing the orphanage's accounts, Wren breezed into Kiera's study, her usual lively self for the first time in the past month. She grinned at Kiera as she alighted on the chair before the desk. "Hard at work, I see."

Kiera grinned back, her chest lightening. Thank the Goddess Wren was better. "Of course, the work never stops at an orphanage." She tilted her head. "I assume you and Hawke settled matters."

Wren blushed but flashed a coy smile. "We did, several times, in fact." She sighed. "Expressing love without pretense is glorious."

Her stomach twisting, Kiera maintained her smile. If only she could experience that joy. Not that she loved King Devon, but he was the closest she'd come, and he was an impossible dream. Her heart warmed when Wren sighed again. Yet seeing her friend's joy was wonderful. She chuckled. "Too bad it took a perilous glamour spell and an unexpected pregnancy for the two of you to admit the truth so obvious to everyone else."

Wren giggled. "Yes, we were a pair of fools. But fortunately, we're past that now." She leaned forward. "We're getting married in four days. We must move quickly to quiet the gossip about our pregnancy. Thanks to Kit, all of court is gossiping about us."

Kiera almost winced. Poor Wren must hate such attention, especially when instigated by her childhood rival. Only gossip about the king hunting a poor orphan of unknown parentage would eclipse Wren and Hawke's scandalous pregnancy. Kiera swallowed. Which hopefully court would never learn.

Wren wrinkled her nose. "Thankfully, Hawke has kept our mothers from interfering, so the wedding shall be only family and close friends. Mel is officiating the ceremony at the Moon Chapel of the Great Temple. 'Tis a bloodbinding."

Kiera nodded. Not surprising. Even without the magical ceremony that would bind their life forces until death, Wren and Hawke had been bound to each other forever, so a bloodbinding was nothing to them. And a small wedding officiated by Hawke's priest brother was perfect for her shy friend. "Sounds romantic."

Wren smiled then reached across the desk and grasped Kiera's hand. "Yes. And I want you to act as my bride witness."

Kiera stiffened despite the warmth flooding her chest. Only Wren would defy the dictates of court and choose a poor orphanage matron as her bride witness. She swallowed. She couldn't possibly stand up before all of Wren's and Hawke's noble relatives. Not only did she not belong, but King Devon might attend the wedding. He *was* Hawke's cousin, after all. "Given the scandal surrounding your wedding, perhaps Selena should be your bride witness instead." Hawke's sister-in-law would be a suitable choice.

Wren's eyes narrowed. "Although I like Selena, she's not my best female friend—*you* are. The only person closer to me is Hawke, and I need you there to support us. Unless there's some reason you can't attend?"

Kiera fought a blush. Being exposed as the king's mysterious mermaid was a compelling reason. Yet she couldn't explain that to Wren. "I'm needed at the orphanage; you know that."

Wren snorted. "Peter and Mary can manage the orphans for a day." Her gaze turned probing. "If you're concerned about your attire, don't. I'm going to purchase a fashionable gown for you." She squeezed Kiera's hand. "'Tis the least I can do for my best female friend, who's gracious enough to act as my bride witness before our noble families."

Kiera glanced down at their clasped hands. Of course, her clever friend had noticed her unease among nobles. But a suitable gown didn't address the king. She lifted her gaze and began to refuse, but halted at Wren's set jaw. Wren would keep insisting until Kiera relented. Besides, she couldn't skip her best friend's wedding. "Very well."

Wren beamed and rose, drawing Kiera upright by their clasped hands. "Excellent. Let's visit a dress shop now to ensure they finish your gown before the wedding. Although not as fashionable as Celeste's, there's a fine shop on Silk Road that should have openings."

After telling Mary and Peter their plans, Kiera and Wren climbed into Wren's carriage. Kiera licked her lips. Surely acting as Wren's bride witness would be fine—doubtless King Devon wouldn't have time to attend Wren and Hawke's wedding. 'Twas hasty and planned to conceal a scandalous pregnancy; plus, he'd the nightmara negotiations to handle. Kiera relaxed with a sigh.

So he'd never realize his vanished mermaid was merely Wren's poor friend.

CHAPTER 11

A little over a week after the fete, Devon chuckled at the wedding invitation and note from Hawke. Wren wearing a glamour spell to seduce Hawke certainly explained his cousin's determination to find his vanished dryad as well as Wren's unexpected pregnancy, which all of court was gossiping about thanks to Lady Blaine.

He grinned. And Hawke's successful hunt might help his own. As promised, his cousin had included the address to Rhiannon's Veils, the witch shop near the docks where Wren had purchased her glamour spell. He'd visit as soon as he'd a few hours free. Even though Moonbud had sworn they were close to finding his mermaid at yesterday's meeting, perhaps a powerful Rhiannon descendant with the reputation of being able to magic anything would have better success.

Unfortunately, thanks to his duties and attending court events to find his mermaid, Devon didn't manage to visit Rhiannon's Veils until the morning of Hawke and Wren's wedding. Although visiting a witch shop near the docks wasn't on the way to the Great Temple, both were beyond the palace and the townhouses of court.

When he and his guards reached the tiny witch shop on

Mountainglass Lane, he eyed the weathered red door. Unremarkable for the powerful Rhiannon descendant that had created the glamour spell which had fooled Hawke for a month, but perhaps the witch preferred a quiet life rather than the renown the royal witch enjoyed.

He shrugged then leapt from his saddle, motioning for his guards to remain mounted. His meeting with Wren's witch should be private. He touched his coat near his heart where he kept the pocketcloth concealing the ragged scrap from his mermaid's enchanted ballgown. Would it be enough for such a powerful witch to trace, despite the royal witch saying its magic was too faint?

Devon attempted to thrust open the witch shop's door, but the weathered wood refused to budge. He blinked. Why was the door locked? 'Twas midmorning and not a festival day, so the shop should be open.

He set his jaw then pounded on the door. He *must* consult with Wren's witch, and who knew when he could return? He pounded until his fist ached, yet no one answered. So he lowered his arm with a sigh. Clearly, the witch wasn't here. Damnation. Why was his hunt for his mermaid so impossible? 'Twas as if the Goddess and her avatar the Autumn Queen, who tracked everyone's fate, were conspiring against him.

He sighed again and trudged back to his black gelding. Unfortunately, he'd no time to wait for the witch shop's owner to return. If he didn't leave now, he'd be late for Hawke and Wren's wedding. So he rode with his guards to the Great Temple on Our Lady's Way.

Devon smiled as he dismounted and handed his reins to a guard. Visiting the magnificent temple always cheered him. Constructed of the same white limestone as the palace and illuminated by elaborate, stained-glass windows, the massive Great Temple was a stunning tribute to the Goddess. A deity worthy of that couldn't be conspiring against him. His impossible hunt was just simple misfortune.

Inhaling a deep breath, he strode through the dazzling nave and sanctuary to reach the covered walkway leading to the Moon Chapel. Although a smaller chapel, doubtless Hawke and Wren had only obtained it because Mel was a priest here and officiating the wedding. The chapels were popular locations for weddings or other intimate ceremonies.

As he slipped inside the gleaming chapel, Devon studied the few guests. Seated in the first pew on the left side, the Duke and Duchess of Childes beamed as they waited. Aragon's parents were clearly thrilled their rakehell youngest son was marrying at last. No doubt the duchess was congratulating herself on matchmaking Hawke and Wren. Behind the duke and duchess were all Aragon's various cousins, except for Lady Blaine. Not surprising, given the fashionable countess had spread gossip about Wren's unexpected pregnancy throughout court. Also on the left were a weathered man and a teenage girl, likely Hawke's merchant friend and the man's daughter. And in the second to last pew sat Selena, but Aragon wasn't beside her since he was Hawke's groom witness. Yet why wasn't Selena with the duke and duchess?

Devon glanced toward the right pews, which appeared empty compared to the groom's side. Sitting apart from the duke and duchess for once, Sir Alaric and Lady Keyes were in the front pew and appeared as smug as their friends about their daughter's marriage. Behind them were Lord and Lady Weston, along with the granddaughters they'd just discovered at Waterstreet Orphanage. The final guest on the bride's side was a veiled woman, no doubt a friend from the orphanage.

Her hair and most of her face concealed by black veils, the unknown woman met his eyes when his gaze touched her. She stared at him for a long moment.

A prickle skittered across his skin. Her probing stare resembled Moonbud's when the nightmara queen-heir's powers pressed against his mind. But surely a human didn't possess the same power over dreams and the mind as a nightmara. So why was the veiled woman staring at him so?

The veiled woman inclined her head then turned back to the front.

Devon exhaled. Surprising that Wren had invited such an eerie woman to her wedding. He slid into the empty seat along the wall beside Selena, forcing his guards to sit behind them. "Morning."

Her freckled face bright, Selena dimpled at him. "Morning. I was wondering if you'd manage to attend." The forthright lady never hesitated to treat him like an ordinary gentleman. His best friend had chosen a wonderful wife.

He winked at her. "I'm pleased to celebrate Hawke and Wren admitting the truth at last." Now if only he could share Hawke's good fortune and find his own mysterious lady.

Selena giggled behind her hand. "So is everyone else."

He eyed her for a moment then coughed and asked, "Why are you sitting alone in the back?"

Selena shrugged and rubbed her gently rounded stomach. "Occasionally, I still suffer nausea, so I wanted to be able to leave without disrupting the wedding. As a pregnant lady herself, Wren completely understood, although Hawke claimed I should make sure to be sick on Mel. He said some places consider it good fortune to start a marriage by vomiting on a priest."

Devon suppressed a chuckle. That sounded like something his impish cousin would say. "I suspect he just wants to stain Mel's robes."

Selena grinned. "Yes, so I said I'd do no such thing. Then Wren told him she wouldn't either and ordered him to stop asking about it."

He smiled then glanced about the mostly empty chapel again. Since he'd visited Rhiannon's Veils first, he'd expected it to be full. "Am I early? There aren't many guests."

Selena shook her head. "I think you're the last to arrive. Hawke and Wren insisted on only family and a few friends. The duchess spent the past week attempting to convince them to invite more people. Hawke threatened to elope if she didn't quit pestering them."

Devon snorted. The duchess adored grandiose affairs, but Hawke was stubborn enough to ignore her, unlike most of court. His gaze drifted to the veiled woman again, and another chill darted through him. "I suppose the veiled woman is a friend of Wren's from the orphanage."

Selena's dark-gray eyes gleamed. "Her? No, she's the witch who created the glamour spell that prevented Hawke from recognizing Wren. According to Aragon, the veiled witch also provides the magical ingredient that makes The Gold Griffin's ale glow when telling the truth."

He nodded, his pulse quickening. So that's why Rhiannon's Veils had been closed. He fingered the pocketcloth concealing his mermaid's scrap of ballgown. He must approach the veiled witch as soon as the wedding ended.

Selena tilted her head. "The only guest from Waterstreet Orphanage is Wren's friend Kiera, the orphanage matron. But she's acting as bride witness, so she's not among the guests. To keep the wedding small, Hawke and Wren decided against inviting the orphans. Instead, they're hosting a party for the orphans at their townhouse two days after the wedding."

Devon flashed a wry grin. "With the wedding so small, I suppose they each only have one witness. I'm surprised the duchess allowed that." Most weddings at court had at least two witnesses apiece.

Selena raised her eyes skyward. "She complained about it in addition to the few guests, but she quieted when Hawke reminded her Mel was officiating and couldn't act as his second witness. It shall be Mel's first time performing a bloodbinding."

Devon swallowed as his ribs squeezed. Of course, Hawke and Wren were seeking a bloodbinding. They'd been devoted to each other forever, and as a younger son, Hawke needn't worry about heirs. If only he could do the same with his mermaid when he found her. "I've never witnessed a bloodbinding before, have you?"

Selena twisted the interlocking hearts on her electrum necklace, the wedding token she and Aragon had exchanged at last year's ceremony. "Unfortunately not, although my parents had one. Aragon and I wanted one as well, but the duke and duchess refused to allow it until we had children."

Devon nodded. Yes, Aragon had grumbled about that. But his parents' refusal was common. Since bloodbound couples could only bear each other's children and often died together, most considered the danger of no heirs too great. He winked to smooth Selena's frown. "Well, you've a start on those children now."

Selena burbled a laugh and caressed her stomach. "So we do." She arched her brows at him. "And have you a start on your mermaid?"

Devon grimaced as weight compressed his chest again. Naturally, Selena would ask about that. "She remains as mysterious as when she vanished, but I intend to speak with Wren's witch after the wedding."

Selena smiled and patted his hand as Mel strode to the altar. "Most fortunate Hawke and Wren invited her then."

Devon nodded as Mel led the opening prayer. Please let the veiled witch help him find his mermaid. Once Mel finished, a lilting waltz from the previous century began, and everyone turned to face the back of the chapel for the arrival of the bride and groom.

Glowing in their simple yet elegant attire, Hawke and Wren glided down the aisle, followed by Aragon and Kiera. But since Devon was seated on the groom's side along the wall, Hawke and Aragon obstructed his view of Wren's orphanage friend at first. Yet his heart fluttered at her half-seen form.

Then Kiera flanked her friend before the altar, and Devon almost leapt to his feet.

She was his mermaid!

Tingling warmth flooded him. Thank the Goddess he'd found her at last. As soon as the wedding ended, he'd beg her to marry him like he should have done at the masquerade. Perhaps he could convince her to marry this afternoon in secret—royal weddings took an age to arrange, especially when a coronation was involved, and he needed her now. If only he'd brought the Vireni betrothal ring. A faegift from Esme the Great, a powerful soul healer and Calator's mentor, the gold and alexandrite ring had been in his family since Calator had proposed to Annalise. 'Twas said to ensure a happy marriage, and when given, the magical ring changed size to fit the wearer until death.

Devon grinned as he eyed Kiera before the altar. Yes, she was the perfect lady to be his queen, even though she'd not been born to privilege. She'd spent years managing the best orphanage in Ormas, and she'd more strength, compassion, and intelligence than any court lady, probably thanks to her poor upbringing. No wonder he'd been unable to resist her. And although a few noble sticklers would object at first, the people would adore her as he did. Plus, Moonbud would approve when he presented Kiera— nightmara couldn't understand why humans chose their leaders by lineage rather than worth.

As Mel read the sacred words and spoke about marriage, Devon continued eyeing Kiera. Her upbringing also explained why she'd not recognized him and his failure to find her at court events. If only he'd taken time to visit the orphanage when Hawke and Wren first began supporting it, instead of simply having his people investigate. He and Kiera would likely be married with several children by now.

Hunger roared through him at making love to Kiera and creating those children. Goddess, he couldn't wait. She was as lovely in her elegant navy gown as she'd been in her sparkling mermaid costume. Her dark-blonde curls and lush figure required no magic to enhance them. As Mel led them in another prayer, Devon leaned toward her and willed her to turn around. She'd fall in his arms once she did.

After Mel began the vows and crowned Hawke and Wren with their bound marriage garlands made of ivy, Kiera finally glanced at the guests. She blushed then paled when her navy eyes met Devon's, but she didn't sway toward him.

His heart pounding in his ears, Devon held his breath and forced himself to remain seated. He burned to storm up the aisle, pull her into his arms, and kiss her. But 'twould ruin Hawke and Wren's wedding. So he must wait until he and Kiera were alone afterward.

Kiera tore her gaze away when Mel asked the witnesses to confirm Hawke and Wren were marrying of their own free will.

Devon sighed and licked his lips. He'd been hunting for Kiera for over a month, so what was another hour? Doubtless he could manage that. He sighed again and scanned the other guests. Had any noticed his exchange with Kiera?

Everyone except Selena and the veiled witch appeared engrossed with Mel tying Hawke's and Wren's left hands together then cutting their palms to begin the bloodbinding ceremony.

The veiled witch winked when Devon's gaze reached her. Clearly, she knew Kiera was his mermaid. No doubt because she'd provided Kiera's enchanted ballgown just like she had Wren's glamour spell.

Her brow furrowed, Selena slanted him a narrow glance as Mel pressed Hawke's and Wren's bloody palms to their marriage tokens, a pair of bracelets, to bind their life forces together. "Are you well?"

Devon simply nodded. Until he spoke with Kiera, he couldn't explain the truth, not even to a friend like Selena.

Once Hawke and Wren slid their marriage tokens about their left wrists, Mel stepped forward and prayed for them before announcing, "I present to you Lord and Lady Beza Hawke."

Everyone chuckled as Hawke winced at his given name like always, causing Wren to shake her head. With joined hands, they followed Mel from the chapel, with Kiera and Aragon trailing behind them.

His pulse surging, Devon narrowed his eyes at Kiera and willed her to return his gaze as she passed.

Yet his erstwhile mermaid kept her gaze firmly at her feet.

He stiffened. Why had she refused to look at him? Surely she felt the same love he did, and a lady bold enough to sneak into the most exclusive event of the season couldn't possibly be shy. Perhaps she just wanted to wait until after signing the matrimony certificate. The king kissing the bride witness before the other guests would overshadow her friends' wedding, even if it had been a rare bloodbinding.

Devon swallowed a sigh and offered Selena his arm. As the groom witness, Aragon would meet them at the reception. "Shall we?"

Selena nodded, but she eyed him as he escorted her through the Great Temple with his guards following. "Are you certain you're well?"

He smiled and inclined his head. "Just moved after witnessing my first bloodbinding." Hopefully, that weak excuse appeared genuine.

Selena hummed but allowed him to hand her into her in-laws' carriage without another word.

Although the duke and duchess invited him to join them, Devon declined with a smile. He required time alone to settle himself before he saw Kiera again. Otherwise, he might seize her like a lusty satyr, and she deserved better than that. He sighed as he and his guards headed to the Keyes's townhouse for the reception. Surely he could remain a gentleman until Kiera agreed to marry him.

CHAPTER 12

Her heart racing, Kiera scrawled her name on Wren and Hawke's matrimony certificate beneath their signatures. With her final duty as bride witness completed, she must leave before King Devon found her. She couldn't face him now that he'd seen her as herself and realized she was nothing more than a poor orphanage matron. 'Twould shatter her when he asked her to become his mistress, especially after all those dreams where he begged her to marry him.

She swallowed as tears pricked her eyes. If only he'd missed Wren and Hawke's hasty wedding like she'd expected. She'd spent most of the ceremony avoiding looking at him. And when she had, their attraction had almost consumed her like a siren's song and compelled her to wreck her ship against the rocks.

So as Kiera handed Aragon the pen to sign the matrimony certificate, she offered Wren a wry smile. "I should return to the orphanage. The Bedsford twins were snickering when I left, and you know how scampish they can be. Goddess knows what mischief they've caused since I've been gone."

Wren frowned as she removed her ivy marriage garland and gave it to Hawke. "Peter and Mary can manage them for the rest of the afternoon. Nothing happened during your dress fitting the other day, did it?"

Kiera smoothed the elegant gown from that trip. The navy silk was the finest real gown she'd ever worn, equal to that of a true lady. Wren was sweet for purchasing it for her. Yet a fashionable gown wouldn't prevent the king from asking her to become his mistress. "No, but I've already been gone longer today, and the orphans are my responsibility."

Wren tsked while Mel began certifying the matrimony certificate. "Kiera, being the orphanage matron doesn't mean you can't have a life outside the orphanage. Please attend the reception."

Hawke flashed a crooked grin. "You met everyone at the last orphanage play, except for the Bufords, Elise's husband, the veiled witch, and Devon." He waggled his brows. "You should ask Devon for those donations we discussed."

Kiera almost blushed. Except she'd met the king before, and she couldn't ask the gentleman she'd kissed and danced with all evening for donations. 'Twould appear grasping.

Wren leaned forward as Hawke accepted the certified matrimony certificate from Mel. "Plus, Cassandra and Amaranth shall be glad to see you again. Please attend, Kiera."

Kiera's heart squeezed. She couldn't disappoint her entreating friend, and seeing the Weston sisters would be wonderful. She just needed to avoid King Devon for a few hours. Surely she could manage that. After all, she'd successfully minded sixty-odd orphans for the past eight years. "Very well."

Wren beamed and took Hawke's arm. "Shall we go then?"

Kiera gritted a smile as she accepted Aragon's arm, and everyone strolled to the carriage. But she chuckled when Wren curled up on Hawke's lap in the forward seat. They were adorable. Her smile no longer forced, she sat in the opposite corner beside the door, while Hawke's brothers took the backward seat.

As the carriage started for Wren's parents' townhouse, Mel

covered his eyes. "Must you two couple with us watching? My eyes are burning."

Kiera grinned when Hawke tightened his arms about Wren and drawled, "Privilege of a newlywed couple."

Wren sniffed and twisted her marriage token, a hawk bracelet on her left wrist. "And we aren't coupling. I'm simply making sure Hawke can't run away."

As Mel lowered his hands, Aragon snorted then said, "He would never."

To tease Wren, Kiera arched her brows and said, "He has the baby to think about, after all."

Wren laughed and pretended to throw something at Kiera. "Wretch. Maybe I shouldn't have invited you to the reception." When everyone ceased chuckling, she hummed then said, "Although, as Hawke mentioned, the reception shall be ideal to ask King Devon for donations. I'll introduce you as soon as we arrive."

Her stomach twisting, Kiera swallowed. 'Twould be a disaster. Neither she nor the king would be able to disguise their attraction, and Wren would instantly realize Kiera was the king's vanished mermaid. "'Tis your wedding day. You needn't do that."

Hawke cocked a brow. "But what about those new clothes, better tutors, and money for trade school you wanted?"

Kiera almost winced. Those would be wonderful, but when she'd mentioned them, she'd not realized the king was her dark-haired squire from the masquerade. She managed a weak smile. "I'll ask the king for donations if we happen to meet at the reception. But don't bother introducing us."

Aragon smiled at her. "Since you don't wish to impose on Wren today, I could introduce you instead. Devon would love to donate to Waterstreet Orphanage. He's devoted to his people's wellbeing."

Warmth flooded Kiera. Yes, he definitely was. His interest in her education goal and his own lofty goal for Calatini demonstrated that. 'Twas one of his most attractive qualities. Yet despite his compassion, he'd never see her as more than charity or a potential mistress, so she must avoid him. "King Devon does possess that reputation, even among those of us near the docks."

Fortunately, before the others could respond, the carriage halted, and Kiera leapt out without waiting for one of Hawke's brothers to help her alight. However, she waved for everyone to proceed her into the Keyes's grand townhouse. As Wren and Hawke entered the drawing room amid cheers, Kiera slipped inside and glanced about the elegant room.

Grinning at the newlyweds, King Devon was beside Selena near the refreshments table with two brawny guards along the wall behind him. Wren and Hawke's other relatives were scattered about the room, and an unknown gentleman, doubtless Lord Farson, was debating the weathered gentleman who must be Hawke's merchant friend Buford Leshane. Also near the refreshments table, the Westons were grinning at whatever Amaranth was chattering about, while Cassandra quarreled with the veiled witch across the room.

Kiera licked her lips. Unfortunately, the drawing room had no alcoves she could use to avoid the king. But perhaps the veiled witch could help. So she bustled straight to her.

Kiera touched Cassandra's shoulder and halted the girl mid-complaint. "How have you been, Cassandra?"

Cassandra beamed and flung her arms about Kiera. "Well enough, Mistress Kiera." She slashed a narrow glance at the veiled witch. "Although I'd be better if *someone* unbound my magic."

Kiera blinked. Magic? Cassandra was a witch? She'd not performed any spells while at the orphanage, had she? There would have been signs of that. And had Wren introduced Cassandra to the veiled witch, or had the two witches found each other through their powers?

Kiera glanced toward the front and tensed. The king was talking to Wren and Hawke, probably congratulating them, but who knew how long that would distract him? She hadn't time to discuss Cassandra's unexpected magic. She squeezed the girl's shoulder. "I must speak privately with the veiled witch. Could you rejoin your grandparents, please?"

Cassandra pursed her lips and sighed. "Very well."

As the girl trudged away, Kiera turned toward the veiled witch and hissed, "He recognized me."

Tiny bells jingling, the veiled witch tilted her head. "That's because you're wiser than your friend and requested a small spell that only lasted an evening."

Kiera's head throbbed. If she were wiser than Wren, she never would have attended that blasted masquerade, no matter how restless she'd been. "You're a Rhiannon descendant. You must know a spell to hide me. Please!"

The veiled witch arched a brow. "But 'tis treason to knowingly deceive a king."

A deep voice interrupted, "Mistress Kiera, I presume? Or should I call you Mistress Mermaid?"

Her breath seizing, Kiera whirled to face King Devon as the veiled witch curtsied and left. Dear Goddess, what was she to do? She must escape before he asked her to become his mistress. Tingling warmth flooded her as she stared at him. Seeing him in person was so much better than in dreams.

His green eyes dark with hunger, King Devon smiled and offered her a flute of sparkling wine. "Sparkling wine? I remember how much you enjoyed it at the masquerade. Your delight made me burn to kiss you."

A blush scorched her cheeks. Oh, Goddess. She stiffened her spine. Perhaps he'd withdraw if she feigned they'd never met. She bobbed a curtsy. "A most indecent remark to a new acquaintance, your majesty. I'm surprised, considering your dutiful reputation."

King Devon sighed. "I see you recognize me now. Pity, I enjoyed being an ordinary gentleman, almost as much as you enjoyed sparkling wine."

Kiera lifted her chin. She must cling to her lie to convince him to withdraw. "I've never tasted sparkling wine, and I told you, we've never met. You must be confusing me with some true court lady."

King Devon chuckled as he thrust a flute into her hand. "If by meet, you mean exchanged names, then yes, we've never met." He leaned toward her, and his voice deepened, "But I possess eyes, and I can see you're my mermaid from the masquerade."

Her pulse pounding in her ears, she clenched the flute between her fingers. How could she end this perilous conversation since her lie had foundered?

King Devon grasped her free hand. "Shall we address our tardy introductions? King Devon Calator Vireni IV at your service, my mermaid." He raised her hand to his lips and kissed it.

As tingling skittered up her arm, Kiera yanked her hand free. Such flirtation was doubtless the prelude to him asking her to become his mistress. She gritted a cool smile. "Kiera, matron of Waterstreet Orphanage."

King Devon smiled and toasted her with his flute. "A pleasure to meet you at last, Kiera. I've been hunting for you the past month. The council and the rest of court have feared I'd gone mad. But their fears shall die when I finally introduce you."

She sipped her sparkling wine and glared at him over her flute. Kings didn't introduce their mistresses. He was simply speaking blandishments to seduce her. "Spending over a month hunting a mysterious lady you met once *is* mad, your majesty."

King Devon shrugged. "Determined, more like." He grinned at her. "Which I assume you understand, given you snuck into the most exclusive event of the season. Only a determined lady could manage that."

Kiera set her jaw. Perhaps he'd withdraw if she attempted her lie again. "I told you, I didn't attend the masquerade."

A frown furrowing his brow, King Devon stilled. "And *I* told you, I recognized you. Please quit lying. A shell mask and an enchanted ballgown didn't disguise you *that* much."

Her shoulders drooping, Kiera sighed and sipped her sparkling wine. She might as well abandon her lie. The king was too obstinate to withdraw. "They weren't supposed to, your majesty. I never intended to meet anyone from the masquerade again."

King Devon tsked and shook his head. "With your best friend belonging to one of Calatini's oldest gentry families? Most short-sighted."

She tensed and glowered at him. "No one would have remembered me—if *you* hadn't danced every dance with me."

King Devon chuckled. "True enough, I suppose." He sipped his sparkling wine. "So why did you sneak into the masquerade, my mermaid?"

Kiera forced a shrug. Because she was a fool? "I burned to experience something new. Wren had always disparaged masquerades, so I was curious if 'twould be as bad as she claimed."

King Devon leaned toward her. "And was it?"

She grimaced. "Parts of it." Like Mr. Winston.

King Devon's eyes narrowed. "Not me, I trust."

Sighing, Kiera licked her lips as her pulse quickened. "No, you were the best part, your majesty. But a fantasy. Why do you think I left before the unveiling?"

King Devon twirled his flute of sparkling wine. "Odd, I felt real to me."

She gaped at him. What did he mean by *that*? She shook her head after a moment. "Of course you're real, your majesty, and so am I. We're just not real together."

King Devon stepped closer, his gaze warm. "Why not?"

Kiera leapt back. "Why not? Because you're the *king*." And kings didn't marry poor orphans of unknown parentage.

King Devon grimaced. "Sometimes being king is a damned nuisance."

Her heart squeezed, and she ached to touch him and soothe his frown. Yet if she did, he'd ask her to become his mistress. An offer she must refuse—she wanted genuine love, like Wren and Hawke shared. So instead she drawled, "Yes, being the most powerful gentleman in Calatini is a wretched burden indeed."

King Devon shook his head. "Sometimes it can be." He tucked a stray curl behind her ear. "Especially when that burden isn't shared."

Tingling flooding her at his caress, Kiera slapped his wandering hand. "Stop that. Simply because I allowed you to kiss me at the masquerade in a secluded garden doesn't mean you can fondle me at a wedding reception before my best friend and her entire family."

King Devon arched a brow. "Does that mean you'll allow me to kiss you if I find another garden? I believe Hawke has mentioned the Keyes's conservatory is quite fine."

She glared at him and drained her sparkling wine. "Perhaps so, but a fine conservatory doesn't tempt me to kiss you." The king alone was enough, but she mustn't succumb.

King Devon sighed. "Pity, I'd hoped to steal a kiss from your sweet lips."

Kiera swayed toward him then jerked back. Goddess, she'd almost kissed the king in public. All from his flirtatious teasing. "Please stop, your majesty."

King Devon frowned then eyed her for a long moment. "Very well. You've been matron at Waterstreet Orphanage for eight years or so, correct? You should be proud of everything you've accomplished there. Although near the docks, 'tis the best orphanage in Ormas."

A chill prickling her neck, she nodded. How did he know all of that? Surely a poor orphanage was beneath the notice of a king.

King Devon winked at her. "And at the masquerade, you assumed I'd not know where you lived."

Kiera swallowed and licked her lips. "Why do you?"

King Devon chuckled with a shrug. "I had Waterstreet Orphanage investigated when Hawke and Wren convinced their families to donate. Too bad I didn't investigate in person. We'd have met years ago."

She froze. He'd had her *investigated*? And he sounded unrepentant too. Only royalty would assume that was normal. Goddess, she was as different from him as a human woman from a triton. Their dealings would only lead to heartbreak or drowning for her. She flicked a curtsy. "I must return to my orphanage, your majesty. I've been gone too long already."

Kiera whirled and fled, not even pausing to bid Wren and Hawke farewell. The king might catch her if she did. And who knew if she was strong enough to escape a second time?

CHAPTER 13

As Kiera bolted from the Keyes's drawing room, Devon's heart wrenched. He'd not asked her to marry him yet. He clenched his flute of sparkling wine. Did she not feel the same love he did? She definitely shared his attraction—when he flirted with her, she'd swayed toward him, and her eyes had darkened. But she'd also become flustered, so he'd relented then praised her work at the orphanage to build toward proposing. Yet mentioning the orphanage had made her flee—again.

He sighed and set down his flute before he shattered it. Clearly, he'd approached Kiera wrong. From their rapport at the masquerade, he'd assumed she'd not care he was the king and would fall into his arms. Yet his rank must have overwhelmed her. He needed to prove that he was still the ordinary gentleman from the masquerade despite being king, and that she was more than equal to being his queen. But how?

Aragon halted beside Devon and coughed. "Are you well? You're pale and tense, and Selena said you were restless during the wedding."

Forcing a smile, Devon yanked his gaze from the door. Although perhaps he should wait until he and Kiera settled matters, he required advice, and Aragon had been acquainted with Kiera for years. "I'm fine. I finally found my mermaid."

Aragon grinned and clapped his shoulder. "Congratulations! No wonder you're restless. You should have brought her to the wedding. Hawke and Wren wouldn't have minded."

Devon snorted a laugh. How had Aragon misunderstood? "I couldn't bring her because I didn't find her until you escorted her down the aisle."

Aragon blinked. "Wren's friend *Kiera* is your mermaid?"

Warmth flooding his chest, Devon inclined his head. Yes, and she was perfect. Except for her unexpected flight.

Aragon's brow furrowed. "How did an orphanage matron manage to attend the most exclusive event of the season?"

Devon flashed a wry smile. "She snuck in, I imagine. Since everyone wore masks and costumes, 'twould be simple enough if she avoided the ushers." And Kiera was certainly clever enough to manage that.

Aragon eyed him. "But everyone claims your mermaid's costume was exquisite. How could she afford it?"

Devon shrugged. She'd probably saved for years, not that her poverty mattered. He didn't need a wealthy bride any more than Aragon had. "Her ballgown was enchanted." He nodded at the veiled witch, who was listening to Lady Farson complain. "Doubtless by the veiled witch. Her shop is near the orphanage."

Aragon rubbed his chin. "Of course..." He chuckled. "Well, from what I know of Kiera, she definitely matches how you described your mermaid. She's perfect for you and shall make an excellent queen—if you can convince court to accept her."

Devon set his jaw. "They'll accept her." He sighed. "Although I must convince Kiera to accept me first. She fled before I could ask her to marry me."

Aragon grimaced. "At least you know where to find her now."

His ribs squeezing, Devon sighed. "True, but I don't know

how to approach her. Everything I attempted today made her more flustered. What would you suggest?"

Aragon hummed. "I'm not sure. I know Kiera more by reputation. I've only met her a few times over the years. But—"

Before Aragon could finish, Selena glided over and touched his arm. "Hawke and Wren just left. Do you think we could go as well? I could use a nap."

Aragon straightened and tucked her hand beneath his arm. "Of course, my love." He nodded at Devon then solicitously escorted his pregnant wife from the drawing room.

Devon smiled after his friends. Hopefully, one day he could escort Kiera home the same way. He sighed. But he must ask her to marry him first. Since Aragon hadn't been able to help, perhaps he should seek Wren's advice. Wren was Kiera's closest friend, so surely she'd know how to approach her.

After saying farewell to the Keyes and the duke and duchess, Devon strode outside with his guards close behind. Although he burned to ask Kiera to marry him, he obviously couldn't bother Wren today, and probably not tomorrow either. But perhaps he could risk the day after, before his fourth meeting with Moonbud.

So two days later straight after luncheon, Devon inhaled then rapped on Hawke and Wren's front door. Let him not be interrupting an intimate moment between the newlyweds. When the door glided open, he asked, "Is Lady Beza Hawke available?"

The butler blinked at him then ushered Devon and his guards inside the townhouse. "Follow me to the study, your majesty, and I'll inquire."

As Devon followed the butler, he arched his brows at the din of rowdy children filling the townhouse. Then he smiled. It must be that party for the orphans Selena had mentioned. His pulse quickened. So Kiera was just down the hall. Should he ask to see her instead?

After a moment, he sighed. No, he should obtain Wren's advice first. He might fluster Kiera again without it, and asking her to marry him was too important to founder twice. Despite his hunger to see Kiera, he must restrain himself.

So Devon strode into the study and sat on the sofa while his guards joined him and flanked the door. As he waited for Wren, he tapped his fingers against his knee. How could he best explain? Wren would surely be protective of her friend. But admitting how he loved Kiera and burned to marry her should help.

Her face flushed but eyes narrow, Wren darted into the study then curtsied. "Good afternoon, your majesty."

He rose and inclined his head in return before waving for his guards to leave. His discussion with Wren should remain private. Not only was his interest in Kiera personal, but being alone should loosen Wren's tongue. He flashed a grin. "Afternoon, Wren. Please call me Devon. We're cousins now, after all."

Wren studied him as she settled at the other end of the sofa and he resumed his seat. "Very well, y—Devon." She hesitated. "Why did you wish to see me?" She blurted, "If 'tis to pen a play in honor of the nightmara, I must decline."

Devon almost laughed. Writing another play for court clearly horrified her. Not surprising. Fortunately for her, a play didn't interest him. "No, 'tis about your friend Kiera."

Wren relaxed and tilted her head. "She's your mermaid."

He blinked. No astonishment shaded her tone. He leaned toward her. "She told you then."

Wren chuckled. "No, I guessed. She turned whiter than an arctic elf when I mentioned your mysterious mermaid. I was too distracted by my tangled relationship with Hawke to make much of it then, but later I suspected the truth. And I was certain of it when she attempted to avoid my wedding reception."

His heart stuttered. Kiera had sought to avoid him? "So you made her attend."

Wren wrinkled her nose. "After my imbroglio with Hawke, I

learned facing matters was better than hiding behind lies." She slashed him a narrow glance. "And if you confronted Kiera at my reception, I could supervise you."

Devon glowered back. From her demeanor, she assumed he'd not consider Kiera his equal. Ridiculous. He set his jaw. "I intend to marry Kiera."

"Do you?" Wren arched her brows. "You realize her parentage is unknown, and she's likely a bastard of some poor sailor."

He tensed as fire flared in his veins. How dare she denigrate Kiera so? "That hasn't stopped *you* from befriending her."

Wren shrugged. "No, but I'm not the king responsible for continuing the Vireni line or involved with court."

Devon gritted a smile. Court's opinions wouldn't stop him from marrying the lady meant to be his queen. And Kiera was the perfect addition to the Vireni line. As the nightmara believed, true nobility came from within, not from bloodlines. He spread his hands. "Kiera's unknown family and poor upbringing mean nothing. 'Tis her maturity, intelligence, compassion, and strength I love." He reared back when tears welled in Wren's eyes. "What?"

Wren sighed. "Your declaration was so romantic. Exactly what Kiera deserves." She dabbed her eyes with a pocketcloth. "I apologize for the tears—pregnancy, you know. I've never cried so much in my life." She grinned at him as she tucked her pocketcloth back into her dress. "Something for you to anticipate."

His chest warmed. Goddess, despite the tears, creating a family with Kiera would be wonderful. And given her dedication and compassion, she'd make an excellent mother.

Wren leaned toward him. "But how do you know your love is genuine and not mere infatuation after just one night?"

Devon waggled his brows. "Not *everyone* is fortunate enough to know the one they love their entire lives." When she flashed a wry smile, he sobered and shook his head. "But my love for Kiera isn't infatuation—it burgeoned from the recognition of a likeminded soul as well as her matching all I ever desired in a wife."

Wren scrutinized him for a long moment. "I see." She smiled. "Kiera is with the orphans in the dining room. Do you wish me to fetch her?"

If only. His ribs squeezed. "As much as I want to see Kiera, no. I tried approaching her at your reception, but she fled like a nymph being chased by a manticore intent on devouring her whole." He sighed. "I require your advice on how to approach her. Everything I attempted just flustered her."

Wren pursed her lips. "Kiera has always been overly conscious of her poor upbringing. When she rescued me and Hawke from the docks all those years ago, she withdrew as soon as she heard our accents. She only relaxed once I began teaching her proper speech."

Devon frowned. Yet Kiera's poor upbringing had shaped her into the lady he loved and provided her insight into Calatini that none at court possessed. She was more than equal to any court lady, but how could he convince her of that?

Before he could ask, Wren tsked and added, "Plus, she probably assumed you meant to make her your mistress."

He winced, his throat tightening. And his flirting had likely reinforced that assumption. Yet he'd never flirted until he met Kiera—he'd been too mindful of raising expectations he'd no intention of fulfilling. But since he truly wanted her, flirting had been natural for once. He sighed. "I suppose I should stop flirting with her then. Although I'm not sure I can help myself."

Wren hummed. "No, keep flirting. It proves you desire her, and she'll trust that even if she trusts nothing else. Just don't go too far."

Devon tapped his fingers against his knee. So nothing more than banter and kisses until Kiera trusted his love. Hopefully, his restraint would last.

Wren leaned toward him. "You'll need time to court Kiera and convince her to trust you and your love." She sighed. "You must remember she's not lived a sheltered life, so she's slow to trust. After she rescued us, it took her a *year* to call me her friend. And she was only seventeen then and hadn't spent nearly a decade managing an orphanage."

He grimaced and rubbed his brow. "Except with the nightmara here and demanding a queen to negotiate the treaty's renewal, I haven't time to court Kiera. I need a queen at once, but she's the only one I'll take."

Wren touched his hand with a gentle smile. "Then you must give Kiera a purpose to interact with you. She cares deeply and loves helping others. And when she commits to something, she always sees it through." She nibbled her lip. "Although that may make it difficult for her to leave the orphanage. She keenly feels her duty to the orphans. But perhaps it shall help that Hawke and I can assume her duties there."

Devon's heart fluttered. He'd not love Kiera half so much if she didn't share his sense of responsibility. Somehow he must convince her that her true duty was to all of Calatini and not just her orphanage. But the nightmara's demands might be his answer.

Wren shook her head. "Also, while she's aiding you, remain steadfast in your support and teach court to accept her. That should help her realize your love is sincere and that she can be queen."

His chest easing, he captured Wren's hands then rose. Her help had been invaluable. "Thank you for your wise counsel."

Wren dug her nails into his palms. "If you hurt Kiera, I *swear* I'll write the most satiric play about you I can imagine and send it to every playhouse in Calatini."

Devon almost smiled. Despite her shyness, she would too. "Kiera holds my heart, so hurting her would be hurting myself."

He swept a deep bow then strode from the study. Late for his meeting with Moonbud, he rode straight to the nightmara stables with his guards. Goddess, please let the nightmara queen-heir understand about Kiera and give him more time.

When they arrived at the nightmara stables, he ordered his guards to remain by the fence then met Moonbud alone, as he had since their first private agreement.

The dappled midnight mare sighed as they began walking abreast through the sweltering paddock. :*Unfortunately, we still haven't located your true mate, and your month is almost gone. Queen Nightsnow and the other dominant mares are becoming impatient, but they don't want a stallion negotiating the treaty.*:

Devon inhaled and clasped his hands behind his back. "I shan't need to. I found my mermaid at my cousin's wedding the other day."

Moonbud's ears pricked forward. "Then why isn't she with you?"

He sighed. If only she was. "Because she's a poor commoner and doesn't believe my interest sincere."

Moonbud snorted and shook her head. :*You humans and your idiotic dwelling on birth.*:

Devon stiffened and hid a glare. "I don't care about Kiera's birth." He drooped. "But she does, so I require another favor."

Her powers pressing against his mind, Moonbud eyed him. :*Which is?*:

He spread his hands in a beseeching gesture. "More time." Please let her agree.

Moonbud's midnight tail swished. :*How shall that help?*:

Devon arched his brows. Hadn't she read that from his mind? "Kiera shall never marry me unless I've time to court her and earn her trust. And I can't do either unless she has a reason to interact with me. But renegotiating the historic Nightmara-Calatini Treaty as my betrothed shall accomplish that. All you must do is stall until she agrees to become my queen in truth."

Moonbud snorted. :*I'll stall as long as I can, but I must only negotiate with her from now on.*:

He relaxed. Thank the Goddess she'd agreed. He flashed a wry smile. Not surprising the nightmara queen-heir only wanted Kiera after dealing with a king for weeks. "Thank you, Lady

Moonbud, but it shall be a few weeks until you meet Kiera. I must prepare her for court and introduce her as my betrothed first."

Moonbud halted. :*I want to meet her as soon as you introduce her. We must start negotiating the treaty.*:

Devon inclined his head. Her impatience was understandable—this treaty renewal had already lasted longer than even the first negotiation of the treaty. He shrugged with a grin. "I must prepare her for that as well. She's never met a nightmara before."

Moonbud snorted again. :*'Twould have been so much easier for us if she had.*:

He frowned. Why would meeting Kiera before have mattered? "What?"

Moonbud tossed her mane. :*'Tis nothing, King Devon.*:

Devon eyed her for a moment. She'd explain if 'twas actually nothing. But he couldn't strain their agreement by probing, so he merely said, "Thank you for your patience about all this, Lady Moonbud."

Moonbud began walking back to the center of the paddock. :*It shall be worth it if we can negotiate with your queen.*:

Devon cocked a brow. "I hope you plan to give her better terms than you did me. Most of your proposals would be disastrous for Calatini." As the nightmara queen-heir had been well aware.

Moonbud snickered. :*Of course.*:

His jaw firming, he nodded at Moonbud then strode from the nightmara paddock. Now that everything was arranged with the nightmara, he must settle exactly how to approach Kiera. He'd visit her right after breakfast tomorrow. Since she tended to flee, he must entice her to remain before he mentioned the nightmara or a betrothal. Offering to support her orphanage should work. Then he'd beg her to marry him. Hopefully, Wren's advice would help him succeed this time.

CHAPTER 14

The morning after Wren and Hawke's party for the orphans, Kiera leapt from bed with a grin. She'd not suffered her impossibly lifelike dream of the king proposing, so she'd managed her first decent sleep in weeks. Yet overtired from the party, the orphans were fractious at breakfast.

The Bedsford twins were especially wild—the Weston sisters had attended yesterday's party, which had reminded the boys how much they missed Amaranth. This morning, the twins had hidden their new pet frogs, which they'd found at a park near Wren and Hawke's, in their pockets to feed them breakfast. But more interested in insects than porridge, the frogs had soon escaped and hopped down the trestle table. The other children's shrieks had been piercing.

After hauling the twins to her study, Kiera frowned at John and Jacob while drumming her fingers on her desk. Again, the scamps appeared unrepentant. "*Why* did you think frogs would want porridge?"

Both boys shrugged, then John said, "Maybe they're princes cursed by a black witch to be frogs until a princess kisses them."

She tsked. Doubtless John and Jacob wished that Amaranth was the princess and they were the frogs. "Such things only happen in one of Miss Wren's plays. You two are old enough to realize that."

An alluring voice rumbled, "I don't know. Sometimes magic happens without warning—like when a mysterious mermaid sneaks into a summer masquerade."

Glancing past the fidgeting twins, Kiera tensed, and her breath caught in her throat. Attired in rough clothes and the silver, melissa torc from the masquerade, King Devon grinned at her from the door. Oh, Goddess. She leapt to her feet. "What are *you* doing here?"

King Devon swept a graceful bow then strode into the study. "Visiting you." He offered her another perfect, peach rose with a warm smile.

She blushed, her heart fluttering. She should refuse his gift. He'd assume she'd become his mistress if she accepted it. But the rose was exquisite and smelled sweeter than a venus's perfume in a seductive dream. So she accepted the thorn-free stem.

John nudged Jacob, and the twins snickered.

Kiera blushed harder. The king had driven the twins from her mind even though they sat before her desk. He truly made her forget herself. She narrowed her eyes at the Bedsford twins. "Go find those frogs. You'll return them to that park when Peter has time to take you. Once you capture them, see Mary for kitchen chores as punishment."

John and Jacob grimaced at each other then hurtled from the study.

She inhaled and laid the peach rose on the corner of her desk then turned back to King Devon. Somehow she must convince him to leave before he asked her to become his mistress. But how? "Thank you for the rose, your majesty. 'Tis exquisite."

As she sank back into her chair, King Devon flashed a grin and sat in the chair Jacob had just left. "Your porter Peter appeared pleased to recognize the rose, although I doubt he recognized me."

Her lips contorting, Kiera snorted. "Us poor folk wouldn't

without your crown and fancy clothes." After all, 'twas why she'd not recognized him at the masquerade.

King Devon tsked and arched his brows. "Don't you like my healer disguise? I thought it appropriate given how we met."

She shrugged. A king disguising himself as a poor healer was hardly appropriate, but then, none of their interaction was. His kiss echoing through her again, she flushed.

King Devon smiled. "To avoid spoiling my disguise, I also ordered my guards to wait with the horses a street away." He chuckled. "They grumbled like trolls perishing in the summer sun when I did."

Kiera frowned at him. "Do you often order them to remain behind?" That didn't seem prudent.

King Devon leaned toward her with a grin. "No, my guards are irksome when I do. They loathe when they can't see the dangers I face. So I only bother when alone in the royal wing or with those I trust."

She blinked. He trusted her that much? But they'd only known each other one night. Yet she trusted him too, even though she probably shouldn't. She lifted her chin. "But should you trust me? I could be dangerous."

King Devon hummed and shook his head. "Not to my person, but to my heart, however..."

Kiera's own heart quickened at the ardent gleam in his green eyes. Given their irresistible attraction and rapport, 'twould be easy for them to fall in love. If only she could be more than his mistress.

But before she could respond, Mary bustled into the study with a laden tea tray that bore a white vase, in addition to the usual tea and sweet biscuits.

Kiera almost winced. Doubtless Peter had told his wife about the king, so she was here to scrutinize Kiera's admirer and matchmake. Oh dear.

King Devon leapt to his feet. "Allow me to take that, Mistress..."

Mary giggled as he set the tray on Kiera's desk beside the peach rose, obviously charmed by his court manners. "Mary. I'm Peter's wife and the cook here."

King Devon grinned and inclined his head. "'Tis a pleasure to meet you."

When Mary beamed back and dropped the rose into the vase, Kiera cleared her throat. She must encourage Mary to leave before Mary declared she'd make an excellent wife and offered the king her hand. "Was there something, Mary?"

Mary turned toward her. "Not particularly. Just wanted to greet your admirer." She slashed the king a narrow glance. "And warn him to cherish you."

Kiera winced when King Devon nodded then said, "Your husband delivered a similar warning. But don't fret; I'll treat Kiera with all the care and respect she deserves."

Mary beamed at him again then pointedly glanced at the peach rose before winking at Kiera. "I'll leave you two alone then. Me and Peter'll handle the mornin' lessons."

As the cook bustled from the study, Kiera rested her face in her hands. "Dear Goddess..." When the king's chair creaked, she jerked up her head to glower at him. "I suppose you find a poor couple threatening their king amusing."

King Devon smiled and shook his head. "I find it wonderful they love you enough to warn your potential suitors."

She stiffened as her stomach tightened. "*You* aren't a suitor." At least not the type interested in marriage, like Mary and Peter assumed.

King Devon cocked a brow. "Aren't I?"

A pang darted through Kiera. He was teasing, of course. She crossed her arms. "Why are you here, your majesty?"

King Devon leaned toward her, his gaze unblinking. "I've a proposal for you."

She glared. She'd never become his mistress. No matter how much she desired him. "No."

King Devon tsked. "Do you always refuse proposals without

hearing them first?" He flicked his fingers. "It shall be worth-while for you to listen. If you do, I'll personally support your orphanage for the next three years."

Her head swirling, Kiera eyed him. With the king's money, she could afford the new clothes, better tutors, and trade school she wanted. And her orphans deserved all of that. Besides, listening didn't mean agreeing. She gritted a brilliant smile as she moved the peach rose from the tea tray to the far corner of her desk then lifted the teapot. "How do you take your tea?"

King Devon straightened and grinned back. "A little sugar."

She hid a sigh as she prepared his tea. The king's simple taste was fortunate. She'd sugar and milk but no lymons to offer him. The orphanage only got those when Wren brought them from her parents' conservatory.

As she handed him his teacup with a sweet biscuit, King Devon arched his brows. "Have you heard about my difficulties with the nightmara?"

Kiera almost winced as she stirred a spoon of sugar into her tea. Difficulties she'd caused by capturing the king's attention at the masquerade. She forced herself to sip her tea with a shrug. "Wren mentioned they want a queen to negotiate, which we don't have since you remain unwed."

King Devon grimaced and set down his teacup. "When I attempted to negotiate myself, the nightmara queen-heir proposed disastrous changes to the treaty, so I'd find a queen."

She nodded, nibbling on a sweet biscuit. Not surprising if the nightmara were matriarchal, like Wren had mentioned. "Like what?"

King Devon shuddered. "Moving from the Nightmara Plains and having the mara renounce their Calatini citizenship."

Kiera shifted in her chair. From his reaction, those changes should alarm her, but she was too ignorant about the kingdom to know why. "But our people would still be at peace. That's the purpose of the treaty, right?"

King Devon sighed and crumbled his sweet biscuit. "Yes, but

over the centuries, the Nightmara-Calatini Treaty has evolved into more than that. Our southern defense is based on the nightmara living in the plains, and the Golddell duchy would go bankrupt if the mara weren't citizens."

She nibbled her lip. Those changes *were* bad. Yet how could she help? "Why are you telling me this?"

King Devon leaned toward her. "The nightmara would accept a future queen to negotiate for Calatini."

Kiera frowned. A poor orphanage matron had nothing to do with Calatini's future queen. "And?"

King Devon shrugged. "And everyone knows I'm mad for my mysterious mermaid from the masquerade." He smiled and eyed her lips. "You."

Despite her pulse quickening at his hungry smile, she snorted. "So?"

King Devon leaned even closer. "So I need you to be my betrothed."

Kiera gaped at him as her teacup clattered on her desk. He was supposed to ask her to become his mistress, not his betrothed. "What?!"

King Devon grinned and repeated, "I want you to be my betrothed."

Cleaning her spilled tea, she suppressed a cackle. She was no future queen. She was poor, a probable bastard of unknown parentage, and had none of the education and resources a true court lady would possess. Even Wren, who despised court events, would make a better queen. He must be mad. She flung aside her sodden pocketcloth and glared at him. "Impossible. No one would accept a poor orphanage matron as your future queen."

King Devon tapped a finger on her desk. "They will when they learn you're my mermaid." He chuckled. "I've been determined to find you. It's been *the* gossip at court for the past month and a half. And the council feared I'd resort to the Mirror of Wisdom."

Kiera swallowed. The perilous faegift his mother had gifted his father could reveal anything but at a terrible price. Surely he'd not have risked using it to find her. "Didn't the Mirror of Wisdom kill your mother?"

Inclining his head, King Devon picked up his teacup. "Yes, so I couldn't risk using it." He winked at her. "I was most fortunate to find you at Hawke's wedding. Finally."

She pursed her lips. 'Twasn't fortunate—more like hapless. Despite his obsession with finding her, she couldn't possibly become his betrothed. Court would despise someone like her becoming queen and savage her. To demonstrate that, she allowed her voice to slip into the coarse accent of her youth, "Fortunate, wot? More like magic. A kin' like yer favorin' a pur chit from the docks."

Yet instead of recoiling, King Devon merely lifted his sleeve to show the three-stranded, gold bracelet on his left wrist. "Not magic. I've a powerful protection charm that prevents enchantments from working on me. And it's worked for years. Father hired the royal witch to create it then gave it to me on my sixteenth natalday."

Kiera blinked. So his obsession couldn't be due to her shell mask from the veiled witch. Yet *why* had he hunted for her then? The veiled witch had implied magic was involved. Shoving that aside, she gritted, "Stop suckin' yer mum's tit, yer majesty. Trut' don't matter. 'Pearance does."

King Devon set his jaw then shook his head. "Appearance does influence people. But in the end, truth shines through."

She sighed and raised her eyes skyward. Why would the obstinate king not listen? She resumed her normal voice, "Dear Goddess, how have you succeeded in politics?"

King Devon chuckled as he drained his tea. "I've learned how to make appearance reveal the truth."

Kiera almost snorted. What truth would possibly allow *her* to be queen? "Your majesty, I've lived a very different life than those ladies at court, and it shows."

King Devon winked again. "That difference is what makes you irresistible, my mermaid."

She glared at him. Must he tease her? "That accent I just used —I spoke like that until I was *seventeen*."

King Devon nodded, his face softening. "When you met Wren."

Kiera stiffened. How did he know about that? Had he learned it when he'd had her and the orphanage investigated years ago? She forced a smile. "After I rescued her and Hawke from the docks, Wren decided we were friends for some reason. She taught me how to speak when she saw how self-conscious I was about it."

King Devon cocked his head. "You learned remarkably well —your accent is indistinguishable from the ladies at court." He smiled at her. "You can learn everything else you need to be my betrothed as well."

Her heart wrenched, and she leapt to her feet, causing the vase with the peach rose to wobble and almost fall off her desk. Why must he keep insisting she become his betrothed? Believing such a fantasy would shatter her when it ended. Glaring, she fisted her hands on her hips. "Impossible! Not even you can hide my past, your majesty. Besides, my education is nowhere near good enough. I didn't even realize the problems with the night-mara's changes until *you* told me. I can't be your betrothed!"

CHAPTER 15

*H*is ribs tight, Devon eyed the glaring Kiera—she was about to flee again. Goddess, if only wrapping her in his arms and whispering reassurances would soothe her. But she'd doubtless flee faster if he attempted that. He swallowed. Perhaps devising how court would accept her would work instead. He forced a grin. "You're correct; we can't hide your past."

Kiera flopped back into her seat, causing the vase with the peach rose to wobble again. Her face was still tight, but at least she wasn't fleeing. She sighed then said, "I'm glad you're seeing sense at last."

His heart squeezed. Although *Kiera* didn't see it, asking her to marry him made perfect sense. He loved her, and she'd become the best queen since Calator's wife Annalise. Yet as Wren had advised, he needed time to prove those truths. So he must convince her to become his betrothed. He leaned toward her with a smile. "Everyone adores romantic tales, so we'll give them one."

Kiera arched her brows.

Devon hummed and rubbed his chin. "You're now a princess of a distant isle who was sent into exile after your kingdom was destroyed. Your caretakers died on the rough voyage, so you grew up in a poor orphanage by the docks." He chuckled. "All we must do is select a suitably distant and uninhabited isle as your erstwhile kingdom."

Kiera gaped at him. "Such pretense. Not even Wren could pen such a fanciful tale." She tilted her head, her dark-blonde curls tumbling against her cheek. "And what happened to truth shining through appearance?"

He shrugged. That Kiera was the lady meant to be his queen was the only important truth. Everyone who knew her saw that, and court would too given time. And so would she. He cocked a brow. "Do you know your parents?" When she shook her head, he continued, "Then our tale could be the truth."

Kiera snorted. "Not likely."

Devon shrugged again. The truth of their romantic tale hardly mattered. "Perhaps not, but we shan't spread the tale ourselves, and never outright claim or deny it. Then we can contend no knowledge of the tale if it unravels."

Kiera pursed her lips. "*Now* I understand how you've succeeded in politics. Your truth is what you want it to be."

Eyeing her lips, he swallowed. If only he could kiss her. But could he restrain himself if he did? "The prerogative of kings."

Sighing, Kiera raised her eyes skyward. "In your tale, how *exactly* did I learn about my royal ancestry, if my caretakers died before I reached Calatini?"

Devon tapped his fingers against the desk. Yes, they should explain that to make their tale more believable. "Your parents, who died when your kingdom was destroyed, left a note in your belongings. You received it at your majority and had a witch perform a translation spell."

Kiera snorted. "Fantastical. No one shall believe it."

He smiled at her. "Enough shall, and the rest shall pretend to. After enough time, no one shall care much either way." Court would have realized how wonderful she was and moved on to another scandal.

Kiera tsked and shook her head.

Devon gritted a smile. *Somehow*, he must convince her to agree to become his betrothed. Perhaps the nightmara's equalitarian beliefs would help. "And your upbringing shall improve your standing with the nightmara, so Calatini shall fare well in the renewed treaty."

Kiera frowned. "They couldn't possibly prefer a poor orphanage matron and probable bastard over a true lady."

He almost chuckled at her patent disbelief. If he persuaded her of that, surely she'd accept his proposal. "They could. In addition to being matriarchal, the nightmara find the concept of royalty and nobility nonsensical."

Kiera blinked. "But they're ruled by *queens*. How do the nightmara select them if not by birth?"

Devon flicked his fingers. "Ability. The mares with the strongest power over dreams and the mind fight for the right to become the dominant mare of their herd, and those mares fight for the right to become queen." So they would appreciate Kiera overcoming her poor upbringing.

Kiera shook her head. "How peculiar. I can't imagine human society working that way."

He flashed a wry smile. "No? I imagine that's how our nobility were born, but they altered the rules once they achieved power to favor their heirs."

Kiera muttered, "I suppose..."

Devon eyed her for a moment. Would she accept him now? He swallowed then asked again, "Shall you be my betrothed?" Goddess, please let her agree this time.

Kiera stiffened but rubbed her chest. "I can't. I'm sorry, your majesty. More than my upbringing prevents me." She lowered her hand and glanced away, toward the peach rose. "I'm not a virgin."

He couldn't help a smile. If that was her only objection, she must be close to agreeing. He reached across the desk to grasp her hands. "Neither am I, but that doesn't prevent me from marrying."

Eyeing him beneath her lashes, Kiera choked a laugh. "You're a gentleman—'tis different."

Devon shrugged. But it shouldn't be. Besides, a wife's virginity was irrelevant if you trusted her, and why marry a lady you didn't trust? And he definitely trusted Kiera. "Not to me. As long as you aren't in love with someone else, bearing his child, or a trollop, your lack of virginity means nothing to me."

Kiera lifted her head to meet his gaze. "You're a most unusual gentleman."

He smiled and nodded. Hopefully, enough to allure the most extraordinary lady he'd ever met. He squeezed her hands. "Which is doubtless why none of the ladies at court appealed to me."

Kiera licked her lips. "And yet I do?"

His eyes never leaving hers, Devon nodded again. She was compassionate, strong, and intelligent as well as lovely. Everything about her appealed to him. "You outshine them like the sun outshines the moon."

When Kiera blushed but shook her head, he set his jaw. He must devise more reasons for her to accept him. His loving ardency and the nightmara weren't enough. Perhaps her goal from the masquerade would work. After all, that worthy idea could only improve Calatini, and 'twas the reason his attraction had blossomed into love. Seeing it become reality would be wonderful and the perfect purpose for Kiera.

He shrugged and smiled at her. "I'd thought to implement your idea about education, but I'm much too busy to do so. As my betrothed, 'twould be ideal for you to handle."

Kiera gaped back and tensed. "Truly?"

Devon almost grinned at the hunger tightening her face. Surely she'd accept him now. He squeezed her hands again. "As long as you include studying other creatures and the world."

Tilting her head, Kiera licked her lips. "Which would further your goal as well."

He tensed as tingling warmth flooded him. Goddess, must she lick her lips? 'Twas almost impossible to resist kissing her when she did. And he couldn't risk that until she agreed to marry him. He forced himself to nod then said, "So what say you to becoming my betrothed?" When she still hesitated, he added, "If you agree, I'll support your orphanage, not just for three years, but the rest of my days." Please, please let that be enough.

Kiera gulped a ragged breath. "By agree, do you mean marry, or simply become your betrothed for the nightmara negotiations?"

Devon clung to his smile. If only Kiera could see he was offering a true betrothal. But she clearly didn't trust him enough for that yet. So he must use their betrothal to court her and prove his love was sincere. He inclined his head. "I mean become my betrothed for at least as long as the nightmara remain." Not exactly a lie.

Kiera scrutinized him for a tortuous moment that seemed to stretch longer than a kraken's tentacles, which were longer than most ships. At last, she murmured, "Very well, your majesty, I'll become your betrothed."

His chest lightening, he leapt to his feet and drew her upright by their clasped hands. He released her left hand to reach inside his coat for the Vireni betrothal ring. "Then you must wear this."

Kiera's eyes widened as she stared at the ancient ring of heavy gold and rare alexandrite. "What is *that*?"

Devon managed a shrug despite his swift pulse. "The Vireni betrothal ring. It dates back to Calator and changes from teal in daylight to purple in candlelight." And, according to family myth, ensured a happy marriage, which he and Kiera deserved.

Kiera yanked her hands free. "I can't possibly wear that. 'Tis much too fine. And much too large."

He sighed. Why must Kiera constantly deny she was meant to be his queen? He gritted a smile. "It magically changes its size to fit the wearer." Until death, but she'd flee if he mentioned that.

He recaptured her left hand. "No one shall believe our betrothal unless you wear it."

Kiera grimaced but allowed him to slide the Vireni betrothal ring on her middle finger. She tensed as it instantly shrunk to the perfect fit, just like she fit him. She eyed it. "How eerie."

Devon relaxed. Kiera had joined the Vireni line when she accepted the ring. Now he must help her realize it. Still holding her hand, he began strolling around her desk. "Although eerie, 'tis tradition to wear it. And my family designs their marriage tokens to match. My parents selected bracelets with alternating teal and purple firegems." After Mother died, Father had always worn hers on a necklace along with the Vireni betrothal ring—to keep her close to his heart, he'd said.

Kiera frowned up at him as he halted before her. "What are you doing?"

His heart quickening at her clean lavender scent, he smiled and arched his brows. Now that she was his betrothed, he could finally risk kissing her. "Sealing our betrothal."

Kiera inhaled then said, "I'm not certain—"

Heat flaring in his veins, Devon tumbled her into his arms. Enough protesting. He captured her lips in a deep kiss. Goddess, she tasted sweeter than ambrosia from Esme the Great's melissae hive at the heart of the royal forest.

For a moment, Kiera remained still, but then she threaded her fingers through his hair and parted her lips to return his kiss with equal hunger. Despite her obstinate refusal to accept his love, even she couldn't deny their attraction.

His body throbbing, he rumbled then drew Kiera closer until their entire bodies touched. How he burned to make love to her. But she'd never trust him or believe he felt more than lust if he seduced her within moments of her agreeing to become his betrothed. So after a timeless moment, he forced himself to wrench his head away and step back.

Kiera wobbled and blinked at him, her navy eyes black with passion.

Devon shuddered as his body hardened further. If only he could kiss her again. But he'd not stop at kissing if he did.

Kiera shook her head then rasped, "You shouldn't have done that. We forget ourselves when we kiss."

Gulping a settling breath, he recaptured her left hand. No, 'twas simply releasing their heartfelt desire. But she'd argue if he said that, so he merely shrugged and asked, "How else were we to seal our betrothal?"

Kiera licked her lips. "A handshake, perhaps?"

Devon swallowed as his hunger flared again. A mere handshake couldn't seal a betrothal. He pressed a kiss on her palm beneath her ring. "We must inure ourselves to kissing now. Everyone knows I want a love match—why else would I have hunted my mysterious mermaid so fiercely? No one shall believe our betrothal if we don't display signs of intimacy."

Blushing, Kiera sagged against the front of her desk, and the vase with the peach rose wobbled. "I suppose."

To lessen the temptation to draw her back into his arms, he released her hand then tugged his shirt and waistcoat straight. "To that end, I'll give you the queen's chambers once I introduce you to court. Don't fret; there's a lock on our adjoining doors if you want it." Although hopefully, she never would.

Kiera bolted upright. "I'm not moving into the palace and abandoning my orphans to *act* as your betrothed."

Devon suppressed a wince. Wren had mentioned that might upset Kiera. To avoid upsetting her further, he murmured, "Then use your quarters to store the wardrobe I'll fund. A queen requires a substantial one, you know. And a maid to attend to it."

Kiera sighed. "Very well." She eyed him. "When do you plan on introducing me to court?"

He hummed and tapped his chin. Although he wanted her by his side now, she required *some* time to prepare herself. "How about Harvestfete?" Held on the equinox later this month, the autumn festival of the Goddess celebrated the harvest and deceased ancestors as well as marked the end of the social season. "Then we'll have two and a half weeks to prepare. I'll host another masquerade to introduce you. That shall entice all of court to remain."

Kiera's cheeks paled, but she inclined a faint nod.

His heart squeezing at her nerves, Devon clenched his hands to avoid pulling her into his arms. He'd do more than reassure her if he did. He managed a smile. "Shall I return tomorrow, so we can discuss our preparations?"

Kiera shook her head. "I'll visit Wren and ask her. Although she despises court events, she's doubtless more aware than you what a lady requires for court."

He muffled a sigh. Wren *would* be better at that, and she'd probably ask her new mother-in-law to help. Aragon's mother adored managing the affairs of others, and she'd successfully presented Selena despite her lack of dowry and her uncle's involvement with a black witch. "Then while you prepare for court, I'll arrange the Harvestfete masquerade and spreading the rumors about my mermaid's royal lineage."

Kiera pursed her lips but nodded.

Tingling warmth suffused Devon anew. But instead of kissing those tempting lips again, he bowed over her hands and kissed them. "Until later, my mermaid."

Although he ached to stay, he strode from Kiera's study. Who knew how much longer he could restrain himself? And going too far would shatter their tenuous agreement. Then Kiera would never trust him enough to marry him one day.

CHAPTER 16

*H*er hands tingling from his last kiss, Kiera stared after King Devon as he strode from her study. How had *she* become the king's betrothed?—a fake one, but still, 'twas as likely as a half-human, half-serpent naga sprouting wings and learning to fly. Grimacing, she sighed. She should have refused, but the chance to help her dark-haired squire as well as further education in Calatini had been impossibly tempting.

She twisted the heavy gold and teal alexandrite ring on her left middle finger. The Vireni magical heirloom was much too fine for a poor orphanage matron. She shuddered. Goddess, what if she lost it? And what would Mary and Peter say when they saw it?

She swallowed and slid the Vireni betrothal ring from her finger. She'd best conceal it, but not in a pocket. Opening her desk drawer, she found a length of ribbon left from the costumes for the last orphanage play. She knotted the ribbon about the royal ring then tied it about her neck. Fortunately, the ribbon was long enough that the ancient ring rested below her high neckline.

Since Mary and Peter were handling morning lessons, Kiera remained in the study until luncheon. She attempted to review the orphanage's accounts, but she kept halting to stare at the new peach rose and muse over the king's unexpected proposal and irresistible kisses. Acting as his betrothed without succumbing to his charms would be near impossible. But she must manage somehow.

Once Kiera joined the orphans for luncheon, Mary bustled over with black bread and a bowl of fish stew. The plump cook grinned at her and asked, "How was your time alone with your suitor?"

Kiera forced herself not to blush. "He's not a suitor. The rose was his gambit to request my help with a delicate matter." She paused. Not that she could say exactly what without encouraging Mary. She swallowed then continued, "So I'll be gone some in the coming weeks. Can you and Peter manage the orphanage? I'm certain Wren and Hawke shall visit more often to help."

Mary beamed. "Of course, we can manage. You mustn't miss this chance. A fine witch healer like that wouldn't trust you with a delicate matter and bring you a rose unless he was interested in courtin' you as well. Doubtless he'll propose before long."

Kiera stiffened. Later she must reveal the king's silver, melissa torc had been a disguise. But she'd wait until she'd decided how to explain the fake betrothal. "No, I'll return to the orphanage as soon as my favor is complete."

Mary pursed her lips but left without another word. Thank the Goddess.

Kiera spent the rest of the day and the next morning busy with the orphans. If she was going to be gone, she must ensure everything was prepared. So she shoved King Devon from her mind and disregarded Mary's and Peter's probing glances. She'd no time for distractions.

After luncheon the following day, she left the orphans playing a riddle game with Mary and Peter then headed to Wren and Hawke's townhouse. She nibbled her lip as she strode across Ormas. What would Wren say when she learned her poor friend was the king's mysterious mermaid?

When she arrived at Wren and Hawke's, Kiera rapped on their front door then smoothed her serviceable dress. Hopefully, Wren wouldn't be too shocked about King Devon's outrageous proposal. She straightened her shoulders as Hobb ushered her inside then led her to the gamesroom and announced her.

The gamesroom door flew open after a faint scuffle. His clothes askew, Hawke flashed a crooked grin. "Afternoon. We were just playing elementball."

Kiera blinked. Why would newlyweds favor a table game? She eyed his clothes and almost blushed. Unless it was more than that. Maybe she should have sent a note first.

Smoothing wrinkles from her dress, Wren glided next to Hawke. Their game definitely involved more than elementball. She smiled at Kiera. "What brings you by? Did an orphan forget something the other day?"

Kiera fingered the ribbon holding the Vireni betrothal ring. Her visit *was* unusual—typically Wren visited her at the orphanage since Kiera had too many duties to leave easily. "No, I need some advice from you."

Her friends exchanged a glance then Hawke chuckled and drawled, "Sounds as if my presence is superfluous, so I'll take myself off. I've some neglected business correspondence to handle, anyway. Being a new husband is demanding." He captured Wren's mouth in a deep kiss before strolling down the hall.

Glowing from Hawke's kiss, Wren eyed Kiera and tilted her head. "Did you wish to stay here or head to the morning room?"

Since callers might interrupt them in the morning room, Kiera strode past Wren and dropped into a chair by the element-ball table. "Here's fine."

Wren turned to the butler still waiting by the door. "A tea tray, please, Hobb."

Once he left, Kiera arched her brows at Wren and asked to tease her, "Were you and Hawke *really* playing elementball?"

Wren blushed as she alighted on the matching chair beside

Kiera. "After a fashion." She coughed then asked, "You wish for some advice?"

Kiera nodded and studied her laced fingers. How to begin? Should she start with the king's outrageous proposal or his summer masquerade? Or maybe the turbulent dreams that had inspired her to attend?

When the silence echoed between them, Wren leaned forward. "Well?"

Kiera swallowed. She'd begin with the most shocking part. She blurted, "King Devon asked me to become his betrothed yesterday." She peeked at Wren through her lashes, but her friend merely nodded. She was about to ask why when Hobb returned with the tea tray. Once the butler left again and shut the gamesroom door, she arched her brows. "You don't appear surprised."

Wren grinned while pouring the tea. "Devon said he would two days ago." She winked and offered Kiera a teacup with several sweet biscuits. "He wanted advice too."

Her fingers numb, Kiera accepted her tea and sweet biscuits. No wonder Wren was so unexpectedly calm. "I suppose you were shocked then."

Wren shrugged as she stirred sugar into her tea. "Not when he said he knew you were his mermaid."

Kiera gulped her hot tea, scorching her mouth. Wren knew that? Why hadn't she said anything? "You saw me at the masquerade?"

Wren sipped her tea with a wry smile. "No, I was too involved with Hawke, but I guessed from your distress when I mentioned the king's mysterious mermaid."

Kiera grimaced and crumbled a sweet biscuit. Not surprising her clever friend had noticed. And Wren probably hadn't quizzed her about it to avoid distressing her further. "I'd no idea he was the king until then. 'Twas quite a shock."

Wren chuckled. "I can imagine. Except for his coronation, I've never seen Devon wear a crown. He dresses and acts more like a country squire than a king." She winked at Kiera. "Dedicated and unpretentious, just like you. You'll make an excellent queen for him."

Kiera forced a laugh, her heart twisting. If only that were possible. "I think not. The betrothal is only to negotiate with the nightmara and shall end when they leave."

Wren paused with her teacup halfway to her mouth. "I see." She arched a brow. "Did Devon give you the Vireni betrothal ring?"

Kiera blinked, but lifted the ancient ring from her dress. Why would Wren ask about that? "Yes, but only so everyone believes the betrothal genuine."

Wren smiled as she sipped her tea. "Of course."

Kiera coughed then dropped the king's ring back into its hiding place. "And to reinforce that belief, King Devon asked me to begin an education initiative."

Wren's smile grew. "Sounds like the perfect purpose for you." She devoured a sweet biscuit. "But such an initiative shall take a lifetime."

Kiera shrugged and sipped her tea. "I'll ensure 'tis well underway before I return to the orphanage." She echoed Wren's smile despite the weight compressing her chest. "Perhaps King Devon's true queen shall undertake the initiative."

Wren hummed. "I imagine so." She tilted her head. "Now, what advice did you need? If 'tis about the orphanage, Hawke and I shall be glad to assume your duties, so you can move to the palace."

Stiffening, Kiera glowered at Wren. "I'm *not* abandoning my orphans to act as the king's betrothed."

Wren sighed. "I didn't say you were. I simply thought managing an orphanage while acting as queen would be too much. I'd not want to attempt it."

Kiera snorted then drained her tea. "I'll manage." She must— she'd a responsibility to the orphans, and King Devon *would* be impossible to resist if they were always together. Seeing the orphans would remind her of her real life. "Although 'twould help if you, and possibly Hawke, visited the orphanage every day while I'm involved with court."

Wren inclined her head. "Hawke and I would enjoy that."

Kiera smiled at her friend. "Thanks, Wren." Then she sighed. With the orphanage handled, now they must discuss court. "Also, I need help preparing for court. I know you despise court events, but you at least know what's expected."

Wren grimaced. "Yes, of course." She set aside her tea then darted to a small cabinet. "I'll need some paper for lists. I believe there's some in here to keep score..."

As Wren rooted through the cabinet, Kiera nibbled her lip. "The only nobles I've met have been your and Hawke's families, who were kind because I was your friend. But I doubt the rest of court shall be as lenient. And King Devon intends to present me as his betrothed at Harvestfete in just two and a half weeks."

Wren chortled when she finally extracted a pen and paper. She returned to her chair and began writing. "First, you'll need a new wardrobe."

Kiera smoothed her serviceable skirt. "King Devon said he'd pay for it." Not entirely proper, but she couldn't afford it otherwise, and she needed one to act as his betrothed.

Wren tsked. "As he should." She tapped her pen against her lip. "I don't care about clothes, so I shan't be much help." She slanted Kiera a penitent glance. "However, Hawke's mother has incomparable taste and would love a chance to outfit a cousin's betrothed."

Kiera grimaced. "His *fake* betrothed." She mustn't forget that. 'Twould lead to heartbreak if she did.

Wren arched a brow. "We shouldn't tell anyone that, not even the duchess. The more people know, the more likely it could spread."

Kiera almost winced. And the nightmara might find out. They'd never negotiate with her if they learned she wasn't the king's true betrothed. "I'll pretend my betrothal to King Devon is genuine with everyone else. But I'm relieved you know the truth."

Wren hummed. "You'll also need to stop calling him 'King Devon.' No one shall believe his betrothed would be so formal. Try to treat him like you do Hawke but act as if you always want to kiss him."

Tingling warmth flooded Kiera at the king's—no, Devon's—irresistible kisses. She *did* always want to kiss him. "Very well."

Wren chuckled then tilted her head. "In addition, you'll need to learn all the nuances of court etiquette. The duchess shall be ideal for that as well. Plus, she can provide details about *everyone* at court, including the councilors."

Kiera swallowed. As the king's advisors who also headed government ministries, the councilors were second only to the king. "Hopefully, those details shall help when I meet them."

Wren patted Kiera's knee. "They shall. The duchess knows how to manage everyone. Besides, Devon shall support you."

Kiera forced a weak smile. True, but the councilors and the rest of court would probably hate that he'd chosen someone like her as his queen.

Wren frowned. "I wonder how we should portray your past. Perhaps the duchess would know."

Kiera grimaced and suppressed a snort. "K—Devon has already decided to spread rumors that I'm a princess of a destroyed kingdom who grew up in an orphanage."

Wren tilted her head again. "I suppose that *does* possess romantic cachet. And most at court shan't bother to dissect your story."

Kiera stiffened as her stomach quivered. But if they did, they'd soon learn 'twas fantasy. "I hope so. Otherwise, our fake betrothal shall likely crumble."

Wren hummed. "What you need are allies at court, in addition to Devon." She began a new list on a separate sheet. "Obviously, Hawke and I shall support you, but I doubt we'll be much use. We'd intended to shun court due to our scandalous pregnancy, and we'll be at the orphanage."

Kiera almost sighed. So her friends probably wouldn't attend many court events while she was acting as the king's betrothed. Too bad.

Wren flashed a wry grin. "Although you'll have Hawke's mother, and she's a formidable ally. And you'll have the Westons—they adore you for caring for their granddaughters." She tapped her pen against her lip again. "But you still need a friend to accompany you and keep you abreast of court ties..."

Kiera arched her brows. "Hawke's sister-in-law or a cousin, perhaps?" Surely one of the ladies she'd met at the last orphanage play would be willing to help.

Wren sighed and lowered her pen. "Selena is further along than I am, and Pippa is too untried, but Elise might do." She straightened. "Although Lady Annalise would be even better."

Kiera frowned. That name sounded familiar. Why? "Lady Annalise?"

Wren nodded as she resumed her list. "Lady Annalise Greysnowe. Everyone assumed Devon would marry her, so if she supports you, your position shall be unassailable."

Kiera swallowed, her skin tightening. Right, Wren had mentioned that before. But would the radiant siren from the summer masquerade really agree to be her friend? "You expect the king's former favorite to support the commoner betrothed he chose over her?"

Wren shrugged. "Devon assured Hawke that Lady Annalise doesn't want to be queen. No one except Devon knows her very well, but he trusts her, and he's astute about people." She winked at Kiera. "After all, he asked *you* to marry him."

Kiera shifted in her chair. "Yes, but not in truth." And only because the nightmara were demanding a queen.

Wren quirked a brow but only said, "Regardless, you can trust Lady Annalise. She saw me seducing Hawke at the masquerade and never spoke about it except with me."

Kiera blinked. And seeing them together would have been fascinating gossip, so Lady Annalise must be remarkably discreet. An ideal friend for a fake future queen. "Very well."

Wren grinned at her. "Then I'll write the duchess and Lady Annalise. The duchess shall probably want to start on your wardrobe and lessons at once. But I'll ask Lady Annalise to meet a few days before Harvestfete—that way you'll feel more prepared when you meet her. Her icy beauty can be daunting."

Kiera muffled a snort. Yes, it was. She arched her brows. "Could I have a pen and paper? I'll write to K—Devon to inform him of our plans."

Wren nodded and passed her some, and they began writing.

Her heart quickening, Kiera forced herself to address the king as simply "Devon" then swiftly wrote everything she and Wren had discussed. At the end, she couldn't help adding that she looked forward to seeing him again soon. She sighed. 'Twas no more than the truth, although she probably shouldn't admit it. She sealed her letter and handed it to Wren. "Could you send this? No one shall notice the king receiving a letter from his new cousin." When Wren nodded, Kiera rose. "I should go."

Her letters half completed, Wren rose as well. "I'll send word once I hear back from the duchess." She embraced Kiera. "This shall succeed, I swear."

Kiera swallowed as she returned Wren's embrace. Hopefully, Devon's and Wren's plans would be enough. Goddess knew what would happen if they weren't. After a moment, she slipped free and flashed Wren a bright smile before returning to the orphanage.

CHAPTER 17

Two days after receiving Kiera's letter, Devon extracted it from his coat pocket yet again, even though he should be preparing for the upcoming council meeting. His chest warmed as he reread the familiar letter. Although she'd reluctantly agreed to become his betrothed, her words demonstrated she felt the same love he did—she just refused to admit it, probably because she believed she wasn't worthy of becoming queen. But she'd forget such nonsense once she acted as his betrothed for a few weeks.

He sighed and caressed Kiera's firm signature. How were her preparations progressing? Yesterday, the duchess had asked to purchase arachne silk from Hawke for Kiera's entire wardrobe. Since a wardrobe of a magical fabric, one that could become any color, would enhance her cachet among the ladies at court, he'd instructed his comptroller to pay whatever the duchess asked.

Devon swallowed to ease his aching throat. But he'd not heard from Kiera since her first letter. Was she excited about her new wardrobe? How did she like her etiquette lessons with the duchess? What had she told everyone at the orphanage about their betrothal? He sighed again. If only he could write her to ask, but she'd been so reluctant to accept his betrothal, she might flee again if he acted too ardent.

He grimaced as he slid Kiera's letter back into his pocket. He must head to the council meeting and reassure them without revealing Kiera. His people had already begun spreading the romantic tale about her, but she must remain secret until the Harvestfete masquerade. Then the rumors would have inflamed the council's and court's interest, which would ease her introduction.

Devon hurried from his study to the council room. His guards halting before the door, he strode inside and eyed his councilors. They'd hushed when he'd entered, and all but Aragon either frowned or watched him with blank expressions. Wonderful, they were upset. Muffling a sigh, he nodded and took his seat at the head of the table. "Morning. Shall we proceed?"

Lord Farson coughed. "It's been a month since the nightmara queen-heir and her delegation arrived. The Nightmara-Calatini Treaty has never taken so long to negotiate—not even the first time. And we're no closer to an agreement than we were when the nightmara arrived." The baron squinted at Devon. "At least, I think so."

Devon forced a shrug. As the representative of the Golddell duchy containing the Nightmara Plains, Lord Farson hadn't appreciated being excluded from the treaty negotiations since the first meeting. Understandable, but hopefully, 'twouldn't blight his support for Kiera. "Lady Moonbud wants a queen to negotiate. She says the nightmara dominant mares shan't accept anything less."

Lord Farson smoothed his beard. "Then we must find them one. 'Twould be disastrous if the nightmara stuck to their initial proposals."

Before Devon could answer, the Duchess of Wildewall hummed and asked, "What *exactly* did they propose? I don't believe anyone said."

Devon grimaced. He'd remained silent to avoid distressing the councilors, so they'd not interfere with his hunt for Kiera, but now that she'd agree to become his betrothed, he might as well tell them. "Signing the treaty every decade, moving from the plains, and having the mara surrender their citizenship."

All the councilors except Aragon and Lord Farson gaped, and their murmurs swept the room.

Devon shrugged and flashed a grin. He'd better soothe them before they erupted like crazed chimeras, who always left behind disaster and often destroyed any nearby buildings. "But Lady Moonbud has admitted those outrageous proposals were to force me to find a queen."

Lady Morwynne snorted. "Which you would have done if not for that mysterious mermaid of yours."

Devon stiffened at the countess's superior drawl. As the Minister of Health and Community, she'd be crucial to Kiera's education initiative. He must soften her disapproval. "Lady Moonbud was intrigued by my mermaid and believes she'll make an excellent queen."

Aragon chuckled. "A lady strong enough to resist a king *would* intrigue the equalitarian nightmara." He slanted Devon a knowing glance, saying without words that Kiera's poor upbringing helped too.

Devon hid his grin. The other councilors would suspect it. He nodded instead. "So Lady Moonbud has allowed me until Harvestfete to find my mysterious mermaid."

The Duke of Osbourne grunted. "Yet you've not found her during the past month and a half. Perhaps 'tis time to settle. Lady Annalise shall make a decent enough queen, and she's available."

Devon glared at the elderly duke, but the Duchess of Wildewall interjected like she had earlier, "Absolutely not. Lord Greysnowe has been calling the king's mermaid a Ravenstone plot since the masquerade. So if King Devon settled for Lady

Annalise, Lord Greysnowe would hector Lord Ravenstone until the young count exploded."

Lady Ducharme, the farsighted Minister of Defense, who typically remained silent until she'd an imperative opinion, inclined her head and said, "Which would cause the Greysnowe-Ravenstone feud to spread beyond Wildewall, and we can barely control it now. So Lady Annalise is an impossible choice." The baroness leaned toward Devon. "But we can't afford to lose the nightmara on our southern border. Your majesty, perhaps you should select another lady to act as your betrothed for the night-mara. Once they leave, the betrothal could end."

Devon arched his brows. "Such a deception would never succeed. Thanks to her power over dreams and the mind, Lady Moonbud would know 'twas fake." Something Kiera fortunately didn't realize—she'd not have accepted his proposal if she had. And hopefully no one would tell her that either. He set his jaw then eyed the councilors around the table. "So it shall be my mermaid or nothing. I refuse to settle for less."

Everyone but Aragon sighed, then the Duke of Oakmoor, the Minister of Foreign Relations, leaned forward. "My people have recently unearthed a rumor that may further your hunt, your majesty."

Devon suppressed a smile. He'd instructed his people to ensure both the Duke of Oakmoor and the Duke of Osbourne heard the romantic tale first. The two dukes always knew the latest court gossip. Osbourne because he was the Minister of Intelligence, and Oakmoor because he was an unwed rakehell who adored intrigue. He cocked a brow. "Oh?"

The suave duke nodded. "Apparently, one of the ladies at the masquerade was a foreign princess. Although none of my people have heard from where yet."

His pulse surging, Devon leaned back in his chair. "And you believe my mermaid is that princess?"

The Duke of Oakmoor shrugged. "'Twould explain why no one recognized her."

As Aragon blinked with a faint frown, Devon pursed his lips to feign doubt. "Perhaps." He turned to the Duke of Osbourne. Getting him to confirm the romantic tale would strengthen it to the rest of the council. "Have your people heard similar rumors?"

The Duke of Osbourne grimaced. "They have, but my people have also heard rumors about your mermaid being seen in the poor neighborhood near the docks. No princess, no matter how foreign, would venture there. So I'm not certain any of the rumors are true. Plus, they just began, and your summer masquerade was over a month ago. I'm attempting to trace the rumors now."

Devon almost winced. Of course the wily duke would suspect such tardy rumors. Damnation. He must deflect the duke before he unraveled the truth. Kiera would never agree to act as queen if anyone at court, besides Aragon's and Wren's families, learned their romantic tale was false. He gritted a smile. "Regardless of their sources, those rumors may lead me closer to my mermaid."

Although Aragon narrowly eyed Devon, Lord Farson, who sat beside Aragon, snorted then muttered, "I hope so—Lady Moonbud only allowed you two more weeks."

Disregarding his friend, Devon nodded at Lord Farson. He'd explain the rumors to Aragon later. "In honor of Lady Moonbud's forbearance and how I met my mermaid, I'll be hosting a masquerade for Harvestfete in addition to the usual feast. Your invitations shall arrive shortly, if they haven't already."

All the councilors except Aragon glanced at one another. Clearly, they knew he was planning something and suspected it involved his mermaid. But as long as they didn't discover Kiera before the Harvestfete masquerade, everything would be fine. Please, Goddess.

Devon straightened with a tight grin. He must distract them. "Let's discuss other matters." He turned to Lord Islaye and Lord Nolan. "Anything new on that mysterious ore in Magehaven?"

Lord Islaye sighed. "Unfortunately not. The ore is too

unstable for the usual spells and has resisted everyone's attempts to identify it. And its influence is still spreading."

Devon frowned and tapped the table. If the ore continued spreading, 'twould disrupt the magic of the Walle. And destroying the wall separating Calatini from the kingdoms ruled by magical creatures could cause another war as catastrophic as the Stone Wars.

Lord Nolan shook his head. "Since my land rangers didn't help, we're meeting with Lady Juliet tomorrow. Perhaps the royal witch shall have some new methods we can try."

Lord Islaye grimaced. "My magic marshals are attempting to extract samples to send to her, although 'tis proving difficult."

Devon gave them a bracing smile, despite the chill prickling his neck. Showing his unease would only rattle them. "Send me reports as you learn more. I'm certain your people shall solve this before too long."

Sobered by the update on the mysterious ore, the council discussed a few other matters then adjourned.

Once the other councilors left, Aragon leaned back in his seat and eyed Devon. "So Kiera is a *princess* now?"

Devon shifted in his chair. How could he explain without concerning his forthright friend? "No, but Kiera was concerned court would despise her, so I devised a romantic tale to help court accept her. We'll never mention the rumors ourselves in case they unravel."

Aragon snorted. "And they might, since the Duke of Osbourne is investigating them." He shook his head. "Although honesty is usually best, your romantic tale shall allow court to get to know Kiera before judging her."

Devon relaxed with a sigh. Thank the Goddess Aragon understood. "Yes, and then they'll realize how wonderful she is and not care about her poor upbringing."

Aragon nodded then arched his brows at Devon. "If you had to resort to devising romantic tales to convince Kiera to marry you, your proposal must have been arduous."

Devon winced and rubbed his chest. "Definitely. It took that tale, mentioning the nightmara's preference for worth over lineage, admitting her irresistible allure, asking her to reform education in Calatini, and offering to fund her orphanage for my lifetime before she'd agree."

Aragon whistled. "Arduous, indeed." He clapped Devon's shoulder. "But she *did* accept you."

Devon's heart clenched. Only because she assumed their betrothal was fake. But he couldn't confess *that*, not even to his trusted friend. So he managed a smile then said, "Kiera wrote your mother is handling her wardrobe and etiquette lessons. How are those progressing?"

Aragon shrugged. "Well, I think. After arranging for a dress fitting later this week, Mother and Lady Keyes visited Hawke's townhouse yesterday afternoon to begin Kiera's lessons. Mother thought they'd be less likely to be interrupted there. Selena offered to help, but Mother ordered her to rest because of the baby."

Devon tensed and tapped his knee. The duchess's refusal must mean her lessons would be grueling. "I hope your mother shan't overwork Kiera."

Aragon flashed a wry smile. "With Mother, who can say? Although if she does, it shall be practice for Kiera's busy life as queen."

Devon grimaced. True enough. Hopefully, 'twouldn't cause Kiera to bolt. The duchess could be overwhelming.

Aragon studied him. "So why did you ask *me* about Kiera's progress? Why didn't you ask her when you wrote her back?"

Devon swallowed, his throat tightening. "I didn't write her back. I was afraid she'd flee if I appeared too ardent."

Aragon snorted. "Writing your betrothed isn't too ardent. She'll be more likely to flee if you *don't* write. She'll assume your love has waned, and a lady like Kiera shan't marry you without love."

His breath freezing, Devon winced. Aragon was right. He

must write back to Kiera at once to demonstrate his steadfast love. He leapt upright. "I must go."

Aragon chuckled as he followed Devon from the council room. "Have fun. Remember to grovel enough to atone for writing late."

His guards trotting to keep up, Devon almost bolted back to his study. Somehow he must write the perfect letter to Kiera—apologetic yet believable, including enough of his daily life to intrigue rather than daunt her, and loving without admitting his love. Goddess, let him be capable of it.

CHAPTER 18

*A*fter her second grueling etiquette lesson, Kiera drooped in her chair in Hawke's study. Goddess, her mind seethed with social customs and deportment rules and court protocol like a hearth witch's brew to purify her home. How was she to remember everything in just two weeks?

Hawke's mother beamed at Kiera while she poured tea for them and Wren's mother, who was also helping prepare Kiera for court. "You're learning remarkably well so far. Devon chose his future queen well."

A blush burning her cheeks, Kiera twisted the Vireni betrothal ring weighing on her left hand. She'd still be wearing it about her neck, but Wren had convinced her the older ladies would expect the king's betrothed to wear it openly. "Thank you, your grace."

Her grin turning impish, the Duchess of Childes handed Kiera a teacup. "Not surprising, given he took an age to choose one. He was so particular I almost feared he'd never marry. Fortunately, after Sarastor risked using the Mirror of Wisdom, he warned us that his son wouldn't find a bride until the nightmara returned."

Kiera gaped at the duchess with her teacup halfway to her

mouth. King Sarastor had seen *her* in the omniscient Mirror of Wisdom? Surely not. Perhaps King Devon's true queen was part of the nightmara delegation. Her stomach twisting, she forced herself to sip her tea.

Lady Keyes chuckled and patted Kiera's knee. "Your dramatic appearance doubtless explains why King Sarastor commissioned that powerful protection charm from the royal witch. He was ensuring everyone would know King Devon's love was genuine and not an enchantment."

Her blush resurging, Kiera managed to hum and bob her head. The king didn't love her, but their attraction was definitely genuine. 'Twas the one true thing in their fake betrothal.

The duchess sipped her tea and tilted her head. "But even so, we must ensure you know *everything* about court before your introduction. So although you're learning quickly, we must expand your lessons from just the afternoon to the morning as well."

Kiera stiffened. She'd never see the orphans then. "What about my duties at the orphanage? I can't just abandon my orphans."

The duchess waved a hand. "You're not. Wren and Hawke shall assume your duties there. You've greater duties to attend to now." She chortled, sounding remarkably like Hawke. "And don't fret about all the etiquette you must learn. As queen, you must learn it, but you needn't obey it if you don't wish."

Kiera sighed. Why must court etiquette be so complicated? 'Twould be more sensible if those at court had serious concerns, like struggling to feed their children.

Lady Keyes winked at Kiera. "You mustn't remake yourself into the perfect court lady—no doubt one of the reasons King Devon loves you is your natural manners."

Kiera blushed again. Given his ravenous kiss at the masquerade and determined pursuit afterward, he *had* appreciated being treated like an ordinary gentleman rather than a king.

The duchess's patrician lips twitched. "Among other things."

Her voice turned dry, "But disregarding etiquette must be a conscious choice rather than lack of knowledge. You must know when others are slighting you. Many at court shall attempt it, and if you don't respond properly, they'll no longer respect you."

Kiera inclined her head. Plus, court would be inclined to disrespect her for her poor upbringing. Knowing etiquette better than any true court lady would be her sole defense against that. "Tomorrow I'll head here straight after eating breakfast with the orphans." That way she'd see them briefly, at least.

The older ladies nodded then rose, and the duchess said, "I'll bring my scrying mirror as well, so we can start reviewing everyone at court, in addition to etiquette. But the day after tomorrow, we'll collect you at the orphanage before breakfast for your dress fitting at Celeste's. I expect it shall consume the entire day."

Kiera suppressed a wince. She was going to be draped and pinned for an *entire* day? No wonder Wren shuddered when she mentioned dress shopping with her mother and the duchess. Kiera gritted a smile as the older ladies sailed from Hawke's study. Yet she must endure it since a future queen, even a fake one, must have a proper wardrobe.

She sighed as she returned the Vireni betrothal ring to the ribbon about her neck. Then she trudged back to the orphanage, reviewing her etiquette lessons as she walked across Ormas. The orphans were just starting dinner when she arrived. As she joined Wren and Hawke at the head table, she eyed the brawny stranger standing along the back wall and watching the orphans with a faint smile. Considering his sword and vigilant air, he appeared a guard of some sort.

Kiera settled beside Wren and nodded at the stranger, who was now watching her without expression. Her neck prickling, she asked, "Who's that?"

Wren chuckled as she devoured her ham and tuber stew. "Smith, a royal guard. He's been waiting since luncheon to carry your response back to the palace."

Kiera blinked and licked her lips. "My response?"

Mary bustled over with another bowl of stew. "To King Devon's letter. Why didn't you tell us the *king* was your admirer and had asked you to marry him?" She beamed at Kiera. "To think, our Kiera shall be Calatini's next queen. Peter, Jane, and I always knew you were meant for more than our poor orphanage, but none of us dreamt you'd fly so high."

Kiera gulped and slashed Wren a wild glance. Goddess, how could she explain the fake betrothal to Mary now?

Sitting on the other side of Wren, Hawke chuckled and flashed a crooked grin. "Kiera was probably afraid to tell you—you might faint when you heard royalty had graced your poor orphanage."

Mary snorted. "I've never fainted a day in my life."

As the plump cook eyed her, Kiera swallowed and shifted in her chair. "I was gathering the courage to tell you. I just hadn't yet." Please let that be enough to appease her.

Mary humphed and pursed her lips but left without another word.

Kiera sagged. When she returned to the orphanage after negotiating the treaty with the nightmara, Mary would be *so* upset. She'd probably storm to the palace and hurl rocks at the windows to punish the king. Hopefully, King Devon would ignore that like he had Mary's warning the other day. She sighed and forced herself to eat despite her tight throat.

Wren grinned as she inhaled her black bread. "I left Devon's letter on your desk in the matron's study. You should attend to it right after dinner, so that poor guard can return to the palace. He's been remarkably patient about the delay, but still. Hawke and I shall distract the orphans with a story, so you've time to reply."

Her pulse quickening, Kiera nodded. Then she asked Wren and Hawke how the day went. As usual under her friends' watch, everything had gone smoothly, except the Bedsford twins had strung torn blankets to the dining hall's rafters and attempted to swing from blanket to blanket. Fortunately, the scamps hadn't broken anything but their pride.

After dinner, Kiera strode to her study with the royal guard trailing behind her. She shut the door then tore open the king's letter.

My dearest Kiera—

My deepest apologies for not writing sooner. I wasn't certain what to write and didn't wish to fluster you. I'm relieved the duchess shall help you prepare for court. She's a formidable lady and adores managing the affairs of others, so she'll be the perfect tutor. Just don't let her overwhelm you. (Nearly impossible, I know—she terrifies even me at times, and don't tell Aragon or Hawke this, but I'm often grateful I'm not related to her by blood.)

How *are* your preparations progressing? Do you enjoy your etiquette lessons with the duchess? Are you excited about your new wardrobe? How have Peter and Mary reacted to our betrothal? Please tell me everything.

I wish we could meet in person, but duties at court make it exceedingly difficult to leave. I spent this morning reassuring the council without revealing your existence, but they suspect something is afoot. Thanks to the romantic tale already spreading through court, they'll be hungry to meet you at the Harvestfete masquerade.

I burn to see you and kiss your delectable lips again. (We must remember to practice often, so court shall believe our betrothal.) I've the afternoon free a week from now, so I can meet you at Hawke's townhouse. But until then, we must settle for letters. My guard shall remain to carry your eagerly awaited reply.

Yours,
Devon

Her heart fluttered as she read his candid words. Although

they weren't truly betrothed, he wrote like they were. If only they could be more. Unable to resist, she answered his plea for news with an outpouring of her nerves and strain and longing to see him again too. Although she itched to destroy her revealing letter, she made herself seal it and hand it to the waiting guard. Hopefully, she'd not regret her unreserve.

She relaxed when King Devon sent his equally open reply the following evening. So she sent another heartfelt letter in return then headed to bed. She'd need the extra sleep to withstand her upcoming dress fitting.

The following morning, Kiera rose before dawn and pulled on the navy silk Wren had given her. 'Twas the only gown she owned that was decent enough to wear to a fashionable dress shop. She downed a cold breakfast of bread and cheese in the still kitchen. Then she slid on the Vireni betrothal ring as she waited for Hawke's and Wren's mothers by the front door. When the duchess's grand carriage halted before the orphanage, she darted outside and settled in the backward seat across from the older ladies.

As the carriage glided forward, the Duchess of Childes flashed an impish grin. "Are you ready for a dress fitting at the best shop in Ormas? Most ladies would barter their firstborn to the fae for an appointment at Celeste's, and we've booked the shop for the entire day."

Lady Keyes chuckled. "Caro used her considerable influence to impel Celeste to cancel all her other appointments, so we'd be the sole patrons."

Kiera swallowed. If only she was as excited as the duchess and her best friend appeared to be. She managed a weak smile. "How nice."

The duchess leaned forward. "'Tis been too long since we bought a lady's entire wardrobe. We're fortunate if Wren or Selena purchase a gown or two a season."

Kiera clung to her smile. "I'm glad you'll enjoy it."

Lady Keyes winked at Kiera. "Contrary to my daughter's opinion, you shall too. Just imagine—you can select any style you wish."

Kiera tensed. Except she'd no inkling what styles would be appropriate for court. "I'll rely on your incomparable taste to guide me."

The older ladies nodded, then the duchess said, "Now let's review your etiquette lessons from yesterday."

The duchess and Lady Keyes quizzed Kiera until the carriage slowed to a stop. When Kiera began to rise, the duchess threw up an arm. "Wait, no one may see you before your transformation."

Kiera arched her brows and glanced down at her navy silk. The elegant gown wasn't fashionable enough? She sighed but returned to her seat. "Very well."

The duchess and Lady Keyes descended from the carriage then waved for Kiera to follow after a few moments.

As she joined them, Kiera glanced about Broad Street. She'd never visited the fashionable area, but given the early hour, the shops were dark and the reported crowds absent. She shrugged and followed the older ladies into the dress shop with Celeste's painted above the door in discreet, blue letters. Elegant, exactly the kind of dress shop a wealthy duchess would patronize.

The duchess inclined her head at the regal dressmaker in the center of the anteroom. "Thank you for seeing us alone, Celeste."

Celeste returned the duchess's nod then turned to Kiera. Her eyes widened when they fell on the Vireni betrothal ring. She swept a deep curtsy. "'Tis a pleasure, your majesty."

As Kiera blushed and struggled not to curtsy in return, Lady Keyes threw an arm about her and said, "Our young friend is a fashion novice and asked us to guide her choices."

When the dressmaker stiffened, the duchess flashed a brilliant smile and added, "If we remain in your anteroom for today's fittings, we shan't violate your rule about only the recipient in the fitting room."

Her stomach quivering, Kiera stepped forward and spread her hands. "Please. I truly require their advice."

Celeste nodded with another curtsy. "As you wish, your majesty."

Kiera swallowed. All this genuflecting would be difficult to handle. Thank the Goddess she was merely the king's temporary betrothed.

Lady Keyes glanced about the anteroom. "As always, we trust your discretion, but your assistants are aware they mustn't discuss today, yes?"

"Of course." Celeste snapped her fingers, and two assistants scurried into the room. "Only my best girls are working."

The duchess beamed. "And you received the fabric from my son?" When the dressmaker nodded and snapped her fingers at her assistants again, the duchess turned to Kiera. "I asked Hawke to send enough bolts of arachne silk for your entire wardrobe. The magical fabric possesses an allure that can't be duplicated."

Kiera blinked. Arachne silk? It must be a fabric Hawke and his merchant friend Buford Leshane were selling, but Wren and Hawke hadn't bothered to mention it. Yet the duchess would know if 'twas appropriate for court. She goggled when Celeste's assistants staggered back into the anteroom beneath stacks of clear fabric. Or maybe not.

Lady Keyes chuckled and patted her shoulder. "Don't fret; the fabric becomes opaque once you're bound to it through a drop of blood. And you can change the color any time you wish with another drop."

Kiera almost whistled. Such a fabric would earn Hawke another fortune. And all these bolts were for *her*? She shook her head but accepted a needle from the nearest assistant then pricked her finger above each bolt and changed them into a pale blue. She licked her lips as she eyed the magical fabric. As the duchess had said, it possessed a magical luster that evinced affluence. Yet her poor finger throbbed when she finished changing the last bolt.

Celeste waved Kiera toward a stool. "Please strip, your majesty."

Kiera sighed but obeyed without protest. The sooner they began, the sooner she could return to the orphanage. The dressmaker hummed then measured Kiera herself, and within moments, Kiera was dressed in the most decadent undergarments she'd ever seen, although they were made of ordinary silk rather than Hawke's latest find. She swallowed when the duchess ordered many of the same. If she was truly the future queen, she'd accept such extravagance.

For the next *fourteen* hours, Celeste and her assistants draped Kiera in arachne silk and fashioned the bolts into gown after gown after gown with the older ladies observing and offering advice. But the gowns soon blurred together—walking dresses cut in this or that style, dinner gowns for specific meals, ballgowns with various furbelows, riding habits both functional and stylish... Thank the Goddess she was permitted off the stool for refreshments every gown or two.

Eventually, the never-ending dress fitting ended, and Kiera was thrust back into her navy silk over her new undergarments, bundled into a voluminous cloak, and dragged into the carriage. She shut her eyes and leaned back in her seat with a sigh. Hopefully, she'd never endure another dress fitting like that. It made running after the orphans seem like nothing. She soon drifted into a doze.

When the carriage halted before the orphanage and Kiera rose, the duchess grasped her wrist. "I almost forgot. Do you have a contraceptive charm?"

A blush scorching her skin, Kiera shook her head. She'd not been intimate since her uncomfortable first time over a decade ago, so she'd never bothered with a contraceptive charm. And although she desired King Devon, she'd not allow him to seduce her, so she'd no need of one now. But she couldn't explain that.

The duchess nodded. "Then we'll visit my healer to procure one." She tsked. "I only wish Hawke and Wren had remembered them last month. 'Twould have spared the families embarrassment."

Lady Keyes giggled. "But if they had, they mightn't be wed now."

To escape *that* debate, Kiera bolted from the carriage and into the sleeping orphanage. Why were sixty-odd orphans easier to handle than two older ladies?

A royal guard met her just inside the door and handed her the king's latest note with a bow. Even though she should head to bed, she jotted a few lines to King Devon about today and gave it to the guard. Although ephemeral, their connection was too wonderful to resist. She rubbed her aching chest. As long as she remembered not to fall in love with him.

CHAPTER 19

a week after sending Kiera his first letter, Devon halted on the threshold of Hawke's study and stared at her as his heart pounded. Exchanging daily letters was nothing compared to *finally* seeing her again. Hopefully, he'd manage to restrain himself. She'd flee if he didn't.

He gulped a breath. But, Goddess, Kiera was tempting. Perhaps remembering everyone would soon know she was his would help. He stiffened when his gaze dropped to her bare hands. Waving his guards to remain outside, he entered the study and shut the door. "Where's your betrothal ring?"

Kiera shifted in her seat on the sofa then lifted the ribbon about her neck to reveal the ancient ring. "Openly wearing such a ring would cause comment at the orphanage, and I was concerned I might lose it."

His chest twisting, Devon strode across the study, untied the ribbon, and slid her betrothal finger back onto her left middle finger where it belonged. Her refusal to wear it revealed she didn't trust him, despite her sincere letters over the past week. He kissed her palm beneath her ring. "According to family myth, the Vireni betrothal ring is impossible to lose once given."

He and Kiera started when Wren murmured, "And since

Mary and Peter know about the betrothal and have told the orphans, you wearing it shan't startle anyone."

He coughed and dropped Kiera's hands. How long had Wren been seated behind Hawke's desk? "Where's Hawke?"

Wren narrowly eyed him as he sat beside Kiera on the sofa. "At the orphanage minding the orphans."

Devon tensed. Why was Wren almost glaring? She'd approved of his betrothal to Kiera before. "I'm surprised you aren't with him."

Kiera smoothed her skirt. "I asked her to join us." She coughed. "As chaperone."

Tingling heat flooding him at their passionate kisses without one, he captured her left hand and kissed her palm again. "Surely we're too mature to require a chaperone. Plus, we're betrothed."

Kiera yanked her hand free. "Not in truth, and only until the nightmara leave."

Devon arched a brow. Was it herself or him she didn't trust? Or both? Their attraction *was* nearly impossible to resist. "We spent the entire summer masquerade dancing together. Court shall never believe our betrothal if we have a chaperone."

No longer stern, Wren chuckled while she rang the bellpull. "I said as much, but Kiera insisted as if you'd pounce like a lusty satyr on a nymph after a Summerday dance."

He flashed a crooked grin worthy of Hawke as Wren alighted in the chair beside Kiera. "I've more restraint than that. I'll wait to pounce until after we review our preparations."

Although her breath quickened, Kiera glared at him. "Your majesty!"

Devon stilled. Despite her using his name in her letters, she still used his formal address when flustered. Another sign she didn't trust him. "I did write we must practice our kissing often."

Kiera pursed her lips. "And you wonder why I insisted Wren act as chaperone."

He grasped her hand and leaned toward her, his pulse stirring as he eyed her lips. They were more tempting than a siren's bewitching song. "You're not afraid of a few kisses, are you?"

A flush suffusing her skin, Kiera swayed toward him. But then Hobb entered with a laden tea tray, and she jerked back.

Devon swallowed as his throat tightened. At least she'd not yanked her hand free this time.

Wren chuckled while waving the butler from the study. Once they were alone again, she said, "If you two are to review your preparations, you may need a chaperone to ensure you don't get distracted."

When Kiera blushed scarlet and tugged on her hand, he sighed and released her. He forced a smile as Wren handed them tea and sweet biscuits. "I suppose we *should* begin reviewing our preparations. Kisses must wait. Unfortunately." He turned to Kiera. "You mentioned in yesterday's letter that the duchess had arranged some appointments this morning. More dress fittings, I assume."

Kiera grimaced and sipped her tea. "No, those were finished when we visited Celeste's, thank the Goddess. The duchess had arranged interviews for a maid to attend to that substantial wardrobe we purchased. 'Twas an experience."

Devon leaned toward her. What did she mean by that? "Sounds as if you didn't enjoy it."

Kiera shrugged. "I've never hired a maid, so the duchess provided me the questions to ask. Some were awkward since all the maids know more about court and fashion than I do. But I did find a maid I liked, so I hired her." She sighed. "I wish I could warn her the position is only temporary."

His jaw tense, he devoured a sweet biscuit to prevent his retort that her being queen wasn't temporary. She didn't trust him enough yet to believe that.

Wren tilted her head. "Don't fret; the duchess can easily find Mia a new position. Her time as your maid shall lend her cachet."

Kiera sighed again. "I hope so." She sipped her tea. "In any case, Mia shall return tomorrow to style my hair, and she'll need access to the queen's chambers as well. The duchess said Celeste has some of my many gowns ready."

Devon nodded. "Have her ask for my valet Simon when she arrives at the palace. I'll tell him tonight to expect her." Warmth filling his chest, he eyed her dark-blonde curls. "I hope your maid doesn't change your hair too much. 'Tis already lovely."

Kiera blushed again as she touched her riotous curls. "Thanks, your majesty."

He tensed. She'd used his formal address again. He must resolve that. Perhaps kisses would work. He glanced at Wren, who was watching them with a faint smile. But later, when he and Kiera were alone.

Kiera coughed and lowered her hand. "Although we met with eight maids, we were careful not to reveal I'll be acting as your betrothed to any but Mia. Rumors about the duchess preparing the future queen would undermine your plan to reveal me at Harvestfete. But speaking of rumors, how is your romantic tale about me faring at court?"

Devon chuckled. So far, that had been the easiest part of their betrothal. "Even better than I'd expected. Half of court is gossiping about your royal lineage, and the other half about your sightings near the docks. All my people must do is bridge the rumors shortly before I introduce you."

Kiera swallowed and crumbled a sweet biscuit. "How delightful."

He flashed a warm smile to reassure her. If only he could embrace her as well. "My plans for the masquerade on Harvest-fete are complete as well. Almost everyone has accepted their invitation."

Wren grinned and set down her teacup. "Including Hawke and myself."

His chest eased when Kiera brightened and whirled to face Wren then asked, "Truly?"

Wren nodded. "Truly. We couldn't abandon you on your first

foray at court as yourself. Mary and Peter can manage the orphans alone for a night."

Kiera chuckled and drawled, "Only if we give the Bedsford twins a sleep spell."

Wren's lips quirked. "I'm sure they can behave for a few hours—maybe." She and Kiera exchanged a grin.

Devon smiled as he drained his tea. Doubtless the Bedsford twins were the two boys Kiera had been lecturing when he'd visited her at the orphanage. They sounded even more scampish than Hawke had been as a child, quite a feat.

Accepting his dishes, Wren cocked her head at Kiera. "Oh, do you still have your mask from the summer masquerade?"

Kiera blinked then eyed Wren while handing over her dishes. "Yes…"

Wren smiled. "Then you must wear it at the Harvestfete masquerade." She winked at him. "At least until Devon introduces you."

He grinned back, energy surging in his veins. A night that couldn't come too soon. He nodded at Kiera. "Wearing the mask *would* prove to court that you're my mysterious mermaid."

Kiera swallowed but returned his nod. "Very well."

Wren hummed. "So the masquerade and Kiera's maid and wardrobe are settled." Her eyes gleamed. "Plus, the duchess mentioned this morning that Kiera has finished learning etiquette and is almost finished memorizing details about everyone at court."

Devon beamed at Kiera. Only a true queen could have learned everything so quickly. Not that she could see that. He tsked. "And you worried your education wasn't good enough."

Kiera grimaced with a shrug. "Thank the Goddess for the duchess's scrying mirror—I'd never keep all the titles and names straight without faces. I've learned so many court titles and names and faces, I dream of them."

He leaned toward her and rumbled, "And here I thought you

dreamt about *me.* I certainly dream about you." And the passionate dreams made sleep impossible at times.

Blushing once again, Kiera shifted and muttered an indecipherable reply. Clearly, she dreamt of him too. At least he wasn't the only one.

His heart light, Devon began a new topic so she could recover, "As the future queen, you'll require guards. Probably six pairs like I have, only all female. My guards are performing discreet interviews now."

Her blush fading, Kiera sighed. "Guards? Must I really?"

He echoed her sigh but inclined his head. Guards were an inevitable precaution for royalty. "Yes, you must. You'll no longer be a simple orphanage matron once I introduce you as my betrothed."

Kiera grimaced. "How suffocating." She shook her head. "But I understand. So after the Harvestfete masquerade, what are the plans?"

Devon straightened with a smile. Convince her he loved her and she was meant to be queen. However, he only said, "The following morning, you'll meet with Lady Moonbud, the nightmara queen-heir. Then the day after that, you'll meet the council. Plus the various court events the duchess recommended we attend."

Her lips wry, Kiera sighed. "Wonderful."

Wren wrinkled her nose. "I don't envy you. Knowing the duchess, you'll have multiple court events each day." She tilted her head. "But it seems we've discussed everything now. If you return to the orphanage, my truant husband can come home."

Kiera grinned as she rose. "I suppose you have some rousing games of elementball to play."

As Wren blushed, Devon arched his brows. The complex table game must be code for a more carnal game. Unusual. He rose and took Kiera's arm. "I'll escort you."

Kiera swallowed. "Surely you've not time for that. No one knows me yet, so I'll be fine alone."

He forced a bland smile as tingling skittered across his skin. They must spend time alone, so he could kiss her again. And an hour carriage ride would allow for plenty of kisses. "Nevertheless, I'll escort you."

Kiera sighed but said goodbye to Wren then allowed him to escort her to the unmarked carriage he'd used to avoid being recognized.

After asking the guards to take the outside seats, Devon climbed in behind Kiera. He scooped her into his arms and settled her across his lap as the carriage began forward. His body tightened when her clean lavender scent surrounded him. Goddess, if only he could always hold her like this.

Kiera stiffened and attempted to jerk free. "Your majesty! What are you doing?"

He strengthened his grip about her waist. He'd make her forget his blasted formal address. He leaned toward her. "You know, Kiera, you must really begin calling me Devon."

With that, he captured her mouth in a deep kiss. At last.

Kiera stilled for a heartbeat then kissed him back and threaded her fingers in his hair.

Heat surging through him, Devon drew her closer and deepened their kiss. She tasted sweeter than the purest faedust and was almost as addictive as the iridescent powder the fae created to enhance their enchantments. Burning for more, he undid the laces along her spine to touch her skin.

At his first caress, Kiera shivered but only kissed him harder.

He rumbled as they devoured each other. Goddess, she was perfect. He ran his hand up and down her bare back. If only he could caress her everywhere. But if he did, he'd never stop at mere kisses. And he must earn her trust first.

Then his guards pounded on the door, and they both froze.

Devon swallowed. The carriage had halted, so they must have arrived at the orphanage. Had it truly been an hour? He sighed then raised his head and relaced Kiera's dress. "Now, what's my name?"

Her navy eyes black, Kiera gulped a breath and licked her lips. "Devon."

He eyed her tempting lips, his body hardening further. If only he could risk kissing her again. "Don't forget it." He caressed her mouth with his thumb. "I'll see you at the masquerade in one week, my mermaid. I'll write tomorrow. Dream of me." He forced himself to release her.

Kiera blushed then tumbled from the carriage.

Devon smiled and leaned back in his seat as the carriage began back to the palace. She'd definitely dream of him tonight. As he would her. Thank the Goddess the Harvestfete masquerade was only a week away. Surely they'd not go mad with unrequited desire before then.

CHAPTER 20

Three days after Devon had kissed her senseless in his carriage, Kiera swallowed as she hid behind a painted screen in Wren's dining room and waited for his former favorite. She extracted his last letter from her reticule and reread it to reassure herself. He'd described Lady Annalise Greysnowe as serene and steadfast, despite her icy beauty and ambitious family. Then he'd assured her she'd like Lady Annalise and could trust her.

She sighed and slid Devon's letter back into her reticule. Hopefully, he and Wren were right about Lady Annalise because everything the duchess had mentioned was unsettling. The most beautiful lady in Calatini and often dubbed Lady Snow for her distant manner, Lady Annalise was the daughter of a wealthy count from Wildewall, a northern duchy renowned for wild magic. Her family had been embroiled in a centuries-long feud with the Ravenstones, another Wildewall family. So when she'd blossomed into a great beauty, her parents had treated her as a means to best the Ravenstones and had thrown her at every unwed lord higher than a count, regardless of their age or disposition—until Devon began escorting her to court events several years ago.

Kiera twisted the Vireni betrothal ring then smoothed her walking dress of arachne silk. Earlier today, she'd transformed the magical fabric into swirls of periwinkle and pale blue to resemble ocean eddies. 'Twas the first she'd worn any of her wardrobe from Celeste's. Plus, Mia had styled her riotous curls into a fashionable cascade. So even though she couldn't match Lady Annalise's icy beauty or affluent upbringing, at least her appearance was worthy of a future queen.

She inhaled a bracing breath when Wren's voice drifted over the screen, "Thanks for attending luncheon, Lady Annalise."

A cool voice replied, "I was glad to attend, Lady Beza, although thanks for not spreading rumors about you and your husband was unnecessary."

Kiera nibbled her lip. Lady Annalise sounded as wintry as her nickname suggested. Perhaps calling it serenity as Devon did would help.

Wren's steps halted before the screen. "Wren, please. I'm grateful just the same."

Silk swished against the screen as Lady Annalise asked, "Where's Lord Beza? From your invitation, I assumed he'd join us."

Kiera almost smiled. At least Lady Annalise wasn't omniscient, as well as beautiful and wealthy.

Wren chuckled. "I banished him to the orphanage. Today's luncheon is only for ladies."

Lady Annalise hummed then replied, "Orphanage? I suppose you mean the one you support."

"I do." Wren paused. "Speaking of Waterstreet Orphanage, I'd like to introduce you to my dear friend from there."

Her stomach quivering, Kiera smoothed her arachne silk dress again. Time to face the daunting Lady Annalise. She lifted her chin then slipped around the screen.

Wren beckoned her. "Kiera, this is Lady Annalise Greysnowe. Lady Annalise, this is Kiera."

Even though she ached to curtsy, Kiera managed a faint smile and inclined her head. The king's betrothed, no matter how temporary or lowborn, ranked above a count's daughter. "Lady Annalise."

Her gaze widening, Lady Annalise gawked at Kiera. "You're the king's mermaid." She glided closer. "Goddess, does he know?"

Kiera flourished her left hand, so the teal alexandrite of the Vireni betrothal ring sparkled. "Of course."

A quicksilver grin warmed Lady Annalise's ice-perfect face. "How wonderful. King Devon must be thrilled."

Kiera blinked. Lady Annalise truly didn't mind losing her royal suitor? But Devon was wonderful and impossible to forget. Even for a lady with no interest in becoming queen. "You're not upset?"

Lady Annalise tilted her head, her white-blonde hair shimmering. "Why would I be? The king has been mad about you since his summer masquerade." Her cerulean eyes flickered. "I'm glad he's fallen in love at last."

Her neck prickling at that flicker, Kiera scrutinized the radiant lady. An almost imperceptible melancholy surrounded Lady Annalise—was she not as indifferent as she claimed? Kiera pursed her lips. "Truly?"

Lady Annalise smiled. "Of course. I love King Devon like a brother, albeit one much less annoying than my own. *He* never dipped my hair in ink growing up like Alex did." She tsked. "Younger brothers..."

Kiera exchanged a glance with Wren. Lady Annalise's story almost made her appear ordinary. Comforting that even the most beautiful lady in Calatini had been tormented by a younger brother as a girl.

Flicking her fingers, Lady Annalise leaned forward. "You're aware of the feud between my family and the Ravenstones, yes?" When Kiera nodded, she continued, "Then you know I could never be queen, even if I loved King Devon, which I assuredly don't."

Kiera eyed Lady Annalise. Her gaze was steady, and her chin relaxed. As Devon and Wren had said, she truly possessed no desire to become queen. So why her melancholy? Kiera hid a grimace. Perhaps because her ambitious parents only saw her as a path to power. Kiera smiled at Lady Annalise. "I believe you." To tease the icy beauty, she arched a brow and drawled, "Although I mightn't if you keep protesting."

Lady Annalise blinked. Then she chuckled and flashed a grin. "I'll endeavor to remember that." Her grin turned wry. "I'm simply not accustomed to other ladies believing I'm uninterested in their gentlemen."

Kiera and Wren exchanged another glance, and Kiera swallowed to ease her tight throat. Doubtless Lady Annalise's extraordinary beauty made other ladies too jealous to see sense. No wonder she'd developed such a distant manner. The poor lady needed a true friend. Kiera straightened. So she'd become one during her foray at court, not just a fake friend for appearances.

Her soft gaze echoing Kiera's resolve, Wren smiled and waved toward the table. "Shall we eat?" Once she rang for luncheon and the servants heaped the table with food then departed, she grinned at Kiera and Annalise. "Don't fret that we'll have more courses. To keep our discussion private, I requested they bring everything at once."

Kiera chuckled as she eyed the shokolat torte. The decadent dessert was one of her friend's favorites. Her mouth watered. And she enjoyed it almost as much the few times she'd eaten it. "Including dessert, I see. I think we should start with that."

Annalise's eyes gleamed. "That seems an excellent plan."

Wren giggled as she split the dessert into three. "I never refuse shokolat torte." She patted her stomach. "Especially now. I swear Hawke's son is even more of a glutton than his father."

Kiera and the others devoured the shokolat torte like manticores devoured a unicorn herd—not a morsel was left behind. She chuckled as they licked their spoons clean. 'Twas fortunate no one had witnessed the carnage. None of them would *ever* be permitted at court, not even the radiant Lady Annalise.

After they sighed and dutifully began their leek soup, Annalise asked, "So why hasn't King Devon announced your betrothal, Lady Kiera? Considering his determination to find you and with the council and nightmara pestering him for a queen, I'd have thought he'd announce it at once."

Kiera smiled at Annalise over her soup. "Call me Kiera. I'm no lady." She grimaced and shook her head. "Which is why Devon hasn't announced our betrothal. I required time to prepare for court."

Annalise nodded. "Court *is* rather different than an orphanage." A grimace flitted across her face. "And the orphanage is doubtless much more fun."

Kiera sighed. How true. She'd still be there if Devon weren't so irresistible and needed her for the good of Calatini. She arched her brows. "You'd know since you're immersed in court."

Annalise winced and glanced down at her full plate. "Not by choice."

Inhaling a roll, Wren leaned toward Annalise. "Regardless, that makes you the ideal lady to become Kiera's closest friend at court." She wrinkled her nose. "Since I rarely attend, I'm no help deciphering court ties."

Annalise swallowed then slanted Kiera a hesitant glance. "I'd be glad to, if Kiera agrees."

Kiera grinned as her chest lightened. "Definitely. I *need* a close friend at court, and you're perfect." She tsked. "Without you, I must feign close friendship to the duchess, and Hawke's mother is intimidating, so I *can't* relax around her."

Annalise giggled and began her glazed duck. "I believe that's the first time I've been called relaxing by another lady."

Kiera shrugged. "'Tisn't as if I must worry about Devon's affections." Even though their betrothal was fake, their wild kisses whenever they were alone—like in a carriage—demonstrated their irresistible attraction. Battling a blush, she added, "After all, he could have wed you ages ago if he wanted."

Annalise blinked at her. "True..."

Kiera forced a blithe smile. "'Tisn't as if Devon allowed my unknown parentage and poor upbringing to prevent him from choosing me." As a fake betrothed.

Tilting her head, Annalise pursed her lips. "But what about the rumors swirling court that you're a lost princess? It didn't seem polite to ask, but I assumed they were true."

While Wren tsked, Kiera snorted and waved a hand. Her new friend shouldn't believe such fantasies. "Of course not. Devon devised those to ease my introduction at court."

Annalise blinked at her again.

Kiera's jaw tightened. Had the truth soured Annalise's esteem? "If you wish to retract your offer to help a poor orphan of unknown parentage, I understand."

As Wren bristled, Annalise started then said, "'Twasn't that. I was simply surprised King Devon had concocted such a grand deception." She smiled at Kiera. "He must love you terribly."

Her skin tightening, Kiera shifted in her seat. Although Wren had advised secrecy, true friends didn't keep secrets so large. She lifted her chin. "Not precisely. Our betrothal is fake, so the nightmara have Calatini's 'future queen' to negotiate with. It shall end when they leave."

Annalise frowned and opened her mouth to reply when Wren interjected, "Annalise, could you pass the roasted tubers?" As Annalise did, Wren locked gazes with her.

Kiera eyed them. Why had Wren interrupted? She swallowed and leaned forward. "Annalise, you were about to say?"

Annalise tore her gaze from Wren and shook her head. "The king isn't one to lie. He must be desperate to stoop to such deception."

Kiera poked her roasted tubers, her heart squeezing. Yes, otherwise he'd never have asked *her* to act as his betrothed. "The nightmara are proposing some disastrous changes to the treaty."

Annalise hummed then winked at Kiera. "It shall be nice having a friend at court, especially a lady. Lady Snow must usually eke by with the few animals her mother allows—but only in private."

Before Kiera could reply, Wren blinked and asked, "You know everyone calls you that?"

Annalise smiled as she finished her plate. "I ensured they did."

While Wren tsked, Kiera chuckled. Of course she had. "Despite your lesser years, I suspect you may be more adept at managing court than the duchess."

Annalise's smile tightened for a moment then burgeoned into a grin. "Which means I'm *definitely* the ideal lady to help you at court." She rose. "When's your introduction?"

Kiera rose as well. "The Harvestfete masquerade." A mere four days away. Oh, Goddess.

Annalise tilted her head. "I should have realized." She sighed. "Unfortunately, I must depart. Mother insists I attend the Valcrests' garden party this afternoon."

Once Annalise glided from the dining room, Wren smiled at Kiera. "That went well."

Kiera nodded. Yes, Annalise had been everything Devon had written as well as adroit and lonely.

Wren arched a brow. "Do you feel better about court now?"

Kiera almost snorted. "Not particularly, but I'll be glad for a friend." That might make it bearable at times.

Wren was about to respond when Hobb announced the duchess and Wren's mother.

Kiera sighed. Back to memorizing details about everyone at court. Although the Harvestfete masquerade still hung over her like a thanatos's scythe ready to collect her soul, at least the interminable lessons about court would end then. Plus, she'd see Devon again. Her heart quickening, she followed the older ladies to Hawke's study.

CHAPTER 21

The day before Harvestfete, Devon woke at dawn and was unable to settle, so he went riding to distract himself right after breakfast. He chuckled while yanking on his riding clothes. With Kiera joining him tomorrow, he was as wild as a child before Longnight waiting to open his gifts. Hopefully, he'd manage to resist unwrapping his gift until she believed he loved her and agreed to marry him.

He sighed as he galloped through the harvested fields to the royal forest with a pair of guards. But Goddess, 'twould be hard to restrain himself, especially after all the passionate dreams he'd suffered since they'd met. And his dreams had become more ravenous since their kisses in his carriage last week. He *would* go mad with unrequited desire soon. Yet surely Kiera burned as he did, and their visceral desire would help convince her to accept him.

Devon leaned over his black gelding to avoid slapping branches as they thundered down the meandering path beneath the thick boughs of the royal forest. From her letter yesterday, Kiera had finished her lessons with the duchess, so she was spending her final day at the orphanage. His heart squeezed. She'd doubtless miss her orphans, but once she'd settled into her duties at court, they could probably visit every week or two. With a king and queen ruling together, they'd have more time than he'd managed alone.

He halted his winded gelding when a melissa, a magical bee as large as a songbird, buzzed before him. Somehow he'd galloped to the heart of the royal forest. He eyed the ancient cottage at the center of the small clearing surrounded by buzzing melissae and their still-blooming plants. Esme the Great's melissae hive was why the royal forest had been created, but most never saw it. Although their ambrosia could cure any ill, a melissae swarm was deadly when angered. 'Twas one reason riding here required royal permission. Yet if approached with caution, the melissae were safe enough. Father had first brought him when he was eight, and he and Aragon had occasionally picnicked here over the years, but he'd never once angered them.

Devon sighed and patted his weary gelding before turning him around. 'Twould take several hours to ride back to the palace, so he'd best return. He'd the final preparations for tomorrow's masquerade as well as reports from across the kingdom to review. Keeping his gelding to a trot to allow him to recover, he returned to Ormas with his guards flanking him.

After a quick bath, he bolted luncheon at his desk while reviewing his reports. But his mind kept drifting to Kiera. Maybe he'd concentrate better once she joined him at the palace. He snorted a laugh. Or maybe not. Then he might be too distracted by not kissing her every moment. He sighed and returned to his reports.

He'd just begun perusing an update from Lord Islaye about the Magehaven ore when a knock interrupted him.

A faint frown furrowing his brow, Lord Ravenstone coughed from the doorway. "May I come in, your majesty?"

Devon tapped his fingers on his desk. Whatever had made the genial count frown so must be serious. He set aside his report and nodded from his seat. "Of course." Once the other gentleman shut the door then settled in the chair before his desk, he leaned forward and asked, "What brings you by?"

Lord Ravenstone sighed and smoothed his beard. "Some troubling rumors concerning the Greysnowes."

Devon echoed his sigh. Not surprising Lord Ravenstone's visit involved them. Yet the count had never approached him about their centuries-long feud, despite becoming the head of his family three years ago. Not even when Lord Alexander had goaded him into that nearly fatal duel on Summerday. So the Greysnowes' latest move must be worse than that. Devon suppressed a wince. "What kind of troubling rumors?"

His amber eyes dark, Lord Ravenstone grimaced. "My people saw Lord Greysnowe approach several known assassins in recent weeks."

Devon tensed. Goddess, that *was* troubling. If the Greysnowe-Ravenstone feud now involved assassins, it might soon spread beyond Wildewall like Lady Ducharme had feared. Damnation, he didn't need that in addition to convincing Kiera to marry him, the nightmara treaty renewal, and the mysterious Magehaven ore. "Assassins?"

Lord Ravenstone inclined his head. "And since the ridiculous feud between my family and the Greysnowes started eleven generations ago, at worst it's been hot words, tragic accidents, and insignificant duels. Never anything so drastic as murder."

Devon forced himself to relax. Appearing upset would only alarm the count. "Did your people determine Lord Greysnowe's target?"

Lord Ravenstone frowned. "No, although I'd suspect myself, or perhaps your mermaid. Lord Greysnowe is convinced she's a plot of mine. Ridiculous." He leaned forward. "You must take care when you introduce her as your betrothed."

Fire flaring in his veins, Devon suppressed a growl. If Lord Greysnowe sent assassins after Kiera, he'd murder the ambitious count himself. Which would *definitely* inflame the Greysnowe-

Ravenstone feud beyond control. He set his jaw. "She'll have the same level of protection as I do."

Lord Ravenstone relaxed. "Good. And I'll be on guard as well." He grimaced. "Almost dying at the hands of a Greysnowe was bad enough. I've no intention of falling prey to a Greysnowe-hired assassin. I've too much left to do with my life."

Devon almost shuddered. Being stabbed near the heart *was* life-altering. He eyed Lord Ravenstone. Although excellent with a sword, he wasn't one to court or cause death. And he'd never participated in his family's feud before then. Devon arched his brows. "However did Lord Alexander goad you into that duel, Lord Ravenstone? You're the most genial gentleman at court, and all your previous sword fights had been for amusement."

Lord Ravenstone sighed. "Young Lord Alexander pestered me since the start of the season and kept demanding duels on flimsy pretenses. So when he accosted me after I'd too many tankards one evening, I decided someone should teach the boy a lesson about challenging more skilled swordsmen."

Devon blinked. True, Lord Alexander was a hellion and deserved that lesson, but still. "I can't imagine how you thought such a *lesson* between a Ravenstone and a Greysnowe could succeed."

Lord Ravenstone winced. "I know. I realized my mistake the next morning once I was sober, but I couldn't in honor withdraw then."

Devon sighed. Of course he couldn't. "At least Lady Annalise and I arrived in time to prevent fatalities."

A wry grimace flashed across Lord Ravenstone's face, but he merely inclined his head.

Devon's eyes widened. Given the count's grimace, their arrival had distracted Lord Ravenstone and allowed his young opponent to slip past his guard and nearly kill him. Such a novice mistake must chagrin the skilled swordsman.

Lord Ravenstone rose with a bow. "I should let you return to your reports, your majesty." A quicksilver grin glinted in his black beard. "I'm anticipating tomorrow evening. It promises to be an interesting occasion."

As Lord Ravenstone left, Devon eyed the report about the final preparations for the Harvestfete masquerade. Tomorrow *would* be interesting. Not only would Kiera be at his side at last, but when court saw her at the masquerade, the romantic tale about her being a princess who'd grown up in an orphanage would explode like a swarm of sprites from an upset nest. His people had informed the best gossips at court of that tale this morning.

He smiled and returned to Lord Islaye's report about the Magehaven ore. He finished that and his other reports then rose with a stretch. At the door, he paused and murmured to his guards, "You heard Lord Ravenstone's news?"

Millier on the left frowned. "Not entirely, your majesty. We heard you exclaim something about assassins, but we couldn't make out Lord Ravenstone's reply through the door." He touched the communication crystal in his ear. "We sent Smith and Stone to contact the count's people to clarify."

Devon sighed. Of course, his guards had already responded. "All Lord Ravenstone told me was that Lord Greysnowe was seen talking to assassins, but he doesn't know if he or Kiera is the target."

Johnson on the right gripped his sword. "We'll inform the queen's guards to watch for assassins."

Devon swallowed, his chest tight. Let Kiera not be harmed by Lord Greysnowe's idiotic scheme. "Have Smith and Stone unearth everything they can about the assassins from Lord Ravenstone's people. I want them neutralized, no matter their target."

Both guards nodded, and Millier replied, "Of course."

Devon strode to his chambers to change then headed to Aragon's for a family dinner. Although he couldn't go often, family dinners at Childes House were one of the few times he could be himself rather than the king. So an evening there was the perfect relaxation before tomorrow's momentous masquerade. If only Kiera would be there too, but doubtless she was enjoying her final dinner with the orphans.

As usual, dinner with all of Aragon's family except Hawke and Wren, who had likely joined Kiera, passed swiftly and was filled with lively discussions, loving jests, and delectable food. Yet everyone was careful to avoid mentioning Kiera or tomorrow's masquerade during dinner, probably to help him relax.

But once his wife and Selena withdrew, the Duke of Childes poured everyone spiritwine then leaned toward him with an avuncular smile. "Are you prepared for tomorrow?"

Devon sipped his spiritwine, his stomach tightening. "I believe so. Although whether court is prepared for Kiera, I can't say."

Mel flashed a wry smile and tugged on his priest robes. "I'm sure you're anticipating tomorrow, but I'm sorry Mother no longer has Kiera's etiquette lessons. I fear she may turn her attention back to my unwed status."

Devon blinked. The duchess adored managing the affairs of others, but to meddle with a priest's marriage? Priests could only marry with their god's permission. "Is she really attempting to matchmake a priest?"

Aragon chuckled. "Of course. Mother is certain the Goddess shall approve once Mother finds the right girl."

Mel sighed and shook his head. "Which the Goddess would, but most mothers possess the deference not to try."

The duke flashed a crooked grin. "I did attempt to persuade Caro to matchmake for others at court instead, but she said no one would listen until *all* her boys were married. Although she didn't dismiss that possibility in the future."

Devon almost shuddered and drained his spiritwine. Thank the Goddess he'd already found Kiera. Otherwise, he'd have been next. Although her help with Kiera had been goddess-sent, the duchess could be more terrifying than the entire council.

'Twas fortunate Aragon and not his mother had assumed the Childes's council seat when his father retired.

Not long after, Devon gathered his guards from the entrance hall and rode back to the palace. Too bad he couldn't risk visiting Kiera at the orphanage. But his restraint might not last if he did, and they both needed their rest before tomorrow. Instead, he returned to his chambers and wrote her a letter describing his day and asking about the orphans.

His pulse quickened as he handed the letter to a guard outside his door. 'Twas his final daily letter to Kiera—tomorrow she'd be with him as his betrothed. At last.

As he waited for Kiera's reply, Devon slipped into the queen's chambers using their adjoining door. Kiera's chambers now— even if the obstinate lady insisted on sleeping at the orphanage still. No doubt she'd stop that after a week full of court events.

He drifted over to the dressing table. Like everything else, 'twas arranged and prepared for Kiera. He removed the stopper from a bottle of perfume and inhaled the clean and fresh lavender scent, nothing like the flowery perfumes most court ladies preferred. He chuckled—her scent alone should have told him his mysterious mermaid wasn't from court.

Returning the perfume, Devon eyed the empty vase beside it. He'd have Mia fill it with peach roses tomorrow and keep it full until the hard frost ended the roses in a few weeks. Kiera had blushed each time he'd given her one. And hopefully, they'd remind her of their rapport in the king's garden retreat at the last masquerade.

He wandered over to the wardrobe and brushed the lustrous arachne silk gowns. Wren dressed in one had enthralled Hawke at the duchess's fete. No doubt he'd react the same to Kiera in one. Could he even focus on court affairs with her beside him in such ravishing gowns? Perhaps once they were married, she'd allow him to whisk her away to *muss* her attire.

Tingling warmth surging beneath his skin, Devon forced himself back to his chambers and read a novel until his guard returned with Kiera's final letter an hour later. He tossed aside the novel to tear open her brief letter. Her nerves were obvious in the short lines, even though she assured him she was prepared for the Harvestfete masquerade.

He caressed Kiera's letter. He'd done everything he could to ease her introduction at court, but he'd remain by her side tomorrow to facilitate her success. He'd not lose Kiera now. If he did, he'd shatter like an arctic elf's ice mirror used by a fire witch.

CHAPTER 22

When the orphans began an early Harvestfete feast, Kiera swallowed her tears then slipped upstairs to change into her navy silk and a voluminous cloak. Although she'd return every night, she'd not see the orphans much while at court. Forcing a bright smile, she embraced a teary yet beaming Mary and Peter then strode out to the unmarked carriage escorted by a pair of female royal guards.

Remaining buried in her cloak as the carriage rumbled through Ormas, she twisted the Vireni betrothal ring and stared out the window at the sprawling white palace drawing closer and closer. She swallowed. Like before, the stunning palace glowed in the afternoon sun and was much too grand for a poor orphanage matron, even if the king had asked her to act as his betrothed.

Her heart quickened. But at least she'd see Devon again. His candid letters over the past two weeks had only proved he was as wonderful as he'd appeared at his summer masquerade and deepened their rapport. And their wild kisses consumed both her waking and sleeping dreams. When would he kiss her again? She sighed and rubbed her aching chest. She should really resist him when he did. His ravenous kisses made it too easy to forget their betrothal wasn't genuine.

Eventually, the carriage halted before the blank palace wall concealing the secret entrance only the royal family, their guards, and their personal servants could find or enter. Devon had written that the entrance had been enchanted when the palace was first built, but was rarely used to ensure it remained secret. However, the secret entrance was the one way she could sneak inside with royal guards and remain unseen, so she must use it tonight.

Kiera gulped a bracing breath then strode after the first guard through the solid-appearing wall with the second guard close behind. She shivered as the entrance's spell caressed her skin like heavy ocean fog at dawn. But soon they were inside the palace, and the guards escorted her through deserted halls to the queen's chambers.

Once she entered, Kiera glanced at the adjoining door that led to Devon's chambers, and her stomach fluttered. How long until he joined her?

Then Mia bustled forward with an arachne silk ballgown, so Kiera pricked her finger and allowed a drop of blood to soak the fabric then pictured her costume from the summer masquerade. Wearing a similar gown and her shell mask would help prove she was the king's mysterious mermaid. After a moment, the arachne silk turned blue-green and appeared studded with pearls, shells, and scales—identical to her enchanted ballgown except for the fitted skirt. She shook her head. Hawke's magical fabric was truly amazing.

Once Mia helped her dress and styled her hair, Kiera donned her shell mask then spun to eye her costume. She gasped at the stranger in the cheval mirror. With a gleaming circlet of pearls and shells adorning her curls and the Vireni betrothal ring sparkling a rich purple on her left hand, she embodied a princess. Most probably wouldn't question the romantic tale Devon's people had spread. Perhaps his mad scheme would succeed after all. At least, if she managed to act the part.

A knock on the adjoining door started her from her reverie. Devon at last. Her pulse leaping, she called, "Come in."

Attired in the same Calator costume as before, Devon strolled into the queen's chambers. He halted and gulped a breath when his gaze reached her. "You're resplendent, Kiera."

She blushed, and tingling warmth flooded her at the hunger turning his green eyes black. If only she could let him kiss her senseless again. She managed a wry smile. "Perhaps. But my appearance is an utter lie. Although I suppose that matches our fake betrothal."

Devon strode forward and captured her hands to press a kiss against her palms. "Don't denigrate yourself so. You appear what you are—a lovely, compassionate, intelligent, strong lady who is ready to captivate court."

Blushing harder, Kiera coughed and freed her hands. She'd only captivate court until they learned the truth. "My, that's a lot of adjectives for a poor orphan."

Devon shrugged. "They're all true."

Her chest squeezed. Doubtless he was attempting to hearten her with exorbitant praise. She flashed a gamine grin. "Flatterer."

Devon held her gaze. "Am I?"

Kiera blinked and swayed toward him, her heart fluttering. He was truly the most wonderful gentleman. If only... She jerked upright. She mustn't succumb to their irresistible attraction again. "Are you ready to go?" She arched a brow. "Or did you wish to praise my attributes for the rest of the evening?"

His gaze intent, Devon drew her into his arms. "Depends on what you mean by praising your attributes."

Warmth kindled in her veins as she stilled and eyed his lips. She really should step back. Except his embrace enthralled her like a siren's song.

Devon smiled and lowered his head.

Even though her pulse surged, Kiera tensed. Kisses were too

dangerous. "I certainly didn't mean that. We'll be late for the masquerade."

His smile growing, Devon rumbled, "Court shall wait." He seized her mouth in a deep kiss.

She whimpered and returned his kiss as heat swamped her. Goddess, she should stop. Kissing like this only made her long for the impossible. Yet when he caressed her back, she clutched his shoulders and kissed him harder. She'd stop in a moment— or two.

Eventually, Devon wrenched up his head. He gulped a breath then said, "We should go. I don't want my praise to destroy your delectable ballgown."

Kiera shivered and licked her lips. What was her ballgown compared to kisses? He could remove it and keep kissing her. But then she stiffened. Such thoughts were why she shouldn't succumb to his dangerous kisses. Her stomach quivering, she lifted her chin then accepted his arm. Time to face court.

When they left the queen's chambers, their four guards joined them with faint smiles hovering on their austere lips. They must know she and Devon had been kissing. How embarrassing.

She blushed and slanted Devon a sidelong glance as they strode down deserted halls. He was relaxed, so clearly the guards' knowing smiles didn't fluster *him*. She shook her head. No doubt he was accustomed to their suffocating presence. Would she ever be the same? Not that it mattered—she'd be gone soon.

Kiera relaxed when they joined Wren and Hawke in the royal anteroom leading to the ballroom. Thank the Goddess for their steadfast support.

Her ivy-patterned arachne silk fluttering, Wren darted across the room and embraced Kiera. "We came to wish you well."

Warmth suffusing her chest, Kiera released Devon to return Wren's embrace. Her shy friend attending tonight despite despising masquerades and court gossiping about her scandalous pregnancy meant so much. She stepped back with a wry smile. "Thanks, I'll need every well-wish I can get."

Wren's eyes narrowed behind her ivy mask. "Nonsense. Everything shall be fine. Devon shall make sure of it." She frowned at him. "Right?"

Devon chuckled. "Right."

In regular evening clothes with a horned mask dangling from one hand, Hawke flashed a crooked grin at Kiera and drew Wren back to his side. "Besides, what's court compared to managing the Bedsford twins?"

Kiera grimaced and swallowed a sigh. Except she understood the scampish boys and knew how to handle them. Court was a mystery, despite everything the duchess had taught her. She tsked. "I can't punish court with chores when they misbehave."

Hawke waggled his brows. "No, but you can have Devon execute them."

Kiera almost snorted at Hawke's ridiculous jest as Devon recaptured her arm then said, "For my betrothed, of course."

Eyeing him, Kiera shook her head. "You'd never do that." He was too dutiful a king.

Devon grinned with a shrug. "Well, maybe not the *entire* court."

As Kiera tsked at his teasing, Wren giggled. Then she reached out and clasped Kiera's hand. "We must join the others. You'll triumph over court with ease." She frowned up at Hawke. "Put on that mask. 'Tis your entire costume."

Hawke sighed but donned his horned mask. Then he and Wren flashed Kiera a final smile, and he escorted Wren into the ballroom.

Kiera gulped a steadying breath. Hopefully, Wren was right, and court didn't learn the truth. Devon's mad scheme depended on it, and so did the renewal of the Nightmara-Calatini Treaty.

Devon squeezed her arm with a tender smile. "Hawke and Wren are right—everything shall be fine. And I'll be beside you the entire time."

Her heart warming, she returned his smile and brushed dark-brown hair from his face. Although their betrothal was fake, Devon would always support and protect her. Her chest tightened. His true queen was a blessed lady. "I know."

Devon led her toward the buzzing ballroom, but paused on the threshold, and squeezed her arm again. "Are you ready?"

Kiera swallowed to ease her dry throat, but she managed a brilliant smile. She'd not fail him. "As much as I'll ever be."

Their guards following, they glided into the back of the ballroom. Silence swept the teeming room as the costumed guests gawked at the king and his mermaid. She suppressed a hysterical giggle. Obviously, none of them expected her to appear again.

In the echoing silence, Devon escorted her to the center of the ballroom with their guards remaining on the outskirts. He nodded at the musicians, who hastily began the first waltz. Devon beamed at her as they twirled alone across the floor. Exactly like a true betrothed would.

The eyes of court weighing on her like gorgons' stone-creating stares, Kiera forced herself to return his smile. When no one else began dancing and the gawking continued unabated, she swallowed and gripped his arms. "If court doesn't cease gawking, I'll trip and fall."

His gaze steady and warm, Devon drew her closer. "Then I'll fall with you, and we'll start the next court fashion."

She grimaced. Doubtless true, considering everything the duchess had said about court. "Delightful."

Devon quirked a wry smile. "Downside to being royalty. Everyone apes your blunders." When she grimaced again, he chuckled. "But Aragon and Hawke shall probably join on the next dance. No doubt their mother ordered them to wait, so court had time to gawk."

Her temples tightening, Kiera sighed then drawled, "How thoughtful of the duchess."

The interminable first dance ended at last. As he'd said, Wren and Hawke, Aragon and Selena, and several of their cousins joined in the second dance. Then by the third, the floor was filled with dancing couples. But court still gawked at her. Lovely.

Devon halted and arched a brow after the third dance. "Shall we make the announcement?"

She swallowed. If only they could continue dancing to delay that. But she'd agreed to act as Devon's betrothed, and she couldn't renege now. So she made herself nod.

Devon escorted her to the front of the ballroom then waved at the musicians to silence them.

She swallowed again as the music quieted and the few not already staring swirled to face them.

Devon flashed a grin. "I'm sure most of you have heard about the mermaid who captivated me at the summer masquerade."

The crowd stirred as whispers flew about the ballroom. No doubt the rumors Devon's people had instigated. Despite her rapid pulse, Kiera gritted the regal smile the duchess had insisted she learn.

Devon kissed her hand with an ardent look. "My mermaid led me on a merry chase. Although I hunted everywhere, I finally found her managing an orphanage near the docks."

While the whispers in the crowd swelled, her hand tingled at Devon's kiss. If only he wasn't feigning adoration to convince court of their betrothal. Allowing her smile to soften, she raised her tingling hand to caress his jaw. A true betrothed would think nothing of such gestures of affection.

Devon kissed her palm then beamed at the whispering crowd as she lowered her hand. "And I knew I must introduce her the same way she burst into court." He paused. "May I introduce Kiera, my betrothed and Calatini's future queen."

Her stomach twisting, she resumed her regal smile and untied her shell mask. "Greetings, lords and ladies. I anticipate meeting you all tonight and hope I'll serve Calatini well as her queen."

Devon squeezed her hand then said, "Please enjoy tonight's

masquerade and this Harvestfete pantomime." He waved toward the stage beneath the musicians' balcony. As the head player began his act, Devon murmured in her ear, "Care to step out for a bit before the introductions?"

Kiera nodded. A brief respite would help her brace herself for that. He was wonderful to think of it. She handed her shell mask to a nearby maid then she and Devon slipped into the balmy gardens. Unlike before, he didn't escort her to that secluded garden but to a stone bench along the palace wall. She sank down with a sigh. She was already weary, and the evening had just begun. "A flute of sparkling wine would be perfect right now."

Devon grimaced while he sat beside her. "I should have fetched some as we left."

She suppressed a chuckle. Even he couldn't remember everything. She smiled and shooed him toward the ballroom. "Go on then."

Devon cocked a brow. "Are you certain I should leave you alone?"

Her heart warming, Kiera caressed his jaw, for herself this time rather than court. Although she wasn't his true betrothed, he was as protective as a gargoyle defending his castle. "I'll be fine here. Go fetch my sparkling wine."

Devon kissed the palm caressing his face then rose and slipped back into the ballroom.

Sighing, she sagged against the palace wall and shut her eyes. She needn't feign verve with no one watching. But then a vicious grip seized her wrist and hauled her upright. She stiffened, and her eyes flew open.

A familiar smirk and cat-like gaze glinted behind a wyvern mask—Mr. Winston. At least the venomous, two-legged, winged snake was more apt than his previous costume. He jerked her toward him. "How far you have risen, my luscious mermaid. I can only imagine the favors you dispensed to achieve your ascent. What would King Devon say if he knew of *our* dalliance?"

Kiera yanked her captured arm but failed to free herself. "You mean when you tried to maul me?" As his grip tightened and smirk deepened, she attempted to gouge Mr. Winston's eyes like she had last time, but he grabbed that hand too.

Mr. Winston snickered with a leer. "I'm wise to your tricks now."

Two shapes burst from the foliage and wrested him to the ground. Over the unconscious man, Holmes, her senior guard, muttered, "Sorry for the delay. Reaching the garden from the opposite end of the ballroom took some time. What shall we do with this vermin?"

Her muscles loosening, Kiera sank back onto her bench. Perhaps the royal guards weren't suffocating after all. "Just escort him from the masquerade."

She gulped a breath as her guards dragged Mr. Winston away. Hopefully, no one inside had heard the scuffle. Rumors she was involved with that cad would negate the romantic tale Devon's people had spread. She'd be no use to him if the nightmara and court thought she was an unchaste betrothed.

CHAPTER 23

$\mathcal{D}$evon strode into the gardens with two flutes of sparkling wine then stiffened at Kiera's guards dragging away an unconscious Winston. How had the cad found her so quickly? He growled. And what had Winston done? The royal guards wouldn't have acted unless he'd become violent.

Setting his jaw, Devon strode toward Kiera. He never should have left her alone, not even to fetch her precious sparkling wine. She was too tempting for the predators at court to overlook. He gritted a smile as he handed her a flute. "Are you unharmed?"

Kiera shrugged while he sat beside her. "Of course."

His fingers clenched about his flute. No thanks to his negligence. He must protect her better or she'd never trust him enough to marry him. "What did Winston do?"

Kiera sipped her sparkling wine. "Grabbed my wrist and threatened to tell you about our encounter at the summer masquerade."

A chill skittering across his skin, Devon leaned toward her. Knowing Winston, their earlier encounter had been as violent as tonight's. "What encounter?"

Kiera shrugged again. "He attempted to seduce me by force, so I knocked him unconscious."

Devon growled as fire flared through him. Winston had gone much too far and must be handled. His flute cracked beneath his fingers. With a curse, he set the broken glass on the bench.

Kiera tsked then set aside her flute to take his hand. While tingling flooded him at her touch, she peered at his fingers. "You're fortunate. I don't see any bleeding."

Despite her moving concern, he suppressed a grimace. Cutting himself was no less than he deserved for leaving her unprotected. Yet he mustn't dwell on that now—he must introduce her to court. He threaded his tingling fingers through hers then kissed her knuckles. "Are you ready to return?"

Kiera sighed. "As ready as I could be."

Abandoning their flutes on the bench, Devon drew Kiera upright and escorted her back to the teeming ballroom. His chest constricting, he eyed her as they rejoined their guests. A faint smile curved her lips, but her encounter with Winston had surely upset her. To hearten her, he must steer her away from detractors until she'd met some sure allies.

But before he could escort her to Aragon or one of his other cousins, a shepherd and shepherdess halted before them. The shepherdess asked, "Mistress Kiera?"

Kiera peered at her. "Lady Weston?"

The older lady beamed and bobbed her head before embracing Kiera. "How lovely to see you again. I can't imagine a finer lady to be our future queen. The girls are always telling us how well you cared for them."

Lord Weston grinned at Kiera as he drew his wife back beside him. "Calatini shall prosper if you care for it like you did our girls."

Devon almost smiled while he reclaimed Kiera's arm. The Westons were the perfect remedy to Winston. And they'd stumbled across the older couple without trying. Fortunate.

Lady Weston clapped her hands. "I can't wait to tell Cassandra and Amaranth. And please attend our musical evening next month. We'll let the girls stay awake late to see you." She curtsied and her husband bowed before they drifted off.

Devon studied Kiera, who was fully smiling now. Yes, meeting the Westons first had been perfect. Next, his cousins. He escorted Kiera to a gargoyle and his naiad. "Evening, Aragon, Selena. I see you're wearing the costumes you'd intended to wear at my summer masquerade."

Aragon shrugged. "No one but family knew these were our costumes for before, and we had to wear them sometime."

Selena patted her rounded stomach. "And fortunately, my costume still fits."

As Devon chuckled at Selena's jest, Kiera leaned toward her with a warm smile. "Thanks for attending tonight to support us, when you'd doubtless rather be in bed."

Selena grinned back. "We're delighted to attend to support Devon's chosen bride at last. Although we shan't stay too much longer."

Devon sighed as Aragon wrapped a solicitous arm about his wife. If only he could embrace Kiera the same, rather than politely holding her arm. But she'd jerk away if he did. After all, she'd protested his kisses earlier tonight, and that had been in private.

Aragon smiled. "Not that we need to stay. Everything is progressing smoothly. Most gossip we overheard seems to favor Kiera, despite her common past."

Selena winked at Kiera. "After all, Devon finding you in an orphanage is downright tame."

Devon muffled a laugh. An orphanage *was* tame compared to a brothel.

Yet Kiera blinked and echoed, "Tame?"

Selena arched her brows. "Didn't Wren or Devon ever mention Aragon found me in a brothel?"

As Kiera gaped at her, Devon almost winced. The brothel had

been years ago, and he'd figured Kiera already knew. Would not mentioning it make her not trust him?

Her eyes wide, Kiera studied Selena. "No... What were you doing in such a place? You're clearly a lady."

Selena grimaced. "I was penniless and desperate to escape my disreputable uncle and his black witch." She smiled at Kiera. "Since you're family now, I'll share the entire tale."

Aragon shook his head. "Not tonight. We should greet a few additional guests then return home so you can rest."

As Aragon whisked his pregnant wife away, Kiera turned to Devon. "Did he truly meet her in a brothel?"

Devon relaxed at her quizzical smile. She didn't appear upset he'd not mentioned that before. He grinned and nodded. "After Aragon brought her home, the duchess handled Selena's presentation at court, and soon court adored her. Although my approval helped."

Kiera sighed and twisted her betrothal ring. "So I'm not the first pariah you foisted on court."

He stiffened. She wasn't a pariah. She was the lady meant to be his queen. But before he could reply, Lord and Lady Escana bowed and curtsied before them.

Devon introduced the Escanas to Kiera, who smiled then asked after their beloved hounds. When they were replaced by the Campbells, she marveled over the wedding tokens they'd redesigned at their recent vow reaffirmation. As they continued meeting members of court, Kiera greeted everyone with warm smiles and personal details as if she already knew them. Some he'd never even heard. Goddess, she was amazing. Her finesse tonight simply proved she'd make the perfect queen.

Warmth suffusing his chest, he squeezed Kiera's arm and handed her a fresh flute of sparkling wine when the introductions slowed. "The duchess's lessons were more thorough than I realized. How did you remember all those personal details?"

Kiera flashed a wry smile as she sipped her sparkling wine. "Many, many sessions with the duchess's scrying mirror with her drilling me until I could recite them without prompting. 'Twas grueling."

As Devon winced, Wren and Hawke halted before them, and Wren grinned then said, "But worth it. Everyone is gossiping about our future queen's warmth and insight." She grasped Kiera's free hand. "I'm sorry to leave so early, but I'm exhausted, and all seems well."

Kiera smiled and shooed her friends toward the back with her flute. "Go, go. Aragon and Selena left a while ago. Pregnant ladies need their rest."

Hawke winked at her. "Have fun charming all of court."

Once her friends left, Kiera drained her flute. "Fun? Ha!"

Devon smiled at her as he passed their flutes to a nearby servant. Watching her charm court was fun, although she probably found it draining. "Shall we keep having *fun*?"

Kiera sighed. "I suppose we must. Although I'd rather head to bed like Wren and Hawke."

His pulse surged. If only they could head to bed together like her friends. He kissed her palm before escorting her to the nearest couple.

Her gauzy Tsarkan veils and bedlah disguising nothing, Lady Blaine stepped back from Lord Ravenstone to eye Kiera. "You're Wren's orphanage friend."

Devon's jaw tensed at her neutral tone. Were her words a sly insult or mere fact?

Kiera lifted her chin with a tight smile. "And you are?"

A flush darkened Lady Blaine's cheeks. "Kit, the Countess of Blaine. Wren and I grew up together."

Kiera arched her brows. "Oh, she never mentioned you. Although you do appear *vaguely* familiar—you attended her last orphanage play, didn't you?" She beamed. "'Twas delightful, wasn't it?"

Devon almost laughed. Wren must have mentioned the sultry countess because Kiera was repaying her habitual needling of Wren in kind.

Lady Blaine stiffened. "Wren's plays always are." She managed a graceful curtsy before she swept away.

Lord Ravenstone's chuckle belied his thanatos robe and scythe. "I'm grateful for your assistance, Lady Kiera. I was almost tempted to use my scythe as more than a prop."

As Kiera blinked at Lord Ravenstone, Devon arched a brow. The genial count would never be so churlish toward a lady, no matter how grasping. He drawled, "Somehow I doubt that."

A grin gleamed amid Lord Ravenstone's black beard. "*Almost* tempted, your majesty, not actually tempted." He glanced beyond them and tensed. "I see the Greysnowes approaching. I must be off to prevent feeding the feud. A pleasure to meet you, Lady Kiera." He bowed then strode into the crowd.

Her tattered white gown and white-blonde hair fluttering behind her, Lady Annalise glided forward to embrace Kiera with a warm smile. "Evening, Kiera."

While Lord and Lady Greysnowe gaped behind their daughter, Kiera beamed and kissed her cheek. "Evening, Annalise. Why are you dressed as a banshee?"

Devon eyed the embracing ladies. Kiera had written they'd met so Lady Annalise could act as her friend at court, but their friendship appeared genuine. Lady Annalise never behaved so open with anyone. He smiled. Of course, his compassionate and perceptive love had befriended the loneliest lady at court despite her extraordinary beauty.

Lady Annalise shrugged as she stepped back and Devon recaptured Kiera's arm. "I thought a banshee costume fitting for a Harvestfete masquerade."

His sultan's robes rustling, Lord Greysnowe glared at Kiera and pulled his daughter between him and his wife. "Or perhaps she foresaw the death of her dreams."

Devon tensed. Not surprising the count would say that. If only he'd never started escorting Lady Annalise and fueled her parents' ambitions.

But before he could respond, Lady Annalise tsked and glided

back to Kiera. "King Devon was no dream of mine. Kiera suits him better than I ever could."

As her husband stiffened, Lady Greysnowe snapped, "And you know this *how*?"

Lady Annalise flashed a cool smile at her parents. "Because we met at Lady Beza's several days ago and became fast friends." She turned back to Kiera. "Are you nervous about meeting the nightmara queen-heir tomorrow?"

Her navy eyes darkening, Kiera grimaced. "Dreadfully."

Devon squeezed her arm. Moonbud would adore her. If only Kiera could believe that.

Lady Annalise beamed and grasped Kiera's free hand. "Let me know if you need my aid." She swept a curtsy at Devon. "Your majesty."

As Kiera watched her new friend and the Greysnowes glide away, Devon caressed her palm with his thumb. Unfortunately, they'd still a lot of court to meet. "Are you ready for harsher critics than the Greysnowes?"

Kiera sighed but inclined her head.

So he escorted her to a cluster of councilors who'd hopefully remain gracious. But he'd start the introductions with the most thorny one. "Kiera, allow me to introduce the Countess of Morwynne." The firecat jerked a brief curtsy. "She's the Minister of Health and Community."

Kiera beamed, probably to build rapport for working together on her education initiative. "A pleasure, Lady Morwynne."

Once the superior countess nodded, Devon waved toward the centaur. "This is the Duke of Oakmoor, the Minister of Foreign Relations." He suppressed a growl when the suave duke kissed Kiera's hand with a suggestive wink. How dare he flirt so with his future queen?

A cool smile on her lips, Kiera tugged her hand free. The duke's inappropriate flirting obviously nettled her as well. She murmured, "Your grace."

Devon squeezed her arm then turned to the auburn owl. "And this is the Duchess of Wildewall, the Minister of Justice."

The duchess smiled and curtsied. "Pleased to meet you, Lady Kiera. I'm glad you weren't fabricated by the Ravenstones."

Kiera chuckled. "Annalise's parents are vexed with me, aren't they? Despite her not wanting to be queen."

As the duchess blinked and tilted her head, Devon nodded at the three councilors. With so many others to meet, they mustn't linger. "We must continue to other guests, but we'll talk more at the council meeting the day after tomorrow."

To avoid more councilors, he led Kiera to a group of young courtiers including Pippa and Edouard. But he and Kiera soon drifted to another group, then another, then another until they met almost everyone. The masquerade was winding to a close when they finally greeted Aragon's and Wren's parents, who were together like always.

Resplendent as an arctic elf, the Duchess of Childes beamed at Kiera. "You're doing wonderfully. Better than Queen Mynee ever did."

Devon grinned and caressed Kiera's palm with his thumb. Of course, she surpassed his mother. One day she'd be recognized as Calatini's best queen since their first, Calator's wife Annalise.

Kiera smiled. "I couldn't have survived tonight without your lessons. You've my deepest thanks."

A wood elf to match his wife, the Duke of Childes flashed a crooked grin. "Caro should be thanking you."

Sir Alaric's wink fit his pirate costume. "Yes, she's never happier than when plotting a triumph over court."

While the duchess sniffed, Lady Keyes twitched her wench skirt and chided, "Must you tease Caro in front of the children?"

Before Wren's father could reply, Devon smiled at the older ladies. Their help had allowed Kiera to triumph tonight. "Regardless, we're grateful for your assistance—no matter the reason."

The two couples bowed and curtsied before gliding from the ballroom.

Devon glanced down at Kiera, who almost swayed beside him. His chest tightened. She could use some rest. He arched a brow. "The masquerade is nearly over. Shall we leave?"

Kiera heaved a sigh. "Yes, please."

His heart fluttering, he kissed her palm then escorted her upstairs to the queen's chambers to change. Tonight had gone even better than he'd hoped, and soon all of court would adore her like he did. Surely her meeting with Moonbud tomorrow would go as well.

On the carriage ride back to the orphanage, Kiera nestled against Devon and dozed. Too bad the obstinate lady had refused to stay at the palace. The extra traveling would soon exhaust her. At the orphanage, he forced himself to release her after a soft kiss. Although he burned for more, she was weary, and he'd ruin tonight's progress if he went too far.

CHAPTER 24

Her stomach quivering, Kiera frowned at the walking dress with pleated trim Mia offered her the following morning. Arachne silk like all of her court wardrobe, 'twas too fancy for an outdoor meeting with the horse-like nightmara. "I'm not certain that dress is right for a meeting in the middle of a paddock."

Mia returned the walking dress to the wardrobe. "You're thinking something more outdoorsy, your highness? One of your riding habits might suit."

Kiera sighed. But the riding habits were also arachne silk, and since she didn't ride, she'd feel an impostor if she wore one. Not what she needed when meeting the nightmara queen-heir for the first time. She shook her head. "Just select the least ornate walking dress."

After Mia helped her dress, Kiera pricked her finger and turned the walking dress a light cream. At least the color was sober, even if the fabric was too fancy. Now she must find Devon, so they could head to the nightmara meeting. She swallowed as she attached one of his peach roses to her dress for luck. She'd not seen him since he'd kissed her at the orphanage last night, but he'd mentioned he spent most mornings in his study handling state affairs. "Mia, could you remind me how to get to the king's study?"

Once the maid explained, Kiera thanked her and strode from the queen's chambers. The guards who joined her at the door were different than the pairs from yesterday and earlier today. They must work eight-hour shifts. Fortunately, they remained outside with Devon's guards when she knocked on his study door and entered.

Devon grinned and dropped his papers on his cluttered desk then strode toward her with obvious intent. "Morning, Kiera."

Her pulse quickening, she shoved the door closed. 'Twas bad enough the guards knew she was kissing Devon without them seeing it too. She should protest, but she burned for another ravenous kiss. So when he drew her into his arms and devoured her lips, she wrapped her arms about his neck and kissed him back.

After a moment, Devon dropped into the nearest chair and pulled her into his lap. He nuzzled her neck. "I could become accustomed to starting every morning this way."

Her already racing heart surging, Kiera threaded her fingers in his dark-brown hair. Goddess, so could she. But then she'd shatter when their betrothal ended. Next time, she really *must* refuse his kiss.

Devon leaned back after a final kiss on her neck. "This morning I received multiple notes congratulating me on my lovely betrothed and inviting us to events in the upcoming weeks. So the masquerade went even better than we thought last night."

She forced herself to remain still. Until he released her, she must pretend he was just another chair. "I hope I can maintain court's favor through the treaty negotiations."

Devon chuckled and squeezed her. "You shall. You'll continue charming them with your natural warmth, insight, and strength."

A blush warming her cheeks, Kiera tsked at his flattery.

Again he was attempting to hearten her. "Right. Now when do we need to meet the nightmara queen-heir?"

Devon shrugged. "Whenever you like. I sent word to Lady Moonbud that we'd meet this morning as soon as you returned to the palace."

She swallowed to wet her suddenly dry mouth. "We might as well go now then." She attempted to rise, but Devon's arms held her fast. She pursed her lips. "You must release me first."

Eyeing her lips, Devon sighed. "If I must." After a brief kiss, he released her and escorted her from his study.

As they silently strode through the cool palace grounds with their guards, Kiera reviewed what she'd learned about the night-mara and the treaty, and her mouth dried further. The powerful nightmara could read thoughts and drive humans mad with their magic. And the only humans nightmara truly trusted were the mara clans who lived among them so they had dreams to consume to prevent becoming feeble and fatigued through dreamsickness. Yet the legendary Nightmara-Calatini Treaty had protected both nightmara and humans for four centuries— somehow she must convince Lady Moonbud, the nightmara queen-heir who was negotiating for the elderly Queen Night-snow, to renew it. She swallowed again. Goddess, let her be able to do that.

When they were in sight of the nightmara stables, Devon squeezed her arm. "Remember, Lady Moonbud has been forced to deal with me for the past month and a half, so she'll be grateful to be dealing with Calatini's future queen finally."

She twisted the Vireni betrothal ring. Too bad Lady Moonbud wasn't dealing with the true future queen. Then she tensed. "What if Lady Moonbud realizes I'm not Calatini's future queen in truth?" After all, the nightmara possessed power over dreams and the mind, and the nightmara queen-heir was the strongest of them all.

Devon smiled. "Don't fret about that. Just remember to be yourself, and treat Lady Moonbud with respect but not deference—as my betrothed, you're equal to the nightmara queen-heir."

Kiera gulped a bracing breath. 'Twould probably be the hardest thing for a poor orphanage matron to remember. But she'd managed to remember that last night amid the opulently costumed court, so surely she would today as well.

Devon halted before the nightmara stable door with a warm smile. "Ready?"

Her temples tightened, but she inclined her head. She had to be. They were here.

Devon kissed her palm. "You'll be wonderful. Remember that."

When he rapped the nightmara stable door, it flew open to reveal a brunette mara woman, who wore trousers and a sword like the royal guards protecting Kiera, and a black nightmara, whose midnight eyes gleamed with fierce intelligence. A hand resting on the saber at her waist, the mara woman beamed and bowed to Kiera. "Your highness, 'tis a great honor to meet you at last. I'm Leila." She waved toward the nightmara beside her. "And this is my partner Nightrose. We're the nightmara-mara pair representing the Flower Herd, the nightmara queen-heir's herd."

Kiera smiled at the mara woman and her partner. Bound to each other until death, such pairs formed the best cavalry in Damensea and were the heart of Calatini's southern defense—part of why she mustn't fail. About to introduce herself, she stilled when Devon coughed behind his hand. What was so amusing?

Devon murmured in her ear, "Leila wasn't *near* so friendly before."

As Kiera blinked, Leila narrowed her eyes at Devon. "Did you have something to share, your majesty?"

Kiera forced herself not to gape at Leila's sharp tone. How could the mara woman behave so rudely toward her king? The nightmara and mara prejudice against males was greater than she'd imagined.

Yet Devon merely shook his head with a smile. "Could you lead us to Lady Moonbud, please?"

Leila pursed her lips but nodded.

As Leila and Nightrose led them through the stables, Kiera finally introduced herself, "I'm Kiera, by the way. 'Tis a pleasure to meet you as well—you're the first mara and nightmara I've ever met." Hopefully, sharing that would please the prickly mara woman.

Her ponytail flying, Leila swung to face Kiera. "Truly?" When Kiera nodded, Leila grinned. "Nightrose and I are honored to be your first."

Kiera sighed as they continued through the stables. If Leila's reaction to her and Devon was typical of the mara and nightmara, no wonder he'd begged her to act as his queen.

They soon exited the stables into the paddock, and Devon waved at the royal guards. "You four remain here. Kiera and I shall be fine alone."

As he spoke, Kiera scanned the paddock. Goddess, please let her not appear too awed or intimidated. Over a dozen nightmara and their mara partners were spread about the paddock in clusters. Ranging from taupe to midnight, the unsaddled nightmara resembled wild horses but for their magical and sentient air. Gliding amid the nightmara and bearing sabers and arrows, the mara appeared more vigilant than the palace guards. As if heeding a silent call, the nightmara and mara paused their various activities to scrutinize her. She swallowed. Oh, Goddess.

Devon drew her arm closer and embraced her hand against his side. Doubtless he was attempting to reassure her without alerting the nightmara and mara.

Warmth easing her chest, she squeezed his arm in thanks. His steadfast support despite her poor upbringing and inexperience simply proved how wonderful he was. If only their betrothal could be genuine.

Then a dappled midnight mare strode through the herd toward them. From her powerful presence, she must be the nightmara queen-heir. She nodded at them. :*Good morning, your majesties. Thank the Goddess you brought your queen at last, King Devon.*:

Kiera tensed as her stomach twisted. She was simply a poor orphanage matron acting as the king's betrothed. Being called *queen* was too much. She lifted her chin. "Future queen."

Her taupe eyes lustrous, Lady Moonbud blinked at Kiera. :*Same difference.*:

As she and Lady Moonbud locked gazes, the oddest tickle skittered inside her skull—the nightmara queen-heir must be attempting to read her. If Lady Moonbud continued, she'd discover the truth and refuse to negotiate. So Kiera shoved Lady Moonbud from her mind then pictured a barbed fence surrounding her thoughts.

Lady Moonbud snorted and jerked back her head. :*You're a most unusual human, your highness.*:

Kiera gritted a smile. Was that an insult or a compliment? But she inclined her head. "Call me Kiera, Lady Moonbud."

Lady Moonbud glided forward and craned toward Kiera, her eyes a mere handbreadth away. :*Only if you call me Moonbud.*:

Her pulse stuttering, Kiera forced herself to breathe. Goddess, the nightmara were massive so close. "If you like."

Moonbud nickered and turned to Devon. :*I'm most impressed by your chosen mate, your majesty. It almost atones for your delay in finding her.*:

Devon beamed at Kiera as he kissed her palm. "I didn't choose her to impress you. I found my true queen."

Kiera caressed his jaw to bolster his pretense, her heart squeezing. If only his words were genuine.

Devon chuckled. "But I hope your approbation means you'll uphold your promise to negotiate more reasonably with Kiera than you did with me."

Moonbud echoed his laugh as she pawed the ground. :*No*

doubt I shall, although we must become better acquainted for me to know for sure.:

Kiera stiffened as heat flooded her. The nightmara had never requested becoming better acquainted before. Could Moonbud sense she was only acting as Devon's betrothed? She arched her brows at the nightmara queen-heir. "How much better do you mean? Queen Sarilee and Nightwind only knew each other a night before laying the foundations for the first treaty."

Moonbud flicked her midnight tail. *:True, but Sarilee was an established queen, and Nightwind had investigated her beforehand. Since you haven't been crowned yet, we don't know what sort of queen you'll be.:*

The heat flooding Kiera ebbed—Moonbud didn't realize the truth. She glanced at Devon, silently asking for advice. When he responded with a faint shrug, she sighed then made herself smile at Moonbud and ask, "How did you wish to become better acquainted?"

Moonbud hummed. *:I assume you'll be busy with your new duties at court, so how about meeting in the morning every three days?:* She narrowly eyed Devon. *:But without pesky stallions like your betrothed interfering.:*

Kiera suppressed a grimace. If only Devon could join them to support her, but the nightmara queen-heir was clearly determined he stay away. Wonderful. Kiera arched her brows at him. "You know better than I—is Moonbud's suggestion feasible?"

Devon smiled and caressed her palm with his thumb. "It should be." He turned to grin at Moonbud. "I suppose since you don't want me *interfering*, you'd like me to leave."

Kiera swallowed. She wasn't ready to face Moonbud alone yet. She forced a wry smile. "I should join him—I must prepare to meet Calatini's council tomorrow."

Moonbud inclined her head. *:Of course. I'll meet you in the paddock midmorning in three days.:*

Kiera returned the nightmara queen-heir's nod. "I look forward to it."

Devon escorted her from the nightmara paddock, not speaking until the nightmara stables had vanished behind them. "That went well."

She exhaled and rubbed her chest. "Did it?"

Devon winked at her. "Certainly better than mine did. And you'll impress her even more without me in future meetings." He squeezed her arm. "Come, luncheon awaits us."

Over luncheon in the royal wing, Devon asked her about the orphanage, no doubt to help her relax. They spent the meal chuckling at the orphans' attempts during breakfast to evade their later lessons. They'd been adorable, but she'd stood firm since their lessons were too important to skip.

Kiera sighed as she and Devon finished their apple tart. If only she'd time to visit the orphanage this afternoon, but they must head to Childes House early for the dinner the duchess was hosting in her honor. The duchess wanted to review how the masquerade went and to offer additional advice about the councilors. And Kiera needed that help—she couldn't fail Devon midway through their fake betrothal.

CHAPTER 25

$\mathcal{S}$hortly before the council meeting the following morning, Devon set down Lord Islaye's latest report about the Magehaven ore then strode from his study to fetch Kiera. Doubtless she was nervous, but she'd shine like she had at the Harvestfete masquerade, the meeting with Moonbud, and at the duchess's dinner in her honor last night. She was a natural queen—but how could he convince her of that?

When he entered her chambers, Kiera stood before her cheval mirror, studying her flowing dress of indeterminate color with a needle poised before her finger.

His heart quickened. Goddess, 'twas wonderful to see her. If only she were the first thing he saw every morning. He coughed from the door. "You should match your betrothal ring. That shall remind the councilors of your future rank."

Kiera smiled at him in the mirror. "Are you certain that's not too obvious?"

Devon chuckled. "No, most of the council would disregard anything subtle." They could be almost as obstinate as Kiera when they chose.

Kiera nodded then pricked her finger. As her blood touched her dress, the arachne silk became ivory trimmed with interlaced knotwork in teal and purple, exactly matching the alexandrite's shifting colors.

He strode forward and kissed her palm beneath her ring. "Perfect as always." When she blushed, he drew her into his arms where she belonged. "I've not greeted you good morning yet, have I?"

Kiera blushed harder. "Don't muss my walking dress. I haven't time to change."

Tingling warmth flooded him. If only he could, but that must wait until she'd agreed to marry him. Yet he needed a few kisses. He squeezed her. "The councilors would understand."

Kiera pursed her lips. "That's what concerns me. They'll believe me no better than a trollop."

His jaw twitched. They'd better not. He gritted a smile. "Or that I passionately love you."

Devon captured her mouth in a deep kiss. Perhaps if he distilled all his love into it, 'twould convince her she was his true queen.

Her arms twining about his neck, Kiera sighed and parted her lips beneath his. Despite her protests, she clearly relished his kisses. She *must* love him as deeply as he loved her.

They continued kissing until a knock interrupted them, and one of his guards called through the door, "Your majesties, the council meeting is about to start."

He groaned but raised his head. If only he could keep kissing Kiera forever. Unfortunately, they'd duties to attend. "We'd better hurry. Tardiness might bias the councilors against you."

Kiera lowered her arms. "You should have remembered that before kissing me."

Flashing a wry smile, Devon kissed her palm before taking her arm. "I did, but kissing you inspires me to forget everything else."

As they left her chambers with their guards following, Kiera blushed and smoothed her dress. "Yes, so we must take care not to forget ourselves entirely."

His heart fluttering, he caressed her palm with his thumb. "Perhaps we're forging new selves together." True couples always did.

Kiera tsked as they turned onto the hall leading to the council room. "By kissing?" She shook her head. "That sounds like something a gentleman bent on seduction would claim."

Devon suppressed a wince. His hungry kisses were only convincing Kiera of his lust, not his love. He must stop until she believed his love was sincere. A few kisses weren't worth losing her. Somehow he must restrain his hunger and demonstrate his love through his steadfast support. Hopefully, 'twould be enough.

He paused when they reached the council room door. His chest tightening, he glanced down at Kiera. Please let the council meeting go smoothly for her. "Are you ready?"

Kiera swallowed but lifted her chin. "As much as I'll ever be."

Aching to kiss his brave lady again, he squeezed her arm instead. "Remember, I can execute any councilors who disrespect you."

Kiera snorted a laugh and returned his squeeze. "I'll remember."

Their guards remaining outside, Devon swept Kiera inside the council room.

The councilors hushed like firebirds before a thunderstorm and squinted at Kiera. Doubtless the weight of their stares amplified her nerves.

To hearten her, he squeezed her arm again, and she smiled at him as they took their seats. Good. He turned to the councilors and nodded. "Morning. Although Kiera has met some of you already, allow me to introduce everyone for those she hasn't."

Starting with Aragon to his right and ending with the Duchess of Wildewall on Kiera's left, Devon introduced the twelve councilors, their duchies, and their ministries. Like at the Harvestfete masquerade, Kiera inclined her head after each introduction then mentioned a political detail, many of which the duchess had reminded her about before last night's dinner.

Given their tight smiles or blank expressions, most of the councilors except Aragon were reserving judgment or mildly opposed to Kiera. Not surprising, but Kiera would soon sway most in her favor.

Devon glanced about the table. "Now that introductions are done, shall we proceed to other matters?"

Silence stretched across the council room until the elderly Duke of Osbourne creaked, "I don't wish to insult Lady Kiera, but how do we know this sudden romance isn't due to an enchantment?"

Devon almost snorted. Until now, the councilors had pressured him to find a queen to negotiate with the nightmara. They were simply annoyed he'd found Kiera without their advice. He arched a brow and brandished the gold bracelet on his left wrist. "Because of the powerful protection charm I've worn the past thirteen years."

Lord Islaye inclined his head. "And Lady Juliet assured me after the summer masquerade that she renewed it this spring, so it couldn't have failed."

The Duke of Osbourne snorted. "Bah, as the Minister of Magic, you know very well that what one witch has spelled another can break."

Devon's jaw tightened, and he was about to respond, when the Duchess of Wildewall interjected, "True, but Lady Juliet is the most illustrious witch in Calatini. 'Twould be nearly impossible to break a spell of hers."

Kiera stirred beside him, probably because a powerful Rhiannon descendant like the veiled witch could manage it. Not that she had. Fortunately, only Aragon and Lord Farson knew about the veiled witch, and the others weren't likely to discover a witch near the docks.

As Devon touched Kiera's knee beneath the table to reassure

her, Aragon chuckled then said, "We could always poison Devon to test the protection charm." When the other councilors stiffened, he snorted and shook his head. "Or perhaps we should simply accept Devon has found his queen at last and ask how their meeting with the nightmara queen-heir went yesterday?"

Lord Farson leaned forward. "If Lady Moonbud accepted Lady Kiera, then we know her sudden relationship with King Devon is no enchantment."

When the councilors eyed them, Devon arched his brows at Kiera. As the future queen who must negotiate with the nightmara, she should answer.

He beamed when Kiera flashed a regal smile and said, "Lady Moonbud was delighted to meet me and has promised to negotiate more reasonably with me than she had with Devon. We'll meet every three days to become better acquainted until she's ready to negotiate the treaty."

His chest warm, Devon chuckled. "Meetings that Lady Moonbud ordered me not to attend. So she must like Kiera."

As all the other councilors except Aragon blinked at Kiera, Lord Farson smiled and smoothed his beard. "Lady Kiera's common upbringing *would* impress the nightmara. With her negotiating, we'll doubtless fare well in the renewed treaty."

When the other councilors blinked again, Devon almost grinned. Good, Kiera had an ally on the council besides Aragon. Aragon's cousin by marriage, but still.

Then Lady Morwynne arched a brow and drawled, "So *Lady* Kiera is ideal to negotiate with the nightmara, but what about after?"

While Kiera tensed beside him, Devon almost glared at the superior countess. *After* Kiera would make the best queen since Queen Annalise.

Lady Ducharme and the Duchess of Wildewall exchanged a glance, then Lady Ducharme said, "According to Lord and Lady Weston, no one would make a better queen."

The duchess smiled then added, "Yes, they told us all about her care of their orphaned granddaughters for upwards of half an hour."

Devon smiled. Two more potential allies. Not as certain as Aragon or Lord Farson, but more than he'd expected so soon.

Kiera blushed and shook her head. "The Westons make too much of my service to their granddaughters. I was merely the matron of the local orphanage."

Aragon arched a brow. "Which happens to be the best in Ormas, despite being near the docks."

Devon squeezed her knee beneath the table then smiled at the other councilors. "And 'twas excellent preparation for caring for all of Calatini."

When the councilors stilled and eyed Kiera again, but with fewer frowns, he almost chuckled. Excellent, they were beginning to see her worth and not just her poor upbringing.

He took Kiera's arm and drew her upright. "That's enough for today. Kiera and I must prepare for petitions at court this afternoon."

The councilors began murmuring to each other as he and Kiera glided from the council room.

They headed straight to the royal wing for luncheon, and as she sipped her orange cucurbit soup, Kiera asked, "How do you think that went?"

Devon beamed at her. "As well as your first meeting with Moonbud did. A third of the councilors support you already, and the others shall soon."

To help her relax, he asked if the orphans had attempted to evade their lessons again, and they spent luncheon discussing the orphanage. They really must visit as soon as everything settled at court. He'd adore meeting all the children she lovingly described.

After luncheon, they changed into court attire, and he barely kept from kissing her. Goddess, she was even more lovely in her resplendent court gown. Yet he must restrain his hunger until she realized he loved her. Hopefully, 'twould be soon—who knew how much longer his restraint would last? He swallowed and offered his arm to escort her to the throne room.

CHAPTER 26

When Devon escorted her into the throne room after luncheon, Kiera almost gaped at the vast chamber. 'Twas even more stunning than the rest of the palace. Sunshine streamed through the many huge windows, and enormous chandeliers blazed with witchlights. Thanks to all that light, the white stone walls and massive pillars almost glowed, and the green and gold tapestries shone.

A matching green and gold carpet split the extravagantly dressed crowd and led to a dais just large enough for the two thrones in white marble and gold. And behind them, the white velvet curtain concealing the perilous Mirror of Wisdom wafted like in a faint breeze. She suppressed a shiver.

Then she forced a regal smile as Devon squeezed her arm and escorted her to the thrones. Once she settled in the left one, she eyed the crowd below and maintained her smile. All the councilors were there, along with many others she recognized from the masquerade.

Devon waved for the petitions to begin, and Kiera kept her regal smile and observed in silence. Whether by wealthy nobles or humble farmers, most petitions were brief, but Devon intently listened to each one then either delivered his decision or promised one at a later time. Her chest warmed at his adroit yet steady manner. He was truly a wonderful king.

Over dinner in the royal wing, Devon arched his brows at her. "You could have spoken during the petitions. The people of Calatini expect to hear their future queen's opinions."

She twisted the Vireni betrothal ring. So they did. "I'll speak more once I'm settled." She touched his hand across the table. "But watching you was enthralling. You were masterful."

Threading his fingers through hers, Devon coughed then flashed a wry grin. "I've enough practice, I suppose. I'll be grateful for a partner to help."

Kiera nodded as her chest squeezed. She'd help however she could while acting as his betrothed. If only she could help him forever. But she must return to the orphanage once the nightmara negotiations were done. Then he could find his true queen to share the burden of ruling.

OVER THE NEXT TWO DAYS, Kiera and Devon attended the many, many court events the duchess had recommended as well as handled state affairs in the morning. The constant social rounds were exhausting, and Kiera spent even less time at the orphanage than expected. Every night, Devon escorted her back to the orphanage well after midnight, but he stopped kissing her at the door, probably because they were both too exhausted.

As soon as she returned to the orphanage, Kiera went straight to bed and collapsed. But even though she needed more sleep, she forced herself to join the orphans for breakfast, so she could see them for an hour at least. Then she headed to the palace for another hectic day at court. And she hadn't even started her education initiative. Hopefully, everything would settle soon, and she could do more than attend party after party.

The morning of her second meeting with Moonbud, Kiera suppressed a wry grimace as she got ready. Although she must face the nightmara queen-heir alone this time, at least 'twasn't another party where all of court stared at her. Then she frowned at the walking dresses Mia offered—they were just too fancy. When she requested a simpler cut, Mia fetched a riding habit with no ornamentation.

Kiera sighed. She didn't ride, but the cut *was* simpler. So she forced herself to nod and let Mia help her into the riding habit. After turning it a purposeful navy, she strode across the crisp palace grounds with her guards close behind. She gulped a steadying breath when she approached the nightmara stables. But before she could knock, the door flew open.

Leila grinned at her. "Morning, Lady Kiera!"

Her stomach easing at the mara woman's exuberance, Kiera smiled at her and her nightmara partner. "Morning, Leila, Nightrose."

The black mare blinked then nodded. :*Morning, Lady Kiera.*:

When the pair led her into the paddock, Kiera waved for her guards to remain by the stables. Not only would that demonstrate her trust for Moonbud, but she'd be free of their hovering. Once the guards were out of earshot, she smiled at Leila and Nightrose. "Do you two always have door duty?"

Leila chuckled. "No, but as the pair representing Moonbud's herd, we're responsible for greeting her visitors."

Kiera eyed Leila's hand resting on her sheathed saber like always, a habit which revealed a fierce vigilance. No wonder the mara and nightmara were renowned warriors. "And guarding her from them, no doubt."

Leila chuckled again, and Nightrose nickered. "Of course."

As they approached, Moonbud didn't glance up from the black nightmara stallion pressed against her. She must be engrossed in their silent conversation.

Leila smirked at Nightrose then coughed into her fist. "Lady Kiera is here."

Moonbud started and tossed her mane. :*Yes, of course. Morning, Kiera.*:

Kiera nodded and suppressed a smile at the nightmara queen-heir's distracted tone. "Morning, Moonbud and..."

:*Darkthorn,*: Moonbud replied. :*He's Nightrose's twin.*:

Kiera almost laughed. He *clearly* meant more to Moonbud than that, but 'twas rude to pry. So she only said, "I can see the resemblance. A pleasure to meet you, Darkthorn."

Darkthorn eyed her for a moment, and his powers prickled against her mind.

Kiera stiffened and strengthened the barbed fence around her thoughts. The nightmara mustn't learn she was only acting as Devon's betrothed.

Darkthorn inclined his head. :*You as well.*: He nuzzled Moonbud then trotted away.

Moonbud leaned toward Kiera, eyeing her riding habit. :*So would you like to ride about the paddock or farther afield?*:

Kiera swallowed. Oh dear. Despite its simple cut, she shouldn't have worn the riding habit. "No, thank you." When Moonbud blinked, Leila gasped, and Nightrose snorted, Kiera licked her lips and added, "Although I appreciate the offer."

Leila gaped at her. "You can't refuse! Don't you realize the great honor she's showed you? Dominant mares are *never* ridden after their training unless they offer, and they rarely do."

Kiera winced. Had her refusal insulted Moonbud? She offered the nightmara queen-heir a wry smile. "I apologize, but I can't ride. 'Tisn't a skill poor orphans learn."

Moonbud cocked her head and chuckled. :*I should have realized. Well, every queen should ride—I'll teach you during our meetings.*:

Kiera swallowed. Wonderful, now she must learn a new skill before people she was supposed to impress. "Thank you, Moonbud." Perhaps having a friend would make the riding lessons more bearable. "Could I bring a friend? Female, of course."

Moonbud flicked her tail. :*Whom did you mean?*:

Her stomach tightening, Kiera made herself smile. "Lady Annalise Greysnowe." If only she could invite Wren, but 'twouldn't be wise in her condition. Besides, she'd be at the orphanage.

Moonbud stilled then replied, *:Tell her not to bring her mount. A nightmara shall carry her.:*

Kiera sighed. At least she'd have a friend to support her when she fell in the dirt. "Annalise shall appreciate that, thank you."

Moonbud blew an almost laugh. Clearly, she could sense Kiera's relief. *:I'll wait until next time to begin your lessons.:* She glanced over at Darkthorn. *:I must return to my earlier conversation. See you in three days.:*

Kiera left, her guards joining her at the nightmara stables. She worried her lip as she strode through the now warming palace grounds. Hopefully, she'd not appear a graceless fool in three days. Perhaps Annalise had some advice to prepare her. She'd ask at tonight's ball.

Not long after she returned to the queen's chambers, Devon rapped on their adjoining door then entered. "How did your first meeting alone go?"

Her heart warming at his smile, she shrugged. "Well. We didn't discuss much, but Moonbud wants to teach me to ride, and she said I could bring Annalise."

Devon blinked. "She *must* like you. Nightmara queen-heirs rarely bear riders."

Kiera grimaced and twisted the Vireni betrothal ring. "So I learned when I attempted to refuse. They were shocked."

Devon strode toward her but halted before touching her. "I'm sure you soothed them."

Her chest squeezed. Why had he stopped? He'd not kissed her since before the council meeting. Was his withdrawal more than exhaustion? Perhaps his attraction had waned once he saw her through the council's eyes. She managed a smile. "I think so."

Devon eyed her for a moment then nodded. "The Campbells' luncheon is within the hour. I'll leave you to change."

Kiera sighed as he left and Mia entered. She should be

relieved he'd stopped tempting her with his ravenous kisses. Yet she ached for them.

When Annalise joined her at the Dracwyns' ball that evening, Kiera leaned toward her friend with a tight smile. "Moonbud is teaching me to ride and said you could join me for the next nightmara meeting. Are you interested? Moonbud said a nightmara would carry you."

Annalise gaped at her then beamed, even more radiant than usual. "Of course! They say riding nightmara is wondrous."

Kiera swallowed. "Is it? I've never ridden before, so I don't know what to expect." Please let her not fall too often.

Annalise squeezed her hand. "Don't fret; riding nightmara is even easier than riding horses. You'll be fine."

Not reassured, Kiera waited at the orphanage until Wren arrived the following morning. Once they were ensconced in her study, she licked her lips then said, "Moonbud offered to teach me to ride, but I know *nothing* about riding and can't appear a fool before the nightmara."

Wren tilted her head. "Don't worry too much. Lady Moonbud offered to teach you *because* you know nothing." She scrawled a note. "But here's a book meant for novice riders. Ask Mia to find a copy. Then at least you can read about riding before your first lesson."

Kiera sighed and accepted the note. A book was better than nothing. She headed to the palace and told Mia about the book while the maid helped her dress. Mia had a copy waiting by luncheon, so after that Kiera spent every spare moment reading it, and by skipping some sleep, she finished it before her first riding lesson. But her stomach roiled while she and Annalise strode to the nightmara stables.

Leila opened the door and beamed at Kiera before inclining her head at Annalise.

Kiera swallowed and managed a smile in return. She waved

her guards to stay behind then introduced Leila and Nightrose to Annalise as they crossed the paddock. Despite their saddles and reins, she almost smiled at Moonbud and Darkthorn nestled together again. Definitely more than Nightrose's twin.

Once everyone exchanged greetings, Kiera introduced Annalise, and Moonbud nodded then said, :*A pleasure, Lady Heart.*:

Kiera frowned and glanced at Annalise. Lady Heart? "I thought your nickname was Lady Snow."

Annalise blushed a delicate rose. "At court. But some at home call me Lady Heart."

Kiera eyed her. Secret meaning echoed in that nickname, but she couldn't ask about it now. She glanced at Moonbud's saddle and swallowed. She'd more pressing concerns, like not falling.

Moonbud nodded at Annalise again. :*Darkthorn has offered to carry you, Lady Heart.*: She turned to Kiera. :*Ready for your first ride, Kiera?*:

Kiera gulped a bracing breath. Goddess, please let this go well. "As much as I'll ever be."

Moonbud glided toward her, and her first riding lesson began.

CHAPTER 27

*D*uring Kiera's first riding lesson, Devon sat by their adjoining door, perusing yet another report on the Magehaven ore while he listened for her return. Success with Moonbud should help convince her she was meant to be his queen. When she returned at last, he abandoned any pretense of reading and began pacing as he waited for her maid to leave.

Once Kiera was alone, he rapped on their adjoining door then strode into her chambers. Tingling warmth flooded him when she smiled at him. Goddess, if only he could kiss her. Restraining his hunger was becoming painful. To keep from drawing her into his arms, he clasped his hands behind his back. "How did your first riding lesson go?"

Kiera sighed then shrugged. "I didn't fall yet, but we kept to the paddock, and Moonbud rarely went faster than a walk. So I suppose I didn't bumble *too* much."

Unable to resist, Devon captured her hand and kissed her palm. "I'm certain you were as graceful as ever."

Kiera blushed and caressed his jaw. "Thanks. Hopefully, I remain so. Moonbud said she shan't negotiate the treaty until I can comfortably gallop and jump, which shall take a while."

His pulse quickening at her touch, he forced himself to smile and release her. They'd best leave her chambers before his restraint shattered. "Shall we head to luncheon?"

Kiera nodded. "Yes, please. Riding is a hungry business. I'm as ravenous as a starved manticore."

Devon almost chuckled. Even when not starved, the rare magical creatures ate half their weight every day and never left remains behind. "Then let's feed you before you start devouring people whole."

After a comfortable luncheon where they discussed their favorite foods, they attended the Blakeleys' garden party then ate dinner and attended the Osteens' ball. Kiera yawned and leaned against him the entire ride back to the orphanage. Their hectic social rounds and her riding lessons were exhausting her.

His heart squeezing, he escorted her to the door then pressed a kiss against her forehead. "Sleep late tomorrow."

Kiera sighed. "I can't. Breakfast is the only time I can see the orphans." She straightened her shoulders with a brilliant smile. "I'll be fine."

Devon scowled after her as she slipped into the orphanage. Not if she kept missing sleep and overworking. Why couldn't the obstinate lady have stayed in the queen's chambers? Then at least she could have gotten more sleep. He shook his head and returned to the palace.

OVER THE NEXT FEW DAYS, Devon kept escorting Kiera to multiple court events every day, and she continued charming court with her warmth and insight. How long until she saw she was meant to be queen despite her common birth? Perhaps then she'd realize he truly wanted to marry her, and he'd no longer need to restrain himself.

Thanks to their hectic social rounds, Kiera dragged more and more each day, and shadows appeared beneath her eyes. He tried suggesting she needed more sleep, but she replied she hadn't time and would be fine. So he swallowed further advice to prevent her from returning her ring and retreating to the orphanage.

Since Kiera had almost dozed the entire ride to the orphanage the previous evening, Devon paced beside their adjoining door as he waited for her to return from her second riding lesson. Hopefully, she'd enough energy for it. When she finally returned, he burst into her chambers after a brief knock. He stiffened at her drooped shoulders. "How was your lesson?"

Kiera shrugged. "Fine, except I was almost late. I only woke when the carriage arrived to take me to the palace." She sighed. "So I missed breakfast with the orphans this morning."

He grasped her hand and squeezed it. No wonder she was upset. "Did you manage to eat before your lesson?"

Kiera nodded. "Mary gave me bread and cheese to eat on the carriage ride, but I'm *starving* again."

Devon escorted her to luncheon, but since she was upset about not seeing the orphans, he didn't ask about the orphanage. Instead, he described the time he was late for a council meeting because he'd gotten locked in a forgotten palace attic without his guards. By their apple tart, Kiera was chuckling at his wild attempts to escape using items stored in the attic.

She sobered when they headed to the council meeting, which had been moved to the afternoon due to her nightmara meeting. At the council room door, Devon paused and asked as he had before, "Are you ready?"

Her smile steady today, Kiera inclined her head and waved for him to enter. Good, she was becoming accustomed to her duties as queen. Their guards remaining outside the door, he swept her to the head of the table then said, "Afternoon, every-one. Shall we proceed? We haven't much time before petitions at court."

Lord Farson leaned toward Kiera. "How are your meetings with Lady Moonbud proceeding?"

Kiera smiled at the Golddell councilor. "Well, I think.

Although we've not discussed matters involving the treaty, Lady Moonbud and I get along. She's even teaching me to ride."

Devon almost chuckled when Lord Farson blurted, "She's letting you *ride* her?"

Kiera arched her brows. "Of course. How else would she teach me to ride?"

All the councilors, even Aragon, gaped at her. They knew how extraordinary that was—the nightmara queens or queen-heirs hadn't carried Calatini's queen since Nightwind had kidnapped Sarilee for their first negotiation.

Devon beamed when Kiera flashed a regal smile and added, "But I must prove my worth as queen to Lady Moonbud. Considering my past, it should involve children. Education, I think."

He kissed her palm to demonstrate his support. Goddess, to pursue her education initiative already just affirmed she'd be a wonderful queen. "An excellent plan, my love."

Her hand remaining in his, Kiera grinned at Lady Morwynne. "We must discuss plans over tea soon. I'm eager to start."

When Lady Morwynne stiffly nodded, Devon squeezed Kiera's fingers. Like the rest of court, the superior countess would soon warm to Kiera. He glanced about the table. "Other matters to discuss?"

Lord Islaye coughed and shifted in his chair. "Despite consulting Lady Juliet almost a month ago, we're still no closer to identifying or counteracting the mysterious ore in Mage-haven." He grimaced. "And its influence continues to spread. Just last week, a journeyman alchemist ignited a magical lantern a mile away, and the lantern exploded."

As Kiera clenched his hand, Devon frowned and tapped the table. Lord Islaye hadn't mentioned that incident in his last report. "How long until its influence disrupts the magic of the Walle?"

The studious count shrugged. "Goddess knows. The ore is so

unstable 'tis impossible to predict its spread. All we know is that it *is* spreading. If only we'd never unearthed it."

Lord Nolan sighed. "My land rangers and Lord Islaye's magic marshals keep attempting to devise new methods to handle the ore, but with no success."

Lord Islaye rubbed his brow. "We need an alchemist who doesn't use magic, but those are rarer than a faebird's teeth, especially in my duchy."

Devon nodded. Unlike the rest of Calatini, witches outnumbered those without magic in Magehaven. The only other duchy with almost as many witches was Wildewall, the other northern duchy.

Kiera leaned forward. "Try searching in a poorer area. Magic is too expensive to use every day there, so you might find an alchemist without magic." She sighed. "Although they mightn't be skilled enough to help."

Lord Islaye straightened. "We'll try there. Thank you, your highness."

His chest warming, Devon caressed her palm with his thumb. Yet again, she'd proved her worth as queen. Did the councilors realize that? He eyed them; some wore blank expressions, but Lord Islaye, Lord Nolan, and several others were almost smiling. Good. "Anything else?"

The Duchess of Wildewall pursed her lips. "Unfortunately, yes." She sighed. "Lord Greysnowe is *still* grumbling about Lady Kiera."

Devon almost snorted. Of course, the ambitious count refused to accept that his daughter would never be queen. Fortunately, the royal guards had neutralized the assassins he'd approached. Devon nodded at the duchess. "Keep monitoring him, and if he does more than grumble, inform us at once." He glanced about the table again. "Anything further?" When no one spoke, he adjourned the meeting.

While the other councilors left, Aragon and the Duke of Osbourne remained seated. The duke glanced at Aragon then said, "Age before youth, I believe." He turned to Kiera. "I hope to see you at my card party next week. Observing your strategy shall be interesting."

Her fingers gripping Devon's, Kiera smiled and inclined her head. "I look forward to it."

Devon almost frowned as the Duke of Osbourne chuckled then bowed and left. Was the wily duke being sincere or snide?

Aragon leaned toward Kiera. "Mother warned you that the duke is a fierce card player, right?"

Kiera sighed. "Of course. And she said winning a difficult hand would increase my standing with him, so she made me practice his favorite game."

Since Aragon wouldn't have delayed them when they'd duties to attend unless he'd news, Devon arched his brows at Aragon and asked, "How's Selena?"

Aragon beamed. "Well. Her nausea and fatigue have eased, and her healer said everything is progressing normally. We should be able to attend more court events again."

Devon grinned as Kiera smiled and replied, "Wonderful. Perhaps she'll tell me about the brothel like she promised."

After Aragon chuckled and left, Devon winked at Kiera. "Today's council meeting went well." If she kept acting like she had this afternoon, all the councilors would soon be staunch allies.

Kiera licked her lips. "Hopefully, they continue to."

Tingling warmth surging in his veins, he swallowed. If only he could kiss those tempting lips. But he must restrain himself. He forced a nod. "They shall. Ready for petitions at court?"

Kiera nodded, and he escorted her to the throne room. As promised, she spoke her thoughts after several petitions, always adding relevant information. Then that evening she enlivened the Landrys' usually dull soiree with her warm wit. The perfect queen, if only she could see it.

• • •

THEIR SOCIAL ROUNDS remained hectic over the following days. Every night, Devon escorted Kiera back to the orphanage well after midnight. Each day the shadows beneath her eyes darkened, even though she admitted to sleeping through breakfast with the orphans most mornings. If she lived at the palace where she belonged, she'd not waste several hours a day traveling. But he forced himself to remain silent to avoid upsetting her.

Then after her next meeting with Moonbud, Kiera was curled on a chair dozing when he came to escort her to luncheon. He frowned and slipped from her chambers so she could sleep until they must leave for Lady Ducharme's fencing party that afternoon.

When he finally made himself wake her, Kiera stumbled upright then shooed him out to change. The entire carriage ride, she yawned while devouring the stuffed rolls he'd saved from luncheon. Then at the fencing party and Elise's rout party that evening, she bustled about in constant motion like she'd fall asleep if she paused. Which she did as soon as she climbed into his carriage just after midnight.

His heart fluttering, Devon drew Kiera into his lap, and she hummed then cuddled against him in her sleep. He swallowed as heat swamped him and his body tightened. Yet he only rubbed her back and kissed her brow then murmured, "My obstinate love, what am I to do with you? I can't allow you to exhaust yourself so."

Her clean lavender scent filling his lungs, he sighed as the carriage rumbled back to the orphanage. Must he end their betrothal just so she'd get some sleep? But if he did, she'd *never* believe he wanted to marry her. Yet matters couldn't continue as they had. Kiera would soon exhaust herself into a coma as if exposed to a nightmara's uncontrolled powers. Perhaps Wren would know how to convince Kiera to rest—he'd visit Wren as soon as he woke to beg her help. He kissed Kiera's brow again. Goddess, please let Kiera listen.

CHAPTER 28

The following day, Kiera jolted awake like a vampire at nightfall then blinked at the familiar bedside table. How had she ended up in her bed at the orphanage? The last she recalled was leaving the ball. She rubbed her gritty eyes as her stomach rumbled. And how late was it? Clearly well past breakfast.

She started when Wren drawled from across the room, "Morning, or more aptly, afternoon."

Kiera winced. She was supposed to be at Lady Dabar's salon now. Hopefully, the Minister of Transportation's wife wasn't too upset. Her crumpled ballgown twisting about her, she rolled over to face her friend. "What are you doing in my bedroom?"

As Kiera sat up, Wren arched a brow and closed her book. "Waiting for you to wake up." She handed Kiera a plate of black bread and cheese. "When Devon visited before breakfast, I knew we must talk as soon as you woke."

Kiera stiffened but began bolting her food. Devon visiting Wren so early didn't bode well. Once she swallowed, she forced herself to ask, "About what?"

Wren slanted her a flat look. "About you falling asleep in Devon's carriage last night and sleeping past breakfast most mornings. You slept past noon today. Usually, you've more energy than a pixie."

Kiera shrugged and devoured another huge bite to avoid answering. As Wren had predicted, acting as both queen and orphanage matron was too much. But she must continue—she couldn't abandon her orphans, and she'd promised to help Devon negotiate with the nightmara.

Wren tsked. "How much sleep have you gotten each night since Devon introduced you to court?"

To placate her, Kiera flashed a brilliant smile while swallowing the last slice of bread and cheese. "About four to five hours." Maybe.

As Kiera rose to change into a serviceable orphanage dress, Wren sighed and shook her head. "Please be smarter about this than I was."

Kiera whirled to glare at Wren. "Our situations aren't at all the same. I'm not in love with Devon." Not yet anyway. "And *I* didn't purchase a dangerous spell to seduce him that drained me and threatened the life of our unborn child."

Wren pursed her lips. "You may not have bought a dangerous spell, but you're exhausting yourself by clinging to the past when everything has changed. Just like I did after seducing Hawke."

Still glaring, Kiera tore off the arachne silk and yanked on her serviceable dress. "I'm not clinging to the *past*. I'm returning here as soon as I finish helping Devon." Hopefully, before she fell in love with him.

She stiffened when Wren eyed her for a long moment then asked, "Regardless, why haven't you accepted Devon's offer to stay at the palace while you're acting as queen? You'd normally be the first to suggest such a sensible plan."

Weight compressing her chest, Kiera dropped onto her bed but gritted another bright smile. "Because me acting as queen is mad, and seeing the orphans helps me remember my true place.

If I stayed at the palace, 'twould be too easy to forget." And succumb to Devon's irresistible kisses.

Wren snorted. "You're too strong-willed to ever forget yourself."

Kiera licked her lips. If only her friend knew how tempting Devon was. But a king would never actually marry a poor orphanage matron, so she mustn't let herself fall in love with him. When Wren opened her mouth to continue, Kiera interjected, "Shall we go find the orphans?"

Wren sighed. "Very well."

The royal guards following several steps behind, Kiera and Wren headed to the library where the younger children were practicing their writing, Kiera's favorite class before she'd begun acting as queen. Once Jace called the boys and girls to order, she asked them, "How are your writing lessons progressing?"

Although most just shrugged, the vivacious Janelle chirped, "Okay, except Miss Wren's a better teacher than Jace."

Kiera's throat tightened as the other orphans bobbed nods. And what about her? They acted as if she'd never taught them.

Wren tsked. "I think Jace manages you hellions very well."

The children giggled, but once they quieted, Roger bounced up and down then asked, "Miss Wren, could you bring us starpeaches tomorrow?"

Wren cocked a brow. "Perhaps. Now, back to your lessons."

Kiera and Wren slipped out as the boys and girls bent over their writing. In the hall, Kiera glanced at Wren. "Why only perhaps?" Wren was usually so generous with the orphans.

Wren sighed. "Because I brought starpeaches just yesterday."

Kiera almost chuckled. Yet Roger asking for more wasn't a surprise. The boy adored starpeaches almost as much as Amaranth.

Wren waved Kiera into the dining hall, and Kiera gaped at the pairs of older children grappling while Hawke prowled about the hall shouting instructions. "What's all this?"

Wren shrugged. "Hawke wanted the orphans to learn proper fighting, in addition to the tricks they learn from the streets."

Kiera nodded. Such skills would be valuable—and help consume the orphans' extra energy. She glanced about the hall. Surprising the Bedsford twins weren't here. Then she winced as Will drove David to the floor. "They appear engrossed. We shouldn't disturb them."

They continued to the kitchen where Mary was showing ten or so children how to roll out crust. Since they also appeared absorbed, Kiera and Wren left and headed to the anteroom by the front door where Peter was teaching carving to the rest of the orphans, including the Bedsford twins.

John tugged Jacob over as soon as she and Wren entered. He poked his twin's ribs and hissed, "Show her."

Jacob shoved his twin back but withdrew a small carving from his pocket and held it before Wren. "'Tis for Amaranth."

Kiera smiled and leaned forward to examine the leaping dolphin. Although not perfect, the carving appeared in constant motion, just like the scampish twins. "Amaranth shall love it."

John beamed. "'Twas my idea for Jacob to carve one—to apologize for the snake prank. His carving is much better than mine."

Kiera and Wren exchanged a grin. Another sign of how much the twins adored Amaranth. Kiera extended her hand and said, "I'll take it to Amaranth for you."

Jacob blinked at her then shook his head. "Miss Wren better do it."

Her chest squeezing, Kiera withdrew her hand. Didn't they trust her?

Jacob blurted, "You're just so busy being queen and all."

Kiera swallowed then forced a smile as Wren accepted the carving. "True, I'm as busy as a melissa in summer." And never here for them.

Once she and Wren returned to the hall, Kiera lifted her chin and said, "I'm going to handle the papers in my study. Could you and Hawke join me for tea after lessons?"

Wren narrowly eyed her but nodded. "Of course."

In her study, Kiera dropped in her chair but simply stared at the papers on her desk. She'd hardly seen the orphans since acting as queen, and today's visit proved how removed she was from their lives. She'd known nothing about recent changes, and the orphans turned to Wren now.

Her heart twisting, she sighed. By acting as both orphanage matron and queen, she could serve neither the orphanage nor Calatini well. So she must surrender her duties here until she finished helping Devon. But since Wren and Hawke loved the orphans as much as she did, she wasn't truly abandoning them —just ensuring they received the care they deserved.

She sighed again and rubbed her aching chest. Besides, her education initiative would greatly benefit her orphans as well as the rest of the poor in Calatini, so she must ensure 'twas well underway before she stopped acting as queen. And she'd be back at the orphanage in a month or so. Hopefully.

When Wren and Hawke joined her for tea, Kiera set her jaw and said, "You're right, Wren. 'Tis sensible for me to stay at the palace while acting as queen, so I must transfer my responsibilities here to you two."

Wren reached across the desk to squeeze her hand. "We'll care for the orphans as best we can."

Her stomach twisting, Kiera sipped her tea. "I know."

Hawke leaned toward her as he devoured his last sweet biscuit. "Do you need help moving your things to the palace?"

Kiera forced a weak smile. "No, I've little to bring." All of her clothes and most of her keepsakes would remain behind. She'd not be at the palace long enough to need more.

After tea, she packed her few items, including last night's ballgown, into one bag then returned to the palace and distributed everything about the queen's chambers. She sighed and dropped onto the bed. Jane's small self-portrait, Mary's embroidered cooking quote, Peter's gargoyle carving, and a recent collage from the orphans *almost* made the sumptuous quarters feel like home—almost. The peach roses from Devon helped too.

Then Devon knocked and strode inside with a warm smile. "Have a nice visit at the orphanage?"

Her heart fluttered. Goddess, how was she to avoid falling in love with him when constantly around his attentive compassion? "Very nice. Was Lady Dabar upset I missed her salon?"

Devon grinned. "Not when I explained you were visiting the orphans."

Kiera sighed. Good. She blinked back the sudden tears pricking her eyes. "Well, I shan't miss court events in the future. I decided I'd best stay here while acting as your betrothed." Her voice cracked, "Wren and Hawke can manage the orphanage."

Without a word, Devon pulled her into his arms for the first time in nearly two weeks.

Although she should step back to protect herself, she leaned into his embrace and laid her head against his chest. If only they could remain nestled like mated griffins forever. But their betrothal was only temporary.

She smiled when his heart quickened beneath her ear and his body firmed against hers. His attraction hadn't waned after all. But why was he suppressing it? Was he afraid to upset her before the nightmara treaty was renewed? Or another reason?

After a moment, Devon kissed her forehead then released her. "Hawke and Wren shall care for the orphans as well as you always have." Then he asked her thoughts about the Islayes' concert that evening, probably to distract her.

The Islayes' concert went well, although Devon eyed her the entire time then escorted her back to the royal wing early. Her heart warmed while Mia helped her into a dressing gown afterward. Doubtless he wanted to ensure she was well after today's momentous decision and got enough sleep. So she started at his knock once Mia left and whirled to face him.

Standing in their adjoining door and also wearing a dressing gown, Devon smiled and lifted two flutes of sparkling wine. "Care for a drink before bed?"

Tingling warmth suffused Kiera at his intimate attire, but she managed to echo his smile and glide forward to accept her flute. "I thought sparkling wine was for parties."

Devon's green eyes gleamed. "Or celebrations."

She hummed as she sipped her sparkling wine. Still as delicious as ever. "What are we celebrating?"

Devon shrugged. "Adequate sleep?"

Kiera grimaced into her flute. Which she'd only achieved by surrendering the orphans. Her throat thickening, she raised her flute. "To adequate sleep."

CHAPTER 29

When Kiera gritted a tremulous smile, Devon clenched his flute of sparkling wine. Her sorrow over leaving the orphans made him ache to pull her into his arms like earlier. Yet embracing her was much too dangerous with them both in dressing gowns. His restraint would turn to ash like a dead firebird.

Tingling warmth flooding him, he glanced away. He'd not joined her tonight to seduce her. He'd joined her so they could spend time alone since they no longer had the lengthy carriage ride back to the orphanage. Perhaps if he joined her every night, she'd come to see their intimacy was natural. Maybe *then* she'd realize he loved her and become his wife.

Devon drained his sparkling wine then forced his gaze back to Kiera. Goddess, she was lovely. And so tempting. He swallowed but flashed a grin. "I mustn't keep you. Please get some sleep. Good night, Kiera."

As she murmured good night, he strode back to his chambers and attempted to follow his own advice. Yet his sleep was restless due to passionate dreams where he'd kissed her instead of withdrawing.

Over the next few days, Devon escorted Kiera to multiple court events every day like before, but since she was now staying at the palace, the shadows beneath her eyes faded. Yet his sleep remained restless, so he began staying in bed longer than usual. Sharing a drink with Kiera in her chambers just before bed was maddening—she was so close, yet as untouchable as ever.

Yet 'twas worth it because by the third night, she no longer gaped when he knocked then entered, this time with a tray of mentha tea. Instead, she smiled at him and prepared his tea with one spoon of sugar like he preferred without asking.

His chest warm, Devon sipped his tea. She'd accepted their intimacy as natural. Surely soon she'd realize his love was sincere. Yet after several sips, he stiffened—she was still stirring her tea. "Is something troubling you?"

Kiera grimaced then set her spoon on the tray. "The council meeting tomorrow."

He blinked at her. The previous two council meetings, she'd proved her worth as queen to more councilors each time. And tomorrow's would be no different. "Why?"

Kiera shifted in her chair. "I was wondering if the councilors would be more censorious now that I'm staying in the queen's chambers."

Devon relaxed and couldn't help a chuckle. "I doubt it." When she arched her brows, he added, "I think only Aragon, and possibly the Duke of Osbourne since he learns everything, realized you were still sleeping at the orphanage. The others couldn't imagine a lost princess residing in squalor when she'd a palace."

Sipping her tea at last, Kiera scowled over her teacup. "Waterstreet Orphanage is hardly squalor."

To soften her indignation, he waggled his brows. "But 'tis no palace."

Kiera sighed. "You should have offered me different chambers then. Everyone shall assume we're anticipating our vows."

Devon sipped his tea. Most at court would assume that regardless of where she slept. But hearing that would simply upset her, so he replied, "But security is much easier with you in the queen's chambers. And so is privacy."

Kiera sighed then drained her teacup. "I suppose it hardly matters now."

As she licked tea from her lips, hunger surged through him. He shuddered and gulped his tea then leapt to his feet and collected the tea tray. "'Tis late; I should go. Forget about the council and get some sleep."

Devon bolted back to his chambers and climbed into his cold, empty bed. Too bad everyone's assumptions weren't true. If they were, *he* might finally get some adequate sleep. Then again, he might not—for a while, anyway.

THE FOLLOWING MORNING, Devon escorted Kiera to the council room but paused at the door to arch a questioning brow at her. He grinned when she simply flashed a smile. Despite her concerns last night, the council no longer fazed her. Their guards remaining by the door, he led her inside and began the meeting.

Once he did, Lord Farson leaned toward Kiera. "Are your meetings with Lady Moonbud still proceeding well?"

Kiera inclined her head. "They are, but 'twould help if I'd more to prove my worth as queen." She narrowed her eyes at Lady Morwynne. "Like my education initiative."

Lady Morwynne shrugged. "We'll meet about it, eventually."

Devon hid his smile when Kiera glared at the superior countess as if scolding the infamous Bedsford twins then said, "Within the week."

Lady Morwynne stiffened but nodded. "Yes, Lady Kiera."

Almost chuckling, he squeezed Kiera's hand beneath the table. The council *definitely* no longer fazed her. Good.

When Devon turned the meeting to other matters, Lord Islaye admitted they'd still not found an alchemist without magic for the Magehaven ore, while Lady Ducharme mentioned a skirmish between the ninth fleet and Tsarkan pirates. However, the other councilors had no news, so he soon adjourned the meeting.

Once all the other councilors except Aragon and the Duke of Osbourne left, the duke smiled at Kiera. "Observing your strategy at my card party tonight shall certainly be interesting. Say you'll be my partner."

Devon almost shrugged when Kiera glanced at him, probably to check his thoughts. Who knew what the wily duke was about?

Kiera nodded at the duke with a wry smile. "If you like, but I must warn you, I've only practiced the elaborate card games you favor."

The Duke of Osbourne bowed. "No matter."

After the duke strolled from the council room, Aragon arched a brow at Devon. "Would you like to partner Selena then?"

Devon leaned back with a sigh. "Yes, please. Gossip would rage fiercer than a wounded hydra with thirty heads if another lady partnered me."

Aragon chuckled. "'Tis almost tempting to allow that just to hear the wild tales." He rose. "I'll ask Selena once I get home and let you know if she declines."

Devon and Kiera exchanged a glance once they were alone, then he led her to the throne room for petitions at court. This time, she spoke her thoughts after almost every petition. He beamed as they left. Clearly court no longer fazed her any more than the council did.

WHEN DEVON ENTERED Kiera's chambers to escort her to the Duke of Osbourne's card party, he grinned at her gown. Yet again, she'd transformed her arachne silk into a statement. Tonight her gown was cream decorated with violets the precise shade of her betrothal ring and his green eyes. He strode forward and kissed her palm beneath her ring. "Your gown is delightful as always."

Kiera chuckled. "'Tis becoming fun to imagine new designs to influence court without saying a word."

He squeezed her arm as they began toward his carriage with his guards following. "The Duke of Osbourne is sure to appreciate your *strategy*." The wily duke adored such mental ploys.

Kiera tossed her dark-blonde curls. "Hence why I ensured my gown was strategic tonight."

And her strategic gown inspired the Duke of Osbourne's first comment after he greeted them, "What lovely violets, Lady Kiera."

Devon almost kissed Kiera when she leaned against him and smiled into his eyes then murmured, "Yes, I like them."

He jerked back at the duke's chuckle. A card party was no place to kiss Kiera. Then the duke requested her arm, and he forced a smile. "My partner and I shall join your game."

The Duke of Osbourne smiled as he escorted them to the head table. "Of course, but where's your partner?"

"Here." Trailed by Aragon with Lady Annalise, Selena glided over with her hands resting on her rounded stomach. "I can't walk fast at the moment."

The duke, Kiera, Selena, and Devon took their seats at the head table, while Aragon and Lady Annalise took the next table and were joined by Winston and his sister. Devon winced at his friend's misfortune. The only worse pairing would have been Lord Ravenstone and Lady Blaine, who were seated across the room. And why had the duke invited the Winstons? They were rarely invited to smaller affairs, given their poverty and Winston's reputation.

He jerked his gaze back to the table when the Duke of Osbourne said, "We'll play wild arcana. Lady Kiera and I shall be white."

Devon almost grimaced. The torturous game with its intricate rules and lengthy play *was* the duke's favorite game. He nodded. "Selena and I shall be black."

The duke began shuffling the deck. "Then red is wild." He smiled at Kiera as he dealt. "How do you find court, Lady Kiera?"

Kiera shrugged and ordered her cards. "Fine. Very different than the orphanage."

Devon suppressed a grin. Such calm was the perfect response to the duke's probing.

The Duke of Osbourne placed the stock pile in the middle of the table. "You were raised at Waterstreet Orphanage, correct?"

Kiera nodded. "I was."

Before the duke could unravel their romantic tale, Devon narrowed his eyes and leaned forward. "Kiera's upbringing shall be a fresh breeze through court."

The duke hummed. "Not all change is good."

Devon set his jaw as he held the elderly duke's gaze. "But 'tis always necessary. If we never changed, we'd have no magic, not even healing spells."

Selena patted her rounded stomach. "And as a pregnant lady, I'm most grateful for those."

The Duke of Osbourne smiled then said, "Enough of this debate. Time to play cards."

With that, the duke began the game then Devon took his turn. Over the course of many turns, Kiera and the duke steadily drew ahead. Although Devon and Selena were both good card players, Kiera was decent for a novice, and the duke was exceptional.

The duke smiled as he played the winning card. "Game to us." He grinned at Kiera. "I knew you'd make an excellent partner."

Kiera grinned back. "Thanks, your grace." She stiffened when Winston leaned toward her with a smirk. Yet she kept her gaze on the duke. "But I suspect our win is entirely your doing."

Devon tensed. How dare Winston smirk at Kiera? While the

duke began shuffling again, he drawled, "Did you check Winston for extra cards tonight? I heard he likes to cheat."

The Duke of Osbourne chuckled. "Even if he brought extra cards, he couldn't use them. I've a spell placed on my card tables and decks that prevents cheating, unless you consider counting cards cheating. But that's really just shrewd play."

As Kiera and Selena exchanged a wry glance, Devon grimaced and leaned forward. He must be blunt for the wily duke to reveal his motives. "Why did you invite him? You never have before."

The duke smiled and began dealing a new hand. "Given the rumors Winston has been spreading about Lady Kiera, observing her reaction promised to be most interesting."

Fire flashing through him, Devon almost growled. The cad was spreading rumors?

Kiera laid her hand on his then asked with a frown, "What rumors?"

The Duke of Osbourne arched a brow. "That you two shared a dalliance at the king's summer masquerade. And then again at the Harvestfete masquerade."

As Kiera grimaced and Selena snorted, Devon clenched his hands to prevent himself from leaping up and punching Winston. 'Twould only inflame the rumors.

Kiera sighed and shook her head. "The only *dalliance* I shared with Mr. Winston was when he attempted to force himself on me, but on both occasions he was swiftly knocked unconscious. The first time by me, and the second by my guards."

The duke quirked a grin. "Somehow, that doesn't surprise me." He arched his brows. "Shall we begin another hand?"

Devon grunted and scowled at his cards without seeing them. He really must devise a way to handle Winston. Unfortunately, he couldn't banish or execute him for spreading rumors. Perhaps he should find a frightful lady for him to wed. But 'twould be cruel to burden any lady with the cad.

He started when Selena prodded his arm and said, "Devon,

would you *please* play a card? 'Tis been your turn for the past fifteen minutes."

Devon sighed and played a random card. Goddess, let this interminable card party end soon.

CHAPTER 30

hen the Duke of Osbourne played the winning card after their second lengthy hand of wild arcana, Kiera scrutinized Devon. His jaw was clenched, and his eyes narrow—he was still furious over Mr. Winston's slanderous rumors. And Mr. Winston's frequent smirks from the next table weren't helping. She'd best remove Devon before he punched the cad. She flashed a wry smile at the elderly duke. "I believe two hands of wild arcana is all my mind can manage."

Selena dimpled. "And the hour is well past when I'm normally abed these days."

The Duke of Osbourne rose. "Of course. I'll take your husband's place so he can escort you home, Lady Treyvan." He smiled at Kiera and Devon. "Thanks for the interesting games."

Kiera relaxed when the duke replaced Aragon without allowing Mr. Winston to rise. Devon's response if Mr. Winston approached wouldn't be polite and would only inflame the rumors.

Devon stopped scowling once they left the duke's, but he was still tense and barely spoke. So over their khamomile tea before bed, Kiera smiled and arched her brows. "Are you upset because court shall believe Mr. Winston's rumors?"

Devon grunted into his tea. "No. Most shan't believe them any more than the Duke of Osbourne did. But I don't like Winston spreading such lies about you."

Warmth filled her chest. As always, he burned to protect her even though she was just a temporary betrothed. So chivalrous. His true queen was most fortunate. She suppressed a sigh then shook her head. "Such lies hardly matter if no one believes them. And refuting them shall only highlight them."

Devon grimaced. "I know."

He left soon after—without attempting to kiss her again.

Kiera twisted the Vireni betrothal ring as she slid into bed. Despite his embrace when she'd moved into the palace, Devon hadn't held her or flirted or kissed her since then. She should be relieved he was treating her like a sister, but she still ached for his irresistible kisses.

Over the following days, her hectic life at court continued unchanged by Mr. Winston's rumors. If they were even mentioned, 'twas with a snort or eyes raised skyward. And her duties at court had become easier now that they were more familiar. Plus, she was slowly improving at her riding lessons with Moonbud and building her rapport with the nightmara queen-heir. So she was performing adequately as acting queen, except for her education initiative.

Although Kiera had demanded they meet within the week, Lady Morwynne still hadn't invited her five days after the council meeting. Clearly, the superior countess didn't respect her. She'd never make a future queen of higher birth wait so long.

Kiera set her jaw as she dressed for a meeting with Moonbud. If Lady Morwynne never invited her, she'd visit unbidden before breakfast on the seventh day. Her education initiative was too vital to keep delaying.

As they strode to the nightmara stables with her guards

following, Kiera grimaced at Annalise. "Lady Morwynne *still* hasn't invited me to discuss my education initiative."

Annalise tsked. "Not surprising. Doubtless she's waiting until the last because you ordered her to invite you."

Kiera suppressed a snort as they reached the nightmara stables. Discussing her education initiative with the Minister of Health and Community would *not* be pleasant. Wonderful.

The stable door flew open, and Leila grinned, even brighter than usual, with Nightrose behind her. At least the mara and nightmara were pleased to see her.

As they bounded through the stables, Kiera eyed Leila. "You appear especially excited this morning. Why?"

Leila and Nightrose chortled together, then Leila replied, "You'll see."

Kiera almost sighed while they entered the paddock and her guards halted. Moonbud's riding plans for today must have excited Leila. If only she could feel the same. Although riding was enjoyable so far and not as difficult as she'd feared, she must excel to impress the nightmara queen-heir. So she couldn't relax and truly enjoy riding.

When they reached Moonbud, the nightmara queen-heir nodded at Kiera then said, :*I think you're ready to ride outside the paddock. Your guards can accompany us on mara ponies.*:

As Annalise began grinning as brightly as Leila, Kiera swallowed and managed a smile. This would be her first true ride— please let her do well. "Where did you want to ride?"

Moonbud's midnight tail swished. :*Just the palace grounds.*:

Kiera relaxed. At least they wouldn't ride far on her first outing.

Once everyone was mounted, Annalise beamed from atop Darkthorn. "Shall we try the path toward the royal bay? 'Tisn't far."

Kiera shrugged then shifted in the saddle. And hopefully, not crowded. Court would surely stare at their supposed future queen riding the nightmara queen-heir. "Sounds fine, except I don't know the way."

Leila chuckled. "We learned all the paths the day we arrived. We'll lead!" She and Nightrose burst into a trot.

Kiera inhaled then pressed Moonbud with her legs and squeezed the right rein to follow them. As sentient creatures who could read their riders' minds, nightmara didn't usually require that, but Moonbud had insisted during their first lesson that Kiera treat her like an ordinary horse, so she'd learn to ride more than just nightmara.

She relaxed after they'd ridden for a few minutes and nothing untoward happened. She'd best start proving her worth as queen again. And she could use information for when she finally met with Lady Morwynne about her education initiative. "What education do nightmara and mara receive? Besides riding, of course."

Moonbud tossed her head. :*Cavalry maneuvers. Most also learn basic history, reading, and arithmetic. Nightmara learn to control their powers, while mara learn weaponry and magic if they possess it.*:

Kiera blinked. They received better education than many in Calatini. Perhaps because they valued abilities rather than birth. "What was most helpful to you as the queen-heir negotiating the treaty?"

Moonbud hummed as they turned onto a well-tended path. :*History, probably. Why the questions?*:

Kiera smiled to greet Lord Nolan, Lord Islaye, and Lord Ravenstone, who were riding together in the opposite direction. As she'd expected, they stared in response. But the two councilors and count were the only ones they passed, so at least the path wasn't crowded. "I've a meeting about my education initiative soon and wanted your input on the matter."

Moonbud nodded. :*Ah....*: Then she began drilling Kiera on riding, and the rest of the ride continued without discussing anything else.

Afterward, Kiera changed to attend tea at Hawke's parents' with Devon. Then after dinner, they attended the Nolans' ball. When they returned, she tsked at the vellum letter from Lady Morwynne.

As they shared spiced cider before bed, Kiera leaned toward Devon sitting in a chair across the room. If only he were beside her on the sofa. She pursed her lips then said, "Lady Morwynne *finally* wrote and invited me to tea tomorrow afternoon."

Devon frowned. "One day before the end of the week you gave her. Not promising."

She hummed as she swirled her mug. *And* the countess had invited her less than a day beforehand. "Any suggestions on how to handle her?"

Devon shrugged. "Be firm like you were at the council meeting. She's accustomed to using wiles to domineer." He sighed. "She's always performed her duties well, but only so she can retain her powerful position." He flashed a warm smile. "Yet if anyone can convince her, 'tis you."

Kiera blushed at his faith. Hopefully, she could fulfill it. Then she sighed when he finished his cider and said good night. No kiss, yet again.

THE FOLLOWING AFTERNOON, Kiera forced a regal smile as she ascended the steps of Lady Morwynne's modish townhouse with her guards behind her. As Devon had said, the countess would ignore her if she appeared weak. And the poor in Calatini, like her orphans, needed her education initiative too much for her to fail.

To reassure herself when the butler opened the door with an almost smirk, she adjusted her final peach rose from Devon she'd pinned above her heart. Too bad she didn't have a crown of them, but this rose was the only one left after the hard frost overnight.

The very superior butler led her to a pristine drawing room, where Lady Morwynne posed liked a statue of refinement in an elegant chair. Lovely.

Her amber silk accentuating her dark hair and gold eyes, the countess pursed a tight smile but gracefully gestured to the matching chair beside her. "Sit, please. The tea shall arrive momentarily."

While her guards stood against the wall, Kiera perched in her designated chair, which was as uncomfortable as 'twas elegant. As soon as she sat, the butler returned bearing a silver tea set adorned with arabesques. More ornate than anything at the palace—the countess must mean to overwhelm Kiera with her sophistication.

Kiera lifted her chin and flashed a brilliant grin as Lady Morwynne served their tea. Although a poor orphanage matron could never actually become queen, the countess's airs made her determined not to show it. When she accepted her gleaming teacup, she drawled, "Your tea set is exquisite."

Lady Morwynne tilted her head but shrugged. "Just one of the trinkets I acquired while my late husband was ambassador to the Tsarkan Empire."

Kiera suppressed a snort. Of course, Lady Morwynne would mention that. But she'd prove she was well-versed about the countess's exalted past. "You served there fifteen years and returned eight years ago when your late husband became ill, didn't you?"

When Lady Morwynne nodded, Kiera sipped her tea and almost choked on the strong, bitter flavor. Goddess! What vile kind of tea *was* that? She should have requested more than her usual spoon of sugar.

Lady Morwynne quirked a faint smirk—doubtless at Kiera's distaste. "Yes, and poor Drake died six months later." She sighed. "I still miss our life in the Tsarkan Empire. Whenever I feel nostalgic, I fetch my Tsarkan tea set and have tea prepared in the Tsarkan style."

Kiera drank another vile mouthful then beamed. She'd not reveal weakness before the superior countess again. "'Tis unique. Thanks for sharing it with me. But enough about tea. We've important matters to discuss."

Lady Morwynne moued and set down her teacup. "That education initiative of yours to impress Lady Moonbud, I suppose."

Heat kindled in Kiera's throat at the countess's drawl. How dare she sneer over something so vital? Kiera gritted a smile. "My education initiative isn't just to impress the nightmara. Calatini needs it."

Lady Morwynne flicked her fingers. "Calatini's education system is perfectly adequate."

Clinging to her smile, Kiera set her teacup beside the countess's. If only she could have slammed the vile brew instead. "No, 'tis not. As an orphan myself then later an orphanage matron, I've witnessed how vital education is to a child's future. *And* how little education the poor receive—most can't even read."

Lady Morwynne shrugged. "And what do the poor need to read for?"

Kiera tensed as heat swamped her again. That harpy. She opened her mouth to retort but was interrupted when a young gentleman who resembled the countess strode in, followed by a lady concealed in heavy Tsarkan veils.

Dark hair flopping before his gold eyes, the gentleman halted and beamed at Kiera. "We've not met, Lady Kiera. I don't bother with many court events, even though Mother says I should. I'm the Count of Morwynne."

Kiera blinked. Despite their resemblance, the affable count acted nothing like his mother. She smiled back. "A pleasure, my lord."

Lord Morwynne gestured to the lady behind him. "And this is Gwen."

Her turquoise eyes brilliant against her dusky skin and dark veils, Gwen swept a silent curtsy.

Kiera inclined her head. If the rest of Gwen matched those striking eyes, she'd rival Annalise in beauty. Amazing. "Nice to meet you, Gwen."

Lady Morwynne heaved a sigh. "Arthur, how many times must I tell you that you needn't introduce Gwen? She's just a servant."

Lord Morwynne grimaced. "But one who's standing right behind me." He dropped into a chair and peered at the tea set. "Is that more of that dreadful Tsarkan tea?" He shuddered at his mother's nod. "None for me then. I can't believe you served *that* to Lady Kiera."

Kiera chuckled. The young count clearly thought the tea vile as well. "'Twas interesting at least." Then she sobered and turned back to his irksome mother. "But returning to our earlier discussion, the poor need to read to understand the agreements they sign and enrich their lives."

Lady Morwynne arched a brow. "Most of the poor are satisfied with their lot. Why foment mutiny when they'd gain almost nothing from further education?"

Her son frowned at her. "How can you say that, Mother? You had Gwen educated with me, and she's not mutinous, are you, Gwen?"

As Gwen shook her veiled head, Lady Morwynne sighed. "But Gwen still has the same position in life despite her education, and although she's suitably grateful, others shan't be."

Kiera stiffened and tapped the Vireni betrothal ring. The countess would *never* support her education initiative, so she might as well leave. She rose with a cool smile. "I must be off to prepare for Lady Blaine's fire ball. Shall I see you there?"

Lady Morwynne scowled and lifted her chin. "No. We've better amusements tonight."

Kiera blinked. Better than attending the fashionable countess's exclusive ball? Perhaps she'd not received an invitation. Curious.

Suppressing her smile, Kiera said farewell then sailed out

with her guards. She sighed once she settled in the royal carriage. Although the Minister of Health and Community wouldn't support her education initiative, she'd not surrender. She just needed other allies. Devon should know whom to approach. She'd ask him when she returned to the palace.

CHAPTER 31

After Kiera left for Lady Morwynne's, Devon tried reviewing Lord Islaye's latest report about the Magehaven ore but couldn't focus. Every few minutes, he glanced at the clock on the mantel. How was Kiera's meeting with the Minister of Health and Community progressing? The education initiative meant so much to her, and if she couldn't sway Lady Morwynne, she might decide she wasn't worthy to be queen. Ridiculous, considering all of her other triumphs at court.

When he glanced at the clock for the sixth time, he sighed and abandoned his report. He'd go riding to distract himself. He hummed as he changed. Given her progressing riding lessons, soon Kiera would be skilled enough to join him. But other company would be nice this afternoon, so he stopped by Aragon's on his way out of Ormas.

He smiled while he sat in the chair across from the sofa where Aragon was reading and Selena sketching. As always, they were so contented together—like mated griffins. His chest squeezed as he leaned forward. "I'm going riding. Care to come along?"

Aragon glanced at Selena, who nodded, then he grinned. "Let me go change."

Once Aragon left, Devon eyed Selena. Somehow she appeared larger than she had at tea yesterday. "How are you feeling?"

Selena dimpled and rubbed her rounded stomach. "Well enough, and the baby has begun kicking often."

He grinned but swallowed a sigh. How long until Kiera was similarly blessed? "Sounds exciting."

Before Selena could do more than nod, Aragon returned in riding clothes and kissed her cheek then glanced at Devon. "Ready?"

Devon nodded, and they strode outside. Once they were heading east through Ormas with his guards, he sighed then said, "I hope I'm as fortunate as you one day." Please, Goddess.

Aragon flashed a grin. "You shall be—after Kiera's coronation. Have you chosen a date yet?"

Devon grunted as he steered his black gelding around a field cart. Kiera must actually accept his proposal first. "No."

Aragon arched his brows. "Mother was wondering why after tea yesterday. I suspect she'll ask you two soon."

Devon winced. Wonderful. "I know 'tis likely impossible, but attempt to convince her not to. Asking that shall only make Kiera flee."

Aragon frowned as they rode through the eastern gate. "Why? She did accept you, which involves being crowned."

Devon winced again. He should finally confess everything to Aragon. "Except she only accepted me to negotiate with the nightmara and intends to return to the orphanage afterward."

Aragon halted his bay mare to gape at Devon. "She what? *Why?*"

Halting as well, Devon coughed and shifted in his saddle. How would his forthright friend react? "Because I, er, implied 'twas why I proposed."

Aragon snorted. "For Goddess's sake, why? You love her."

Devon sighed and urged his gelding forward. "Yes, but I

couldn't convince her of that. She assumed a king would only make a poor orphanage matron his mistress."

Aragon shook his head. "A fake betrothed is hardly better."

Devon grimaced, his throat tightening. "I know, but 'twas the only way she'd agree. And Wren thought if Kiera had a purpose to become my betrothed and I remained steadfast in my support and taught court to accept her, then she'd eventually realize my love was sincere and that she was meant to be queen."

Aragon tsked. "I suppose Wren knows Kiera better than I..."

Devon drooped and rubbed his aching chest. "But I can't so much as kiss Kiera—it only convinces her I want to seduce her. And restraining myself is driving me mad. I don't know how much longer I'll last."

Aragon shuddered. "I felt the same before Selena and I resolved matters." He nodded at the fence across a nearby field. "Race you there and back?"

Devon relaxed at his friend's attempt to distract him. He waved his guards to remain behind. "Yes, but after that, I must return to the palace." Kiera should hopefully be back.

They prodded their mounts forward and galloped around the fence. When he won by a head, Devon grinned and said, "Losing must be a family trait—I beat Hawke two months ago too."

Aragon smirked at him as they began back to Ormas. "We only take pity on you because you're our cousin."

Devon arched a brow. Or he was just a better rider. "Right..."

They rode in silence until they reached the intersection their paths separated. Then Aragon clapped his shoulder. "Don't fret. Even though she doesn't believe you love her, an honest lady like Kiera wouldn't have agreed to a fake betrothal unless she secretly felt the same."

Devon sighed when he continued to the palace with his guards. Goddess, let Aragon be right. And let Kiera admit her love before his restraint shattered.

As soon as he returned, he knocked on their adjoining door and entered Kiera's chambers to escort her to dinner. He stiffened at the frown creasing her brow. Her meeting mustn't have gone well. Had that convinced her she wasn't meant to be queen? Yet he waited until they began eating to ask, "How was tea with Lady Morwynne?"

Kiera's frown burgeoned into a scowl. "Vile. She tried to choke me on Tsarkan tea and told me the poor have no reason to read. Her son was nice, however."

Devon shuddered. The pungent Tsarkan tea *was* vile. He leaned forward over his mushroom soup. "I should have warned you about that tea. I'd forgotten Lady Morwynne likes to serve it to those she wants to impress."

Kiera snorted. "Or those she wants to intimidate." She shook her head. "But I shan't let her obstruct my education initiative. I just need other allies. Who should I approach?"

His heart surged. Lady Morwynne's resistance had only spurred Kiera. Thank the Goddess. He smiled at her. 'Twas precisely why she'd make the perfect queen. She was willing to fight to help others. If he didn't already love her, her conviction would have made him fall in love. Not that he could tell her that. So instead, he replied, "Try Mel. He probably knows other priests who share your passion and would be glad to help."

Kiera blinked at him over her duck terrine. "I never considered them, but priests *are* everywhere. Thanks, Devon."

He nodded, and they soon finished dinner then returned to their chambers to dress for Lady Blaine's fire ball. All of court had been chattering about the unprecedented autumn event for the past week. With Kiera beside him, he could risk attending, unlike the countess's water party three months ago.

When Devon joined Kiera in her chambers again, tingling warmth flooded him at her stunning ballgown. She'd turned the arachne silk a luxurious cream patterned with vivid firebirds that flickered like flame.

Kiera grinned and smoothed her ballgown. "Too much?"

He swallowed as he took her arm. "No, you're as alluring as a fire witch leaping through a Summerday bonfire." How was he to resist kissing her?

Kiera squeezed his arm, and he almost shuddered. She said, "That *was* the idea."

Devon escorted her to his carriage and handed her inside as their guards took their outside seats. Then he forced himself to drop her arm. Touching her was too dangerous. Yet he couldn't help watching Kiera the entire ride. Her flickering gown lit up the carriage and accentuated her lovely face. Goddess, he burned to kiss her. But she'd assume he only wanted to seduce her if he did.

He sighed when they finally reached the fire ball. He'd managed to restrain himself. Then he tensed at the beggars lurking outside the garden holding the fire ball. Although the event was exclusive, the garden was outside the fashionable area of Ormas—'twas one of the few large enough for so many fires.

Once they greeted Lady Blaine, Kiera leaned forward. "Is Mel here yet?"

Lady Blaine scowled. "Why would you want *him*?"

Devon suppressed a chuckle despite hungering to kiss Kiera. Mel and his cousin by marriage were always bickering about something.

Kiera beamed at the countess. "I've a proposal for him, and I can't imagine he'd missed *your* event."

Lady Blaine almost smiled. Then she sniffed and tossed her head. "Mel finds my events frivolous. He's yet to attend one—unless it's a family event and the duchess forces him."

Devon's mouth twitched. Considering what Mel had said over the years, 'twas more than her events he found frivolous.

Yet Kiera tsked. "How puritanical."

When they moved on, Devon murmured in her ear, "I'll write to Mel and ask him to join us for luncheon in the next few days." Then he stiffened as her clean lavender scent swamped him. So tempting.

They spent an hour mingling amid the open braziers and

enjoying spiced cider, wild music, and fire dancers. Yet despite the exotic entertainment, he kept glancing at Kiera. She was as irresistible with her flickering firebirds as she'd been in her mermaid costume. When she caught his hungry gaze and licked her lips, he couldn't help drawing her into his arms. Surely he'd not go too far in public.

They spent the rest of the fire ball dancing every dance nestled together like they had at the summer masquerade. Except tonight, he stole kisses between songs. And she never pulled away or stopped him. Instead, she deepened every kiss—exactly like a lady in love with her betrothed. Perhaps she was warming to their betrothal at last.

On the ride back to the palace, Kiera leaned against him and chuckled. "Lady Blaine may be Wren's childhood rival, but she definitely knows how to entertain. Her fire ball was the most diverting court event I've attended so far."

Devon nodded, but his body hardened at her lush curves pressing against him. 'Twould be so easy to scoop her into his lap and kiss her until they couldn't breathe. Surely she'd twine her arms about him and deepen his kisses like she had at the fire ball. Would she stop him from sliding his hands up her skirt or lowering her neckline?

He began to reach for her but then jerked back. If he seduced her before she realized he loved her, she likely never would. She'd negotiate the nightmara treaty then retreat to her orphanage convinced he only wanted her as a mistress.

His hunger crumbling to ash, Devon eased away from Kiera. His restraint would shatter if he kept touching her. He swallowed when she stiffened and eyed him. As she drew breath to speak, he interjected, "I suspect Lady Blaine is compensating for last year. She couldn't arrange any events since she was in mourning."

After a long moment, Kiera relaxed into her seat and lowered her gaze. "That must have been difficult for a fashionable lady like Lady Blaine."

They remained silent the rest of the carriage ride and through the palace. At her door, he let himself kiss her palms. "Good night, Kiera."

Her navy eyes black, Kiera stared up at him then darted forward to press a kiss beside his mouth. "Good night, Devon."

As she whirled into her chambers, he touched his tingling cheek. That sweet kiss had been the first sign of affection—not passion—she'd offered. She was definitely warming to their betrothal. Thank the Goddess.

CHAPTER 32

*H*er heart pounding, Kiera darted across the queen's chambers. How could she have kissed him like that, so near a bed? Especially after they'd acted like starved venuses at Lady Blaine's fire ball. 'Twas almost begging him to seduce her.

She licked her tingling lips as Mia helped her into a dressing gown. And if he kissed her when he brought their evening drink, she'd let him seduce her, despite all her vows not to become his mistress. He was just too tempting to resist any longer.

As Mia left, Kiera smoothed her dressing gown with trembling hands. Then she perched on the sofa like usual and faced the adjoining door. Oh, Goddess.

But for the first time since she'd moved into the palace, Devon didn't join her for their drink before bed.

After waiting for an hour, she crawled beneath her covers, foolish tears pricking her eyes. Was he being chivalrous by staying away? Or had his ravenous kisses at the fire ball been to convince court of their betrothal? She should be grateful for his restraint, but she ached to kiss him too much.

The following morning, Kiera stiffened when Devon joined her at breakfast. If he meant to kiss her now, she was no longer interested. She was listless after a restless night plagued by sensual dreams. Besides, 'twas fortunate he'd stayed away—otherwise she'd have surrendered her dream of genuine love for an evening of passion.

Yet Devon merely sat across from her with a weak smile. He swallowed then said, "I wrote Mel, asking him to join us for luncheon the day after tomorrow. And he already wrote back to accept."

She almost winced. To discuss the education initiative she'd forgotten about because of Devon's kisses. She crumbled her toast. He truly made her forget everything. She managed to echo his smile. "Wonderful."

Over the next few days, Devon returned to treating Kiera like a sister. He mustn't want to risk the nightmara treaty by succumbing to their irresistible attraction. But he did bring their evening drink every night, although he still sat across the room. And whenever she looked away when they were together, she could sense his hungry eyes caressing her skin. But he only feathered a fleeting kiss against her palm before their evening court events, probably to encourage her. When he did, she sighed and rubbed her tingling palms against her gown. Would he ever truly kiss her again? And would she ever stop aching for those kisses?

Kiera relaxed when Mel joined her and Devon for a quiet luncheon. She'd only met Hawke's middle brother a handful of times, but the young priest was always compassionate and perceptive. The perfect ally for her education initiative. Plus, she couldn't contemplate kissing Devon with a priest beside her.

Midway through luncheon, Mel grinned and leaned forward. "So what inspired your royal invitation? The high priest shall wail like a banshee portending a family death if you ask me to officiate your wedding ceremony."

She blushed. Since he'd officiated both his brothers' wedding ceremonies, not surprising he assumed they'd invited him to discuss another. She glanced at Devon, who smiled and nodded for her to speak.

Kiera sipped her tea to hide her blush then replied, "Nothing like that. I intend to make basic education—like reading, arithmetic, history, self-defense, and rudimentary spells—mandatory for all children in Calatini, but I require assistance implementing my initiative."

Mel gaped at her. "Quite an initiative." He smiled then eyed his cousin. "No wonder Devon is mad for you. Nothing would win his heart faster than a plan to improve his people's lives."

Another blush burned her cheeks as Devon kissed her palm beneath the Vireni ring and said, "Exactly. My Kiera shall become the best queen since Calator's wife Annalise."

She tugged her hand free. Doubtless his adulation was to convince his perceptive cousin of their betrothal.

Mel chuckled. "Appropriate considering your resemblance." He grinned at her. "How can I help?"

Kiera straightened, her chest lightening. His ready agreement was the antithesis of Lady Morwynne's. Wonderful. "Do you know other priests who share my passion for education and would be interested in joining my initiative?"

Mel slowly nodded. "I think I do, and I'll ask the high priest to send out a call to all the temples in Calatini." He rose. "I'll contact you as soon as I know more."

Once Mel strode out, she laughed and flung herself against Devon. "Thank you! Your suggestion was perfect. Lady Morwynne shan't be able to obstruct my education initiative now."

Devon swallowed. "'Twas nothing."

As his body firmed against hers, Kiera shivered and eyed his lips. 'Twould be so easy to kiss him. Goddess, why did he tempt her like a singing siren? She began leaning forward.

But just before their lips met, Devon jerked back. "I must go.

I've reports from yesterday's council meeting." He leapt upright and bolted.

She sagged, her heart clenching. She *must* stop almost kissing him. She was merely a fake betrothed who was helping him negotiate with the nightmara. And she could never be more.

HER CHEST still tight after dinner the following day, Kiera sighed as she prepared for the Westons' musical evening. Perhaps wearing her favorite evening gown would cheer her. Simple and elegant, its high waist and flowing skirt enhanced her rounded figure and almost made her appear a true queen. To further hearten herself, she touched her pricked finger to the arachne silk then pictured pink and cream butterflies against a brilliant blue sky.

She was eyeing her creation in the cheval mirror when Devon rumbled from the adjoining door, "Lovely, as always."

Tingling warmth flooding her, she managed a serene smile and turned to face him. Why must he be so tempting? "Thanks. Shall we go? I'm eager to see Cassandra and Amaranth again."

Devon nodded then escorted her to his carriage but shifted away once they sat. And neither spoke as they rode to the Westons' townhouse. Nothing like their intimate carriage rides to the orphanage when she'd first begun acting as queen. She sighed.

When they arrived, Lady Weston immediately embraced Kiera. "Good evening, your majesty. Thanks to tonight's harpist, we're more crowded than usual, so Amaranth shan't join us for the performance, but Cassandra is with Hawke."

Kiera sighed. "I was anticipating seeing both girls."

Lord Weston chuckled. "You shall. A maid went to fetch Amaranth when you arrived, but she'll return upstairs once she sees you."

A small whirlwind burst into the room and flung her arms about Kiera's skirt. "Mistress Kiera!"

Her chest warming, Kiera bent and embraced the little girl. She was better than any cheerful gown. "How have you been?"

Amaranth giggled. "Wonderful! Grandma is teaching me to play the keyharp, and Grandpa is teaching me to ride, and they tell me stories about Mama as a girl every night."

Kiera grinned and smoothed the girl's loose curls. How lovely she was so happy with her family. "I'm learning to ride too. The nightmara queen-heir is teaching me."

Amaranth gaped then began chattering more about her life with her grandparents until the Westons firmly but lovingly sent her to bed.

Once the little girl left, Lord Weston beamed at Kiera. "We heard you're beginning an education initiative. Just let us know how we can help."

Lady Weston clapped her hands, appearing remarkably like her young granddaughter. "Yes, 'tis marvelous. Exactly the thing a generous lady like you would champion."

Kiera blushed. "You're too kind."

Devon chuckled once he drew her past their hosts. "More allies for your initiative. I wonder how many you'll receive."

Kiera shrugged but tugged him toward Hawke and Cassandra. She must talk to the girl before the concert began. She beamed and embraced Cassandra while Devon and Hawke exchanged greetings. "How are you?"

Cassandra smiled back then murmured, "Well enough. It's been an adjustment living with Lord and Lady Weston, but they love us and want us to be happy. They've never once insulted Papa, even though I know they forbade Mama to marry him. And they weren't upset when they learned about my magic lessons with the veiled witch, although they did insist on meeting her."

While Devon teased Hawke for leaving Wren at home so she could rest, Kiera squeezed Cassandra's hand. The teenage girl wasn't as effusive as her sister, but she was clearly happy too and learning to trust her grandparents. "I suspect losing your mother made them reevaluate their prejudices, and if they'd found her again, they'd have reconciled."

Cassandra's mulberry eyes darkened. "I wish they'd had the chance. Mama always missed them."

Her throat aching, Kiera embraced the grieving girl again. "She'd be glad they've found you now."

Cassandra hugged her back then stepped free. "I know." She gestured to Hawke beside her. "Hawke was just updating me on the orphanage."

A pang darted through Kiera's chest. Thanks to her hectic social rounds at court, she'd not found time to visit since she'd left. She managed to smile at Hawke. "And how is everything there?"

As Devon eyed her, Hawke flashed a crooked grin then replied, "Well. The orphans are performing another of Wren's plays in a couple of weeks."

Kiera twisted the Vireni betrothal ring. Goddess, she'd missed so much being gone for merely two weeks. "Let me know when, and I'll make sure to attend."

Hawke winked. "Of course. The orphans shall be excited to perform for royalty." When she grimaced at him, he arched a brow. "Anticipating tonight's performance?"

As Devon nodded, Kiera shrugged. She only cared about seeing the girls. "Not as much as you."

Hawke chuckled. "So no." He began to continue, but stiffened when Lady Blaine approached with Lord Ravenstone.

Kiera almost winced when Hawke ignored Lady Blaine but nodded at her companion. Not surprising he was still furious over the rumors Lady Blaine had spread about Wren.

Despite that, Lady Blaine leaned toward him. "Hawke, I must speak with you and Wren."

Kiera gripped Devon's arm. Oh dear.

His face as stony as a gargoyle's in sunlight, Hawke glared at the sultry countess. "No."

Lady Blaine blushed when he grasped Cassandra's arm and

strode across the room. Then Lady Blaine flashed a brilliant smile at Kiera and Devon. "I'm sorry for subjecting you to family squabbles."

Devon arched a brow. "No matter. We're part of the family."

When Lady Blaine swallowed, Kiera took pity on her and leaned forward with a smile. After all, the fashionable countess had arranged that diverting fire ball where Devon had kissed her senseless. "Are you anticipating tonight's performance?"

Lady Blaine relaxed. "Oh, yes. The harpist is said to be the finest in Calatini."

Annalise glided forward beside Kiera. "She is. I heard her at a concert last year." She greeted everyone else then paused and nodded at her family's ancestral enemy. "Lord Ravenstone."

Kiera gripped Devon's arm again as the count eyed Annalise without his usual genial smile. Why had Annalise risked approaching and inflaming the feud? Greysnowes and Ravenstones couldn't resist flinging insults whenever they met, and her younger brother had almost killed Lord Ravenstone four months ago.

Eventually, Lord Ravenstone bowed at Annalise and drawled, "I suppose I should thank you for staunching my wound after your hellion brother stabbed me. Doubtless I owe you my life."

Her white-blonde hair shimmering, Annalise lifted her chin with a cool smile. "'Twas nothing. You owe your life to the Goddess and your healer."

Kiera sighed as Lord Ravenstone inclined his head before escorting Lady Blaine to a nearby chair for the performance. Then she eyed Annalise. "Why didn't you wait to join us?"

Devon frowned at Annalise. "Yes, that could have gone very badly."

Annalise grimaced. "I know, but Mr. Winston began pestering me." She shuddered. "Apparently, I've become prey again since you two announced your betrothal."

Kiera glanced across the room, so they could avoid the cad.

She stiffened at the scowl darkening Mr. Winston's face as he scrutinized them. If he had a dagger, he'd stab someone.

Annalise widened her eyes and leaned forward. "Do you mind if I join you?"

Her chest tightening at her friend's pleading, Kiera smiled and threaded her free arm through Annalise's. "Please do."

Devon echoed her smile then escorted them to the front row, and they settled in to enjoy the harpist's performance. Hopefully, 'twould be as splendid as promised.

CHAPTER 33

In Kiera's chambers that evening, Devon grinned at her over his spiced cider. Her husky humming of the harpist's last song was adorable. "So how did you like the Westons' musical evening?"

Kiera shrugged. "The harpist was as splendid as promised, and 'twas wonderful to see Cassandra and Amaranth again. They've adjusted well and appear happy with their grandparents." Her shoulders drooping, she sighed and swirled her spiced cider. "Too bad the rest of my orphans weren't fortunate enough to find their families."

He strode across her chambers and kissed her palm beneath her betrothal ring. If only he could wrap her in his arms and kiss the frown from her lips. But he'd not stop at a kiss. He smiled at her. "Perhaps they'll create their own families. Like you did with Wren and Hawke." And him when she finally accepted him in truth.

Licking her lips, Kiera caressed his jaw. "True, and created families can fit better than blood ones since you choose them."

His body hardening, Devon released her and jerked back. Even kissing her palm was too much. How much longer until she agreed to marry him, so he could make love to her at last?

He forced himself to say good night then strode back to his chambers.

Over the next few days, he still joined Kiera for a drink before bed, but he no longer let himself kiss her palms. And he avoided touching her as much as possible. His restraint was too weak. She began watching him with a frown between her brows, but he couldn't explain without revealing how desperately he loved her, and 'twould make her flee to the orphanage.

Meanwhile, Kiera's triumphs at court continued. She charmed almost everyone at the court events they attended. And word about her education initiative spread through court, thanks to Aragon's mother and Kiera's other allies. Many appeared to approve, and the high priest was especially eager—he'd written an exuberant letter as soon as Mel mentioned it.

Her riding lessons were also progressing well. The morning of the Duchess of Wildewall's autumn garden party, Kiera galloped with Moonbud for the first time. But that gallop made them the last to arrive to the duchess's event.

After they greeted the duchess, Kiera leaned toward her with a grin. "I'm sorry we're late. My nightmara ride delayed us."

Her frosted auburn hair mirroring the vibrant flowers behind her, which still bloomed thanks to the frost-prevention spell on her garden, the Duchess of Wildewall smiled back at Kiera. "Royalty is never late, your highness."

Devon almost chuckled when Kiera pursed her lips. She was too responsible to approve of that. Another sign she was his perfect queen—he'd always felt the same.

The duchess grinned. "The Duchess of Childes mentioned yesterday that you're progressing with an education initiative. I'd be interested in hearing more about it over tea one day soon."

Devon almost beamed as he and Kiera moved on and their guards drifted to the outskirts. The Duchess of Wildewall definitely saw Kiera's worth as queen. He squeezed Kiera's arm. "Another ally, I think."

Kiera nodded, and they headed to the refreshments table.

They'd just accepted mugs of spiced cider when Lord Farson and his wife intercepted them.

Lord Farson grinned at Kiera. "I heard you successfully galloped today. Lady Moonbud is impressed with your improvement. She said you're doing well for a non-mara adult."

Devon chuckled when Kiera sipped her cider then drawled, "What praise."

Elise flashed a wry smile. "To a nightmara it is. Mara are the only humans they truly like."

When Kiera sighed, Devon winked to hearten her then said, "Doubtless 'twas kinder than what Lady Moonbud said about *me*."

Lord Farson shook his head. "Her only criticism about you was regarding your inability to find a bride."

Since he couldn't go too far in the duchess's garden, Devon let himself kiss Kiera's palm. Goddess, she tasted sweet. "Perfection always takes time."

Kiera arched a brow but didn't pull away. "I'm hardly perfect."

Disregarding everyone watching, he held her gaze and risked revealing part of the truth, "You are for me."

As a blush darkened Kiera's cheeks, Elise chuckled. "You two are more adorable than Hawke and Wren at their wedding."

Devon sighed when Kiera tugged her hand free and faced the baroness to say, "Not hardly."

Elise smiled and shook her head. "We'll let you get some luncheon." She darted a curtsy then tugged on her husband's arm.

Once Lord Farson bowed and escorted Elise away, Devon and Kiera filled their plates then stood by a bed of yellow daisies to eat.

They'd barely begun when Lady Annalise glided over beside Kiera with a mug and a full plate. "Afternoon."

Kiera grinned at her. "It's been *too* long since we've met. What, two hours?"

Lady Annalise giggled. "If that."

Devon blinked. He'd never heard the icy beauty giggle before. He smiled. Kiera's friendship was helping her. Like Kiera would do for the rest of Calatini as queen.

Lady Annalise sobered and peered at the other guests. "Did either of you see Mr. Winston?"

Devon scowled as he devoured a stuffed mushroom. He still hadn't devised a way to handle the cad. "I doubt the Duchess of Wildewall invited him. She never has to previous garden parties."

Lady Annalise sighed. "Thank the Goddess. He's becoming vexing to avoid."

Kiera gave her friend a warm smile. Then she sighed and nodded toward the approaching Lord Ravenstone and Lady Blaine. "Although the duchess *did* invite both the Greysnowes and Ravenstones."

Devon tensed. Why was Lord Ravenstone approaching? They were fortunate his encounter with Lady Annalise at the Westons' musical evening hadn't erupted. Why risk another so soon?

Lady Annalise's cerulean eyes darkened. "As the head of our duchy, she must invite both. 'Twould inflame the feud if she didn't. But it always adds a dash of tension to her events."

He suppressed a snort as Kiera grimaced then said, "Exciting."

Lady Annalise sighed. "Not particularly." She flashed a brilliant smile. "I'd best go before Lord Ravenstone arrives."

As her friend glided away, Kiera shook her head while finishing her food. "Ridiculous feud."

Devon sighed and handed their empty plates to a nearby servant. True. Too bad they couldn't end it without destroying both families and the Wildewall duchy. "Very. But both sides refuse to abandon it."

After a genial nod toward Devon, Lord Ravenstone grinned at Kiera. "How is it riding nightmara?"

Kiera shrugged. "Very nice, although I can't say how it compares to riding horses."

Unable to resist praising her, Devon beamed and said, "She galloped for the first time today."

As Kiera blushed and slanted him a narrow glance, Lady Blaine smiled and leaned toward her. "That must have been incredible." Then Aragon strolled over with Selena, and Lady Blaine released Lord Ravenstone to grasp Aragon's elbow. "Could I speak with you for a moment? Please."

Aragon and Selena exchanged a glance, then he nodded and escorted the fashionable countess out of earshot.

Devon almost chuckled when Lord Ravenstone arched a brow at Selena and asked, "Should you be concerned about your husband?"

Selena smiled, her hands resting on her rounded stomach. "No. I suspect she wishes to talk to him about Hawke and Wren. Hawke has been refusing to speak with her and barred her from their townhouse."

Devon tsked and waved over a servant bearing cider. Doubtless Lady Blaine was hoping his eldest brother could convince Hawke to relent. 'Twasn't likely to succeed—Hawke was too stubborn and rightly furious with her. "Nothing shall convince Hawke to forgive Lady Blaine for how she treated Wren."

Kiera smiled as she accepted a fresh mug of cider. "Except Wren herself, but I doubt she'll bother." She shook her head. "Although perhaps she should. Without Lady Blaine, they probably would have pretended they were just friends forever."

Selena giggled. "Not if the duchess could help it."

After glancing at Lady Blaine leaning toward Aragon, Lord Ravenstone bowed to Devon and Kiera. "I see someone I must greet. Good luck with your riding lessons, Lady Kiera."

As the count darted to a hidden corner, Devon chuckled. He appeared like a firecat escaping a tempest. "Do you suppose Lord Ravenstone doesn't wish to become Lady Blaine's next husband?"

Kiera snorted into her cider. "From the manner he bolted, yes."

Selena sighed as Lady Blaine fisted her hands on her hips. "I'd better go rescue my husband."

Once Selena waddled away, Lady Ducharme and Lord Morwynne strode over, then Lady Ducharme arched her brows at Kiera and murmured, "Young Lord Morwynne here mentioned his mother was dismissive of your education initiative when you met the other week. No wonder you didn't mention it at the last council meeting."

Lord Morwynne gestured with his mug, causing cider to surge over the rim. "I found the idea most intriguing, despite Mother's detractions."

Devon blinked at the young count. Though Kiera had called him "nice", him opposing his mother was surprising. 'Twould be interesting dealing with him when he reached his majority in a couple of years.

Kiera lifted her chin as she handed her mug to a nearby servant. "I'll discuss my progress at the council meeting tomorrow. Since Lady Morwynne refused to help, it took a bit longer to get everything arranged."

Devon hid a grin and passed over his mug too. But Kiera had done it. Because she was meant to be queen.

Lady Ducharme smiled and leaned forward. "I'm eager to hear more."

"More of what?" the Duchess of Childes asked as she, her husband, and Wren's parents joined them.

Lady Ducharme arched a brow. "Lady Kiera's education initiative."

Devon beamed when the two older couples nodded and Lady Keyes murmured, "A worthy undertaking."

Lady Ducharme smiled again. "Yes." Then she bowed, forcing Lord Morwynne to hurriedly echo her before she drew him away.

The duchess grinned at Kiera. "All of court has your compassion and wisdom on their lips."

Devon almost laughed. And Aragon's mother had made sure of that by discussing Kiera whenever possible. Her meddling could be useful at times.

Kiera pursed a tight smile. "Lovely."

Devon sobered and eyed her. She could use some respite. He glanced about the garden. Other guests had begun to disperse, so they could manage a moment. "Come, we should take a turn about the garden before we depart."

He nodded at his cousins' parents then whisked Kiera to a secluded bench.

Kiera sat with a sigh and eyed the vibrant asters before her. "Thanks. Although I'm not shy like Wren, 'tis overwhelming to be reminded all of court is discussing your every move."

His heart squeezing, Devon sat beside her and draped an arm about her. She appeared so weary. Please let being queen not crush her. "I know. I imagine 'tis harder not having grown up with it."

Kiera curled against him and laid her head on his shoulder. "How do you handle it?"

He sighed. He'd never discussed the burden of ruling, not even with Aragon, but she deserved the entire truth. To distract himself from his confession, he twined a dark-blonde curl about his finger, and his pulse quickened as her clean lavender scent weaved around him. "Practice, I suppose. Although I strive to act genuine with everyone, I'm always aware my actions shall be scrutinized and restrain myself accordingly."

Kiera's chuckle vibrated against him. "You didn't act very restrained at your summer masquerade or Lady Blaine's fire ball."

Devon swallowed as tingling warmth surged in his veins. "No? I think I did, considering I burned to toss you over my shoulder and haul you to my bed."

Kiera stilled and remained silent for a long moment. Finally, she murmured, "I suppose you were restrained, after all."

He shuddered and released her. His restraint would shatter if he continued holding her, despite being in the duchess's garden. Plus, he must confess the remaining truth about ruling. "Lack of privacy is one of my greatest challenges as king." Convincing Kiera he loved her was the other. He sighed again. "Most assume being royal means you've power to do as you wish. And I suppose that's true, but good kings—or queens—must always uphold the trust the people place in them and act in a way that benefits the kingdom."

Kiera caressed his face. "Devon, you're a *very* good king. Better than even Calator. I only pray I can equal you while I'm acting as your betrothed."

Warmth flooding his chest, Devon couldn't help kissing her palm. Only a true queen would fret about that. And ruling together with her made the burden infinitely lighter. Thank the Goddess he'd found her at the summer masquerade. "You already do. Shall we return to the palace?"

Kiera nodded, and he escorted her from their secluded bench back to their courtly stage.

CHAPTER 34

*B*efore the council meeting the following morning, Kiera kept pondering her conversation with Devon in the Duchess of Wildewall's garden. Goddess, being an unwed king must be lonely—even more than being a poor orphanage matron with no family. If only she could do more to help him than acting as his fake betrothed for a few months.

She eyed him as they strode to the council room. Well, she'd be the best acting queen she could while she was here. She'd return his steadfast support, no matter what happened. She'd improve Calatini's agreements in the Nightmara-Calatini Treaty. And she'd ensure her education initiative was well underway.

When they reached the council room, Devon escorted her inside without pausing at the door like he had her first few meetings. She smiled as they took their seats at the head of the table. He trusted she was prepared to face the council. And she was.

Devon opened the meeting, and they discussed the Magehaven ore, her progress with Moonbud, and those Tsarkan pirates from before. Once the councilors quieted, Kiera straightened and flashed a regal smile. 'Twas time to reveal her plans for her education initiative.

As Devon squeezed her hand beneath the table, she glanced

at each of the councilors in turn. "I've mentioned my education initiative in council meetings, but everything is finally arranged, so I can share the details with you."

Lady Ducharme leaned forward with a faint smile. "What do you intend to do?"

Kiera's chest lightened. The baroness was as eager as she'd said. Perhaps because she understood in a way the other councilors didn't—although Calatini's best war strategist in generations, as a gentry lady, she'd had to fight to secure her position as Minister of Defense. Kiera returned her smile. "Make basic education like reading, arithmetic, history, self-defense, and rudimentary spells mandatory for all children in Calatini."

A hush swept across the council room as the councilors studied Kiera. Lady Ducharme, the Duchess of Wildewall, Lord Farson, and Aragon smiled at her, while most of the others eyed her with blank expressions. And Lady Morwynne glowered.

While Devon caressed her palm with his thumb but remained silent, Kiera smiled and lifted her chin. He knew she could handle them and would let her lead. "Having raised many orphans, I've witnessed how vital education is to success." She paused and shook her head. "Yet many of the poor can't even read their own name."

Lady Morwynne sniffed. "Which most of the poor don't miss."

Before Kiera could reply, the Duchess of Wildewall pursed her lips. "Don't they? Or do they simply not know anything else?"

Kiera narrowed her eyes at the superior countess. If only another councilor was the Minister of Health and Community. "Precisely. And the poor deserve the chance to improve their lives. Basic education provides that."

As Devon beamed at her, the Duke of Osbourne creaked, "Your idea is noble, but 'tis a massive endeavor. How exactly do you intend to accomplish it?"

She nodded at the elderly duke. His face was blank as an

empty mirror—did he approve or detest her education initiative? "The high priest was eager for his priests to act as teachers if the kingdom provides the books and other resources." She tilted her head. "Although I suspect we must also hire additional teachers to supply the education the priests can't. These teachers would travel about Calatini offering more advanced lessons."

Aragon rubbed his chin. "Educating everyone is right, but can the poor afford to send their children to school? Most need them to help with housework or earn money for the family."

Although Devon sighed, Kiera flashed a wry smile. Not surprising that would concern a dedicated gentleman like Aragon. "True. So lessons shall only last the morning for ages six to sixteen, and at the end of lessons, luncheon shall be provided for the participating children. This way, the children can still help in the afternoon, and their family can save money on food."

The portly Lord Osteen, the Minister of Finance, choked. "Your education initiative sounds ruinously expensive. How do you plan to fund it?"

As Devon grimaced, Kiera sighed but managed a smile. Appearing uncertain would ensure the councilors didn't support her. "Money *is* the most difficult aspect. I hope to solicit much of the funding from donations."

The Duchess of Wildewall hummed. "If you found someone to promote your initiative as worthy, you might raise enough." She chuckled and nodded at Aragon. "And I believe the Duchess of Childes is already doing so."

Kiera and Devon exchanged an amused glance at Aragon's sigh, and she swallowed a chuckle. His mother did love to influence court.

Then Devon glanced about the table and spoke at last, "This education initiative is vital to Calatini's future, so the government shall cover whatever funds can't be raised. But I shan't raise taxes to cover it. We'll reduce spending elsewhere instead."

The councilors shifted and glanced at each other, but no one else raised further concerns.

Devon arched a brow at Kiera, obviously asking if she'd more to add. When she smiled and shook her head, he adjourned the council meeting, and all the councilors except Aragon left.

On his way out, the Duke of Osbourne bowed to Kiera with an almost smirk. "An interesting strategy indeed, Lady Kiera."

Kiera blinked. Again, did the wily duke approve or not? She turned to Devon and Aragon when they were alone. "How do you think that went?"

Humming, Devon tapped his finger on the table. "Reasonably well, but we'll know more later—by the amount of donations."

Aragon snorted. "I'm certain Mother shall convince court to donate enough. And make them believe 'twas all their own idea." Then he rose. "I'd best get back to Selena."

Once his friend left, Devon offered his arm. "Shall we?"

Kiera nodded as she threaded her arm through his, and they headed to the throne room with their guards to hear petitions at court.

ALTHOUGH COURT HAD HEARD about her education initiative before, after the council meeting, people kept asking about it at court events and anywhere else they saw her. The constant questions were heartening, yet daunting.

After several people waylaid them on their way to the nightmara stables, Annalise tsked and shook her head. "I can't believe the enthusiasm over your education initiative."

Kiera chuckled. "All the Duchess of Childes's doing. I swear she could convince harpies and nagas to form a treaty." And the bird-human and serpent-human magical creatures were fiercer enemies than the Greysnowes and Ravenstones.

Annalise tapped the hollow of her throat, covered by her riding habit. "You need a relaxing event with no queenly duties. How about we skip the Reids' kahve party and eat luncheon at my family's townhouse? I'll invite Wren as well."

Kiera brightened. She'd not seen Wren since she'd left the

orphanage over two weeks ago. Then she sighed. "She might be too busy at the orphanage."

Annalise's eyes narrowed. "I'll make sure she attends."

So around noon that day, Kiera bounded up the steps to the Greysnowes' townhouse with her guards behind her. Had Wren been able to attend? When she burst inside, she beamed at Annalise's parents, who were doubtless headed to the Reids'. "Afternoon, Lord and Lady Greysnowe."

Their faces stiff, Annalise's parents glared at her for a moment before turning away without a word.

Kiera blinked. Not even Lady Morwynne behaved so rudely. Only Mr. Winston was worse.

Annalise glided into the entrance hall and frowned at them. "Mother, Father, how could you act so churlish? Kiera is our future queen and my friend."

Lady Greysnowe sniffed and shook her head, her white-blonde hair shimmering like her daughter's. "She shan't be *our* queen. The Ravenstones chose her."

Kiera almost winced. She wouldn't be their queen, but not because of the genial count's family.

Annalise pursed her lips. "You know they did no such thing." She turned to her father. "Please don't allow the feud to delude you."

His matching cerulean eyes narrow, Lord Greysnowe snorted. "We're not deluded. We simply know what treacherous ogres the Ravenstones are." He offered his wife his arm, and they whisked outside without another word.

Annalise covered her face and muttered, "I apologize for their shocking manners."

Kiera sighed. Poor Annalise. Sometimes parents could be more of a burden than a blessing. Perhaps 'twas fortunate she didn't know hers. She flashed a wry smile to reassure Annalise. "At least they behave honestly. A rare thing at court."

Annalise grimaced as she lowered her hands. "I should have informed them that I'd never marry King Devon when he first began escorting me. But 'twas such a relief that they ceased foisting gentlemen on me."

Kiera nodded. Understandable. And with parents who seemed to only value her as a means to further their ambitions, no wonder Annalise appeared melancholy at times. But discussing that would only upset her, so Kiera asked, "Was Wren able to attend?"

Annalise relaxed with a grin. "Yes, she's waiting in the family dining room."

Her heart lightening, Kiera beamed. Wonderful. She followed Annalise into the family dining room and tsked at Wren dozing in her seat. "Waiting, you said? Sleeping, more like."

Remaining motionless, Wren replied, "I'm awake. Just resting my eyes until there's food."

As Annalise rang for luncheon, Kiera sat beside Wren and nudged her shoulder. Her lively friend must be exhausted to doze around noon. Managing the orphanage every day must be too much. "Don't lie."

Her eyes popping open, Wren flung her arms around Kiera as Annalise sat across from them. "I'm not. 'Tis wonderful to see you finally. How has acting as queen been going?"

Kiera squeezed her back, warmth suffusing her chest. Then she drew back with a shrug. "Well, I suppose. Still hectic, but now that I'm staying at the palace, I can get adequate sleep." She arched her brows at Wren. "Unlike you, clearly."

Annalise frowned and leaned toward Wren once the servants brought luncheon then left. "You do appear tired."

Wren chuckled while she began her creamy tuber soup. "No doubt." She grinned then paused and patted her stomach. "Thanks to the twins."

Their spoons halfway to their mouths, Kiera and Annalise chorused, "Twins?"

Kiera beamed as Wren bobbed a nod then replied, "Yes, our healer confirmed the double heartbeats two weeks ago."

Her dancing pulse stilling, Kiera gaped at Wren. "But I saw Hawke at the Westons' last week, and he never said a word."

Wren's lips twitched as she resumed devouring her tuber soup. "I threatened to wallop him if he divulged our news. I wanted to tell you myself. In fact, you two are the first besides us to know."

Annalise blinked but began eating as well. "Why the secrecy?"

Kiera almost sputtered mid-swallow. The duchess probably.

Wren shrugged as she finished her soup and began her grilled fish. "We wanted time to celebrate without enduring the fuss our families, particularly the duchess, shall make."

Annalise flashed a wry smile and fingered the heart-shaped, sapphire firegem flickering in the hollow of her throat. "Understandable."

Kiera eyed the delicate, pale-electrum necklace. It echoed Annalise's ice-perfect beauty and must have been hidden beneath her riding habit this morning. "Your new necklace is exquisite. That mixture of electrum perfectly matches your hair. But how did you find a firegem the precise shade of your eyes?"

Annalise blinked and lowered her hand. "I believe a nature witch enchanted it."

Kiera and Wren exchanged a wide glance. Only an extremely powerful nature witch could alter hardened dragon flame. Annalise's witch must be a Rhiannon descendant. However, Kiera merely murmured, "It suits you."

A blush tinged Annalise's cheeks as she thanked Kiera. Then she asked about the orphanage, probably to distract them from the necklace.

As they discussed the orphanage, Wren's latest play, the nightmara rides, and court during luncheon, Kiera gaped at how much Wren devoured—'twas more than her and Annalise together. But Wren *was* eating for three now.

The servants had cleared the table, but Kiera and her friends were still talking when Wren blanched and leapt to her feet.

Kiera winced as Wren bolted from the room. Doubtless she was about to lose everything she'd just devoured. Bearing your beloved's children was wonderful, but the consequent ailments weren't. Perhaps she should be grateful she'd never experience them. Her ribs squeezing, she twisted the Vireni betrothal ring. Yet somehow she wasn't.

CHAPTER 35

*H*aving attended the Reids' kahve party alone so Kiera could see her friends, Devon was about to leave when the Greysnowes intercepted him.

Lord Greysnowe scowled and leaned forward. "Your powerful protection charm may defend you from enchantments, your majesty, but not the Ravenstones' treacherous schemes."

Lady Greysnowe sniffed. "That Kiera creature is no more than a soul-stealing venus fabricated by the Ravenstones to beguile you from our daughter."

Fire flaring beneath his skin, Devon forced himself to smile at Annalise's parents. Punching the ambitious count and snarling at his wife would only inflame the Greysnowe-Ravenstone feud. "Kiera had never met Lord Ravenstone until I introduced him at the Harvestfete masquerade." When the Greysnowes began to speak, he leaned toward them and added, "Such accusations about your future queen are almost treasonous."

He strode from the room before they could reply. He *would* punch Lord Greysnowe otherwise. How dare he and his wife denigrate Kiera? 'Twas amazing they had birthed a serene and steadfast lady like Lady Annalise.

When he returned to the palace, Kiera was humming in her

chambers. He stilled in their adjoining door as tingling warmth surged through him. Goddess, her joy made her more radiant than an angel at dawn. If only he could kiss her. He swallowed then strode inside. "How was your luncheon with Wren and Lady Annalise?"

Kiera beamed and whirled to face him. "Wonderful." She paused for a moment then shook her head and asked, "How was the Reids' kahve party?"

Devon eyed Kiera. From her pause, Wren or Lady Annalise must have revealed a secret she couldn't share. So he only replied, "Fine, until the Greysnowes approached me."

Her face dimming, Kiera winced. "I encountered them as well. 'Twasn't pleasant. I don't envy Annalise her parents."

He sighed. He'd tarnished her joy—he should have remained silent. The Greysnowes' animosity was inconsequential, anyway. "Me either. But at least we needn't worry about anyone believing them. All of court knows not to trust any tales Greysnowes or Ravenstones spread about each other."

And his prediction proved correct over the next few days. No one at court listened to the Greysnowes' rumors any more than they had Mr. Winston's. Instead, they continued discussing Kiera's education initiative as well as the sudden chill and the perfect autumn leaves.

WHILE KIERA WAS at her next riding lesson with Moonbud, Devon was reviewing Lady Ducharme's report about the Tsarkan pirates when pounding vibrated his door. He jerked and called, "Enter."

His face flushed, Lord Islaye burst into the study and panted, "The ore. Exploded. Killed twelve. Wounded thirty-eight."

Devon leapt to his feet. Goddess! "Summon the council and Lady Juliet. I'll fetch Kiera." He needed her by his side to face this.

With his guards close behind, he strode to the nightmara

stables. But he gritted a smile the entire way and made sure not to run. A king must always appear composed during a crisis.

An unfamiliar mara man opened the door with a taupe night-mara behind him. The mara blinked at him. "Your majesty?"

Keeping his tone even, Devon asked, "Where's Kiera?"

The mara glanced at his nightmara partner. "Darkstar says Moonbud and the others are riding on the palace grounds."

Devon turned to Darkstar. Hopefully, the nightmara couldn't read him—gossip would only worsen the crisis. "Could you ask Lady Moonbud to return? We require Kiera at once."

The nightmara inclined his head.

Clasping his hand behind his back, Devon forced himself to remain still while he waited for Kiera. Please let her be nearby.

Within moments, Moonbud galloped to the stables with Kiera clinging to her back. Thank the Goddess.

Her dark-blonde curls wild, Kiera slid to the ground. "What's wrong?"

He grasped her arm, his blood not stirring for once. "The Magehaven ore exploded, killing twelve and wounding thirty-eight. I called a council meeting and invited the royal witch."

Kiera clutched him and paled whiter than a grieving banshee. "Dear Goddess."

Devon nodded at Moonbud, keeping his mind open so she could read him. "I apologize for disrupting your ride, but we must go."

Moonbud nodded back. :*Goddess keep you. I'll tell Kiera's guards where to find you once they return with the others.*:

While they hurried back to the palace as fast as they could and still appear calm, Kiera eyed him. "Do you have any further details?"

He sighed, his stomach roiling. "No, not yet."

Kiera whispered again, "Dear Goddess."

They soon strode into the palace, but he paused before the council room door. Handling today's crisis was different than anything Kiera had undertaken. He squeezed her arm. "Ready?"

Lifting her chin, Kiera nodded and returned his squeeze.

Devon almost smiled as his chest warmed despite his concern about the Magehaven ore. Thank the Goddess she was here.

His guards flanking the door, he and Kiera strode inside the council room to the head of the table. All the councilors were assembled except Lord Farson, Lord Dabar, and Lady Morwynne, probably because they lived farther from the palace than the rest.

While everyone else waited in tense silence, Lord Islaye, Lord Nolan, and Lady Juliet muttered to each other.

Devon gripped Kiera's hand beneath the table but kept his shoulders straight. Hopefully, the missing councilors wouldn't be long. When they rushed into the room, he waved for Lord Islaye, Lord Nolan, and Lady Juliet to begin. Please be better than he feared.

Lord Islaye inhaled. "Shortly after dawn, the mysterious ore in Magehaven exploded and destroyed the encampment studying it. None of my magic marshals know why—no one was testing the ore when it exploded. Preliminary reports estimate twelve killed and thirty-eight wounded, but they're still confirming that."

A shocked murmur swept across the council room, and many of the councilors paled. However, both Devon and Kiera remained still and clung to their serene expressions, although they did clutch each other's hands beneath the table.

The studious count rubbed his forehead as he continued, "Use of magic or enchanted items has been banned near the ore, so we only learned about the explosion thanks to Lord Nolan's pigeons. Thank the Goddess he convinced us to switch to them last month."

Devon nodded. Without those pigeons, 'twould have been twelve days before news would reach Ormas by even the swiftest horse.

Lord Nolan shrugged. "I thought they'd be useful, considering the ore's instability. My family has used pigeons for centuries since there's never been a thimble's worth of magic among us."

Lord Islaye drooped in his seat. "The explosion decimated my best magic marshals and Lord Nolan's land rangers, and I'm not sure what we can do about the ore now."

Devon and Kiera glanced at each other. Yet left unchecked, the Magehaven ore would soon destroy the Walle and start a catastrophic war with magical creatures. They must do something. He turned to the royal witch. "Your thoughts?"

Lady Juliet pursed her lips. "The ore in Magehaven is *impossible* to study with magic. When I attempt to scry it, the area is now blank, even though it had been visible to scrying before the ore was unearthed. And attempting to neutralize the ore using magic is worse. *If* you can get your spell going, it's likely to explode—or the ore will."

Lord Islaye grimaced. "Even magic meant to shield the ore causes explosions, so we've no way to protect anyone from it."

As Devon stiffened, Kiera leaned forward and asked, "Any success locating an alchemist without magic? One might find a solution."

Lord Islaye shook his head. "We've not been able to locate one who has the expertise we require."

Devon tapped his fingers on the table. Damnation, they needed that alchemist. "Redouble your search. Contact people outside of Calatini if need be."

As Lord Islaye nodded, the Duke of Osbourne frowned and asked, "The ore caused no disruptions until 'twas unearthed, correct?" At Lord Islaye's and Lady Juliet's nods, he continued, "Perhaps we should simply bury it again."

Lady Juliet shrugged. "We could try that, but I doubt 'twould be enough now that the ore has been exposed."

Devon glanced at Kiera to check her thoughts, and she squeezed his hand with a faint smile. He turned back to Lord Islaye. "Once everyone is accounted for, cover that ore with the amount of earth originally removed. Even if that doesn't work entirely, perhaps it shall dampen the ore enough to give us time to decipher how to neutralize it."

Kiera pursed her lips. "We should also move the encampment back several miles outside of the ore's influence and post guards at the ore deposit. We don't want anyone messing with it."

Devon nodded as the councilors winced. They definitely didn't. Goddess knew what would happen. He glanced about the table. "Other precautions we should take?"

Aragon frowned. "Perhaps restrict the use of magic in the area? We could send notices to the villages and post signs along the road."

Devon set his jaw. "Do it. Anything else?" When no one spoke, he continued, "Burying the ore is only a temporary solution. We must decipher how to neutralize it—and soon. Finding an alchemist without magic shall help, but we should explore other strategies."

The Duchess of Wildewall hummed. "How about consulting the elves? They don't often offer their wisdom to mere humans, but the ore shall impact their kingdoms north of the Walle if it keeps spreading."

Lord Farson smoothed his beard. "The elves might be more amenable if we have the nightmara approach them."

Kiera nodded. "I'll ask Moonbud this afternoon. I'm certain she'll agree." Then she arched her brows at Devon.

Devon squeezed her hand beneath the table. Doubtless she wanted to reveal the veiled witch. An excellent idea. They needed the help, even if it might rile Lady Juliet.

Kiera turned back to the councilors. "We should also consult a witch on Mountainglass Lane who has the extraordinary reputation of being able to magic anything."

Lady Juliet frowned and smoothed her fashionable gown. "An overblown reputation, surely."

Devon suppressed a snort. Not hardly.

Kiera shook her head. "The veiled witch created my

enchanted ballgown and Wren's glamour spell for the summer masquerade, and neither could be traced back to her or to us."

The royal witch gaped. "She created the enchanted bird Lord Beza showed me?" When Kiera nodded, Lady Juliet grumbled, "*'Twas* extraordinary. Perhaps we should consult her, after all."

Devon almost coughed. The royal witch sounded as peevish as a molting basilisk.

Lady Morwynne drawled, "If this witch is so extraordinary, why did she open a shop in *that* part of Ormas? She must be a black witch."

Lady Juliet tsked. "No, evil didn't taint her spells. But she *is* an incredibly powerful Rhiannon descendant."

Devon nodded with a wry smile. "And having met the veiled witch, I suspect she prefers not to be noticed." He glanced about the table again. "Anything else to suggest?" When no one answered, he said, "Then we'll adjourn until our regular council meeting in three days."

Once the other councilors and Lady Juliet left, Aragon glanced at Devon and Kiera. "Do you need any help?"

Devon sighed. What he needed now was to hold Kiera in his arms. But could he risk testing his restraint? Probably not. He shook his head. "Not at the moment. Go embrace your wife." At least one of them should embrace the lady he loved.

Aragon nodded and squeezed Devon's shoulder before leaving as well.

Devon and Kiera remained silent as they returned to the royal wing with both their pairs of guards following. He requested tea then sat beside Kiera on her sofa rather than across her chambers. Although he couldn't embrace her, he must keep her close.

Over their tea, he gave Kiera a tender smile. She'd been so strong and insightful today. Precisely the queen he needed by his side to share the burden. "How did you enjoy your first crisis as queen?"

Kiera grimaced and sipped her tea. "I'd rather have avoided

it. How often have crises like that happened since you've been king?"

Devon suppressed a shudder. The swarm of sea serpents attacking their ships his second month as king. And the Blackham wildfires last summer. "A few times."

Her navy eyes darkening, she caressed his face. "Does it ever get easier to handle?"

Devon sighed. "Not particularly." He kissed her palm. "But having you beside me helped immeasurably." When she blushed, he said to distract her, "We'll visit Moonbud after luncheon."

Kiera blinked. "We?"

His chest tightening, Devon nodded and drained his tea. "Yes, we. Although Moonbud would prefer to deal only with you, a crisis like this requires us both."

CHAPTER 36

As they strode back to the nightmara stables with their guards, Kiera kept glancing at Devon. He wore a calm smile, but his green eyes were dark. The crisis troubled him as it did her. And this wasn't the first he'd had to handle as king. How had he managed them alone?

She sighed. She wasn't his true queen, but thank the Goddess she was here to support him this time. If only she could do more. She licked her lips. Perhaps kissing him would cheer him. Then she shook her head. No, 'twas only her hunger for more ravenous kisses.

At the nightmara stables, their guards remained behind as usual, but Leila didn't speak as she and Nightrose directed Kiera and Devon to Moonbud in the paddock, who was nestled against Darkthorn. When they halted beside Moonbud, Leila and the other nightmara drifted to the fence.

Moonbud craned toward Kiera and Devon. :*How did things go?*:

Devon glanced at Kiera, and she nodded that he should start due to the severity of the crisis. So he sighed then replied, "The casualties and injuries remain the same, but we're no closer to understanding why the explosion happened."

Kiera leaned forward. "And to help learn that, we require your help." Please let her agree.

Moonbud blinked at them. :*I'm not certain how a nightmara could help with a magical ore.*:

Devon held her gaze. "We want to approach the elves for help."

Moonbud flicked her midnight tail. :*And assumed a magical creature would receive a better response.*:

Kiera flashed a wry smile, her stomach tightening. Was the nightmara queen-heir upset by their assumption? "In essence."

She relaxed when Moonbud nickered and said, :*You're probably right.*: Then Moonbud cocked her head. :*There's an elf in Ormas we can approach. Meet me in the paddock early tomorrow.*:

Kiera sighed. Thank the Goddess Moonbud had agreed. She smiled at the nightmara queen-heir. "Thank you. If you're willing, we've another visit to make—the witch who provided my enchanted ballgown for the summer masquerade. She's a powerful Rhiannon descendant with the extraordinary reputation of being able to magic anything, so she may provide help."

Moonbud hummed and flicked her tail again. :*Of course. That visit should prove most interesting.*: She turned to Devon. :*Don't bother with a mount tomorrow; Darkthorn shall bear you. Your guards can ride their own horses though—we shan't outpace them through the city.*:

Kiera and Devon inclined their heads at the nightmara queen-heir then swept from the paddock. Hopefully, their consultations tomorrow would prove successful.

As they returned to the palace with their guards, Devon squeezed her arm. "We'd better rest this afternoon. We must appear composed at the sirenic play opening tonight."

She arched her brows. Although she'd been anticipating seeing her first sirenic play since Wren had called them stunning with flying battles, exquisite duets, and passionate romances, surely 'twas too frivolous given the Magehaven ore explosion. "We're still attending?"

Devon grimaced. "Yes. Doubtless rumors about the explosion are spreading through court, and altering our plans would only alarm everyone further. We can only do that if essential."

Kiera sighed but nodded. Ruling a kingdom was a lot like managing an orphanage. Always appear calm and move forward no matter your strain or panic or loneliness.

So she followed his advice and remained in the queen's chambers to rest, even though she couldn't sleep. After a while, she found a novel to distract herself until 'twas time to dress for the evening.

Once dressed, she eyed her arachne silk gown in the cheval mirror. Although as frivolous as the sirenic play, she must choose an appropriate design for tonight. Court expected it. After a moment, she pricked her finger and transformed the arachne silk into navy flecked with gold. Almost sober yet still resplendent.

Then Devon joined her for dinner, and despite her tense stomach, Kiera forced herself to eat. Appearing composed would be hard enough without fainting from hunger. As she sliced her roast quail, she arched her brows at Devon. "I did mention Annalise was accompanying us tonight, right?"

Devon nodded and sipped his wine. "You did." He studied her for a moment then said, "I know this may be difficult considering the explosion, but enjoy yourself tonight. Sirenic plays are beyond compare, and I know you've never been."

Kiera sighed as she finished eating. "I'll try."

Once Devon finished as well, they left for the sirenic play. Her chest warmed when he draped an arm about her as they settled in the carriage—he'd not held her so since Lady Blaine's fire ball. And although they didn't kiss or speak during the ride, his embrace heartened her more than her earlier rest had.

The carriage paused at Greysnowe House, and Annalise glided to the backward seat with a faint frown. "I heard rumors of an explosion in Magehaven. I assume 'twas why our nightmara ride was halted. How serious was the explosion?"

Since Annalise was invariably discreet, Kiera grimaced and

replied, "Serious, but we're pretending 'tis nothing to maintain appearances."

As Devon echoed her with a nod, Annalise winced. "I understand. I'll endeavor to assist you."

Kiera smiled back. Annalise always supported her. A true friend, despite knowing each other less than two months. "Thanks."

At the theater, Devon took Kiera's arm then escorted her and Annalise through the crowd to the blessedly empty royal box. While their guards stood along the back wall, he sat beside Kiera and draped an arm about her again.

Tingling warmth filling her, she snuggled into his embrace like a besotted betrothed. Not that she loved him, right? She sighed as she rested her head against his. She'd crave this when she returned to the orphanage.

Kiera leaned forward when the curtains opened. Then an ethereal siren glided onstage with her wings folded behind her. Goddess, sirens were as radiant as everyone said. Once the theater quieted, the siren laid her hands over her heart and began to sing.

Kiera glanced at Annalise as the siren's dulcet song about lost love echoed through the theater. In her costume from the summer masquerade, Annalise would almost appear the siren's twin. Although the siren's singing was more like Amaranth, not Annalise.

Then a knock from the back of the royal box disturbed the performance. Kiera stiffened as she and the others turned to face it. Was it more news about the Magehaven ore?

Her gaze fixed on Devon, the Duchess of Wildewall pursed a tight smile. "Could I have a word, your majesty?"

Kiera and Devon exchanged a glance. The duchess had probably come about the Greysnowe-Ravenstone feud, rather than the Magehaven ore, but for her to disturb them mid-play was concerning.

After a moment, Devon removed his arm from Kiera's shoulders and rose. "Of course."

Kiera arched her brows at Annalise after Devon and the duchess left followed by his guards. "Do you know what that was about?"

Returning her gaze to the stage, Annalise fingered the heart-shaped firegem flickering in the hollow of her throat. "No. But the duchess appeared worried, and that usually means my family or the Ravenstones have done something outrageous to inflame the feud."

Kiera sighed. Wonderful. Then she began watching the stage again as well.

A male siren with outstretched wings had just strode onstage and joined the female siren's song when something rustled behind Kiera and Annalise. Although likely one of the royal guards, they turned to check then stiffened.

Mr. Winston smirked at Kiera and strode toward her. "Enjoy the play while it lasts, my dear."

Her neck prickling, Kiera turned back to the stage to feign nonchalance. Why was Mr. Winston pestering them? "I'd enjoy it more if you left."

Annalise flashed an icy smile at him. "King Devon shall return any moment."

As Annalise also turned to the stage, Mr. Winston drawled from behind Kiera, "'Tis shameful we must restrict our passion to furtive moments when your patron is absent."

Still blindly watching the sirenic play, Kiera clenched her hands into fists in her lap. Goddess, if only she could punch the cad. But with the entire theater watching, 'twould only inflame the slanderous rumors he kept attempting to spread. She set her jaw. "The only passion I have for you, Mr. Winston, is *loathing*."

A sultry voice behind them purred, "But Mr. Winston has so little experience with passion, he often mistakes the two."

Kiera blinked. Was that Lady Blaine? She turned around again and tensed. It was—escorted by Lord Ravenstone. She glanced at Annalise, who paled as she eyed the enemy count. Kiera swallowed. At least her guards were here if matters devolved.

His smile a baring of teeth rather than his usual genial expression, Lord Ravenstone clapped Mr. Winston's shoulder. "And I believe we should discuss the difference between passion and loathing, Winston."

As the count impelled Mr. Winston from the royal box, Lady Blaine sashayed forward and took Devon's seat beside Kiera. "Wretched cad. He was pursuing me this season until," she snickered, "I made it clear how *expensive* I was."

Kiera almost smiled. Not surprising the fashionable countess had managed that. She was nearly as skilled as Hawke's mother at influencing court. Although she tended to do so for herself rather than to help others like the duchess did.

Annalise grimaced. "If only iciness worked as well on Mr. Winston."

Lady Blaine glanced at Kiera. "I was pleased to rescue you, but Lord Ravenstone was the one to observe Mr. Winston pestering you and insist we must remove him."

Kiera blinked but nodded. That explained the countess's unexpected rescue. 'Twas fortunate Lord Ravenstone had noticed. His sense of chivalry wouldn't allow ladies to be pestered by a cad like Mr. Winston, even if one of them belonged to an enemy family. She smiled at Lady Blaine. "I'm grateful to you both."

The countess tossed her head, and her cinnaspice perfume swamped Kiera. "If you weren't in love with King Devon, I'd be jealous of the attention Lord Ravenstone pays you, Lady Kiera."

Kiera blinked again as she twisted the Vireni ring. Lord Ravenstone was genial, but he'd never regarded her in an amorous way.

Annalise snorted. "Lord Ravenstone is probably attempting to cozen up to you, so he can trick you into acting against the

Greysnowes."

Kiera arched her brows. Surprising that Annalise was acting as prejudiced as the rest of her family, especially after their civil interaction at the Westons' musical evening. Kiera frowned at her friend. "I doubt that."

Lady Blaine echoed her, "Despite your families' centuries-long feud, Lord Ravenstone isn't the sort for such spite. Now Mr. Winston, however..."

Kiera and the other ladies grimaced then returned their attention to the stage where the male and female siren were locked in an embrace and singing while gazing into each other's eyes. She sighed. Definitely as stunning as Wren had said.

Halfway through the duet, Devon and his guards returned to the royal box.

As Kiera's heart quickened, Lady Blaine rose then curtsied. "Good evening, your majesty. I should return to my box."

Devon sat and draped his arm around Kiera. "Was Lady Blaine pestering you?"

She nestled against him again. Yes, she'd definitely miss this. "No, quite the opposite." But given his fury about Mr. Winston before, she didn't elaborate. He'd enough to handle without adding Mr. Winston. "What did the Duchess of Wildewall want?"

Not glancing at Annalise, Devon murmured in Kiera's ear, "Lord Ravenstone's mother, who never visits Ormas, arrived today."

Kiera swallowed. What else could go wrong today? Hopefully, Lady Ravenstone's arrival wouldn't inflame the feud too much. Had the countess attended tonight? As she glanced about the theater to check, her gaze stilled on Lady Staghorn's box holding the Winstons. Sitting beside his sister, Mr. Winston scowled at Kiera and cradled his stomach. Lord Ravenstone's discussion must have involved punches. Good.

She sighed as Mr. Winston's scowl pricked her skin—he clearly burned to stab her more than ever. Yet she could do nothing about his hatred, Lady Ravenstone's arrival, or the

Magehaven ore tonight, so she returned her gaze to the sirenic play and attempted to enjoy it like Devon had requested.

CHAPTER 37

*A*s they rode through Ormas the following morning, Moonbud told Devon and Kiera, :*Morideryn owns the witch shop Over the Walle. She's friendlier to humans than most. Plus, she's cousin to the king of the northern wood elves.*:

Devon suppressed a grimace. Friendlier than most didn't mean an elf would deign to help mere humans. Since they lived for centuries, elves often considered humans ignorant and akin to mayflies. And a royal elf would be even more likely to condescend.

Kiera swallowed and shifted in her saddle. "Friendly sounds promising. Anything special we need to know about approaching her?"

Moonbud flicked her midnight tail. :*Allow me to explain matters, but be honest if she asks you something."*

Devon sighed. Please let that be enough. They needed the elves' wisdom and magical prowess to neutralize the Magehaven ore. As they turned onto Amaryllis Road, he forced himself not to pull Darkthorn's reins. Treating Darkthorn like an ordinary horse might insult the stallion, which might damage negotiations with the nightmara queen-heir, given his importance to her.

He shook his head. Not steering his mount was odd, but the ride was the smoothest he'd ever enjoyed. And Darkthorn's power surged beneath him. If only they could ride outside Ormas. The nightmara stallion would be extraordinary at a gallop.

They soon reached Over the Walle, and the nightmara bypassed the front door and turned down the alley beside the witch shop. They must know a special entrance.

When the nightmara halted behind the shop, Devon and Kiera dismounted, but he gestured for their guards to stay mounted. Moonbud's elf would be more likely to help if they demonstrated they trusted her.

As Moonbud raised her hoof and knocked on the massive back door, he inhaled then captured Kiera's arm and drew her to his side. Goddess, please let this succeed. His chest warmed when she squeezed his arm.

The door glided open to reveal a brunette elf wearing a robe cut like massive merlin wings. Definitely a wood elf. Her dark-green, slitted eyes flicked over everyone, then she smiled at the nightmara queen-heir. "What brings you by, Moonbud?"

Moonbud sighed. :*We've a matter to discuss with you, Morideryn. This is King Devon and his future queen, Lady Kiera.*:

Morideryn cocked her head, causing the merlin feathers behind her pointed ears to flutter. "I know of them, but we have never met."

A prickle skittering up his neck, Devon gave Morideryn a respectful nod, and Kiera echoed him. Hopefully, the wood elf would listen. He murmured, "Pleased to meet you."

Kiera flashed a brilliant smile. "You're the first elf I've ever met, so please excuse any blunders."

Her winged brows quirking, Morideryn waved them inside. "Come in to discuss your matter in private."

His eyes widened as everyone but the guards entered the witch shop's exotic sitting room. 'Twas like entering a northern forest.

Light trickled through the oak, maple, and beech trees painted on the walls, verdant carpet covered the floor like plush moss, faint birdsong drifted through the air, and all the furnishings resembled items from nature. He glanced at Kiera, whose eyes were similarly wide. He squeezed her arm as they sat on a feather-shaped divan.

Darkthorn behind her, Moonbud reclined on a fluffy, green pallet along the wall then asked, :*Have you heard about the explosion up north?*: When Morideryn nodded, the nightmara queen-heir continued, :*We could use counsel from the elves to unravel matters.*:

Curled on a leafy hanging chair, Morideryn eyed Moonbud and quirked a brow. "Do you, or do they?"

Devon and Kiera exchanged a glance. The wood elf's reply didn't sound promising.

Moonbud tossed her head. :*Both. The fate of the nightmara is entwined with that of Calatini's people. But this ore threatens other magical creatures too.*:

Devon grimaced and leaned forward. He *must* prove the ore a threat. "The ore disrupts all magic, and its influence keeps spreading. If we can't neutralize it, it shall destroy the Walle and devastate your kingdoms up north too."

Kiera nodded. "And we don't expect elves to neutralize the ore themselves. We'd just like advice and, perhaps, assistance. No one understands magic better than elves."

Her dark-green gaze probing, Morideryn inclined her head. "I suppose I can send word to my cousin. Since I am relaying your request, he shall probably pass it on to his fellow kings. However, I cannot guarantee a response. Although your quandary may intrigue a lore master or two."

Devon smiled and muffled a sigh. Thank the Goddess she'd agreed to that much. "Relaying our request for aid is all we can ask."

Kiera beamed at the wood elf. "Our deepest thanks."

Morideryn nodded again then ushered them out.

Once Devon and Kiera mounted, Moonbud flicked her tail. *:So how do we get to this other witch shop of yours?:*

Kiera shrugged and glanced at him. "I've never been to this part of Ormas, so I can't say."

He hummed. Since 'twas near the docks, the veiled witch's shop was across Ormas, so they should use main streets. "Go back to Center Street then head toward the docks. When we reach Mermaid Street, turn right then take a left onto Mountain-glass Lane. Rhiannon's Veils is the first door on the left."

The nightmara followed his directions through Ormas, and when Devon and Kiera dismounted at the witch shop, he waved for their guards to remain mounted. Again, they must demonstrate their trust.

With Moonbud's head craning over her shoulder, Kiera rapped on the weathered red door, but it remained motionless.

He and Kiera glanced at each other, and he grimaced. Was the tiny witch shop closed again? Surely the veiled witch wasn't attending another wedding.

As Kiera turned back to the door and raised her hand to knock again, the door at last creaked open, and the veiled witch peered at them, her gaze darting from Kiera and Devon to Moonbud and Darkthorn. A chuckle undulated her black veils. "I suppose the nightmara explain why you knocked rather than entered." She arched her brows. "How can I assist you, your majesties? I've little experience with unraveling nightmara magic."

Devon blinked. Few beyond the nightmara themselves or the witches among the mara did. So why would the veiled witch assume they'd approach others about nightmara magic?

Kiera smiled and shook her head. "We've another matter to discuss with you."

The veiled witch's exotically lined eyes narrowed. "My shop is too tiny for nightmara to enter." Bracelets and tiny bells jingling, she gestured toward the alley between her shop and the miscellany shop. "Go around back to my garden."

When the veiled witch disappeared, Devon took Kiera's arm. Was the veiled witch intrigued or irritated? He sighed as everyone headed around back. The guards remaining in the alley, he and the others strode through the green, wooden gate.

He and Kiera gaped when they entered the veiled witch's garden. The crisp autumn wind warmed to a balmy summer breeze carrying the heady scent of wild roses and apples. Lush wildflowers, herbs, and fruit trees hummed with butterflies, faebirds, and melissae. A paradise, despite being in the heart of the poorer part of Ormas and so late in the year. The veiled witch was powerful indeed. Not even the royal witch had a garden like this.

Shutting the back door of her shop, the veiled witch sashayed into her magical garden. "So what did you wish to discuss, your majesties?"

Devon swallowed, a prickle skittering across his skin. The veiled witch's dark gaze was as intense and eerie as before, but today he was close enough that her magic swamped him like waves during a hurricane.

However, Kiera flashed a brilliant smile. "Before we start, allow me to introduce our companions." She gestured toward the nightmara in turn. "This is Lady Moonbud, the nightmara queen-heir, and Darkthorn, a member of her herd."

Their eyes locking, the veiled witch and Moonbud exchanged nods. Then Moonbud murmured, :'Tis an honor to meet a *Rhiannon descendant with such an extraordinary reputation.*:

The veiled witch tilted her head. "'Tis an honor to meet a nightmara queen-heir with such inspiring powers."

As Moonbud flinched and Darkthorn's nostrils flared, Devon and Kiera glanced at one another. Why would mentioning how the nightmara chose their queens fluster them? Yet 'twas irrelevant to securing the veiled witch's help. So he leaned forward and asked, "Have you heard about the explosion in Magehaven?"

Breaking her locked stare with Moonbud, the veiled witch

turned toward him and Kiera. "Yes, caused by an ore that disrupts magic."

He blinked. Impressive that she already knew that.

Kiera leaned forward. "We hoped you could help us determine how to neutralize it."

The veiled witch drawled, "Didn't you ask the royal witch?"

Devon sighed. The veiled witch and Lady Juliet clearly shared a mutual disdain. Hopefully, the two Rhiannon descendants could set that aside enough to handle the Magehaven ore. "We did, but she said the area became blank to scrying since the ore was unearthed."

Her eyes widening, the veiled witch stiffened. "Wait here."

As she swirled back into her shop, he and Kiera traded a glance. Was she going to help then?

Moonbud snorted. :*Is the veiled witch always so cryptic?*:

Kiera quirked a wry smile. "Of course. Why else would she wear veils that conceal all but her eyes?"

Then the veiled witch returned, bearing a large quartz bowl and an opalescent leather flask. She set the bowl on a nearby table then emptied the flask into the bowl. The magical garden seemed to still as she peered into the crystalline water for a long moment. Finally, she said, "To decipher the ore's secrets, you'll need the magicless alchemist, the warrior priest, and the crippled elf lore master."

Devon and Kiera frowned at each other. Was that a prophecy? Like most, 'twas too vague to act on. They required details to neutralize the ore. He frowned at the veiled witch. "We've been hunting a magicless alchemist to study the ore for a month, with no success."

Kiera pursed her lips. "And we requested help from the elves today, but we don't know if any shall respond."

He shook his head. "Plus, how could a priest help?" If a warrior one even existed.

The veiled witch sighed. "I assure you, you'll need those three." She turned back to her scrying bowl and waved her hand over it. "The alchemist is near and shall approach you soon." She waved again. "The priest is already in place." She waved a third time. "The elf is still beyond the Walle, but your request shall call him before long."

Devon and Kiera traded another glance. That was more information, but no less cryptic. Wonderful.

Kiera leaned forward. "Is that all you can tell us?"

The veiled witch lifted her gaze from her scrying bowl. "It is."

Devon suppressed a sigh but inclined his head. At least they knew that neutralizing the Magehaven ore was possible, even if they didn't know exactly how. "Thank you, madam witch."

Kiera smiled at the veiled witch, and Moonbud and the witch exchanged another nod while Darkthorn eyed them. Then Devon and the others left the veiled witch's magical garden and returned to the palace. Please let her prophecy come true soon.

YET NOTHING CHANGED with the Magehaven ore, and no one approached them over the next two days. So after Kiera's early riding lesson, a brief council meeting spent discussing the explosion, and petitions at court, Devon returned to his study to scour Lord Islaye's latest reports about the Magehaven ore and the explosion. If the veiled witch's warrior priest was already there, surely he'd be mentioned *somewhere*.

He was about to crumple the useless reports when Kiera knocked and drew Miss Winston inside.

Kiera smiled at him as she sat beside him and gestured for Miss Winston to sit before his desk. "Miss Winston said she must speak with us."

Devon blinked as he took Kiera's hand. Miss Winston had never requested a private meeting in all her years at court. When Miss Winston swallowed, he smiled to reassure her. "Go ahead."

Miss Winston straightened but toyed with the worn gloves resting in her lap. "Before I start, I want you *both* to know I've nothing to do with Herrick's scheme."

He tensed as Kiera gripped his hand, and they exchanged a frown. What had Winston done now? He should have handled the cad as soon as Kiera had mentioned his attack at the summer masquerade.

Miss Winston shifted in her seat. "Over our parents' protests, he hired some new servants last week. We can ill afford them, despite them being rougher than any I've ever seen."

Devon blinked. Why was she explaining about their servants? Yet he nodded to encourage her to reveal what her brother had done.

Miss Winston bit her lip. "Then just after luncheon today, I overheard Herrick instructing them to kidnap Lady Kiera."

Fire flared through Devon. Winston had done *what*? He'd eviscerate the cad and feed his entrails to a rabid hellhound. He clenched his free hand to avoid growling at Winston's innocent sister. He must appear calm, so she'd reveal everything.

CHAPTER 38

Kiera gaped at Miss Winston. *Kidnap* her? Mr. Winston had scowled like he burned to stab her, but actually plotting to kidnap the king's betrothed was treasonous. Perhaps she'd scrambled his brains when she'd bashed his head at the summer masquerade.

She swallowed and clutched Devon's hand. He'd been furious over Mr. Winston's slanderous rumors, so how would he react to a kidnapping attempt? She glanced over then almost winced. Although his face was smooth, his green eyes were black, his body tense, and his free hand clenched. He resembled a chimera about to erupt.

To prevent him from destroying poor Miss Winston like a crazed chimera had the Goddess's Great Temple in Oress during the catastrophic Stone Wars, Kiera leaned forward and offered the other lady a gentle smile. "Thanks for telling us. It required great courage. Did you overhear anything else?"

Miss Winston grimaced. "No. I was afraid if I lingered, Herrick would find me, and I knew I must warn you at once."

Devon inclined his head with a tight smile. "We're most grateful. Please let us know how we can repay you."

Kiera swallowed a sigh and squeezed his hand. Thank the Goddess he'd restrained his fury.

Miss Winston brightened. His feigned calm must have reassured her. "There *is* something..."

Kiera tilted her head. From everything the duchess had mentioned about Miss Winston and what she'd observed at court, Miss Winston wasn't the sort to pursue influence. Unlike her brother.

Yet Devon merely waved for Miss Winston to continue.

Miss Winston's eyes, the same green-gold as her brother's yet not predatory at all, glowed as she leaned forward. "Although 'tisn't ladylike, I adore the reactions of elements, so I've studied alchemy for years. My mentors said I was the most talented pupil without magic they'd ever seen."

Kiera almost gasped. Miss Winston must be the veiled witch's magicless alchemist. Perhaps the veiled witch's help the other day hadn't been nonsense, after all.

Miss Winston sighed. "I heard about the explosion in Magehaven and would love to study the mysterious ore. But my parents would never allow that—unless the king and his future queen commanded it."

Kiera and Devon exchanged a glance. Although they needed a magicless alchemist to neutralize the Magehaven ore, did Miss Winston truly understand the risks?

After a moment, Devon turned back to Miss Winston. "The Magehaven ore is no lark. You understand studying it may kill you?" When she nodded, he continued, "Very well. Return home for now and say nothing to anyone about our meeting. Once we handle your brother, we'll send you up north."

Miss Winston flashed a glittering smile, darted a curtsy, then left. An echoing silence filled Devon's study in her wake.

Eyeing him, Kiera swallowed. His utter stillness was unnatural. Surely he'd erupt soon. She squeezed his hand again. "Devon?"

Devon started then called, "Millier, Stone, Holmes, Walker,

could you enter?" Once their guards stood before his desk, he arched his brows. "Did you hear Miss Winston?"

Millier, his senior guard, nodded with his hand resting on his sword. "Yes, your majesty."

She shivered at Devon's cold smile as he said, "Neutralize those kidnappers, but make sure Winston doesn't know. I mean to handle him myself. I expect a report tomorrow. You may go."

Once their guards bowed and left, Kiera caressed his clenched jaw. "Are you well?"

Devon's blank mask vanished, and he yanked her into his arms and buried his face in her neck. "No. You could have been kidnapped."

Tingling warmth swamping her, she sighed and rubbed his back. If only she could kiss him, but he'd jerked away from their almost kisses since Lady Blaine's fire ball. "But I wasn't."

When Devon merely grunted, Kiera pursed her lips. He required physical exertion before he erupted and hunted down Mr. Winston. "We can do nothing about Mr. Winston until tomorrow. Why don't you go riding? If you leave now, you've time for a long ride before dinner."

Devon raised his head with a scowl. "I don't want to leave you alone."

Extracting herself from his embrace, she stood and drew him upright. Her heart warmed. Of course he didn't. He always protected her like the fiercest gargoyle. "Escort me to the queen's chambers. I'll remain there with my guards while you're gone. 'Tis the safest part of the palace, so I'll be fine."

Devon frowned as they strode down the hall flanked by two pairs of fresh guards. "I don't know..."

At the door to the queen's chambers, Kiera narrowed her eyes at him. "Well, I do. Go riding." She darted forward and kissed his cheek—all she could risk, despite burning for a genuine kiss. "Now."

Devon sighed. "Very well. If you *promise* to remain safe in the queen's chambers while I'm gone."

She winked at Devon. "I shan't leave even for Wren." Before he could reply, she retreated into the queen's chambers as promised. Then she prowled about the room. Too bad she couldn't go riding with him, but she wasn't skilled enough to match the grueling pace he needed. Eventually, she sighed and found a novel to distract herself.

Kiera smiled when Devon joined her for dinner before the Dracwyns' card party. He was no longer scowling and almost relaxed. The ride had helped. Thank the Goddess tonight was a smaller affair that the Winstons wouldn't attend. But she'd remain close to avoid worrying him.

THE FOLLOWING MORNING, Kiera and Devon both waited impatiently for their guards' report. Fortunately, since they spent most mornings handling state affairs, they needn't feign calm at a court event. And their senior guards joined them in Devon's study straight after luncheon.

Once Devon waved for them to start, Millier said, "Mr. Winston instructed three servants to grab Lady Kiera when she visits the orphanage tomorrow then deposit her in an abandoned shack on the road to Blackham."

Kiera and Devon frowned at each other. How had Mr. Winston known she meant to attend Wren's latest orphanage play?

Fingering her sword, Holmes added, "We paid the servants to disappear tomorrow, rather than kidnap Lady Kiera." She chuckled. "Then we threatened to kill them if they reneged. The kidnappers are neutralized."

Millier nodded. "After our discussion, the servants returned to their posts, so Mr. Winston suspects nothing. He plans to meet them at the shack late tomorrow afternoon."

Kiera tensed as Devon inclined his head. His expression was too smooth again. He folded his hands on his desk then said,

"Thanks for your report. I'll skip the St. Claires' tea party to meet Winston in that shack."

Her chest tightening, she fisted her hands in her lap. Devon mustn't meet Mr. Winston alone. His restraint might shatter, and Goddess knew what he'd do. And if he went too far, he'd never forgive himself. So she smiled and lifted her chin. "I'll join you."

Devon jerked to face her with a scowl. "No. I don't want you anywhere near Winston."

Kiera held his gaze as warmth filled her at his protectiveness. Yet she couldn't allow him to go too far. She caressed his jaw. "I'll be fine. You'll be there to protect me."

Still scowling, Devon shook his head. "Too dangerous."

She arched a brow. She'd not relent until he agreed. "If you don't take me, I'll follow you, which would be *much* more dangerous."

Devon rubbed his face. "Goddess, why are you so obstinate?"

A blush warming her cheeks as their guards almost smiled, Kiera shrugged. She was only obstinate because she *must* protect him, even from himself. She replied, "Bad upbringing?"

Devon snorted. "Likely excuse." He sighed. "Just promise to stay hidden."

She inclined her head. "I shan't reveal myself unless absolutely necessary." Because he was about to go too far.

Devon turned to their guards. "Have a carriage ready tomorrow when Kiera would have left for the orphanage."

Kiera winced. How could she have forgotten about the orphanage play? The orphans would be upset if she didn't attend. And she couldn't forsake Wren without a word.

Their guards began to rise but halted when she said, "I'll pen a note for a guard to deliver to Wren about tomorrow."

Devon frowned at her. "Is that wise?"

She glared back. His worry had driven him mad if he believed her friends a threat. "Wren or Hawke *weren't* how Mr. Winston discovered my plans at the orphanage. And they'll never reveal anything I ask them to keep secret."

Devon winced. "I know, but I wish we knew how Winston learned of your orphanage visit. You only confirmed it the other day, and I doubt you spoke of it to many."

Kiera pursed her lips. True, she hadn't. So either Mr. Winston possessed a spy at the orphanage, which seemed unlikely, or he'd used a listening spell, which was also unlikely given their expense. She hummed. "To be safe, the guard delivering my note should stay hidden, and I'll tell Wren and Hawke not to speak of my changed plans aloud even between themselves."

Devon sighed but handed her a pen and paper. "Hopefully, that shall be enough."

Her skin prickling, she nodded then scrawled a brief note and handed it to Holmes.

She and Devon soon left for Lady Morwynne's ball, but tomorrow's confrontation with Mr. Winston kept troubling her. How *exactly* did he intend to handle the cad? Perhaps if he had a plan, he'd not go too far.

So over their khamomile tea before bed, Kiera leaned toward Devon and asked, "What are your plans when you confront Mr. Winston tomorrow?"

From his usual chair across the room, Devon arched his brows. "I'm not certain. I'd *like* to rip his head from his shoulders, but I'm no bloodthirsty orc."

She glared at him over her teacup. Since when was he as flippant as Hawke? "Be serious."

Devon gritted a cold smile. "I am. I shan't allow anyone to threaten you. Ever."

Kiera swallowed, her chest warming. His protectiveness was endearing, especially after needing to defend herself her entire life. If only she could remain by his side forever. But she was nothing more than his fake betrothed, and he'd find a true court lady to marry once she returned to the orphanage.

She tossed back her khamomile tea then set aside her teacup, so she'd not hurl it against the wall. Goddess, she loathed that perfect lady, whomever she was. She'd sacrifice almost anything

—the orphans, her dignity, her soul—to be that lady. Yet not because she wanted to be queen. That was merely a burden, but one she'd accept to stay.

Her heart pounding, Kiera stared at Devon across the queen's chambers and forced herself not to leap into his arms. No, she burned to be his queen because she loved him.

He wasn't just the *kind* of gentleman she could love—he was the one she *did* love.

And she had since he'd shared his lofty goal for Calatini at the summer masquerade. How could she not love him? He was compassionate, unpretentious, and purposeful, and he tended to the kingdom the same way she had her orphanage.

But since a king and a poor orphanage matron could never marry, she'd convinced herself 'twas merely irresistible attraction. Yet he was so irresistible *because* she loved him. Goddess, how had she been so blind?

Devon eyed her as he finished his khamomile tea. "Kiera, are you all right? You appear flushed."

She gulped a shuddering breath but managed to smile. "Only because I drank my tea too fast. After such a fraught day, I'm eager to retire."

Devon blinked yet merely said good night then strode to his chambers.

Once Kiera crawled beneath her covers, she rubbed her aching chest. Somehow, she must hide her realization while she acted as his betrothed. If he discovered she loved him, his sense of chivalry might compel him to marry her. Yet she wasn't worthy of being queen, and he didn't return her love. She loved him too much to steal his chance for genuine love. So once the nightmara treaty was renewed, she'd return to the orphanage where she belonged.

CHAPTER 39

Right after luncheon the following day, Devon frowned as he handed Kiera into an unmarked carriage headed to Winston's abandoned shack. He and their guards would be there, so the cad wouldn't likely endanger her, but she should still stay far, far away from Winston. He arched his brows as he settled across from her in the backward seat. "Are you *sure* I can't drop you at the orphanage? You could see Wren's play."

Kiera's eyes narrowed. "I'm coming with you."

He hid a sigh. Not surprising, but he had to ask. Yet he couldn't force her to remain behind—if he coddled her when she didn't wish it, she'd return to the orphanage before the night-mara treaty was renewed. Besides, her strength was one of the reasons he loved her.

Neither spoke as the carriage rumbled through Ormas, out the eastern gate, and to Winston's shack. He glanced at her throughout the ride, but her set jaw as she stared out the window silenced him. She'd not welcome an interruption, and he might beg her to return if he spoke.

When they entered the tiny shack, Devon and their guards arranged a plan. Kiera would crouch behind the small privacy screen, but 'twas the only place to hide, so he and Millier would stand beside the door out of immediate sight. Adams had remained with the carriage, so Holmes and Smith would conceal themselves outside to watch for Winston and block his escape.

Devon led Kiera behind the privacy screen. Goddess, let this ragged screen be enough to protect her. He arched a brow. "All right?"

Kiera nodded and caressed his jaw. "I'm fine—are you?"

He echoed her nod and pressed a kiss against her palm. For now, but his calm would doubtless vanish when Winston arrived. Hopefully, he'd not murder the cad.

From beside the door, Millier touched the communication crystal in his ear. "Smith says Mr. Winston is approaching."

As Devon began moving, Kiera yanked his head down for a fierce kiss then released him.

Tingling warmth flooding him, he forced himself to dart into position. If only he'd time to return her kiss. But then Winston would certainly spot her.

He swallowed his growl when a smirking Winston strode inside. Clearly, the cad expected Kiera helpless before him. As Winston's smirk faded to a frown, Devon drawled, "Expecting someone?"

Winston whirled to face him. "Y-your majesty, what are you doing here?"

Devon gritted an almost smile despite his surging pulse. He must remain calm. "Kiera bound and gagged by those wretched servants of yours, perhaps?"

Winston blanched. Then he lifted his chin with another smirk. "Bound and gagged, no. I expected her willingly enough."

Fire flaring through him, Devon lunged forward and punched Winston in the lower ribs. He smiled when Winston doubled over gasping. Then he punched Winston's nose with a satisfying crunch. He grinned as Winston fell to his knees with blood gushing between his fingers. Definitely broken.

He was about to punch Winston a third time when Kiera burst from behind the privacy screen. "Devon, stop!"

As she grasped his elbow, he gulped a shuddering breath. She was right. He mustn't allow his fury to control him. The royal guards could handle Winston. He flicked his fingers at Millier, who jerked Winston upright then captured his arms.

Devon glared at Winston. "What shall I do with you?" He shook his head. "I'd love to execute you, but I can't without explaining why, and I don't want to reveal your kidnapping attempt."

Despite his broken nose and captured arms, Winston smirked at him.

Devon stiffened. Too bad he couldn't punch Winston until that smirk was no longer possible. But he'd never punch a captured man. So he only said, "I believe I'll inform your family you've pressing concerns on your family estate and are unable to return to Ormas—indefinitely."

He grabbed Winston's cravat and yanked until their noses almost touched. "But if I *ever* see you again, I'll kill you, regardless of the havoc it causes." He chuckled as Winston's smirk vanished. At last. "Do you understand me?"

When Winston swallowed and nodded, Devon released him, and Millier dragged him from the shack. He sighed. The cad would never threaten Kiera, or any other lady, again. He smiled and offered her his arm.

Kiera pursed her lips but accepted his arm. "Did that go as you planned?"

He flashed a wry grin as he escorted her back to the carriage. "More or less."

When he handed her inside and began to sit across from her, Kiera drew him beside her and nestled against him as the carriage rumbled forward.

His body tightening and blood surging, Devon swallowed but laid an arm about her shoulders. He couldn't deny her seeking comfort after facing Winston, even though her lush curves and clean lavender scent made him burn to kiss her.

When the carriage slowed near the palace, Kiera drew back and studied his face. Then she caressed his cheek and kissed him. The first true kiss she'd given him, other than that brief one in the shack.

He forced himself to remain still, but when Kiera kept kissing him, his restraint shattered. He deepened their kiss and tumbled her into his lap.

Her lips never leaving his, Kiera purred and wrapped her arms about his neck before undulating against him.

Devon groaned and flipped her beneath him. More, he needed more. Throbbing hunger consuming him, he slid his hand under her skirt and up her legs.

A pounding on the carriage door halted him, and his blood froze. *What* had he almost done? Ravaging Kiera like a lusty satyr would never convince her of his love. She might decide to flee, and he couldn't bear to lose her. He thrust himself backward. What could he say to atone?

Her dark-blonde curls wild and lips swollen, Kiera giggled as she sat up and smoothed her dress. "I suppose those tales about danger heightening desire are true."

Devon winced. He needed no danger to heighten his desire for Kiera. When she grinned at him, he almost shuddered. He must leave, or he'd kiss her again. And if he did, he'd not stop. So he jerked a silent bow then bolted.

Unable to face Kiera, he locked himself in his study and spent the evening writing letters. He first wrote to Lord and Lady Winston about their son's banishment and their daughter's assignment. Then he wrote letters of introduction for Miss Winston to take to Magehaven. Once the Winstons were settled, he devoured dinner then headed to bed.

$\bullet$ $\quad$ $\bullet$ $\quad$ $\bullet$

AFTER A RESTLESS NIGHT plagued by explicit dreams, Devon rose at dawn and bolted breakfast then went on a lengthy gallop in the royal forest with his guards. He couldn't risk seeing Kiera until he'd not ravage her when they met. But the crisp air and trees shedding their red and yellow leaves settled him.

'Twas almost luncheon when he returned to Ormas, but instead of the palace, he rode to Aragon's. Seeing the steadfast love Aragon and Selena shared would remind him of what he sought with Kiera.

His guards remaining behind with the exhausted horses for once, Devon strode into the rear sitting room and dropped in the chair closest to Aragon, who was again reading on the sofa with Selena sketching beside him. Definitely as content as mated griffins.

Aragon arched his brows and lowered his book. "Here to invite me riding again?"

Devon managed a smile despite his aching chest. Goddess, would he and Kiera ever be like them? "No, I've just come from that."

Selena eyed him as she set aside her sketch journal. "You do appear weary."

Devon sighed, his shoulders sagging. "My ride isn't the only reason I appear weary. My sleep was disturbed last night."

Aragon frowned and leaned forward. "Did something happen with the Magehaven ore?"

Devon shrugged. Only Miss Winston, but she'd not arrive for a month. "Not really. 'Tis a personal matter, and I need your advice." When Selena rose, he waved for her to sit. "Stay, please. I could use a lady's opinion as well."

Rubbing her rounded stomach, Selena hummed. "I think our discussion would be better over luncheon. You might collapse mid-sentence otherwise."

Once Selena requested luncheon, they headed to the family dining room. From the variety of cooked dishes when they arrived, the servants had anticipated her request. She waddled into the seat Aragon pulled out, smiling at the hovering servants. "Very nice, everyone. We'll serve ourselves today. Thank you, you may go."

Devon relaxed as the servants bowed and left. Without them, he could reveal everything to his friends and not worry about gossip. As Selena had doubtless intended. He almost smiled while he served himself and Aragon served Selena then himself.

After they'd finished their parsnip soup, Selena arched her brows at Devon. "Now tell us your problem."

Devon sighed and cut his beefsteak into pieces. He'd best be blunt to get past their shock. "After I prevented Winston from kidnapping Kiera yesterday, I almost seduced her."

Aragon's heaped fork paused midway to his mouth. "Winston *what*?"

Devon grimaced. "Attempted to kidnap Kiera. But his sister overheard and told us, so our guards and I easily prevented it." He forced a shrug. "No, the problem came afterward."

Buttering a roll, Selena frowned. "Because you 'almost seduced' Kiera? I can't see how that's a problem." When her husband choked, she slanted him a narrow glance. "What? They *are* betrothed, and surely the duchess ensured they'd contraceptive charms after Wren and Hawke's unexpected pregnancy."

Aragon arched his brows at Devon, saying without words he'd not explain Devon's pretend fake betrothal.

Devon sighed. Fair enough. He coughed and shifted in his seat. "Kiera believes our betrothal is only to negotiate with the nightmara."

Selena dropped her roll. "Why would she believe something so ridiculous?"

Devon winced and speared a piece of beefsteak. "Because I used the nightmara as an excuse when I proposed. Despite our intense rapport, Kiera couldn't believe I truly wanted to marry her. A fake betrothal was all she would accept."

Selena tsked. "If you ever want to marry her, you'd best tell Kiera you love her at once."

As Aragon nodded, Devon grimaced into his wine. How would simply telling her help? He'd spent the past two months demonstrating his love, and she still didn't realize his love was sincere. "She'll flee back to the orphanage if I do."

Selena snorted and picked up her roll. "If Kiera flees for good, then she's not strong enough to be your queen."

Devon scowled. Kiera was plenty strong. She just didn't see it or trust that anyone could truly love her. Probably because she'd grown up without a family. He sighed, his heart squeezing.

Aragon coughed then sipped his wine. "So what did you do with Winston?"

Devon relaxed at Aragon's attempt to end his wife's scold. "I banished him from Ormas." He chuckled. "But I broke his nose first."

Selena sniffed as she buttered another roll. "The ladies of court shall be glad to be rid of the cad." She glanced at Devon. "How was the new sirenic play last week? I tire too early to attend such late events now."

Devon shrugged but described the new sirenic play, what little he'd seen of it. Then he and his friends discussed the latest novel they were reading, a comedy about a flock of sprites, tangled love affairs, and a grumpy centaur. Selena was even sketching the more hilarious scenes while Aragon read aloud.

After luncheon, Devon returned to the palace then headed to the queen's chambers. If he continued avoiding Kiera, she *would* believe he didn't love her. Please let his restraint last. He sighed when Mia said Kiera had just left for her riding lesson with Moonbud. So he went to handle this morning's reports while he awaited her return.

CHAPTER 40

*H*er breath misting in the cool autumn air, Kiera sighed as she left the palace with her guards to meet Annalise for her riding lesson with Moonbud. Devon had been avoiding her since their wild kisses yesterday. Like after Lady Blaine's fire ball, he'd skipped their drink before bed, but this time, he'd also not joined her for breakfast. Almost seducing her in his carriage *must* have perturbed him.

Her heart squeezed. His fierce protectiveness yesterday had incinerated her intention to hide her love while acting as his betrothed, so she'd been unable to resist kissing him. And like whenever they indulged their attraction alone, their kisses soon burgeoned far beyond mere kisses. Tingling warmth suffused her yet again as his hand on her leg echoed through her.

Kiera twisted the Vireni betrothal ring. From how he'd bolted and avoided her since, he'd not intended to go so far. He was too chivalrous to seduce a lady he considered under his protection—unless he meant to marry her later. But their betrothal was only to negotiate with the nightmara and would end once the treaty was renewed.

She blew another sigh. Whenever she finally saw Devon, she must treat him like a brother until he was comfortable again. No more kisses, no matter how she burned for them or what wonderful things he did. But, Goddess, now that she knew she loved him, hiding it took all her restraint.

Kiera forced a smile as she joined Annalise, and they strode to the nightmara stables. Halfway there, she coughed then said, "You no longer must fret about Mr. Winston."

Her white-blonde hair shimmering, Annalise cocked her head. "Why?"

Kiera leaned closer. Although no one was in sight, court shouldn't overhear this. "Devon banished him from Ormas for planning to kidnap me."

Annalise gaped at her. "Mr. Winston what?" When Kiera opened her mouth, Annalise waved a hand. "I heard you—I just couldn't believe it."

Kiera shrugged in reply as they reached the nightmara stables. Mr. Winston's kidnapping attempt *was* mad.

At her knock, the nightmara stable door flew open, and like always, Leila beamed at them with Nightrose behind her, then the pair escorted them to Moonbud, who was entwined with Darkthorn again.

Kiera smiled when the nightmara stallion nuzzled Moonbud's neck and Moonbud leaned against him. That must be the nightmara version of a kiss. Adorable.

Nightrose nickered as they halted beside her brother and the nightmara queen-heir.

Moonbud craned her neck to face Kiera without extracting herself from Darkthorn. :*Is it that time already?*:

Kiera shrugged with a wry smile. Moonbud would clearly rather cuddle with Darkthorn. She wasn't even saddled today. "It is."

Moonbud tossed her mane and began toward the stables. :*I was thinking we could go on a longer ride today. The royal forest, perhaps?*:

Kiera shrugged again. A longer ride would allow Devon

more time before he saw her again, which might help settle him. "That should be fine. I've nothing until after dinner."

Moonbud eyed her as they reached the stables. :*A long ride can soothe the thorniest problems.*:

Kiera nodded while saddling Moonbud. Hopefully so. Then she mounted, and she and the others trotted through the palace grounds with her guards following. But when they entered Ormas, her guards moved before and after Moonbud while the nightmara rode on either side of their queen-heir.

Kiera sighed at the habitual maneuver. She was outside but still surrounded. She leaned down and murmured to Moonbud, "Their protection can be smothering at times, right?"

Moonbud snorted. :*Definitely. They forget we can protect ourselves.*: She bobbed her head as they rode through the eastern gate. :*Shall we remind them?*:

Kiera chuckled, her pulse quickening. "Let's."

Moonbud surged forward and shot past the others. Darkthorn and Nightrose soon accelerated to match her, but the mara ponies bearing Kiera's guards fell behind. Although the mara ponies lived among the nightmara, they'd been bred for endurance, not speed. Besides, no ordinary horse could ever match a galloping nightmara.

As the nightmara raced down the road, their silent laughter echoed in Kiera's mind, and she, Annalise, and Leila all beamed like djinns freed from their bottles. Such speed was exhilarating —no wonder it relaxed Devon.

Plus, she held her seat with ease the entire ride. Amazing that she'd never ridden until a month ago, and now she could comfortably gallop. She beamed broader. Which meant she was halfway to negotiating the nightmara treaty.

When they reached the thick boughs of the royal forest, the nightmara slowed, and Kiera gaped at the massive trees bearing half their scarlet and gold leaves. Goddess, these trees were ancient. But the royal forest *had* been created at Calatini's founding a millennium ago to protect Esme the Great's melissae hive.

As they began down the meandering path, Moonbud nickered then said, :*Nightrose, join Kiera's guards so they don't lose us.*:

Nightrose and Leila sighed but halted to wait for the mara ponies.

Tossing Darkthorn a coy glance, Moonbud darted off the path, and he dashed after her with a whinny.

Kiera blushed as she clung to her seat. Although still exhilarating, being atop nightmara during their courtship gallop was like ogling a kissing couple. Did Annalise feel as awkward? She'd glance back, but she couldn't while Moonbud weaved through the trees.

As they galloped deeper into the royal forest, a buzzing began and grew increasingly louder. Could that be the bee-like melissae? Or just the wind rustling the autumn leaves? Then Moonbud burst into a small clearing, and the strident buzzing halted as if shorn by a knife.

Kiera blinked at the antique cottage in the center of the clearing, surrounded by magical bees as large as songbirds. How had they reached the melissae hive already?

Then the strident buzzing revived and became deafening as the melissae surged toward Kiera and Moonbud.

Kiera gasped as her pulse pounded in her ears. Oh, Goddess! A melissae swarm defending its hive was deadly.

Moonbud squealed and whirled to escape, but even she wasn't fast enough to evade the furious melissae.

Kiera and Moonbud shrieked as the melissae stung them, and violent spasms wracked their entire bodies. Boiling agony like a fire witch's curse swamped Kiera, and she wheezed as tears coursed down her cheeks.

Over their screams and the melissae's buzzing, Annalise shouted, "No!"

The melissae quieted then hurtled away from Kiera and Moonbud and whisked back to their cottage.

Her blood still boiling, Kiera slid from the saddle onto the ground while Moonbud crumbled beside her. She gasped and writhed as the melissae's venom coursed through her veins. Her heart sped faster and faster then stuttered. Oh, Goddess, she was about to die—without Devon knowing she loved him.

Then gentle hands cupped her face. Relief swept through her like ice water dousing flame, and the excruciating pain vanished as if it had never been. When the hands left, she opened her eyes and stared as Annalise pressed her palms against Moonbud.

After a moment, Moonbud's spasms also stilled, and the nightmara queen-heir lurched to her feet.

Darkthorn caroled, :*Moonbud!*: then bounded to her side and began nuzzling her.

Kiera staggered upright as well. Miraculous she still could. How had Annalise managed to heal her? One melissa sting was often too fatal for even the best witch healer, and she and Moonbud had been stung countless times. She eyed Annalise, who was staring into the forest and fingering the heart-shaped firegem flickering in the hollow of her throat. "What just happened?"

Still looking away, Annalise shrugged. "The melissae were startled when you burst into their clearing and attacked to defend their hive. I explained 'twas an accident to the melissa queen and asked her to halt the attack."

Kiera nibbled her lip. That explanation didn't address her true question. "But how did you heal our melissae stings?"

Her fingers clutching her firegem, Annalise swallowed. "I'm a soul healer, a very powerful one."

Kiera frowned. Like the Goddess's Spring Queen? Weren't they incredibly rare? She'd always assumed they were a type of witch healer, but their powers must be different if they could heal melissae stings. Not that she could ask, considering her normally serene friend's agitation.

Annalise leaned forward, whiter than a banshee before a family death. "Swear you shan't tell King Devon I'm a soul healer." When Kiera blinked, Annalise reached out to grip her hands. "*Please*. 'Tisn't a state matter, and 'tis vital no one knows."

Kiera scrutinized her. *This* was the secret Annalise had been hiding. Her eyes flicked to Annalise's pale-electrum necklace. Lady Heart, a heart-shaped firegem... hearts *were* akin to souls. She squeezed Annalise's hands. "I shan't tell him unless absolutely necessary."

Annalise beamed and flung her arms about Kiera. "Thank you."

Then they whirled to face Nightrose, Leila, and Kiera's guards when they thundered into the clearing.

Kiera lifted her chin and smoothed her riding habit. To keep Annalise's secret, they must pretend nothing had happened. She called to Moonbud, "Shall we ride back to the palace?"

Moonbud separated from Darkthorn and inclined her head at Annalise. She'd known Annalise's nickname, so the nightmara queen-heir must have always known but hadn't revealed Annalise's secret. No doubt she'd continue to do so.

Once Kiera and Annalise mounted, everyone rode back to Ormas. Unlike the gallop out, the nightmara kept to a trot the tired mara ponies could match, so it took a couple of hours to reach the palace.

Yet Kiera's mind whirled the entire ride. Without Annalise, she and Moonbud would have *died*. And her last thoughts would have been about Devon and her hidden love. Not that she could brazenly tell him, but perhaps she could show him until he realized it.

She sighed when the nightmara left them at the palace rather than the nightmara stables. Thank the Goddess. Her entire body ached, and her stomach was gnawing her innards, so the walk across the palace grounds would have been brutal.

As soon as Kiera entered the queen's chambers, she ordered a hot bath and dinner. The bath refreshed her, but she was too hungry to dress before dinner. She'd just begun inhaling her whitekrab soup when Devon knocked then joined her.

His green eyes darkening, Devon stared at her silk dressing gown and swallowed. "How was your nightmara ride?"

She blushed as tingling warmth flooded her at his hungry gaze. Plus, she was naked beneath her dressing gown. But since she couldn't reveal Annalise's secret, she only replied, "Interesting. We rode to the royal forest, and the melissae gave us a fright."

Devon paled. "Are you all right?"

Kiera nodded then gestured toward her dinner to distract him. "Yes, but I'm *starving*. Join me?"

Devon swallowed again, his eyes returning to her dressing gown. "I should go. You're not dressed."

Her heart surging, she flashed a coy smile. Making love to him would be the perfect way to show her love. Doubtless he'd realize she'd not do that unless she loved him. Besides, she'd almost died this afternoon. What if she never had another chance to make love to him? She waved toward the other chair at the tea table. "I'm certain you can restrain yourself." Through dinner, at least.

Devon stiffened but sat across from her. "You trust me too much."

Kiera hummed and leaned forward, allowing her dressing gown to loosen. "Because you inspire trust." And love.

Devon shuddered then yanked his gaze from her chest and heaped his plate with food. He began eating without looking at her again.

She smiled as they devoured their dinner in silence. His restraint would shatter if she flirted again. But they must eat first. When he rose to leave, she darted toward him until their chests almost touched, but he still didn't look at her. "Why won't you look at me?"

Devon shuddered again. "Because I'll seduce you if I do."

Her pulse throbbing, Kiera pressed against him and unraveled his cravat. "Perhaps I want you to seduce me."

Devon remained rigid. "Since when?"

She kissed his throat then unbuttoned his waistcoat. Since she realized she loved him and wanted to express it somehow. "Since now."

Although his body hardened further against hers, Devon grasped her hands and jerked free. "You'll be grateful for my restraint in the morning."

Kiera swayed, her stomach twisting. His chivalry had triumphed over his desire? She set her jaw. She'd not let him deny what they both needed tonight. As he began striding away, she called, "Devon, please don't go."

Devon stilled then glanced back. "I mu—"

Before he could finish, she gulped a breath then allowed her dressing gown to slide down her body and pool at her feet. Surely seeing her naked would drive chivalry from his mind.

His eyes black and face tightening, Devon gaped at her like a sailor bewitched by a siren.

Kiera's heart surged. His restraint was almost spent. She stepped forward and captured his face in her hands then purred, "Come to bed."

With that, she lowered his head and kissed him.

Devon remained frozen for a moment then groaned and yanked her against him before deepening their kiss.

Heat swamping her, she sighed and threaded her fingers through his dark-brown hair. He'd not stop this time. Finally.

As they devoured each other's mouths, Devon tore off his clothes between ardent caresses. Then they tumbled into bed and came together in a storm of wild kisses and fiery hunger.

Afterward, Kiera beamed and nuzzled his chest. Goddess, that had been *transcendent*. So much better than her uncomfortable first time. Being in love turned the physical into so much more. How soon until they could make love again?

CHAPTER 41

As Kiera nuzzled his chest, Devon fisted the hand not buried in her riotous curls. Now that he'd ravaged her like a lusty satyr, would she *ever* believe his love was sincere and marry him? True, she'd been determined to seduce him—what *exactly* had happened on that nightmara ride with the melissae? —but he should have resisted until she realized he loved her.

He kissed her brow and inhaled her clean lavender scent then sighed. He'd almost escaped, but then she'd dropped her dressing gown, and his restraint had vanished. After all, he was a man, not some sexless angel, and seeing his beloved's lush curves bare was too much temptation.

His body hardened anew when Kiera undulated against him. And feeling those curves were even worse. Goddess, he burned to make love to her again and again and again. But he mustn't. Not until she truly agreed to marry him. Then he might not let her out of bed for *days*. He grimaced. Or at least until state affairs intruded, which they always did.

Devon forced himself to release her. Keeping his gaze averted to avoid further temptation, he murmured, "I should go."

Kiera wrapped her arms about his neck. "No, we should make love again."

He swallowed as his pulse surged. Goddess, save him. Unable to speak, he shook his head.

Kiera brushed a kiss against his lips. "Why not? Making love was too transcendent not to repeat." She fingered a gold earring. "And we needn't fret about pregnancy thanks to the contraceptive charm the duchess bought."

Devon attempted to slip free. An unnecessary precaution since the removable strand of his protection charm prevented pregnancy. Which the duchess should know, but she'd probably wanted to be doubly certain after Hawke and Wren.

Kiera suddenly stiffened, and she released him. "Unless you don't *want* to make love to me again."

His chest clenched. His withdrawal had hurt her. And he couldn't let her believe he didn't want her. So he'd stay tonight and make love to her until they collapsed. He'd figure out the rest tomorrow. He captured Kiera and flipped her beneath him. "I want you too much."

Kiera beamed and twined her arms about his neck again. "Prove it."

Devon seized her mouth in a ravenous kiss. Oh, he would. He caressed and kissed her everywhere, trying to make love slower this time, but when she returned his kisses with equal hunger, their lovemaking became as fiery and explosive as before.

Afterward, he kissed her brow and refused to release her. She was right—'twas transcendent. Perhaps she *was* beginning to realize he loved her and was returning that love.

Devon made love to her twice more before they collapsed into slumber, nestled together like mated griffins. They only woke when Simon and Mia rattled the door and burst inside Kiera's chambers.

As Mia laid out dressing gowns for them then whisked away the remnants of last night's dinner, Simon waited with a heaped breakfast tray. His face blank, the valet murmured, "You've luncheon with the high priest in two hours, but we figured you'd want to eat now, regardless."

While Kiera blushed, Devon sighed then glanced at the clock on the mantel. They'd not eat much at luncheon, but if they didn't eat now, they'd be unable to focus enough to discuss her education initiative with the high priest. Plus, they probably shouldn't appear so disheveled when meeting with a priest.

Once Simon deposited the breakfast tray then bustled out with Mia, Kiera coughed and slipped into her dressing gown. "I can't believe 'tis so late. No wonder I'm as ravenous as a starved manticore."

Devon shrugged as he tossed on his dressing gown. "So am I. Making love is famishing—especially when repeated as often as we did." Too bad they couldn't make love again. But they hadn't time, and he must make sure she realized his love first.

Kiera blushed again as she served their tea. "We *were* incessant. I thought perhaps that was normal for you."

He snorted while he heaped his plate with eggs, bacon, tubers, and toast. Normal? Last night she called it transcendent. "Not hardly."

Her buttered toast halfway to her mouth, Kiera studied him through her lashes. Adorable. "Because we were in the queen's chambers rather than yours?"

His heart squeezing, Devon leaned toward her. Confessing his love might fluster her, but surely hinting at it wouldn't. "No, because I was with you. Once a night was usually enough with the few lovers I've had over the years. Plus, none visited my chambers, and I certainly never slept with them after."

Kiera's blush deepened as she devoured her toast. "We'd a lot of suppressed attraction to expend. And we were both exhausted afterward, so 'tisn't surprising we slept."

He stopped eating and reached across the tea table to take her hand. She clearly needed reassurance. "No, I slept with you because I trust you." And because he couldn't bear to release her.

Kiera blinked but threaded her fingers through his. "I trust you too."

His pulse leaping, Devon grinned. For her to repeat that when not about to seduce him *must* mean she loved him and realized he loved her too. He caressed her palm with his thumb and leaned forward to ask her to marry him again.

But before he could speak, Kiera licked her lips then murmured, "Perhaps we should remain lovers while I'm acting as your betrothed. Restraining ourselves was tortuous, and all of court already believes we are. Besides, being lovers shall help the nightmara believe our fake betrothal."

His chest froze, and he struggled to breathe. Goddess, *why* couldn't she *see*? Should he confess his love like Selena had said? He swallowed. No, if Kiera couldn't see he loved her after he'd admitted how irresistible she was and that he trusted her, saying he loved her wouldn't be enough. And if she didn't believe him, she'd end their betrothal and flee back to the orphanage.

He almost shuddered. And he couldn't lose her now. So he'd continue to support her and help her realize she was meant to be his queen. But he'd also make love to her with all the love blazing inside him. She was right, restraining themselves had been tortuous. And likely impossible since they'd already succumbed. But perhaps their lovemaking would finally convince her—something so transcendent couldn't be attributed to mere lust.

Devon squeezed her hand and forced a smile. "Convincing others is no reason to remain lovers, but if *you* truly wish to continue, I'd enjoy that."

Kiera licked her lips again. "I truly wish it."

Tingling warmth flooding him, he rose and pulled her upright by her captured hand. At least she couldn't deny their irresistible hunger. "Shall we seal our agreement?"

His body hardened as Kiera pressed against him and threaded her arms about his neck. Nothing like her protests when he'd suggested sealing their betrothal two months ago. He seized her mouth in a deep kiss. When she purred and slid her hands beneath his dressing gown, he began trailing kisses along her throat. He'd make love to her slowly this time, no matter how ravenous she made him.

But then their door rattled, and Simon coughed.

Devon wrenched up his head to glare at his valet, who watched them from the door with Mia. "What?"

Simon's mouth twitched. "You'll be late for your luncheon with the high priest if you don't dress now."

Devon and Kiera exchanged a wry grimace. They'd both forgotten about that. Too bad they couldn't move the luncheon to another day, but the high priest was almost as busy as they were, and her education initiative was too vital to delay. He squeezed her but didn't kiss her again. Too dangerous. "We'll continue this tonight."

Kiera hummed with a coy smile. "I'll look forward to it."

With a sigh, he made himself release Kiera then joined his valet to dress for their luncheon. Then he returned to her chambers and escorted her to their private dining room to meet the high priest.

A beam illuminating his austere face, High Priest Theodag leaned toward them as soon as everyone sat. "I've secured priests to act as teachers in all the cities, towns, and villages across Calatini. If you send them the books and resources they need, we should be able to start your education initiative after the Longnight season."

Kiera beamed back over her tuber-leek soup. "That's excellent news. Handling the ore explosion in Magehaven delayed us, but we can start sending resources this week, so your priests should have everything before then."

Devon grinned, his chest swelling. Goddess, she was such a perfect queen. "Fitting that such a momentous initiative shall begin at the start of a new year."

The high priest chuckled and toasted them. "Definitely."

Devon and Kiera continued reviewing her education initiative with the high priest over luncheon, which they actually ate since they'd been too distracted to eat much of their tardy breakfast. After their apple tart, Devon rose then risked a brief kiss. He chuckled when she blushed and glanced at the high priest, who only smiled. As she and the high priest began discussing further details, Devon headed to his study to address other state affairs. She could handle everything here.

He worked until shortly before dinner. Then he changed and entered Kiera's chambers but halted inside the threshold at her arachne silk gown. Tonight's sleek creation was the same purple as her betrothal ring. Goddess, he burned to remove it and take her to bed. His body hardened. And he could now—if she agreed.

Devon strode behind her and wrapped his arms about her waist then kissed her neck. "We should miss the art gala tonight. Aragon's mother is family. She'll understand."

Kiera chuckled and folded her hands over his. "The duchess would understand only too well. And so would the rest of court."

He sighed into her neck. A stuffy gala was much less pleasurable than making love, especially to her.

Kiera squeezed his hands. "If we miss tonight, 'twould be our third evening in a row not attending court events. We must go, but—" she purred another chuckle, "we could leave early."

His blood surging, Devon flipped her in his arms. "Hopefully, *very* early."

Kiera brushed a kiss against his lips. "Perhaps. Now let's leave before you kiss me senseless yet again."

He sighed but forced himself to escort her outside to their carriage with their guards close behind.

Yet when he began to sit beside her, Kiera shooed him toward the backward seat. "You'd best sit over there. Our restraint can't be trusted."

Devon chuckled as he took his designated seat. How true. "We do tend to forget ourselves during carriage rides."

Kiera tsked as the carriage rumbled forward. "And I thought my restraint was good until I met you."

He chuckled again, warmth filling his chest. At least he wasn't the only one. "Likewise."

Kiera beamed then sobered and said, "Before I forget, Wren wrote this afternoon and asked me to visit the orphanage in a few days. The orphans want to redo her play for me."

Devon smiled. Of course they did. "Let me know when so I can attend."

Kiera twisted her betrothal ring. "I think I'd better go alone. A king visiting would make the orphans too nervous. Perhaps another time."

He stiffened, his ribs tightening. Kiera had said that every time he'd mentioned visiting the orphanage. Why was she so ashamed of her poor upbringing? He loved how strong, compassionate, and wise it had made her. And 'twasn't like he'd never visited before. But he made himself nod.

Then the carriage halted at Childes House, and Devon escorted Kiera inside. They enjoyed a lively family dinner with Aragon, Selena, and Aragon's parents before enduring the art gala. But as Kiera had promised, she pled pressing duties halfway through, and they left. Thank the Goddess.

On the return ride to the palace, they nestled together, but he never kissed her despite the hunger throbbing beneath his skin. If he kissed her, he'd not stop, and the carriage ride wasn't long. A king and future queen should appear dignified when exiting their carriage. He leapt out once the carriage halted then whisked her upstairs with their guards following. Soon he'd be making love to her again.

Inside her chambers, Kiera released his arm and waved him toward their adjoining door. "Now that we're lovers, Mia and Simon should remove our evening clothes prior to our drink before bed."

Devon chuckled but left, his heart quickening. More of her gowns would remain intact that way. He swiftly changed then returned and accepted his spiced cider. "Since we'll now be together all night, do you still want to share a drink before bed?"

Kiera smiled into her mug. "I like the habit."

He flashed a wry grin. Their shared drink was his favorite part of the day, other than making love to her. "I only started it so we could spend time alone together, but I didn't trust myself with my hands free."

Her smile turning coy, Kiera drained her cider. "How flattering."

Devon shuddered. He needed Kiera now, no more waiting. He set aside his half-empty mug and scooped her into his arms. To prove she eclipsed any past lover, he carried her to his chambers and laid her on his bed and climbed beside her. His body painfully hard, he pressed gentle kisses along her arms. Although he burned to possess her, he *would* make love to her slowly tonight. Surely such tenderness would help her realize he loved her.

CHAPTER 42

For the third morning in a row, Kiera woke to Devon making love to her. Tingling warmth flooding her, she pressed against him and returned his ravenous kisses. After they both shuddered their release, she clung to him and breathed in his scent. If only they could make love forever.

She smiled as they remained entwined and exchanged a languorous kiss. Since she'd seduced him, they'd been as insatiable as starving venuses. He was always wild or tender or both, but whatever his mood, he never failed to enrapture her. The world couldn't touch her in the midst of their passion.

Eventually, Devon sighed then shifted until he lay beside her. "What are your plans today?"

Kiera nuzzled his chest, her body tingling anew at his crisp hair and salty skin. Goddess, 'twas amazing they ever managed to get out of bed. "After luncheon, I'm visiting the orphanage, remember?"

His fingers buried in her curls, Devon stilled beneath her. "Are you certain I shouldn't attend?"

She sighed. If only he could. Yet Wren had requested she visit alone, so Wren doubtless had private news about the orphanage, although it must be unusual if Devon couldn't know it. She kissed his chest. "Yes..."

Instead of making love to her again, Devon stiffened then rose from bed, hers today, and donned his abandoned dressing gown.

Kiera eyed him, her heart squeezing. He must have a lot of state affairs to handle for him to rise so abruptly.

Yet Devon still bent and captured her mouth in a deep kiss before he strode out the adjoining door.

Breathless from his kiss, she flopped back onto her bed but rose when Mia entered with a full breakfast tray. The maid helped her dress, and she'd just sat down to eat when Devon rejoined her. She beamed at him, and he grinned back then asked what she thought Wren's latest play was about. They spent breakfast chuckling over increasingly wild possibilities, like a walleyed wyvern.

Once Devon kissed her again and left, Kiera spent the morning handling details for her education initiative. At least half of the books and resources had been sent, and rest would go today or tomorrow. Then her education initiative would be well underway. She grinned as she sealed her final letter. The lives of the poor in Calatini would soon be so much better.

She bolted luncheon then left for the orphanage with her guards. As the carriage rumbled through the streets of Ormas, she hummed and relaxed in her seat. Now that Mr. Winston had been banished, her duties at court had been smooth. More at court appeared to accept her, and some had even begun seeking her counsel. And during their first ride since their nearly fatal one, Moonbud had said they'd start jumping soon, although she didn't mention Kiera's successful gallop, the melissae, or Annalise's secret powers. So the only true concern remaining was the Magehaven explosion, but Miss Winston must arrive at the ore before any progress could be made there, and that wouldn't be for almost four weeks.

Her heart quickening, Kiera smiled and straightened. For a poor orphanage matron, she'd performed remarkably well as acting queen. Perhaps her becoming queen *wasn't* so mad. If Devon loved her as she loved him, maybe they could transform their fake betrothal into a genuine one. Then she could remain by his side forever, and they could share each other's burdens.

She grinned. Considering the way Devon made love to her, he *must* return her love. And a love as deep as theirs deserved to be heeded. 'Twas a blessing from the Goddess. Her stomach fluttered. So tonight at their drink before bed, she'd confess her love. Then surely he'd confess his and propose to her in truth.

When the carriage halted at the orphanage, Kiera grinned harder and leapt down. As her guards moved to follow, she waved for them to stay with the carriage. No danger threatened her here, and Wren *had* written alone.

Peter flung open the door and crushed her in a fierce hug. "Our own Mistress Kiera, at last!"

Her grin wobbling, she almost winced. Despite her hectic days at court, she should have returned before now. She squeezed the burly porter. "I'm sorry 'tis been so long."

Peter released her with a beam. "I'm sure you've been mighty busy with all those court dos. Mary and I be proud as mama rocs of you." He patted her shoulder. "Everyone's waitin' for you in the dinin' hall."

When they entered the dining hall, the orphans on the floor whooped and bounced. Warmth flooding her, Kiera grinned back. 'Twas wonderful to see their familiar faces, although the older children and the Bedsford twins were missing. They must be helping manage the play. After a moment, she thanked the rowdy orphans and waved for silence so the play could start.

While the orphans settled, Mary bustled over and enfolded her in a hug as fierce as her husband's. The plump cook whispered in her ear, "You're glowin' brighter than the sun, Mistress Kiera. That king of yours is cherishin' you right."

A blush burned her cheeks as Kiera freed herself from Mary's arms. He truly did. But she only replied, "Hush, the play is about to start."

Mary chuckled then bustled back to the refreshments table.

Kiera sat in her chair of honor along the back wall as the curtain rose and the orphans acting in the play tumbled onstage. She grinned as she watched Wren's new play, which wasn't about a walleyed wyvern but about a boy who befriended and protected an orphan nightmara stallion long before the treaty. After a rousing finale where the boy rescued the nightmara from an evil knight, she leapt upright then clapped until her hands were numb and embraced any orphan that approached.

Eventually, the orphans drifted away to devour their refreshments and talk with friends, and Kiera embraced Wren, whose gently rounded stomach pressed against her. "Delightful, as always." She drew back. "Where's Hawke?"

Wren stilled. "He went home to fetch something. He'll return shortly. Let's head to the matron's study."

Kiera eyed her friend, a chill prickling her neck. Wren must mean to disclose her mysterious news. She nodded and followed Wren from the dining hall.

Once they sat before the desk in the matron's study, Wren smiled at her. "So what exactly happened with Mr. Winston? Your notes didn't include many details."

Kiera grimaced. "In case someone else found them." She described everything that had happened with Mr. Winston, including her wild kisses with Devon after. A blush warming her cheeks, she paused to collect herself before revealing her melissae encounter, becoming lovers, and her plans for tonight.

As she was about to continue, Wren leaned forward and grasped her hand. "I'm glad everything is progressing well at court. Things are here too. Hawke and I just started an apprenticeship program to secure the orphans' livelihoods after they leave."

Kiera beamed and squeezed Wren's hand. *That* must have

been why the older children were missing today. She'd always wished she could start such a program, but basic education was all she'd been able to afford. Yet Wren and Hawke could sponsor more, thanks to his shrewd investments. "That's wonderful. I suppose your plays and Hawke's music trains the orphans who want to become entertainers. What about the others?"

Wren released Kiera's hand to flick her fingers. "Our servants are training the orphans interested in those trades. And Buford, Hawke's merchant friend, is training those interested in becoming merchants or sailors. Since he came from the streets, he was excited by our program and even invited all the orphans to tour his warehouse." She flashed a grin. "The Bedsford twins were *spellbound*. I've never seen two boys more sea mad."

Kiera chuckled. Being sailors would suit the scampish twins. And perhaps cheer them after losing Amaranth.

Wren wrinkled her nose. "Although twelve was younger than we'd intended for our program, we succumbed to their pleas and allowed them to apprentice with Buford. And Buford says the twins are doing marvelously."

Kiera smiled and chuckled again. That explained why they'd also been missing today. "They finally have the perfect outlet for their exuberance." She leaned forward. "Have you approached Mel about the orphans with a calling to be priests or healers?"

Wren nodded. "Hawke asked him last week. Now we just need a fighter for those who wish to enter the military or the marshals."

Kiera hummed then tilted her head. "Approach Lady Ducharme. She's been eager to support my education initiative."

Wren straightened with a grin. "I'll write her tonight then. The Minister of Defense would be a conquest for our little program." Then a knock, surely Hawke's, extinguished her grin.

Kiera tensed. Why wasn't Wren excited to see her husband? It must involve what he'd gone to fetch. Her stomach quivered as she turned toward the door.

His usual crooked smile absent, Hawke ushered a woman concealed by a dark cloak into the matron's study.

Kiera inhaled, her stomach twisting.

The woman flung aside her cloak as soon as the door closed then smirked at Kiera.

Nausea swamping her, Kiera eyed the older version of herself. The same dark-blonde curls but streaked with gray. The same soft face but beginning to wrinkle. The same rounded figure but wearing a garish fuchsia. Only the woman's eyes were different: bright blue rather than navy.

Kiera swallowed. Dear Goddess, let that not be... She lifted her chin and gritted a cool smile. "Who is this?"

The woman tittered. "Don't ya know yer own ma?"

Fire kindling in her chest, Kiera clung to her smile. This woman was *not* her mother. She'd never hugged her when she'd fallen or taught her to read with a proud beam or lightened every problem using her wisdom. This woman hadn't even *named* her. Jane had done all of that. Kiera murmured, "A mother doesn't abandon her infant daughter on the steps of an orphanage near the docks."

The woman moued then lifted a shoulder. "She do when the babe's pa threaten to toss 'er out on the street if she don't. The good trader didn't want his rich wife to find out his doxy bore his child—wifey held the purse strings, ya see."

Kiera suppressed a cackle. So her father wasn't some poor sailor, but a merchant not decent enough to support his bastard daughter. She grimaced as the woman adjusted her bosom. And this woman was *no* mermaid—or a dead princess from a distant isle. Kiera arched her brows at her. "Why have you appeared after twenty-eight years?"

The woman fluttered her lashes. "Yer pa died a few years back, and I didn't know where ya got to until I saw ya at that fancy bonfire with the king last month." She smirked. "Sure doin' well for yerself."

Kiera twisted the Vireni betrothal ring. The woman must

have been one of the beggars lurking outside Lady Blaine's fire ball. Thank the Goddess it had been too dark for the guests to see her resemblance to their king's betrothed. Kiera almost shuddered. If they had, Devon's romantic tale about her parentage would have exploded, and all of court would have savaged her.

Kiera eyed the smirking woman. Doubtless she wanted money. She could have easily found her daughter at the orphanage where she'd left her, but she'd never bothered until she saw her daughter acting as the king's betrothed. Kiera suppressed a snort. Not that she could give the woman any money. All her apparent wealth belonged to Devon. But even if she had any, the greedy woman would bleed her until she'd none. Extortioners always did.

Wren coughed then nodded at Hawke. "Take Bobbi back to the townhouse. Kiera needs time to reflect."

Bobbi leaned toward Kiera and drawled, "Be seein' ya." Then she wrapped her dark cloak about herself and let Hawke lead her from the study.

Once they were alone, Wren sighed. "Bobbi visited the orphanage shortly after our luncheon at Annalise's. She said she'd attempted to enter the palace to no avail."

Kiera shuddered. Thank the Goddess no one at court had seen her there either.

Wren shook her head. "After Bobbi found us, I hid her at our townhouse and bought her whatever she asked to keep her there." She grasped Kiera's hand. "I'm sorry I didn't tell you about her sooner, but Hawke and I wanted to investigate her first. And I couldn't disclose her in a letter."

Kiera squeezed Wren's hand then slipped free. No wonder Wren had requested she visit *alone*. She swallowed and rose. "I must go."

Wren enfolded her in a tight embrace. "I'll see you soon."

On the ride back to the palace, Kiera stared out the carriage window, her eyes pricking and chest hollow. Goddess, she was such a fool. How could she have ever believed that *she* could actually marry Devon? The bastard daughter of a greedy whore and a dead cad could *never* become queen. No matter how much she loved him and he might love her, all they could ever be was temporary lovers. Sometimes not even the deepest love could be heeded.

CHAPTER 43

When Kiera returned to the palace, Devon strode into her chambers then froze. Pale and still, she was sitting on her sofa and twisting her betrothal ring. His heart squeezed. *What* had happened? Aching to wrap her in his arms, he forced a smile and sat beside her. "How was the orphanage? Was Wren's play about a walleyed wyvern?"

Kiera started. "No, 'twas about a boy who befriended a night-mara stallion."

When she fell silent again, he leaned forward and took her hand. She'd not effused about the orphans like normal. Something was definitely troubling her. "Did something happen?"

Kiera slipped her hand free then flashed a glittering smile. "Not really. I was simply pondering the apprenticeship program Wren and Hawke just started. They've only been managing the orphanage for a month, but they're already surpassing me."

Devon frowned. That couldn't be why she was so upset. What was she hiding? But from her smile, she wasn't ready to share whatever it was. He sighed. Would she ever learn to trust him? Please let demonstrating his steadfast love succeed soon. He forced a smile and asked, "Are you anticipating the Landcastles' ball?"

Kiera shrugged. "I suppose." She glanced at the clock on the mantel. "We'd best change if we don't wish to be late."

He nodded then kissed her palm beneath her betrothal ring. Perhaps 'twould hearten her, at least a little.

During the ball that evening, Devon kept glancing at Kiera. No one else could probably see her bright smiles were fake, but he could. And in his bed later, she clung to him, but her eyes shimmered with tears.

His chest tight, he pulled back to scrutinize her. She appeared almost desperate, as if he'd vanish like a shattered mirage. So he risked asking, "Is everything all right?"

Kiera flashed the same glittering smile from before. "Of course. You're making love to me." Then she pulled down his head and kissed him.

Although his blood quickened, Devon stiffened and made himself return her kiss. Perhaps making love to her would soothe her. Then maybe she'd talk to him. So he made love to her with all the love burning inside him. But she remained silent. He sighed as he wrapped her in his arms, and they succumbed to slumber.

OVER THE FOLLOWING DAYS, Kiera continued feigning cheer, but her smiles faded whenever she thought no one was watching. Yet she never told Devon what was troubling her. He began making love to her even more often because 'twas the only time she appeared carefree. And she barely slept—whenever he awoke, she was lying stiff beside him and pretending to sleep, and faint shadows reappeared beneath her eyes like before she'd begun staying at the palace.

Yet regardless of her melancholy, Kiera still continued being the perfect queen as the days grew colder, and outdoor court events ceased. Nearly all at court accepted her now, even Lord and Lady Winston, despite their son's banishment. Only Lord and Lady Greysnowe continued denigrating her. And at the recent council meeting, many of the councilors appeared pleased her education initiative would start in the new year. Then during petitions at court afterward, several petitioners requested her decision rather than his. So everyone in Calatini accepted her as their future queen, except for Kiera herself. When would she finally realize the truth?

Kiera's riding lessons with Moonbud were progressing as well. After her third lesson since they'd become lovers, she pursed a tight smile as they began luncheon and said, "Moonbud said she'll begin teaching me to jump on our next ride."

Devon forced himself to swallow the savory venison stew clogging his throat. Once the nightmara queen-heir taught her to jump, she and Kiera would negotiate the treaty. And Kiera wasn't even close to accepting him in truth. He echoed her tight smile. "Exciting."

Kiera grimaced and sipped her tea. "As long as I don't fall."

His chest squeezing, he touched her hand across the tea table to encourage her. "Moonbud shan't allow you to be injured."

Kiera's navy eyes flickered, and she shifted from his touch to take a roll. "I'm not worried about that. I can't appear a fool before the nightmara while I'm attempting to prove my worth as queen."

Devon sighed. Even if Kiera fell a hundred times, she was still the lady meant to be his queen, and Moonbud knew that. He made himself smile and eat more stew. "I doubt Moonbud cares how well you ride. Your lessons were an excuse to become acquainted."

Kiera snorted as she buttered her roll. "Unlikely. Moonbud repeats her lessons until I can perform them without thought. So she *must* care." She shook her head. "Sometimes it feels as if my riding lessons shall never end."

He almost winced. Not because Moonbud truly cared about Kiera's riding, but because she was attempting to provide the delay he'd requested. He gritted a warm smile. "Riding requires time to master."

Kiera sighed. "True, but when I agreed to act as your betrothed, I never realized 'twould take so long to negotiate the treaty. I thought I'd be back at the orphanage within a month, and 'tis been nearly two."

Devon stiffened. Was *that* what was troubling her? Did she feel a failure because she'd not succeeded yet? Or had seeing the orphans reminded her how much she missed them? What if she decided to leave him for them? He leaned forward. "Don't worry about the delay. 'Tis entirely my fault. Moonbud just requires extra reassurance, since I wasn't even betrothed when they arrived."

Kiera straightened and almost smiled. "I'm sure you're right."

He eyed her as she began her roll. Had he reassured her, or was she still pretending? Perhaps a distraction would help. He flashed a grin. "Did Wren ever tell you about learning to ride the pony who jumped sideways?"

When Kiera shook her head, he began the humorous tale from one of his summers with his cousins. He relaxed as she smiled, a genuine one, at his description of when he'd fallen into a scummy pond after attempting to jump a stream. Perhaps more such tales would help her realize being royal didn't require being perfect. And maybe *then* she'd see she was meant to be his queen.

KIERA WAS STILL relaxed when they shared dinner before the Duke of Oakmoor's soiree that evening. His humorous tale had definitely helped. So Devon described when the now deceased Orandian ambassador had vomited on him at one of the duke's soirees, and she was smiling again by their cinnaspice apple sweetice. He grinned as he changed clothes. Hopefully, soon she'd forget whatever was troubling her.

When he returned to escort her to the carriage, he beamed at her elegant and strategic gown. Navy in the fitted bodice, the arachne silk faded to blue, purple, or teal at the high waist and flowing sleeves, and those colors faded into white at the hems. He wrapped his arms around her from behind. "Echoing your betrothal ring again, I see."

As he kissed her neck, Kiera hummed but stepped from his arms and smoothed her gown. "I wanted to remind the ambassadors at the duke's soiree that I'm your betrothed."

Devon captured her hand and twirled her back against his chest. Tingling warmth flooded him. "I could kiss you a few times in front of them to reinforce that."

Kiera tensed and arched her brows. "A soiree hosted by the Minister of Foreign Relations shall be too formal for public kisses. Even if he is a rakehell known for his flirtations."

He lowered his head until their lips almost touched, and his body hardened as her clean lavender scent surrounded him. Goddess, he'd never get enough of her. "How about I make sure you appear well-kissed when we arrive instead?"

Kiera tsked. "Sometimes you're more of a rakehell than even the Duke of Oakmoor."

His chest light, Devon smiled and rumbled, "You inspire me, remember?" Then he kissed her like a lonely griffin meeting his newfound mate.

Kiera stilled then hungrily returned his kiss before drawing back. "We'd better leave. Surely I appear well-kissed now."

He grinned when they left the royal wing with their guards. If only they could skip the soiree. "We should kiss in the carriage to make sure."

Kiera's mouth twitched as she shook her head. "Rakehell."

Yet when they sat in the carriage, she drew him beside her then eyed him for a long moment before brushing a kiss against his lips. His heart fluttered as he deepened their kiss. 'Twas the first she'd initiated since her visit to the orphanage. They spent the short ride kissing, and both sighed when the carriage halted.

As he helped her alight, Devon murmured in her ear, "We'll continue this later."

Kiera swallowed and looked down. "We can't."

He stiffened while he escorted her up the front steps with their guards close behind. Why did she appear guilty at their ravenous kisses? "Why not?"

Kiera blushed as they entered Oakmoor House. "I'll explain later. A councilor's townhouse isn't the place to discuss it."

Devon forced a nod, a chill prickling his neck. Her refusal must be related to whatever was troubling her.

Then he and Kiera exchanged a glance at Lady Blaine greeting guests with the Duke of Oakmoor. The husband-hunting countess had deserted Lord Ravenstone for a rakehell who'd never sought marriage? Perhaps the arrival of Lord Ravenstone's mother had deterred Lady Blaine.

The Duke of Oakmoor flashed a suave smile when they reached him. "Good evening, your majesties. I hope you'll enjoy tonight."

As Devon and Kiera nodded, Lady Blaine leaned forward. "The Duke of Oakmoor's events are always *so* exclusive." She arched her brows at Kiera. "No cads like Mr. Winston to avoid." She caressed the duke's arm. "I was elated when the duke requested I act as hostess."

The duke kissed Lady Blaine's hand with a smoldering glance. "Your talents as hostess are renowned throughout court, so my soiree can only be enhanced by your aid. I do pity Lord Ravenstone though..."

Devon and Kiera exchanged another glance. Flirting or courtship? Perhaps the rakehell duke had decided 'twas time to produce an heir.

Lady Blaine chuckled. "Don't waste your pity on him." She glanced behind Devon and Kiera then smiled. "Evening, Lady Annalise. Where are your parents?"

Lady Annalise glided forward beside Kiera. "They're in the hall conversing with Lady Morwynne."

Devon suppressed a sigh as they continued into the drawing room. Wonderful. The one councilor who *definitely* didn't like Kiera's education initiative was talking to her only detractors at court. He stiffened when the trio joined them while he was handing Kiera and Lady Annalise flutes of sparkling wine. Although Lady Morwynne's nod encompassed both him and Kiera, the Greysnowes only nodded at him. Such disrespect to their future queen was inexcusable.

Lady Morwynne smirking beside him, Lord Greysnowe said to his daughter without glancing at Kiera, "You squander entirely too much time with this Ravenstone pawn."

As Lady Greysnowe nodded, Devon clenched his sparkling wine. How dare they? He opened his mouth to retort but halted at Kiera's gentle touch on his arm.

Kiera beamed at Lady Annalise's parents. "I'd not call enjoying time with a friend squandering."

Her white-blonde hair shimmering, Lady Annalise lifted her chin. "Neither would I."

Devon blinked. Had the peaceable lady just defied her parents in public? Kiera's friendship *was* helping her.

Lady Greysnowe moued. "You should be dancing. 'Tis unfortunate Lady Blaine landed the elusive Duke of Oakmoor. He's eminently suitable, even if he invited the treacherous Ravenstones to his soiree."

Lady Annalise's cerulean eyes darkened. "I don't want to *land* an *eminently suitable* gentleman."

As Devon gaped and Kiera smiled, Lady Greysnowe turned to her husband and said, "Why did the Goddess curse us with such an obstinate child?"

Her smile vanishing, Kiera took Lady Annalise's arm. "Good fortune, perhaps? Come, Annalise." She drew her friend across the room.

Devon strode after them, warmth filling his chest. Typical that the Greysnowes' treatment of their daughter irked Kiera more than their treatment of herself.

Halfway across the room, Lord and Lady Weston beamed and waylaid them. Then Lady Weston embraced Kiera and drew her aside to discuss their granddaughters.

While Kiera and the Westons talked, Devon remained beside Lady Annalise. Perhaps she knew what was troubling Kiera. He murmured, "Have you noticed a secret weighing on Kiera recently?"

Lady Annalise fingered the heart-shaped firegem flickering in the hollow of her throat. "I don't believe so."

He sighed. Kiera's melancholy must be too subtle for even her friends to see, so seeking advice from them wouldn't help. But perhaps Kiera would finally reveal what was troubling her tonight.

To hasten that, when the first guests began to leave, Devon took Kiera back to the palace. They sat beside each other in the carriage but didn't touch or speak during the short ride. Whatever she had to share would be best done when they were alone in her chambers.

After escorting Kiera there, he yanked on his dressing gown then returned to her. His stomach fluttered. Please let her revelation be something he could help her solve and not involve leaving him.

Wrapped in a thick dressing gown and almost frowning, Kiera handed him his mentha tea without a word.

Sitting beside her on the sofa, Devon swallowed but nodded his thanks. She'd only worn flowing nightgowns since they'd become lovers. Why would her revelation alter that?

Kiera shifted then murmured into her teacup, "So we can't continue our kisses in the carriage because, er... my courses started this afternoon."

Almost flushing, he shifted as well. *That* was what was troubling her? At least it didn't involve leaving him. He frowned. But she'd been melancholy the past few days. Maybe visiting the orphanage had reminded her about children, which had in turn reminded her about her upcoming courses. His heart twisted. Did she fear he'd not want her if they couldn't make love? Or were her courses painful? He sipped his mentha tea to brace himself. "Are they paining you?"

Her gaze still lowered, Kiera sighed. "No, they never do. I just can't make love right now. You should return to your chambers once you finish your tea."

He nodded, his throat easing. Thank the Goddess she wasn't in pain. "I see no reason to return to my empty bed. I'd much rather share yours."

Kiera raised her head and stared at him. "Even without making love?"

Devon held her gaze and nodded again. She *had* feared he'd not want her. "I'll miss making love, of course, but sleeping beside you is almost as nice." He shrugged. "We might even recoup some sleep." Which she needed after her recent sleepless nights.

Kiera blinked. "You're too wonderful to be real."

A blush warmed his cheeks. He wasn't. Just desperately in love. But revealing that would fluster her, and she needed comfort right now. He drained his teacup. "Nonsense. Shall we retire?"

Kiera smiled and set down her teacup to take his outstretched hand.

Light suffusing his chest, Devon kissed her palm then led her to bed. He smiled as she curled against him and fell asleep. Relaxed and trusting him at last. Hopefully, soon she'd realize he loved her and accept his heartfelt proposal.

CHAPTER 44

Kiera woke the following morning with Devon curled around her like a griffin around his mate. Tears pricked her eyes as she nestled closer. From the way he held her, he definitely loved her as she loved him. If only she could remain with him forever, but someone would soon discover Bobbi, and his romantic tale would explode. She must negotiate the Nightmara-Calatini Treaty then return to the orphanage before that happened. Although leaving would surely shatter her.

As her eyes burned and chest clenched, she gulped then quashed her tears. If she began to cry, she'd never stop, and Devon would certainly ask why she was crying. Yet she couldn't possibly tell him about Bobbi. He was too wonderful to think any less of her, but coming from such a greedy creature was mortifying. At least Jane, along with Peter and Mary, had raised her instead—although she and Jane weren't related by blood, the warmhearted orphanage matron was her true mother and who she'd emulated her entire life.

Devon stirred behind her then pressed a kiss against her cheek. "How did you sleep?"

Warmth swelling in her chest, Kiera turned and brushed dark-brown hair from his face. Dear Goddess, she loved him. Not that she could ever tell him when they must part after the nightmara treaty was renewed. "Well, thanks to you."

Devon sighed then flashed a smile. "Good. Shall we have breakfast? Perhaps we should request beefsteak and shokolat along with our regular food."

She chuckled as her stomach rumbled. It obviously approved. "Yes, please."

Devon's tenderness continued throughout her courses. He acted content simply to hold her every night, and he made sure she ate and slept well. Plus, he requested shokolat for breakfast and their drink before bed, and the sweet, rich beverage always soothed her cravings. If she hadn't already loved him, his solicitude would have made her fall in love. The only time it bothered her was before her next nightmara ride.

Over breakfast, Devon coughed then gestured with his shokolat. "Considering your courses, should you attempt learning to jump today?"

Kiera narrowed her eyes as she sipped her shokolat. Her courses didn't make her an invalid. And negotiating the nightmara treaty had been delayed too long already. "No, I should be fine. Besides, my courses end today."

She softened when he grasped her hand then said, "Just wanted to check." He kissed her palm. "You're so dedicated I sometimes fear you'll forget to care for yourself."

She chuckled and caressed his jaw. The dear man. "I could say the same about you."

He flashed a wry smile and kissed her palm again. "'Tis why we can't resist each other."

Her heart twisting, Kiera swallowed and extracted her hand. And their dedication was why she would eventually leave. She was too dedicated to him and Calatini to remain when they both deserved a worthier queen. And he was too dedicated to stop her when he knew the same, even if he did love her. She forced herself to smile. "No doubt."

After breakfast, she met Annalise, and they strode to the nightmara stables. They were halfway there when Annalise coughed then said, "At the Duke of Oakmoor's soiree, King Devon asked if I'd noticed a secret weighing on you."

Kiera almost winced. She should have realized he'd seen her continued upset over Bobbi, even if he'd not asked about it since the first day. She eyed Annalise. "What did you tell him?"

Annalise shrugged, fingering her heart-shaped firegem. "What could I tell him? I knew 'twas my secret weighing on you." A grimace flitted across her ice-perfect face. "I feel so guilty for coming between you and the king."

Kiera twisted the Vireni betrothal ring. Bobbi had made her forget about her friend's secret. Annalise being a soul healer was trivial compared to the woman who could make acting as Devon's betrothed impossible. She managed a smile. "You didn't. If you'd not healed me, I never could have made love to him that night."

Annalise gaped at her. "You? Oh..."

Kiera blushed. "I know our betrothal is only temporary, but I couldn't resist him any longer." That should make Annalise assume their hopeless affair was what had been weighing on her.

Annalise released her pale-electrum necklace with a sigh. "Because you love him."

Her blush burning her cheeks, Kiera inclined her head. Doubtless her love was obvious to anyone who knew her, including Devon. Hopefully, she'd not confess her love aloud to him—'twould only make their inevitable separation hurt more. But to prevent that, she should go visit Wren and confess everything. Since Wren already knew about Bobbi, she'd understand why Kiera couldn't stay with Devon, regardless of their love.

• • •

So after a successful first lesson about jumping, which involved nothing more than trotting over poles, Kiera ate luncheon with Devon then headed to the orphanage while he met with the Duke of Osbourne.

Once she arrived, Peter grinned and hugged her. "Another royal visit so soon?"

She tsked while returning the burly porter's embrace. Silly man. Then she instructed her guards to remain with him and strode to the matron's study to see Wren.

When Kiera knocked and entered, Wren glanced up from her papers then beamed. "Kiera! What brings you by? Did your hectic social rounds magically cease?"

Kiera grimaced as she sat in a chair before the desk. If only. "No, I skipped the Merrileas' shokolat party so I could visit." She leaned forward, her chest tightening. "Is Bobbi here?"

Wren wrinkled her nose. "No, she's still hidden at our townhouse, spending gold as if 'twere copper."

Kiera sat back with a sigh. Good. Then she needn't deal with extortion while confessing everything to Wren.

But before she could, Mary bustled in with a tea tray. The plump cook set the tray on the desk then hugged Kiera. "You look tired."

Kiera shrugged while Wren began serving their tea. "Acting as queen is even more taxing than being an orphanage matron." Especially while worrying when court would discover her true parentage.

Mary tsked. "I'm sure you're surpassin' everyone's expectations, other than your own. Like always." With that, she bustled from the study.

Once they were alone, Wren narrowed her eyes at Kiera over her teacup. "Something is different about you. I noticed last week, but Bobbi arrived before I could ask."

Kiera blushed as she sipped her tea. After all her claims that their betrothal was temporary, Wren might be surprised by her confession. "Devon and I became lovers."

However, Wren simply nodded. "Ah..." Looking remarkably like her husband, she flashed an impish grin and devoured a sweet biscuit. "Who seduced whom?"

Kiera blushed harder but shrugged. Wren acted as if she and Devon becoming lovers had been inevitable. No doubt her clever friend had noticed her love long before she'd admitted it to herself. "I did."

Arching a brow, Wren tilted her head. "What made you finally realize your love and act on it?"

A touch of that day's boiling agony echoing through her, Kiera shuddered and gulped some tea. "Moonbud and I were stung by melissae on our ride in the royal forest. After nearly dying, I knew I must demonstrate my love before 'twas too late."

Wren blanched. "Esme the Great's melissae hive, dear Goddess. How *did* you survive?"

Kiera leaned forward. "Annalise is a soul healer and healed us. But don't tell anyone, not even Hawke. She begged me to not tell Devon, so 'tis secret."

Blinking, Wren echoed, "Annalise is a *soul healer*? They're so rare I can't name another living today." Then she shook her head and sipped her tea. "Although it makes sense. Soul healers are always female, and, according to legend, many are irresistible. Plus, the Greysnowes are descended from Esme the Great, who was a powerful soul healer. As her descendants, the Greysnowes produce soul healers every generation or two. In fact, 'twas a soul healer who caused the Greysnowe-Ravenstone feud. And knowing her parents, I'm not surprised Annalise has kept her powers secret."

Kiera frowned. Annalise and her family were descended from Calator's mentor? The duchess hadn't mentioned that *or* the cause behind their centuries-long feud with the Ravenstones. "So the melissae hive belonged to Annalise's ancestor? No wonder she could calm them."

Wren hummed as she devoured another sweet biscuit. "Not exactly. She could calm them because she's a soul healer. The

Goddess made them the defenders of the melissae, so 'tis said they can communicate directly with them."

Kiera inclined her head. From what Annalise had said, she clearly could. "Is that why she could heal us too?"

Wren hummed again. "No, soul healers can heal nearly any ailment by meshing their soul with whomever they're healing."

Kiera gaped at her friend. Annalise had meshed their *souls*? Her powers were *definitely* different than an ordinary witch healer's, who only used spells to heal.

Wren frowned and leaned forward. "Did Annalise heal you or Lady Moonbud first?"

Kiera blinked, her skin prickling at her friend's palpable concern. "Me. Why?"

Wren eyed her as she drained her tea. "Perhaps *that's* why you seem different, not seducing Devon." When Kiera opened her mouth to ask Wren to explain, Wren continued, "The first time a soul healer heals a fatal ailment, she forms a lifelong soul-bond with whomever she heals."

Tingling skittering through her, Kiera rubbed her chest. No wonder Wren had appeared concerned. Such a bond would surely complicate matters. "I don't feel connected to Annalise in any way besides friendship. And gratitude, of course."

Wren relaxed. "If you'd a soulbond, you'd know it. 'Tis said the pull is irresistible." She shook her head. "Annalise must be soulbound to someone else—but who?"

Kiera pursed her lips then finished her tea. "I don't recall her being drawn to anyone, so that must be secret too. Doubtless 'tis someone her parents wouldn't accept, a childhood servant or tenant, perhaps?"

Wren grimaced and nodded. "That seems likely." Then she sighed. "Poor Annalise. With such secrets, no wonder she's so reserved." She leaned forward. "But enough troubles. Let's discuss a happier matter. Have you and Devon decided to have a private wedding before your public one? A royal wedding shall take an age to plan. Especially since yours shall involve a coronation as well."

Weight compressing her chest, Kiera tensed and lifted her chin. Of course, Wren would assume that. "Just because we became lovers doesn't mean our betrothal is genuine. I'm still returning here once the nightmara treaty is renewed."

Wren gawked at her. "But you love each other. You should marry."

Kiera glared back. How could Wren be so obtuse? "We *can't*. Someone shall soon discover Bobbi, and court shall never accept a queen with such sordid parentage." When Wren began to protest, Kiera leapt to her feet. Discussing her impossible love for Devon hurt too much. "I must return to the palace."

Back at the palace, her heart squeezed when Devon joined her for dinner. If only Wren's assumption were possible. Too bad he wasn't the country squire she'd believed at first—given their deep love, she'd risk marrying him if he was. But her marrying the king would harm Calatini, and she couldn't risk that.

Despite her aching chest, she managed a bright smile when he asked about her visit to the orphanage. She clung to her smile during the concert they attended that evening and their shokolat before bed, but tears pricked her eyes again as he curled around her and they drifted into slumber. If only...

The following day, Kiera remained cheerful throughout the council meeting and petitions at court. If not for the threat of Bobbi being discovered, such duties would no longer trouble her. She could now handle the intricacies of court with ease.

Plus, her courses had ended, so she and Devon could finally make love again. She blushed as she turned her arachne silk ball-gown cream with ivy the same green as his eyes. Hopefully, they'd not stay long at the Magehavens' ball. Although she did want to see Annalise first. Now that she fully understood her friend's secret, maybe she could find some way to help.

Yet when they arrived, Annalise wasn't there, so Kiera approached her parents, but the Greysnowes coldly refused to tell her why. Her stomach tightened. Please let Annalise be well. She'd write to check, but Annalise's parents would probably destroy her note unopened. Shoving aside her concern, Kiera turned to Devon with a coy smile. Since Annalise wasn't here, they might as well return to the palace and start the exciting part of the evening.

CHAPTER 45

*D*evon's heart quickened when Kiera slanted him a coy smile after the Greysnowes had rudely ignored her questions about Annalise. Since her courses had ended yesterday, that smile must be an invitation to make love again, and she was clearly as eager as he. She leaned toward him and murmured, "Shall we go?"

He forced himself to nod and calmly escort her from the ball instead of tossing her over his shoulder. A king, even one desperately in love with his queen, couldn't behave so scandalously. But as soon as they leapt into the carriage, he pulled her into his arms and captured her mouth in a ravenous kiss. At last, thank the Goddess. When the carriage halted, he swept her to his chambers, and they made love for half the night.

And when they woke late the following morning, they remained in bed, making love for most of the day. Fortunately, Mia and Simon brought them a tray of cold meat, cheese, and rolls around noon, so they didn't starve. But they did miss Lady Morwynne's salon that afternoon.

They exchanged a laughing glance when Simon returned an hour before dinner and began preparing a bath then mentioned Mia was preparing one as well. Clearly, their servants had decided they should rise. So after a lingering kiss, Kiera slipped from bed and returned to her chambers to dress for tonight's pantomime. Devon sighed and did the same.

Fortunately, the pantomime was brief, and no one joined them in the royal box since Lady Annalise was still missing and he asked their guards to only admit family or someone bringing dire news. So soon, they were ensconced in the royal wing again.

Tingling flooding him, Devon sat beside Kiera on her sofa. A bottle of sparkling wine in one hand, she was reading a note in the other. Interesting. "What's that?"

Kiera glanced up and set aside the note. "An apology from Annalise for abandoning me the past few evenings. She's felt unwell." An adorable frown creased her brow. "I wonder if she'll be well enough for tomorrow's nightmara ride."

He wrapped an arm about her shoulders to comfort her. "I'm sure she'll recover soon. Lady Annalise is rarely ill. But if she isn't, I can join you on your ride."

Kiera quirked a brow. "Would Moonbud allow that?"

Devon chuckled. The nightmara queen-heir would probably snort when she saw him. "If I swore to not negotiate the treaty." He nodded at the sparkling wine. "May I?" When she nodded, he took the bottle then whistled as he read the label. "'Tis an exquisite vintage."

Kiera flashed a wry smile. "Annalise knows my weakness for it."

He grinned, warmth filling his chest. Her delight wasn't a weakness, 'twas irresistible. "She's a dear friend indeed, to send such a vintage as an apology."

Her navy eyes gleaming, Kiera hummed. "We should drink it instead of the khamomile tea Mia brought."

Devon arched his brows and muffled a laugh. Definitely irresistible. Yet to tease her, he said, "But we've no flutes."

Kiera winked at him. "I'm willing to drink sparkling wine from teacups if you are."

His mouth twitching, he tsked. He'd drink it however she liked. "A connoisseur would say that spoils a fine vintage."

Kiera smiled and plucked two teacups from the tea table. "Nonsense. Open the sparkling wine."

Devon heaved a feigned sigh. "If you insist." He popped open the sparkling wine and poured. As he handed her a teacup, he waggled his brows and toasted her. "To apologies from *dear* friends."

As he intended, Kiera began giggling.

While she giggled too hard to drink, he gulped half his teacup and grimaced. Although a prized vintage, the sparkling wine was almost bitter. Then the middle strand of his protection charm became molten gold and scorched his left wrist.

Goddess! The strand defending against poisons had been activated. He dashed Kiera's teacup from her lips. "No! Did you drink any?"

Kiera gaped at him, her gaze wide. "N-no..."

His pulse skittering, Devon flung aside his own teacup and crushed her in his arms. "Thank the Goddess!"

Kiera shoved his chest until he released her. "Devon, what was that about?"

Although he ached to embrace her again, he shuddered and pointed at the still-fiery strand on his bracelet. "That charm I showed you when I asked you to marry me. Only the top strand defends me from enchantments. The middle strand defends me from poisons."

Kiera blanched whiter than a wraith under the full moon. "So that sparkling wine was *poisoned*?"

Devon clasped her icy hands. "Yes." Goddess, he could have lost her. How could he have survived that? He kissed her palm beneath her betrothal ring. "I always worried what Father had seen in the Mirror of Wisdom to compel him to hire Lady Juliet then order her to create this charm for me. When you appeared at the summer masquerade, I knew the enchantment strand was so everyone would realize our... attraction was genuine.

But I hoped the poison strand was nothing more than a precaution."

Kiera shivered. "Which it clearly wasn't." She paused then asked, "What does the bottom strand do?"

He shrugged and kissed her palm again to reassure her. "'Tis a removable contraceptive charm. I never worried about that one."

Kiera snorted an almost laugh. "No wonder you didn't appear concerned when I mentioned pregnancy before." Her eyes drifted to the shattered teacups on the floor then the bottle on the tea table. "What are we to do about that sparkling wine?"

Fire flaring beneath his skin, Devon swallowed a growl. "First, we must speak with Lady Annalise." The serene and seemingly steadfast lady must have betrayed them. Perhaps she was more like her ambitious parents than he'd believed.

Kiera jerked her hands free. "Annalise had *nothing* to do with this."

He grunted. Of course, Kiera trusted her supposed friend. But the events didn't agree. "Yet she sent the sparkling wine. And her father met with assassins in the weeks before I introduced you to court."

Kiera blinked at him. "Lord Greysnowe did what?" Then she crossed her arms. "Regardless, Annalise would never harm *anyone*, let alone a dear friend. And she mightn't have even sent that sparkling wine. We've never exchanged notes, so I'd not recognize her writing. It could have come from someone pretending to be her."

Some of his tension eased. Hopefully, Kiera's faith in her friend would be proven true. She'd be hurt if it wasn't. "Even if Lady Annalise didn't send the sparkling wine, it must have come from someone at court. Only the affluent could afford that vintage."

Kiera leapt upright. "Annalise might know who'd impersonate her. I'll write asking her to join us for breakfast tomorrow."

Devon sighed. If only Lady Annalise could visit now, but 'twould scandalize court for an unwed lady to visit the royal wing so late, even with the future queen present. "Very well. I'll summon Lady Juliet to handle the poison."

While Kiera penned her note, he told their guards outside their door about the poisoning attempt then asked one to fetch the royal witch.

After handing her note to one of her guards, Kiera coughed and gestured toward her flowing nightgown. "Should I dress before Lady Juliet arrives?"

His heart fluttering, he drew her back to the sofa. "No, we should be fine." He flashed a playful leer to cheer her. "As long as I can resist kissing you. If I don't, we might be naked by the time she arrives."

Kiera tsked but cuddled against him as he wrapped an arm about her. Then she sighed and asked, "Do you think that poison was meant for just me or both of us?"

Devon echoed her sigh and kissed her dark-blonde curls. If only he could offer comfort, but 'twould be a lie. "Since 'twas sent to you, I suspect just you."

Kiera grimaced against his chest. "But who drinks a bottle of sparkling wine alone?"

He hummed. Sparkling wine *was* saved for balls and parties or private celebrations. "True, but we shan't know for certain until we unearth the poisoner."

Nestled together, they lapsed into silence as they waited for the royal witch.

Fortunately, Lady Juliet burst into Kiera's chambers within a quarter of an hour. Uncharacteristically disheveled, her modish gown was also marred by her bulging satchel. "What's this about poison?"

His jaw tightening, Devon nodded at the bottle on the table and forced a calm tone as he replied, "That sparkling wine there, as well as the shattered teacups on the floor, but test everything."

Lady Juliet dropped her satchel on the floor and extracted a silver pendant from inside. Straightening, she muttered a singsong chant while dangling the pendant by its chain. The pendant first swung toward the bottle of sparkling wine then drifted to the teacups but pointed nowhere else. After a moment, she coiled the pendant. "Only the sparkling wine was poisoned, although I can't tell by what. I'll need to take it back to my workroom to test it."

As Kiera sighed beside him, he nodded. "Collect whatever you need to unearth the poisoner as soon as possible." Then he'd try them for treason—no one should threaten the lady meant to be his queen.

Lady Juliet grimaced as she carefully collected the shattered teacups into a wooden box. "I'll try, but unless the poison is magical, tracing it shall be difficult."

Devon suppressed a scowl. Of course it was. "Do your best." He pointed at his protection charm, whose middle strand appeared ordinary gold again. "But first, create a protection charm like mine for Kiera."

Kiera drew back from his embrace to eye him. "Is that necessary?"

He held her gaze. Why was she questioning that? "While there's an unidentified poisoner about? Yes."

Lady Juliet sighed while she tucked her wooden box into her satchel. "Your protection charm was a difficult spell, your majesty. It shall take me at least a week to create one for Lady Kiera."

Devon grimaced. Wonderful, another delay to unearthing the poisoner. "I understand, but complete it as soon as possible." He turned to Kiera once the royal witch nodded. "In the meantime, before you eat or drink *anything*, I'll try it first to make sure 'tis safe."

As Lady Juliet tossed a glittering powder where the shattered teacups had been and muttered another singsong chant, Kiera sighed and arched her brows at him. "Poison can be in more than food and drink, you know."

Finishing her chant, Lady Juliet handed her silver pendant to Kiera. "I'll show you how to test for poisons with this. The enchantment on it should last until I have your protection charm." Once the royal witch showed Kiera how to use the pendant and took some blood for Kiera's protection charm, she added the bottle of sparkling wine to her bulging satchel. "I neutralized the poison with a general remedy, so the mess should be safe to clean."

After Lady Juliet left, Devon and Kiera stared at each other then she drawled, "Well, that was exciting."

He snorted. Terrifying, more like. "I hope never to be so *excited* again." He pulled her into his arms where she belonged. "Shall we retire now?"

Kiera drew his head down for a deep kiss before leading him to bed.

Since they both needed comfort, Devon made love to Kiera with tender passion then enfolded her in his arms. Keeping her close and safe, he drifted into slumber.

The following morning, they dressed then strolled to their private dining room. He relaxed when Kiera tested breakfast with Lady Juliet's pendant, and no poison tainted any of their food or drink. He threaded his fingers through hers and caressed her palm with his thumb as they waited for Lady Annalise.

When Lady Annalise finally trudged through the door, Devon stiffened and almost gaped. The most beautiful lady in Calatini looked *dreadful*—her porcelain skin was bloodless, dark shadows underscored her cerulean eyes, and her white-blonde hair was dull. Were her ravaged looks related to Kiera's poisoning attempt?

Kiera darted to her friend. "Annalise, are you ill?"

Lady Annalise eked a tremulous smile. "I fell ill a few days ago, but I'm recovering."

He narrowly eyed Lady Annalise as Kiera helped her to the table and said, "I'm sorry to disrupt your recovery."

Crumpling into her chair, Lady Annalise shook her head.

"Nonsense. Kiera wouldn't have written 'twas urgent unless it was."

As Kiera began to protest, Devon nodded and continued scrutinizing Lady Annalise. He'd not trust the icy beauty until she proved she'd nothing to do with Kiera's poisoning attempt. "And despite whatever Kiera may say now, it *is* urgent."

CHAPTER 46

Kiera almost scowled at Devon as she sat beside him. Must he treat Annalise so brusquely? Especially when she clearly wasn't well enough to handle it—she resembled the banshee she'd dressed as at the Harvestfete masquerade.

Yet Annalise only nodded and said, "Tell me."

Since her friend appeared like she'd collapse without sustenance, Kiera interjected before Devon could start, "We should begin breakfast first. I'm famished."

Annalise chuckled. "So am I. Could you pass the beefsteak?"

As Devon's brows rose, Kiera hummed then passed the platter and said, "Substantial food for this early." One that she and Devon had only requested during her courses.

Annalise shrugged and speared the largest beefsteak. "My family just allowed invalid fare while I was ill, and my body needs beefsteak to hasten my recovery."

Kiera and Devon exchanged a glance as they filled their plates. Mia and Simon must have brought the beefsteak for Annalise. So word of her illness had spread to the servants' quarters, even if most of court hadn't heard.

While everyone ate, Kiera kicked Devon's shin whenever he

opened his mouth to speak. Annalise needed some food in her before they revealed the poisoning attempt.

Once Annalise finished her beefsteak, she eyed them but continued eating. "Are we ever going to discuss your urgent matter?"

Kiera almost smiled when Devon arched his brows at her, silently saying she should start. She leaned toward Annalise. "Did you send me a bottle of sparkling wine to apologize for being ill the past few days?"

Her laden fork halfway to her mouth, Annalise blinked. "No..."

Kiera nodded as she extracted the note and passed it to Annalise. Surely she'd be able to decipher something from it. "This note, supposedly from you, came with the bottle."

Annalise set down her fork and frowned at the note. "I didn't write that. Why would anyone bother to impersonate me?"

Kiera suppressed a grimace, her chest sinking. From her frown, Annalise knew as little as they did and couldn't help unearth the poisoner.

Devon narrowed his eyes at Annalise. He obviously still suspected her. Ridiculous. "Because the sparkling wine was poisoned, *whoever* sent it knew Kiera would drink a gift from you."

Annalise paled, her gaze darting between Kiera and Devon. "Poisoned? Are you two well?"

Kiera smiled to calm her friend. "Yes, thanks to Devon's protection charm."

Annalise relaxed back into her chair. "Praise the Goddess."

Devon still narrowly eyed Annalise. "Any idea who sent that bottle?"

Kiera glowered at him. Annalise had nothing to do with the poisoned sparkling wine. Besides being her friend, Annalise was a soul healer, and murder violated a healer's most basic tenet.

But before Kiera could protest, Annalise stiffened and lifted her chin then asked, "Do you suspect me, your majesty?"

Kiera grasped Annalise's hand across the table to reassure her. "No, but you might know who could impersonate you."

As Kiera squeezed her hand, Annalise held Devon's gaze. Doubtless she read his suspicion. She leaned forward. "Given my parents' ambitions, I comprehend why you might suspect me, but I swear I'd never poison anyone, much less Kiera."

Devon inclined his head. "I suspect everyone right now."

Kiera almost humphed. Although endearing, his fierce protectiveness had led him astray this time.

Yet Annalise nodded back. "Understandable." She studied the note again. "The writing appears an imitation of mine, and few outside my family knew I was ill. But despite their faults, my family wouldn't poison our future queen."

Kiera sighed. Hopefully, Annalise was right about her family. She waved toward the platter of beefsteak. "The servants knew you were ill. The poisoner must have heard you were ill through them."

Annalise frowned but hummed. "I suppose. Are you protected from future attempts?" When Kiera nodded, Annalise squeezed her hand. "Good. Let me know if you ever need me."

Although Devon blinked, Kiera nodded and returned Annalise's squeeze. No doubt she was offering to heal any fatal wounds or ailments with her secret powers. "Of course."

Sighing, Annalise released Kiera's hand and rose. "I must return to bed. Unfortunately, I'm not well enough for our night-mara ride today. Perhaps next time."

Her throat tightening, Kiera rose as well and embraced her. "Rest well." She clearly needed that. Once Annalise swept a deep curtsy then trudged out, Kiera frowned at Devon. "You can't still suspect Annalise."

Devon sighed and tapped a finger on the table. "No, she was sincerely concerned for you. Her parents though..."

She grimaced and drained her tea. "Might be my poisoner. But so could several others at court. Although most are polite, there's no warmth behind it, and they hunt for my blunders to gossip about. And half the council still doesn't accept me, either openly like Lady Morwynne or behind their blank masks like the Duke of Osbourne."

Devon shook his head. "More at court like you greater than you realize. People adore gossiping about royals, no matter what they do. And I suspect most of the inscrutable councilors accept you but refuse to show it."

Kiera shrugged. Perhaps... But that someone would risk attempting to poison her and being tried for treason just proved a poor orphanage matron could never become queen. And no one at court knew about Bobbi. She swallowed. Or did they, and that's why they attempted to poison her?

Devon kissed her palm. "Lady Juliet shall unearth the poisoner as soon as she finishes your protection charm."

She forced a smile. But the royal witch had said that would take a week. Plus, she'd not sounded certain the poisoner could be traced with magic. Kiera worried her lip. Perhaps the veiled witch could manage it. After a moment, she sighed. No, trusting such a mysterious witch with a treasonous poisoning attempt wasn't prudent, especially if the veiled witch couldn't determine more than the royal witch. So what else could they do to unearth the poisoner?

Devon drew her upright. "I'll join you on your nightmara ride like I mentioned yesterday. With an unidentified poisoner about, I don't want you alone."

Kiera eyed their guards while she and Devon returned to their chambers to change into riding clothes. Alone? Since acting as his betrothed, she was never alone unless locked in the queen's chambers. But she'd enjoy riding with him, so she didn't protest.

As they strode to the nightmara stables with their guards following, she shoved the poisoning attempt into the deepest corner of her mind—Moonbud wouldn't negotiate with a future queen whose subjects were attempting to assassinate her before she was even crowned.

Thankfully, when they greeted her, Moonbud only snorted then asked, :*Where's Lady Annalise?*:

Kiera shrugged with a wry smile. "She's not feeling well, but I didn't wish to ride alone." Even if Devon *had* let her.

Devon inclined his head. "I swear not to negotiate the treaty."

Moonbud snorted again. :*Very well. Come on, we'll start with the poles again.*:

Kiera's second jumping lesson proceeded smoothly, then she and Devon returned to the palace and spent the afternoon handling state affairs. He never once left her side during the day, and he glowered at any food or drink until she tested it with Lady Juliet's pendant. After dinner, he swept her into his bed rather than attending the Linwicks' ball. She sighed as she returned his ravenous kisses. His fierce protectiveness and hunger were enthralling.

THE FOLLOWING DAY, Kiera remained in the queen's chambers until after dinner. She'd intended to attend Selena's art salon in the afternoon, but Devon had insisted he'd join her, so she stayed at the palace. The king attending an event for ladies would engender too much gossip.

When they attended Lady Ducharme's reception that evening, she couldn't help scrutinizing everyone as if they'd never met. One of them must be her poisoner. And although Devon remained close, her skin prickled the entire time. Plus, she couldn't risk the sparkling wine or other refreshments. Testing them with Lady Juliet's pendant would be too noticeable. Fortunately, they didn't stay long.

As they shared spiced cider before bed in the queen's chambers, Kiera sighed and nestled against Devon on the sofa. Living like this for the next week or more would be trying. Soon court would begin gossiping about their odd behavior, and constantly scrutinizing everyone was exhausting. She must hasten unearthing the poisoner. But how?

She inhaled a ragged breath when Devon's protection charm gleamed as he set down his cider. His father had known his son would need that charm after consulting the Mirror of Wisdom. She could do the same about her poisoner *and* Bobbi. But since using the powerful yet perilous mirror had killed his mother, Devon would never allow her to risk herself. Yet they needed answers.

So once Devon's breathing slowed into the steady rhythm of slumber, Kiera slid from his arms then silently donned her nightgown and dressing gown. Her stomach quivering, she lit the candle on the dressing table then pocketed a few hair pins to unlock the throne room door. She swallowed as she glanced back at Devon. Good, he was still asleep. With luck, he'd never notice she'd left.

The four guards flanking the door started and gripped their swords when she slipped from the queen's chambers, but she set her jaw and waved them to silence. She *must* consult the Mirror of Wisdom. She skulked down the hall with her two guards close behind.

At the throne room door, Kiera nibbled her lip and slid her hair pins into the lock. Thank the Goddess she'd learned how to pick locks as a child from another orphan. A true court lady would need to steal the key. She began sweating when the lock refused to open. She'd not picked a lock in years, so her meager skills had deteriorated. Would she ever unlock it?

When the door *finally* clicked open, she sighed and waved her guards to remain then slipped inside the throne room and latched the door. She twisted the Vireni betrothal ring as she approached the thrones. At night, the vast chamber was eerie—shadows pressed against her, and her steps echoed despite the plush carpet. Plus, she could almost feel the mirror watching.

Kiera shivered as she climbed the dais and eyed the white velvet curtain concealing the Mirror of Wisdom. Although never still, tonight it rippled like before an open window during a storm. She gulped a breath then drew aside the curtain.

A chill skittering across her skin, she eyed the Mirror of Wisdom. Even in her candle's dim light, its mahogany frame of crescent moon faces and flowing vines gleamed with an opalescent sheen. To avoid activating the mirror before deciding what to ask, she kept her gaze from the shimmering glass.

She should only ask one question for both her poisoner and Bobbi. The Mirror of Wisdom would draw its power from her, so it could kill her if her question was broad or she asked too many. And although her poisoner must be unearthed soon, asking about that wouldn't help with Bobbi. What she really must know was how to handle them both. She sighed. *Maybe* she could risk asking her poisoner's identity after her first question.

Kiera swallowed then looked at the shimmering glass and whispered, "Oh mighty mirror, show me what I must know to handle my poisoner and Bobbi."

She shivered again as the glass began glowing a milky white with a faint hum. Then her breath froze and her blood surged when an image of Lady Ducharme's well-equipped sparring hall appeared. She leaned forward to scrutinize the scene.

Her hand resting on her pommel, Lady Ducharme talked with young Lord Morwynne as they observed Lord Ravenstone crossing swords with a gentleman who resembled Annalise. It must be the nearly fatal duel between the count and Annalise's hellion younger brother, Lord Alexander, on last Summerday.

Kiera wobbled as the mirror turned white. Then her head whirled and pulse raced as a new image appeared. A black and brown spider the size of a cat was weaving an elaborate yet clear web. The scene swept back to show many other webs and villages dotting an isle amidst the vast ocean. At the largest village, a ship, The Blonde Nymph, was loading bundles of clear fabric onboard. Arachne silk, surely.

Her heart thundering and spots dancing before her eyes, she ripped her gaze from the mirror. Goddess! If she kept watching, she'd faint or die from angina. Risking a second question was impossible. She released the curtain then staggered to the queen's throne and collapsed.

Gasping, Kiera rubbed her chest. She'd asked about her poisoner first, and the first scene had only involved members of court, so that must be about handling her poisoner. But how could a duel five months ago help? Yet it must—imbued with the magic of nature, elves, and seers, the mirror had never once been proved wrong.

She shook her head. Regardless of the puzzling first scene, the second must be about Bobbi—exile to a distant isle *would* prevent further extortion or discovery. Since only Buford Leshane traded with that isle, she'd visit Hawke and request a meeting with his merchant friend.

Weak as a newborn angelkitten, she lurched to her feet and stumbled back to the queen's chambers with her guards following. Then she curled beside the mercifully still asleep Devon and plummeted into a death-like slumber.

CHAPTER 47

*A*fter Devon woke the following morning, he nuzzled Kiera's neck then kissed her, but she didn't stir. He drew back to eye her—although 'twas well after they normally rose, she appeared exhausted. To avoid waking her, he slipped from bed then read the novel on her bedside table. His chest tightened when she continued slumbering as still as a gnome during a stone nap. Something must be wrong. He leapt upright when she finally woke just before luncheon. "How are you feeling?"

Kiera stretched. "Starving." Her eyes flicked to the clock on the mantel. "Goddess, is that truly the time?"

He forced a calm nod as Mia burst in with a heaped luncheon tray. Once they were alone again, he arched his brows at Kiera. "Did attending the reception exhaust you, or did you have trouble sleeping?"

Kiera stirred her orange cucurbit bisque. "Neither." She glanced at him then lowered her gaze. "After you fell asleep, I asked the Mirror of Wisdom about my poisoner."

Devon tensed, his heart clenching. *How* could she have risked herself like that? Yet he swallowed his scold—from her downcast eyes she already knew how reckless she'd been. So he only said,

"You shouldn't have used that cursed mirror, but did you learn anything?"

Kiera winced. "Maybe. The mirror showed the duel between Lord Ravenstone and Annalise's brother, although I'm not certain why."

He narrowed his eyes and almost growled. "I am. The Mirror of Wisdom must be hinting the Greysnowes are involved in your attempted poisoning." But the genial Lord Ravenstone couldn't be.

Kiera frowned and began her orange cucurbit bisque again. "I suppose..." She sighed, and they fell silent as they devoured the rest of luncheon. Once they finished, she rubbed her brow. "I'm going to return to bed."

His stomach lurching, Devon wrapped her in his arms and kissed her. Goddess, let more sleep be enough for her to recover. Then he strode to his study but couldn't focus on state affairs. So after checking on Kiera and doubling her guards, he left to visit Aragon. Confiding the poisoning attempt to his friend might help settle him.

Sitting beside Selena on the sofa in the rear sitting room, Aragon lowered his book with a smile. "We've not seen much of you recently. Doubtless because you and Kiera succumbed to your attraction at last."

Devon blushed as Selena giggled then murmured, "Yes, the looks you two exchanged at the duchess's art gala were ardent." She arched a brow. "Have you confessed your love yet?"

His blush flaring, Devon shifted in his chair. "Not yet. But she's not confessed her love either. Recent matters have distracted us."

Aragon frowned and leaned forward. "The Magehaven ore again? You mentioned nothing at the last council meeting."

Devon grimaced. If only. "No, the evening after that, someone at court sent Kiera a poisoned bottle of sparkling wine." When Aragon and Selena both gasped, he reassured them, "She's fine thanks to my protection charm, but we're waiting for Lady Juliet to unearth the poisoner."

Aragon shuddered. "Goddess, no wonder you've avoided court events lately. Just let us know if we can help."

Devon sighed and relaxed slightly. He could always count on his steadfast friends to offer support.

Her freckled face pale, Selena rubbed her rounded stomach. "We'll divert court gossip from your unusual behavior as much as possible. Can we tell the duchess so she can help too?"

Devon nodded with a faint smile. That should keep the poisoner ignorant of their hunt. "Please do."

Settled enough to focus because of his friends' support, Devon left soon after and returned to his study to handle state affairs. Then he joined Kiera for dinner, but they skipped the young Duke of Golddell's musical evening because she was still weary. And for the first time since her courses, he didn't make love to her but simply wrapped her in his arms.

THE FOLLOWING MORNING, Kiera woke Devon with a hungry kiss then proceeded to seduce him. As they lay entwined afterward, he grinned and kissed her riotous curls. She'd recovered from using the Mirror of Wisdom. Thank the Goddess.

Yet they still had her poisoner to unearth, so during breakfast he offered to join her nightmara ride again, but she frowned and said Annalise had written she could ride again. He suppressed a smile as she sailed out for her nightmara ride. Yes, definitely recovered.

Then as they rode to the Duchess of Wildewall's ball that evening, Kiera lifted her chin and said, "I need to drink some sparkling wine tonight."

Devon scowled. Until her poisoner was found or she had her protection charm, she couldn't risk not testing her food and drink. "Using Lady Juliet's pendant is too noticeable."

Kiera squeezed his hand. "Perhaps you could test my drink before you give it to me?"

He stared at her and snorted. Such odd behavior would be noticed as well. "Why do you *need* to drink anything?"

Kiera blushed and shifted beside him. "After our nightmara ride, Annalise mentioned her parents had asked her if I was with child because we haven't attended many court events recently and I've not drunk sparkling wine at those we had. I suspect the rest of court is gossiping as well."

Devon almost chuckled. Of course they were. When she glared, he coughed and replied, "That gossip shall die as soon as you've your protection charm from Lady Juliet and you can drink at court events again."

Kiera poked his chest. "Fine. But I'll send anyone who hints I'm pregnant to you, so *you* can answer them."

Warmth flooding his chest, he captured her hand and kissed her palm. He couldn't wait until he could tell everyone she was pregnant. "If you like."

Then the carriage halted, and he escorted her inside Wildewall House with their guards following. After greeting their hostess, they circulated the ballroom, and he listened for insinuations about Kiera being pregnant but heard none. Perhaps 'twas only the Greysnowes who were gossiping.

Midway through, he arched his brows when Lady Annalise and her brother approached them. The hellion had been notably absent from court events since almost killing Lord Ravenstone. And although not bleak like after that Summerday duel, the young lord's expression was much more serious than it had been at the start of the season.

Her icy beauty restored, Lady Annalise beamed at Kiera. "Evening. Kiera, allow me to introduce my brother, Lord Alexander Greysnowe."

Kiera smiled at Lord Alexander. "A pleasure finally to meet the imp who dared dip Annalise's hair in ink growing up. I'm surprised tonight is the first we've met."

Devon suppressed a laugh. Ink? Ruining their daughter's perfect beauty must have infuriated the Greysnowes. No wonder they often watched their son like broody basilisks.

Lord Alexander shrugged, his blue eyes flickering. "Much to Mother and Father's dismay, I've decided most court events are too dull to attend." He smirked at his sister. "I only attended tonight because Annalise begged me. She didn't want to be saddled with a bounder on her first evening out since her illness."

As Devon blinked at Lord Alexander's candor, Lady Annalise stiffened and elbowed her brother. "Alex! If you attended more often, you'd remember to leash your tongue."

Devon and Kiera exchanged a smile when Lord Alexander arched his brows and drawled, "Why? Their majesties are your friends, aren't they?"

Her white-blonde hair shimmering, Lady Annalise leaned forward. "Yes, but those who might overhear are not."

As Lord Alexander shrugged and Lady Annalise glared back, Devon and Kiera exchanged another smile. Sibling squabbles. Hopefully, one day they'd be blessed enough to have those to mediate.

Then the Greysnowes swept over, and once again, they nodded at Devon but ignored Kiera.

Fire flaring beneath his skin, Devon forced himself to smile at them. The Greysnowes *must* be involved in attempting to poison Kiera.

Lord Greysnowe glowered at his daughter. "Why aren't you circulating? You've been missing from court for five days."

Lifting her chin, Lady Annalise gestured toward Devon and Kiera. "What do you call conversing with the king and his betrothed?"

Devon eyed her. Even after her illness, Lady Annalise was defying her parents in public. Interesting.

Lady Greysnowe sniffed. "While King Devon is taken, you must pursue other opportunities."

As Kiera arched her brows, Devon lost his polite smile. While? That sounded like the countess soon expected Kiera gone. Annalise's ambitious parents were definitely involved in Kiera's attempted poisoning.

Lord Alexander snickered. "Yes, the Duke of Osbourne is free. Who cares that he's ancient and hasn't noticed any lady since his wife died eight years ago?"

Ignoring his son, Lord Greysnowe sneered at Kiera. "I'd thank you to cease poisoning our children with your common opinions."

As Lady Annalise paled and Kiera blinked, Devon stiffened and swallowed a growl. How dare the count flaunt their attempt to poison Kiera? He almost snarled, "What do you mean by that?"

While the Greysnowes started and gawked at him, Kiera tugged on his arm then said, "Come, the Duchess of Childes is hailing us." She drew him away and tsked. "Confronting them in a crowded ballroom shan't keep the poisoning attempt a secret."

He winced. "I know." Kiera being in danger made him forget discretion. He couldn't lose her. "But we must confront them as soon as possible tomorrow."

STRAIGHT AFTER AN EARLY breakfast the following morning, Devon and Kiera took a carriage to Greysnowe House, and he gave her the two-month-old report about Lord Greysnowe's meetings with assassins.

While she read it, Kiera's brows rose. "You mentioned the assassins the other day, but no wonder you suspected Annalise at first. Why didn't you confront the Greysnowes before?"

He sighed and tucked the report back into his satchel as the carriage halted. If only he had, then Kiera wouldn't have almost been poisoned. "The count never contacted assassins again. I assumed he'd abandoned whatever mad scheme he was plotting against the Ravenstones." And drawing attention to their schemes only inflamed the Greysnowes and Ravenstones to wilder ones.

When Devon escorted Kiera into Greysnowe House with their guards close behind, the refined butler goggled to see them so early, but he led them to the breakfast room where the Greysnowes were still eating. As they entered, Lord Greysnowe choked on his bacon and eggs, Lady Greysnowe dropped her toast, and Lord Alexander halted with his laden fork halfway to his mouth. Only Lady Annalise remained calm, although she did pale, probably suspecting the reason behind their early visit.

While Kiera sat beside her friend and squeezed her hand, Devon sat beside Kiera and narrowed his eyes at Lord and Lady Greysnowe. When they paled like their daughter, he flashed a cool smile. Good, they finally realized this was serious. "We're here to finish the discussion we began last night."

As their son blinked, Lord and Lady Greysnowe swallowed and exchanged a glance. Then Lord Greysnowe thrust out his chin and replied, "I'm not certain what you mean."

His pulse surging, Devon inhaled to retort but halted when Kiera laid her hand on his and said, "You claimed I was poisoning your children with my opinions. Did you repay that by sending me a poisoned bottle of sparkling wine supposedly from Annalise?"

Silent for once, Lord and Lady Greysnowe gaped and jerked back, while Lord Alexander paled but leaned forward and replied, "Father and Mother have acted almost treasonously toward Lady Kiera, but they'd never poison anyone."

Devon extracted his report from his satchel and tossed it before Lord Alexander. The young lord's faith in his parents would vanish after reading it. "Then why was your father seen with assassins in recent months?"

As her brother began reading and paled further, Lady Annalise recoiled from her parents and whispered, "What?!"

Lord Greysnowe stiffened and muttered to his plate, "I've not met with any assassins in the last two months."

His jaw tight, Devon glared at the ambitious count. "Which is why I never pursued the matter, other than having my guards neutralize those assassins. But they could have sold you a poison at your first meeting."

His wife grimacing beside him while his children stared, Lord Greysnowe waved a hand. "Not hardly. They were all incensed that I approached them in public and refused to offer their services, which suited me fine."

Devon and Kiera exchanged a glance, and he almost sighed. Such convoluted schemes were typical of the Greysnowes, yet attempting to poison Kiera couldn't be ignored like their usual ones against the Ravenstones.

Lord Alexander frowned at his parents. "Why would you approach assassins if you didn't wish to hire them?"

Lord and Lady Greysnowe merely glanced at each other then shrugged, clearly unrepentant.

Her cerulean eyes black, Lady Annalise shuddered and fingered the matching heart-shaped firegem flickering in the hollow of her throat. "You *must* explain why—poisoning Kiera is treason as well as evil."

Lady Greysnowe lifted her chin and blurted, "'Tis all that whelp Ravenstone's fault."

CHAPTER 48

As Annalise turned whiter than a mourning banshee at her mother's accusation, Kiera and Devon exchanged a frown then Kiera almost snorted. The genial count was too honorable to associate with assassins.

After a moment, Devon narrowed his eyes at Annalise's father. "Explain."

Lord Greysnowe sighed. "After his duel with Alexander on Summerday, Ravenstone sent us letters requesting we meet to end the feud. Claimed almost dying made him want peace. As if we'd believe *anything* a treacherous Ravenstone claimed." He chuckled. "Well, those public meetings with assassins were my answer."

Kiera squeezed Annalise's shoulder as Annalise whimpered and covered her face with her hands then murmured, "Oh, Father."

Although Lord Alexander gaped at them as well, Lady Greysnowe beamed at her husband. "He was quite clever about it. He made sure to meet when Ravenstone's people were watching. But he had to pretend not to notice them."

Kiera and Devon glanced at each other again. That mad scheme sounded exactly like another incident in the

Greysnowes' ridiculous, centuries-long feud with the Ravenstones.

Devon sighed and shook his head. "I expect you to write to Lord Ravenstone and explain at once. I don't want your feud escalating any further."

As Lord Greysnowe grimaced but nodded, Lord Alexander grinned and resumed eating his eggs. "Don't fret, Father. Lord Ravenstone shall remain gracious, like when I apologized for almost killing him. He seems a decent sort."

Kiera suppressed a laugh when the count glared at his son, who ignored him with a bright smile. Annalise's younger brother was definitely a hellion, although he didn't seem to embrace the feud any longer.

Devon rose. "We must go. Mention the poisoning attempt to no one."

Kiera embraced Annalise then took Devon's outstretched hand and rose as well. She paused and eyed Annalise's parents. Despite not being involved, perhaps they still could help unearth her poisoner. "Who knew Annalise was ill?"

Lady Greysnowe sniffed. "We knew, and our servants, of course. But we kept her illness quiet. We don't want any suitable gentlemen believing Annalise can't bear them strong sons."

Her jaw tensing, Kiera swallowed her retort when Annalise drooped. Her poor friend didn't need to endure any further embarrassment. So she tugged Devon toward the door. On the carriage ride back to the palace, she leaned against him and sighed. With the Greysnowes eliminated, her poisoner must be a councilor or one of her other detractors. Hopefully, Lady Juliet would finish her protection charm soon, so she could begin unearthing the poisoner.

OVER THE FOLLOWING DAYS, Kiera and Devon continued avoiding most court events, and not staying long or consuming refreshments when they did. Her neck prickled whenever they arrived

—from everyone's stares, the gossip about her pregnancy must be flaring. And since Devon accompanied her everywhere except her nightmara rides, she never managed a private meeting with Hawke to discuss Buford Leshane.

So she couldn't help a grin when she received Lady Juliet's note just before the next council meeting. The royal witch had finished the protection charm at last. They could silence that embarrassing pregnancy gossip, and she could begin arranging Bobbi's exile. Thank the Goddess.

As she bounded to her desk and began jotting a note to Wren and Hawke, Devon arched his brows at her. "What is it?"

Kiera beamed at him as she sealed her note. "Lady Juliet finished my protection charm. I'm writing Wren to ask if we can meet at the orphanage tomorrow morning. I didn't want to risk it without that charm, but I've been impatient to see her and confide everything." And obtain Hawke's help.

Devon grinned back. "Finally! We'll fetch it before the council meeting."

She arched her brows when he took her arm. "That shall make us late." Which would irritate the councilors, one of whom might be her poisoner.

Devon shook his head as they left the queen's chambers. "Fetching your protection charm is more important."

Kiera nodded and handed her note to one of her guards. Especially considering the unidentified poisoner could try again at any time.

As they strode to the royal witch's wing with their guards, Devon glanced at her. "If I rearrange my meeting with Lord Islaye, I could join you at the orphanage tomorrow."

Her throat tightening, she swallowed. "Don't bother." She almost winced when his eyes narrowed, clearly suspicious why she kept dissuading him from visiting the orphanage. Once she handled Bobbi, she must have him join her on a visit as well as confess about Bobbi. But she'd wait—she couldn't bear his pity at her true parentage, and handling Bobbi herself would brace her.

When they knocked on Lady Juliet's door, a little maid in starched livery ushered them inside. "Right this way, your majesties."

As Devon waved for their guards to remain by the door, Kiera blinked at the royal witch's immaculate and stylish chambers. No signs of magic or the usual clutter most witches possessed. She almost chuckled. Lady Juliet always wore fashionable attire with an elaborate coiffure—she should have expected her chambers to match.

The maid led them to a bright and airy workroom, which did possess magical accoutrements, but meticulously arranged rather than cluttered. "Their majesties, Lady Juliet."

Her modish gown protected by a canvas apron, the royal witch continued grinding herbs in a marble mortar and pestle. "Thank you, Lara. You may go." Once her maid left, Lady Juliet removed her apron and gestured toward the sofa near the door. "Sit, please, your majesties."

Kiera's mouth twitched as they sat. Of course, the royal witch had to discard the plain apron as soon as anyone could see her. It marred her fashionable air.

Kiera inhaled as Lady Juliet whisked to the cabinet in the corner then crooned and weaved a pattern of light before it. The door creaked open, and she extracted a cloth packet from inside. Then she weaved another pattern of light before the cabinet, which locked with a click, and glided over to them before unwrapping the packet. "Your left hand, please, Lady Kiera."

Kiera swallowed as the royal witch slid a smaller version of Devon's three-stranded, gold bracelet onto her left wrist. With an almost inaudible hum, the bracelet warmed and welded against her skin. Removing it when she returned to the orphanage might be difficult.

As Devon relaxed beside her, she licked her lips then said, "I assume the strands are the same as Devon's: the top preventing enchantments, the middle poisons, and the one by my wrist pregnancy."

Lady Juliet smiled. "Yes. Did he show you how to remove the contraceptive strand?" When Kiera shook her head, the royal witch continued, "Just turn it counterclockwise. Don't fret about damaging the other two; they're fused together and almost indestructible."

Devon chuckled. "I've had mine for thirteen years, and it still appears new."

Lady Juliet nodded, her eyes gleaming. "I'll need to renew the protection charm once a year, but otherwise you're set. Any questions, Lady Kiera?"

Kiera eyed the slender bracelet. Only how to remove it, but if she were Devon's true betrothed, she'd not care about that. Perhaps 'twould loosen when its power faded after a year. She smiled and handed the royal witch her silver pendant. "No, but thank you for creating it for me. I feel much safer now."

As Devon nodded his thanks, Lady Juliet beamed at them. "Of course. I'll start testing that bottle of sparkling wine and attempting to trace your poisoner as soon as you leave. If I unearth anything, I'll send word at once."

Kiera and Devon rose then left. As they began toward the council room with their guards, she tugged her sleeve until the protection charm was hidden. Her poisoner might be forewarned if they saw a bracelet exactly like the king's protection charm. Fortunately, with Longnight under four weeks away, the weather was cold enough to wear long-sleeved gowns without comment.

They swept inside the council room, and Devon apologized for the delay without explaining why then began the meeting. Since her poisoner might be a councilor, they'd not inform the council about the poisoning attempt until her poisoner was unearthed. Yet she had to resist fingering her new protection charm throughout the brief meeting where they discussed the Magehaven ore and the Tsarkan pirates but nothing else.

Her skin prickled at the councilors' piercing stares, especially Lady Morwynne's and the Duke of Osbourne's. Doubtless the councilors were scrutinizing her for signs of pregnancy. But she lifted her chin and met their eyes without blushing. She'd nothing to be ashamed of. They'd see she wasn't pregnant at the Dabars' ball later. And she'd performed well as acting queen over the past two months.

As soon as they arrived at Dabar House that evening, Kiera asked Devon for sparkling wine. Then they remained at the ball until well past midnight, dancing every dance and drinking sparkling wine in between. *That* should prove to court she wasn't pregnant. When they finally returned to Devon's chambers, they forwent their evening drink and went straight to bed, although not to sleep.

As THEY FINISHED breakfast the following morning, Devon arched his brows and asked, "Are you certain I shouldn't join you at the orphanage?"

Kiera swallowed and forced a smile. Yes, he was definitely suspicious. "I want some private time with Wren today." When he opened his mouth, probably to suggest he'd visit Hawke, she added, "And Hawke shall be busy managing the orphans during our talk."

Devon sighed. "Very well. I'll see you at luncheon then."

Her heart squeezing, she leaned forward and kissed him. He was so wonderful to trust her to handle matters even when he suspected something. Then she left for the orphanage. Once there, she embraced Peter and waved for her guards to remain with the carriage before stopping by the kitchen to see Mary then continuing to the matron's study to join Wren and Hawke.

Hawke sprawled in a chair beside her, Wren folded her hands on the desk and leaned forward. "So why did you ask to meet with both of us alone? I assume 'tis about Bobbi."

Kiera grimaced but nodded. She'd not mention her plan for Bobbi came from the Mirror of Wisdom—using such a perilous enchanted item would horrify Wren, and pregnant ladies should be kept calm. "Bobbi is the first reason. I've decided that she must be exiled to end her extortion." She turned to Hawke. "And your friend Buford Leshane can help with that. When his next ship sails to procure arachne silk, I want Bobbi to be a passenger. Could you arrange a meeting with him for me?"

As Hawke inclined his head, Wren quirked a wry smile then said, "An isle across the ocean is certainly distant enough to make her extortion impossible."

Hawke rubbed his chin. "I'll write to Buford today, but he mightn't respond immediately. His daughter ran off with Winston, and Buford is still attempting to find her."

Although she'd only met the teenage girl at Wren and Hawke's wedding, Kiera paled at such an innocent being tangled with that cad. "Dear Goddess."

Wren sighed and shook her head. "I'm certain poor Marianne is how Mr. Winston learned of your visit for the orphanage play. During their apprenticeship, the Bedsford twins doubtless mentioned something, which she told her secret lover."

Kiera slowly nodded. So Mr. Winston *had* possessed a spy, but not at the orphanage itself. She turned to Hawke. "Thanks for writing for me. Hopefully, Mr. Leshane responds soon."

Hawke cocked a brow. "Wren and I shall be poorer than the orphans if he doesn't. Bobbi has *very* expensive tastes."

Kiera winced. No doubt the greedy creature did. If only she'd money to reimburse them, though they'd probably not accept it. She coughed and leaned forward. "About my second reason for visiting, I'd have told you sooner, but I couldn't trust this to a letter."

Wren paled then exchanged a frown with Hawke before saying, "You wrote us about Mr. Winston's kidnapping attempt, so I assume this is worse."

Kiera twisted the Vireni betrothal ring. "Someone sent me a poisoned bottle of sparkling wine, supposedly from Annalise. But Devon drank some first, and his protection charm neutralized the poison, then he prevented me from drinking any."

While Hawke stiffened, Wren paled further and clutched his arm then whispered, "Dear Goddess."

To reassure them, Kiera flashed a bright smile. "Everything is fine." She lifted her left sleeve to reveal her protection charm. "Devon had Lady Juliet create this for me, and she's hunting the poisoner now and should unearth them soon. I can't negotiate with the nightmara while there's an unidentified poisoner sabotaging me."

Hawke leaned forward. "Just let us know how we can help."

As Wren nodded, Kiera hummed and flicked her fingers. Simply being here and always supporting her was help enough. "What would help most would be a relaxing visit with the orphans before I must return to the palace."

Wren leapt upright and enfolded her in a fierce embrace. "Come, they'll be ecstatic to see you."

To cheer Wren, Kiera winked as she drew back then jested, "Only because they believe I'm the future queen."

CHAPTER 49

As they began luncheon after Kiera's visit to the orphanage, Devon beamed at her over his mushroom soup. Perhaps 'twould encourage her to share why she'd not wanted him to join her. "How was your private time with Wren?"

Kiera stilled for a moment and studied her soup. "'Twas a relief to unburden myself finally."

He eyed her. Then why did she appear almost guilty? But confronting her about that wouldn't encourage her to tell him. He must simply continue his steadfast support until she realized she could trust him with anything. So he hummed and nodded. "I felt the same after telling Aragon. We're fortunate to have such dear friends."

Kiera relaxed and began her mushroom soup. "We are."

His chest warming at her relief, Devon resumed eating as well. "How were the orphans?"

Kiera grinned. "Excited about the upcoming Longnight season. They all reminded me that 'twas less than two weeks away. I promised to return in the days before Longnight and bring a surprise." She peeked at him through her lashes. "Would you care to be it?"

His pulse surged. At last, she was trusting him enough to

invite him to the orphanage? He restrained his broad grin. "Very much."

Kiera sighed as she began her steak pie. "Hopefully, Lady Juliet shall unearth the poisoner before then. It shall dampen the Longnight season if she doesn't. Plus, my jumping lessons are progressing well, so Moonbud shall want to negotiate the treaty soon, but a poisoner still seeking to assassinate me proves I'm not accepted as queen, and she may decide I'm not worth negotiating with."

His grin fading, Devon captured her hand across the tea table. "Moonbud shan't decide that." He squeezed her hand. "But Lady Juliet shall contact us soon. She's the most illustrious witch in Calatini—testing that poison and unearthing your poisoner shan't take her more than a few days."

Kiera returned his squeeze. "I hope you're right."

Yet despite his reassurance, they heard nothing from the royal witch over the following days. What was delaying her? Surely a simple poison wasn't that complicated to unravel. And every day the poisoner remained unknown, Kiera grew a bit more uneasy. No doubt she didn't feel safe at the palace, and she assumed the poisoner represented how all of court regarded her. How long until her unease convinced her to return to the orphanage?

So during luncheon after Kiera's next nightmara ride, Devon grimaced while he drained his tea. "I can't believe Lady Juliet hasn't unearthed the poisoner yet."

Kiera sighed as she finished her baked pear with vahnila sweetice. "'Tis only been three days since she finished my protection charm. And although you thought she'd contact us soon, she *did* say tracing the poison would be difficult unless 'twas magical."

He frowned. True, yet with the poisoner free, if Kiera *finally* realized he loved her, she'd still refuse him because she assumed court wouldn't accept her as queen. But once the poisoner was caught, she'd see the poisoner was just one person, not all of court. He shook his head. "We need a report on her progress at least."

Kiera quirked a wry smile. "Perhaps she didn't wish to bother you with minimal progress. You've plenty of other state affairs to handle."

Devon set his jaw and tapped his fingers on the table. The royal witch *was* a perfectionist who only revealed her completed work. But they must know her progress this time. He rose and offered Kiera his hand. "Shall we go visit Lady Juliet?"

Kiera took his hand but arched a brow as she rose. "Just don't treat her as brusquely as you did Annalise when we divulged the poisoning attempt. We don't want the royal witch cursing all of Calatini because you insulted her too much."

He forced a shrug as they began toward the royal witch's wing with their guards. "I'll remain civil when I demand Lady Juliet reveal her progress."

Her mouth twitching, Kiera tsked. "Demand doesn't sound civil to me."

Devon grimaced. Remaining civil *was* difficult when Kiera was threatened. She was too dear for him to lose. "I'll try at least."

When he knocked on the royal witch's door, it creaked open, and her little maid blinked at them. "Your majesties, Lady Juliet isn't expecting you."

Squeezing his arm before he could reply, Kiera flashed a bright smile. "We know, but we must speak with her."

The maid pursed her lips. "Very well, but Lady Juliet is deep scrying, so we mustn't startle her. She could lose her powers, mind, or sight if she surfaces in the wrong manner."

Devon and Kiera exchanged a glance. The royal witch must be deep scrying to unearth the poisoner.

He waved the maid forward, and with a sigh, she led them to the royal witch's workroom. Gesturing for them to wait near the door, she whispered in her mistress's ear.

Her pupils wide and blank, Lady Juliet gazed into a massive

silver bowl filled with steaming water. She blinked slowly at her maid's whisper, and expression returned to her face. She swirled her hand over the bowl, and the water ceased steaming. "How may I serve you, your majesties?"

Devon and Kiera sat on the sofa near the door while their guards stood along the wall. He gritted a smile. Be civil, be civil. He replied, "We wish to hear your progress unearthing the poisoner."

Lady Juliet smoothed her modish gown. "I've determined the poison. Ground seeds from the kuchla tree found in tropical regions of the Tsarkan Empire."

He tensed. If Kiera died and couldn't negotiate the Nightmara-Calatini Treaty, the nightmara and mara might leave the Nightmara Plains, and the Tsarkan Empire would be quick to invade Calatini like it had invaded their other neighbors. "Do you suspect the poisoner is Tsarkan?"

Lady Juliet sighed. "Likely not. Although kuchla seeds are a popular poison in the Tsarkan Empire, Calatini traders have imported kuchla seeds for a century or more. They usually market the seeds as pest control."

Devon almost growled when Kiera snorted a laugh then drawled, "A pest is surely how my poisoner views me."

Frowning, Lady Juliet tapped her lip with her finger. "Albeit readily available, kuchla seeds aren't often used as poison in Calatini. Arsenic, hemlock, or death mushrooms are the typical natural poisons." She sighed again. "And unfortunately, natural poisons like kuchla seeds can be used by anyone, and there's no magical trail to trace. I'm attempting to scry more, but that shall take time."

He stiffened, narrowing his eyes at the royal witch. Didn't she see how pressing this was? "Time shall simply allow the poisoner to try again."

Kiera laid a hand on his knee. "With the protection charm Lady Juliet created for me, we can afford some time. I doubt a poisoner would be so brazen as to attempt a more direct method of murder."

His heart squeezing, Devon kissed her palm. Who knew what a treasonous poisoner would attempt? "Hopefully not. I couldn't bear if harm befell you."

A blush darkening her cheeks, Kiera glanced at the royal witch then tugged her hand free.

He suppressed a sigh. If she believed his love was sincere, such public tenderness wouldn't fluster her. He turned back to the royal witch and arched his brows. "Do you require assistance to unearth the poisoner? The veiled witch was invaluable in helping with the Magehaven ore. We can consult her again."

Lady Juliet stiffened as if turned to stone by a gorgon's gaze. "When I require that *poseur's* assistance, I'll no longer be fit to bear the title of royal witch."

Devon inclined his head. "Fine. But I want an answer before the Longnight season." Then Kiera could have a cheerful Longnight. He narrowed his eyes at the royal witch again. "If not, I'll summon the veiled witch regardless of your dislike." Taking Kiera's arm, he rose. "We'll leave you to your hunt."

Once they left the royal witch's wing with their guards, Kiera murmured, "That was you acting civil, was it?" When he shrugged, she tsked. "You're outrageous when people don't do as you wish."

He tensed, a pang slicing through him. He always attempted to respect others and only be peremptory when imperative. Good kings listened to their people. But unearthing her poisoner *was* imperative. "I am not. I simply want you safe."

Kiera hummed. "You acted much the same when you stormed into my orphanage and demanded I become your betrothed. I wasn't threatened then."

His chest tightening, Devon turned to Kiera then relaxed at the teasing gleam in her navy eyes. She must be attempting to lighten his frustration. And her tender solicitude did precisely that. He'd worry about her poisoner and everything else later.

Echoing her teasing, he arched a brow as they entered her chambers. "Perhaps not, but you accepted my demand, and as my betrothed, 'tis your duty to stop me when I become outrageous."

Kiera wrapped her arms about his neck. "However do I manage that?"

Tingling heat swamping him at her clean lavender scent, he lowered his head until their lips almost touched. "Kisses work well."

Kiera smiled against his lips. "Only when we're alone."

Devon made himself remain still. He mustn't appear *demanding*. "We're alone right now."

Kiera purred a laugh. "So we are." With that, she captured his mouth in a ravenous kiss.

Deepening their kiss, he tumbled them onto her bed. Goddess, he loved her. When she yanked off his cravat then attacked his waistcoat, he chuckled and captured her hands. "Oh no, we're making love slowly this afternoon. I must prove I'm not always demanding."

Flashing a coy smile, Kiera rolled them until she was on top. "A better way to prove that would be to let me lead." She freed her hands then wrenched open his waistcoat and kissed him again.

His body painfully hard, Devon rumbled as he returned her kiss. Letting her lead would be perfect. They could go slowly another time. So they made love like starving venuses who'd been locked in a convent for a year.

After they'd shuddered in explosive release, he buried his fingers in her dark-blonde curls when she nuzzled his chest. He said, "I can never get enough of you." Being desperately in love did that.

Kiera hummed. "Nor I you." She kissed his chest. "Shall we make love slowly now?"

Devon grinned, his heart leaping. If she felt the same and was willing to admit it, surely she returned his love. As soon as her poisoner was tried, he could renew his proposal, and she'd happily accept this time. He kissed her then tenderly made love to her again.

Yet they both sobered when they dressed for the Valcrests' reception that evening. As king and queen, they could only be so carefree when alone. Plus, her poisoner was still about.

Over the next several days, they heard nothing from Lady Juliet about the poisoner, and every day he forced himself not to write to demand updates. He'd definitely not be civil if he did. While they waited for news, Kiera's unease returned until she almost started at anything unexpected.

Then at breakfast before the next council meeting, Kiera received a note and exhaled a shuddering breath as she opened it.

His stomach twisting, Devon stiffened and lowered his laden fork. Something must be wrong. "What is it?"

CHAPTER 50

At Devon's question, Kiera swallowed and glanced up from Buford Leshane's note stating he could meet tomorrow. She could *finally* arrange Bobbi's exile. Thank the Goddess.

His green eyes dark, Devon leaned toward her. "Kiera?"

She stared at him, her heart squeezing. He looked ready to wrap her in his arms and protect her from the entire world, and as always, his fierce protectiveness lured her like a siren's song. Although she'd meant to wait to confess so she could handle Bobbi herself, she couldn't continue hiding the truth from him any longer. And leaning on him while they were together surely wasn't wrong, even though she'd ache for his support once she returned to the orphanage. She sighed and set the merchant's note on the tea table. "Something *did* happen when I saw Wren's latest orphanage play, but I was too ashamed to admit it then."

Devon paled but swept her to the sofa then wrapped her in his arms. Exactly as expected. "Did someone hurt you?"

Kiera nestled against him. He was so wonderful. "Not really." After a moment, she drew back and brushed dark-brown hair from his face. "But she did threaten to unravel your romantic tale about my parentage."

Devon frowned. "What do you mean?"

She managed a weak smile. "The greedy woman who birthed me found me. She was a beggar lurking outside Lady Blaine's fire ball. When she saw me, she realized she could extort money from the royal coffers. Wren and Hawke hid her until I could decide how to handle her."

Devon stiffened but kissed her palm. "And you were so ashamed of her that you hid her from me as well? I don't care about your parentage and would have gladly helped however I could."

Kiera winced, her throat tightening. Keeping Bobbi secret had hurt him. "I never doubted that. I just wasn't strong enough to tell you." She brushed a kiss against his lips. "But your embrace," and unspoken love, "eventually gave me enough strength to confess."

His face softening, Devon returned her kiss. "I'm glad you told me." He inclined his head at Buford Leshane's note across the queen's chambers. "Was that note another extortion attempt?"

She licked her lips. "No, 'tis from Hawke's merchant friend. When I asked the Mirror of Wisdom about my poisoner, I also asked about Bobbi, and the mirror showed me the arachne's isle, so I began planning her exile." She eyed him. Had mentioning when she'd risked the Mirror of Wisdom upset him?

But although his jaw twitched, Devon merely nodded and said, "She can't extort anyone from there."

Kiera sighed at his calm reply. "Exactly. So I'm meeting with Buford Leshane tomorrow afternoon to arrange everything."

Devon frowned. "At his warehouse near the docks?" When she nodded, he hummed. "I'll move my meeting with Lord Osteen about taxes, so I can join you. I'll have our guards secure an unmarked carriage."

Her chest warmed at his ready support, but she shook her head. "You might make Mr. Leshane nervous. I'd better go alone."

Devon captured her mouth in a fierce kiss. "You're not going alone. But I'll remain in the carriage if you prefer." He drew her upright. "Come, we must finish breakfast."

Kiera smiled at him as they returned to the tea table and resumed eating. He was truly the most wonderful gentleman. If only she could confess her love as well, but then she'd shatter when she returned to the orphanage.

After breakfast, they headed to the council meeting with their guards. Unlike last time, only Lady Morwynne and the Duke of Osbourne scrutinized her during the meeting, probably because they didn't approve of her as queen. Now that the pregnancy gossip had vanished, the other councilors treated her as they had before.

Her skin prickling, Kiera forced herself to ignore the two staring councilors as Lord Islaye leaned forward and said, "I just received word that Miss Winston shall arrive at the ore deposit in Magehaven tomorrow. My magic marshals and Lord Nolan's land rangers are eager to assist her as soon as she arrives. Hopefully, with an alchemist who doesn't use magic, we'll finally make progress identifying and counteracting the ore, so I'll have good news at the next council meeting."

Kiera smiled. "I'm sure you shall. Despite her wretched brother, Miss Winston is clever and determined. Plus, she adores alchemy and was excited to study a mysterious ore." And the veiled witch had said Miss Winston would succeed.

Devon nodded at Lord Islaye. "Have a detailed report ready for the next meeting. It shall be a relief to solve the Magehaven ore at last." He glanced about the table. "Does anyone have anything else?" When no one spoke, he adjourned the meeting.

As they returned to the royal wing, Kiera sighed. Solving the Magehaven ore would be a relief, as would arranging Bobbi's exile tomorrow. Now if only they could unearth her poisoner as well.

· · ·

After a passionate night where Devon made love to her until well past midnight, Kiera rose late and barely arrived to her nightmara ride on time. Despite that, her jumping lesson went well. Then she returned to the queen's chambers and changed into her plainest arachne silk dress. She pricked her finger and turned her dress a sober charcoal before wrapping herself in a black cloak. She swallowed and eyed herself in the cheval mirror. She was as anonymous as she could be dressed in such rich fabric.

Wearing plain clothes as well, Devon knocked on the adjoining door then strode beside her. "Ready?"

She smiled in reply and took his arm, and he escorted her to the unmarked carriage, which rumbled out the secret royal entrance with their guards disguised as drivers and outriders. She leaned into his embrace as they rode through the crowded streets of Ormas toward the docks. "How was the meeting with Lord Osteen?"

Devon shrugged. "Productive yet tortuous. Meetings about taxes always are. Be grateful you'd your ride with Moonbud. How did that go?"

Kiera suppressed a laugh. She *was* grateful for her riding lessons. They were excellent exercise and a great distraction from her concerns, whether court gossip, the Magehaven ore, Bobbi, or her poisoner. Although she did have to make sure to bury those concerns lest the nightmara queen-heir read them. "Well. We'll start high jumps next time. Moonbud thinks I've only a few more lessons left."

As Devon stilled, her heart twisted. And once those lessons were done, she could negotiate the treaty. Then she'd return to the orphanage where she belonged, and she'd never see him again except from a distance. If only she could delay the treaty forever.

They rode in silence for the rest of the ride, but when the carriage halted outside Buford Leshane's warehouse, Devon squeezed her hand. "Are you certain you don't want me to join you?"

She smiled and brushed a kiss against his lips. So protective. "I'll be fine. But I'm glad you're here to support me."

Kiera alighted then asked an idle cabin boy where to find the merchant. Glancing about for the Bedsford twins but not spotting them, she followed the boy's directions up the mezzanine to the merchant's office then entered while her guards remained outside.

Lines creasing his weathered face, Mr. Leshane glanced up from his papers then rose with a deep bow. "Good afternoon, your majesty."

She beamed and settled before the desk then waved for him to sit. He looked exhausted. "Thanks for agreeing to meet. Have you found your daughter yet?"

Mr. Leshane dropped into his chair. "Not yet. I've people all over Ormas, but none have found a trace of her. That cad Winston must have hidden them well."

Kiera's chest tightened. Poor Mr. Leshane. "I doubt your daughter is in Ormas if she's still with Mr. Winston. Devon banished him on pain of death if he returned."

Mr. Leshane paled. "Dear Goddess." Then he straightened. "So how may I serve you, your majesty?"

She leaned forward, her stomach tensing. "I've a passenger I want on your next ship sailing for arachne silk, but you must speak of her to no one."

A frown creased Mr. Leshane's brow. "To Mist Isle? The arachne and humans living there are strict on who they permit to come and go. Most of my crew isn't allowed ashore."

Kiera shrugged. Yet the Mirror of Wisdom had shown that isle, and the powerful mirror was never wrong. "She wishes to visit the isle." Or she would soon.

Mr. Leshane echoed her shrug. "On your friend's head be it. My next ship sailing for Mist Isle is The Blonde Nymph in six days." He drooped again. "She's my best ship—named after my daughter, you know."

She almost winced. Perhaps discussing business would distract the poor man. "Your passenger is currently Wren and Hawke's houseguest and has expensive tastes. She'll require luxurious quarters on your ship." So she'd not balk until 'twas too late. "Ask Wren and Hawke for suggestions. I'll pay whatever you deem fair. Any questions?"

His eyes narrowing, Mr. Leshane shook his head. Clearly, he understood his task was royal business and refused to pry. Wise man.

Kiera flashed a smile and rose. The merchant was as helpful as Hawke had always said. "Thanks for your assistance in this matter. Once your ship is ready to sail, please send me a note with your fee and when you'll collect your passenger."

After she rejoined him in the carriage, Devon arched his brows. "How'd it go?"

She threaded her fingers through his, her heart softening at his concern. "The ship sails in six days. Now I must convince Bobbi to be on it."

They again fell silent as they rode to Wren and Hawke's townhouse, but again when the carriage halted, Devon asked, "Should I join you?"

Kiera shuddered. Bobbi would imagine never-ending wealth if he did. "No, she might never leave then."

Waving her guards to remain behind, she strode inside her friends' townhouse then followed Hobb to an upstairs sitting room. When she entered, she coughed at the sickly sweet scent of faesmoke and the middle strand of her protection charm warmed. It must be protecting her from the highly addictive mixture of faedust and herbs. Hopefully, the pregnant Wren had stayed far away.

She glanced about the room, and her brows rose. The plush furniture, vibrant rugs, and velvet curtains were a garish fuchsia that clashed with Bobbi's equally garish scarlet dress.

Plus, decanters of spiritwine and platters of delicacies surrounded the sofa where Bobbi lounged smoking. Expensive tastes, indeed.

Blowing a stream of faesmoke, Bobbi smirked at her. "Finally visitin' yer poor ma?"

Kiera eyed the mirrorlike stranger as she perched on the chair farthest away. "You may have birthed me, but you're not my mother." Jane was.

Bobbi eyed Kiera and slurped her snifter of spiritwine. "Ungrateful whelp. Shoulda had a healer cut ya out when I learnt I's breedin'."

Her skin tightening, Kiera arched a brow. Not surprising Bobbi would say that. "Why didn't you?"

Bobbi waved her snifter and sloshed spiritwine on the sofa. "Yer pa hadn't got brats off that rich wife of his. I thought he'd get rid of 'er and marry me if I bore ya. But he didn't, so I made him pay to not tell wifey about ya. I left ya at the orphanage as living proof. Ya should be grateful."

Kiera inclined her head. Yes, she was definitely grateful she'd been raised at the orphanage rather than by this greedy creature. "I am, so I've arranged a trip to repay your kindness."

Bobbi lurched upright and puffed on her faesmoke pipe. "Have ya now?"

Kiera nodded again. "To Mist Isle." She pricked her finger and turned her dress a vivid sky-blue. That should impress Bobbi. She gestured toward her dress. "Where the weavers of arachne silk live."

Bobbi's eyes glittered as she drained her spiritwine. "They must make a bundle off that magicked fabric."

Kiera suppressed a smile. Bobbi was already convinced. She murmured, "I believe so. They rarely allow anyone on their isle, and we've not yet sent a royal envoy." She lifted a shoulder. "Royal envoys receive many gifts to bring home to their king and queen, but as a blood relation, you may keep whatever they give you."

Faesmoke billowed from the smirk curving Bobbi's lips. "Suppose I could help ya with that."

Kiera rose. "I'll make arrangements for your trip." She slipped from the sitting room before Bobbi could reconsider. She went downstairs then requested a pen and paper to write her friends about the arrangements for Bobbi. Handing Hobb her note, she said, "Please give this to Wren."

Then gulping air to cleanse her lungs, she strode outside to rejoin Devon in the carriage. Thank the Goddess he was waiting for her.

CHAPTER 51

When Kiera climbed into the unmarked carriage, Devon wrapped an arm about her shoulders and asked like he had earlier, "How'd it go?"

Kiera nestled against him as the carriage began toward the palace. "Bobbi was easily convinced."

His pulse quickening at her lush curves pressing against him, he kissed her brow. She was so strong to handle her painful parentage without tears or wavering. "Are you certain you wish to exile your mother?"

Kiera sighed. "That greedy creature may have given birth to me, but she's not my mother. Other than shock at first and later disgust, I felt little when facing her. Jane, the previous orphanage matron, was my true mother—thank the Goddess. Bobbi would have been a horrid mother, while Jane..." Her voice softened, "Jane was compassionate and strong and wise."

Devon kissed her palm beneath her betrothal ring, his heart warming. And Kiera had clearly patterned herself after that wonderful lady. "Like you."

Kiera hummed and shifted against him. "I try to be."

He lifted her chin until her gaze met his. "You succeed, you know." Which was why he loved her, and why she'd make the perfect queen.

Kiera blushed but flashed a coy smile. "Flatterer. Are you attempting to seduce me?"

Devon waggled his brows. Doubtless she wished for a diversion after handling Bobbi. Not that he minded. "I would, except we're almost home, and 'twouldn't do for a king and queen to be seen disheveled. You know how we get in carriages."

Kiera giggled. "And anywhere else we're alone."

He kissed her nose as the carriage halted. So adorable. If only he could actually kiss her. "I blame you. You're too irresistible."

Her navy eyes bright, Kiera tsked but took his hand to descend from the carriage. "Of course, blame an innocent lady for your rakehell behavior."

Devon chuckled and swept her upstairs to his chambers. His body hardened as he scooped her into his arms and carried her to bed. As he had last night after her revelations, he must prove he still loved her despite her parentage.

OVER THE FOLLOWING DAYS, Devon and Kiera's time alone was as joyously ardent as when they'd first become lovers. Hiding Bobbi had truly oppressed Kiera. Perhaps now she'd realize he loved her and agree to become his wife. If only they could unearth that treasonous poisoner.

Unfortunately, Lady Juliet had provided no further news about the poisoner since their meeting over a week ago. *What was taking so long?* The royal witch had never failed to complete a task on time before. Yet they still heard nothing by the first day of the Longnight season.

During dinner before the Duchess of Childes's ball to open the Longnight season, Devon sighed as he finished his Longnight cake, a rich dessert only served then—a massapan-covered fruitcake soaked in spiritwine. "Since we've heard nothing from

Lady Juliet, we must write to the veiled witch tomorrow about your poisoner."

Kiera grimaced over her eggmilk punch. "I suppose. Although I'd rather not trust a witch we know so little about with treason. We've no idea of her true allegiance. She may not even be from Calatini."

He tapped his finger against the tea table. True, but they *must* unearth that poisoner. "At least we know she's a powerful Rhiannon descendant with the extraordinary reputation of being able to magic anything."

Then a knock sounded on Kiera's door, and Lady Juliet sailed inside. "You don't need that poseur, your majesties. 'Twas a delicate bit of magic, but I finally unearthed Lady Kiera's poisoner."

Devon and Kiera exchanged a glance. How opportune that the royal witch would join them at that exact moment. Yet now they could finally move past Kiera's poisoner. His blood surging, he smiled and leaned forward. "At last. Who is it?"

Lady Juliet smoothed her festive snowflake gown. "If you'd follow me to my workroom, I'd prefer to show you, else you mightn't believe me."

He almost snorted. He'd probably believe the poisoner was anyone at court, other than Aragon and his family. But he waved for the royal witch to proceed. They'd arrive late to the duchess's Longnight ball, but this was too imperative to delay. Besides, the duchess was family and would understand.

Kiera licked her lips as she accepted his arm. She must be nervous to learn her poisoner.

His chest tightening, Devon brushed a kiss against her tempting lips. Then he arched his brows, silently asking if she was all right. When she nodded, he escorted her down the hall behind Lady Juliet with their guards following.

Once they entered her workroom, Lady Juliet donned her apron and waved for them to approach the table with the poisoned bottle of sparkling wine, a silver bowl, and several herbs, powders, and potions. "As I explained before, kuchla seeds are a natural poison with no magical connection to the poisoner. However, the other day, I realized I could modify a kin spell to find seeds related to the ones in the sparkling wine."

While Lady Juliet poured sparkling wine into the silver bowl then added the other ingredients on the table, he smiled and nodded. Soon they'd know the poisoner. He squeezed Kiera's arm against his side to hearten her. "Very clever, but what if most of the kuchla seeds in Ormas came from the same merchant?"

Lady Juliet hummed. "I assumed many would be, so 'twas a final effort to unearth something. What I found, however..." She shook her head then murmured a singsong chant in the melodic witch's tongue.

The mixture in the silver bowl evaporated into a glowing mist that hovered over the table until Lady Juliet pointed at the massive map of Ormas pinned on the wall. The glowing mist flew across the room to hover a fingerbreadth from the map.

Lady Juliet gestured for them to follow her to the map. "The mist condenses where the related kuchla seeds are. I repeated my spell several times, even with a map showing all of Calatini, but my results remained the same."

Their guards close behind, Devon hurried across the room with Kiera. As they leaned toward the map, she murmured, "'Tis only one spot."

Heat kindling in his chest, he growled. True, and one he should have suspected at once. The superior countess had been blatantly against Kiera since the start. "Morwynne House."

Kiera frowned. "I doubt young Lord Morwynne is involved —unless his affability is a clever facade, which seems improbable. So Lady Morwynne must be the poisoner. Not surprising 'twas a councilor, especially that one."

As she shivered, Devon drew her closer then scowled at the damning map. "And since her husband was the ambassador to the Tsarkan Empire, she could possess kuchla seeds unrelated to the rest in Calatini."

Kiera twisted her betrothal ring. "Lady Morwynne doubtless believes she's rescuing Calatini from me. 'Tis clear she despises my common birth. But why did she wait two months to poison me?"

He sighed and kissed her palm. Goddess knew. But at least they could try Lady Morwynne for treason now. "We'll ask her when we confront her." He turned to the royal witch. "Thanks for unearthing Kiera's poisoner." Finally.

Lady Juliet's mouth twitched, almost as if she heard his thoughts, but she only inclined her head. "Of course, your majesty."

As Devon and Kiera turned to leave, his eye caught on the poisoned bottle of sparkling wine, and he almost chuckled. 'Twould be perfect for confronting the countess. He nodded at the bottle. "Could we take that?"

Lady Juliet arched her brows but corked the bottle then handed it to him. "Be careful. Since altering the sparkling wine might have hampered my ability to unearth the poisoner, I've not yet neutralized the poison."

He grinned and passed the bottle to Millier. 'Twas a better threat then. "Good."

As they left the royal witch's wing, Kiera eyed him. "What do you intend to do with that bottle?"

Devon flashed a wicked grin and squeezed her arm. "Share it with Lady Morwynne." She deserved it.

Kiera tsked while he led her outside toward the carriage. "We can't just poison her."

He grimaced and handed her inside then leapt after her. True, good kings pursued justice, not revenge. "We shan't. She'll be tried before the council at the next meeting." He smiled and sat beside her. "But we can confront her with the poisoned bottle. Seeing it shall unnerve her."

Kiera's lips twitched as the carriage rumbled forward. "Good." She nudged him with her hip. "We could *offer* to share it with Lady Morwynne but not allow her to drink."

Devon chuckled. The superior countess's dismay would be marvelous. "I like it."

They soon arrived at Childes House, and he escorted her into the crowded ballroom.

The Duchess of Childes beamed, her gaze probing. "At last! I was afraid you weren't attending. Everything all right?"

Devon inclined his head and forced himself not to glance at Kiera. Aragon's perceptive mother would see something was amiss if he did. "Sorry, state affairs delayed us."

The Duke of Childes arched his brows. "Nothing serious, I hope."

Kiera pursed a wry smile at the duke. "Unfortunately, they often are."

The duchess tsked then shooed them toward the twirling couples. "Well, forget about them and go dance."

Devon began to lead Kiera out, but she resisted him to ask, "Are Wren and Hawke still here?"

The duchess shook her head. "They already left, as did Aragon and Selena. Pregnant ladies tire early. Now go dance."

As ordered, he and Kiera danced several Longnight reels. Since her poisoner had been unearthed, they could enjoy the cheerful Longnight she'd wanted. Then they fetched flutes of sparkling wine and circulated the ballroom.

Twirling her flute before her lips, Kiera frowned at the crowd. "I don't see Annalise here either. I'm surprised her parents allowed her to leave already."

Devon shrugged. "Maybe their brush with treason scared them into sense." Although 'twas unlikely. "Or maybe she left without their permission." Like at the summer masquerade. "For such a beauteous lady, she's excellent at slipping away unseen."

Kiera hummed and eyed her sparkling wine.

His brows rose. From Kiera's expression, Lady Annalise had developed that unexpected skill for a reason. Hopefully, whatever it was wouldn't inflame the Greysnowe-Ravenstone feud. But since 'twas doubtless a confidence between friends, he'd not pry. So he glanced about the ballroom and drawled, "I don't see Lady Morwynne either—fortunately. I don't trust myself to remain calm around her."

Kiera shuddered. "Her poisoning attempt would surely become court gossip then."

Devon smiled at her as he handed their half-empty flutes to a nearby servant. He must distract her. "Shall we dance a few more reels before we leave as well?"

Kiera grinned back, and they danced several more songs then returned to the palace. They must face Lady Morwynne straight after breakfast tomorrow, and permanently end her threat. Then he could resume convincing Kiera to become his queen.

THE FOLLOWING morning as they left for Morwynne House, Devon frowned when Kiera handed one of her guards a note. How odd. "Who's that for?"

Kiera shrugged while he escorted her down the hall. "Lord Morwynne. He and Lady Ducharme were witnesses at that duel the Mirror of Wisdom showed me. Considering his mother is the poisoner, I suspect 'tis happening now rather than last Summerday, and we'll need him to handle his mother."

He grimaced and handed her into the carriage. Too bad she'd not mentioned the witnesses. They might have realized Lady Morwynne was responsible sooner. "Doubtless you're right. There were no witnesses to Lord Ravenstone and Lord Alexander's nearly fatal duel, until Lady Annalise and I interrupted."

Kiera sighed as she leaned against him. "I should have described the scene more, but I wanted to cease discussing it, so you'd not scold me for risking to use the Mirror of Wisdom."

Devon shuddered and wrapped an arm about her. "The information you obtained has been useful, but please swear never to risk that cursed mirror again." He couldn't bear it killing her like it had his mother.

Kiera shuddered as well. "I never want to. I'd say we should destroy it, but I doubt we could, and Calatini might need it one day."

He grunted. 'Twas why he'd kept the perilous Mirror of Wisdom. Then the carriage halted, and he inhaled a steadying breath and glanced at Kiera. "Ready?"

Kiera inclined her head. "Are you?"

Devon echoed her nod. Hopefully. He helped her from the carriage then accepted the poisoned bottle of sparkling wine from one of his guards.

As they began climbing the townhouse steps, Lord Morwynne, dressed in sword clothes, bounded up to meet them. "Good morning, your majesties. How did you know I was at Lady Ducharme's? And what brings you by so early?"

Devon and Kiera exchanged a glance. The young count's opinion of his mother would suffer worse than Lord Alexander's had of his parents. "An urgent matter to discuss with you and Lady Morwynne."

Lord Morwynne frowned but waved them inside. "Mother should still be at breakfast. Follow me."

Their guards close behind, Devon and Kiera followed the count to the breakfast room. As he sat beside his mother, they settled across from the countess with tight smiles.

Unlike the Greysnowes two weeks ago, Lady Morwynne continued eating with languid nonchalance. "Good morning, your majesty. Would you care for some breakfast?"

Devon stiffened as fire flared in his veins. The superior countess obviously felt no remorse for her poisoning attempt and would try again whenever she could. But he'd make sure she'd never threaten Kiera again. Too bad she wasn't a man, so he could punch her like he had Winston.

CHAPTER 52

hen Devon stiffened, his green eyes turning black, Kiera laid a hand on his knee. He resembled a chimera about to erupt again. Like with Mr. Winston, she must make sure he'd not go so far that he'd not forgive himself later. She flashed a glittering grin at her poisoner. "Thank you, Lady Morwynne, but we ate breakfast earlier."

His jaw tight, Devon set the poisoned bottle on the table with exaggerated care, as if he'd smash it otherwise. "We're here to discuss this."

Lord Morwynne leaned forward to peer at the bottle. "A fine vintage. Mother and I drank some three weeks ago."

Kiera suppressed a wince. The young count clearly had no idea what his mother had done with the bottle shortly after that.

Devon bared his teeth in an almost smile. "Perhaps you'd care for another glass, Lady Morwynne."

Laying her utensils on her empty plate, Lady Morwynne lifted her chin and arched her brows. "Much too early for me."

Kiera blinked at the superior countess. *That* was her objection? Goddess, she was brazen—her gold eyes hadn't even flickered when confronted with evidence of her treason.

Lord Morwynne frowned as he glanced between his mother then Devon and Kiera. "What's this about, your majesties?"

Devon glared at Lady Morwynne. "Do you wish to explain, or shall I?"

Lady Morwynne sniffed. "There's nothing to explain."

Kiera gripped Devon's knee when he stiffened more than a gargoyle turned to stone by sunlight. She'd better explain before he erupted. She offered the count a soft smile and waved toward the bottle. "I received this bottle almost three weeks ago—'tis poisoned with kuchla seeds from Morwynne House."

Devon leaned forward. "Considering the vintage, the sparkling wine could have only come from you or," he glared at the countess again, "your mother."

All color leached from Lord Morwynne's face. "Dear Goddess..."

Kiera winced, her throat constricting. The poor count. Learning of his mother's treasonous poisoning attempt must be worse than when she'd met Bobbi. She'd felt little since the greedy creature hadn't raised her. Unlike Lord Morwynne and his mother.

Lady Morwynne tossed her head. "You've no proof that poisoned sparkling wine came from here. 'Tis impossible to trace non-magical poisons."

As Devon growled beside her, Kiera squeezed his knee again. Of course, the devious countess knew that. Kiera tsked then replied, "Unfortunately for you, Lady Juliet discovered how to do so. She performed a kin spell on the kuchla seeds in the sparkling wine, and Morwynne House was the sole result."

Lady Morwynne tensed but said nothing, while her son somehow blanched further.

Kiera leaned toward the countess. "So we *know* you attempted to poison me, but we don't know why you waited so long."

Lady Morwynne eyed her without expression for a long moment, then her blank mask shattered. She flushed, and a sneer warped her face. "Because I *knew* your betrothal must be a sham to appease the nightmara. Which was fine—until the other councilors accepted your ruinous education initiative. And then King Devon began skipping important court events, like my salon, to *cavort* with you, as if he were truly in love and meant to marry you."

Kiera released Devon's knee and twisted the Vireni betrothal ring. Given Lady Morwynne's opposition, she should have realized her education initiative had been a motive. She sighed. Yet insulting the countess's sense of status had been the final provocation. Not surprising.

Taking Kiera's hand, Devon eyed Lady Morwynne like a firecat eyed a faebird. "Believe me, I *do* mean to marry Kiera."

Her heart clenching, Kiera forced herself to not tug her hand free. He sounded so sincere, probably because he did love her and wished they could marry. But regardless of their love, a bastard daughter of a greedy whore could *never* be queen. 'Twould harm Calatini if the truth ever emerged.

Devon snorted. "Besides, even if you had succeeded in poisoning Kiera, I'd have made certain her education initiative continued."

Smirking, Lady Morwynne quirked her brows. "You might have *tried*, but without her as inspiration, 'twould have soon foundered."

Kiera blinked. The countess overestimated her influence. Once underway, her education initiative didn't need her.

His gold eyes a muddy brown in his still pale face, Lord Morwynne stared at his mother. "You were so against the poor receiving a decent education that you sent Lady Kiera poisoned sparkling wine? You might have murdered King Devon in addition to our future queen."

Lady Morwynne touched his hand and frowned when he jerked away. "Oh no, 'twas no chance of that. King Devon's protection charm would neutralize the poison if he drank any of the sparkling wine."

Kiera swallowed and clutched Devon's hand. And it had. If he'd not tried it first, she'd be dead now. Murdered by this conniving harpy.

Devon leaned forward, his jaw twitching. "Poisoning your future queen is just as treasonous as poisoning your king."

When Lady Morwynne smirked and opened her mouth to retort, Kiera interjected before the countess could exacerbate Devon's fury, "How did you know to send the sparkling wine as a gift from Annalise?"

Lady Morwynne snickered and flicked her fingers. "I befriended the feud-obsessed Greysnowes because they're *so* easy to manipulate, and Lady Greysnowe couldn't help complaining about her annoyingly ill daughter. And I knew you'd not question a gift from your *dear* friend."

Kiera grimaced. How perceptive of Lady Morwynne. Both about her trusting a friend and Annalise's parents.

Devon narrowed his eyes at the countess. "You'd be wise to show remorse for your crime, my lady."

Lady Morwynne moued. "My only *crime* was that I failed."

As Devon tensed again, Kiera dug her nails into his palm to restrain him. She shook her head when he turned toward her. Confronting Lady Morwynne further would gain them nothing.

Devon inhaled a breath then turned back to the countess. "Lady Morwynne, you'll remain confined here until your trial at the next council meeting." He beckoned Millier, who grasped Lady Morwynne's arm and escorted her out with Holmes. Once the countess was gone, Devon turned to her son. "A pair of royal guards shall remain to watch her and handle her communication mirror linked to the council room during the trial. I expect you to attend the council meeting in her stead."

Lord Morwynne swallowed but bowed in his seat to Devon. "Yes, your majesty." He repeated his bow to Kiera. "I apologize for any trouble Mother has caused you, Lady Kiera."

Kiera inclined her head and smiled at Lord Morwynne. The poor boy had aged a decade this morning. "Please remember her sins aren't yours. None of us can choose our parents." She certainly wouldn't have chosen Bobbi.

Devon collected the poisoned bottle of sparkling wine then drew her upright. "We must return to the palace."

After Lord Morwynne rose then bowed again, Kiera and Devon left and rode back to the palace in silence with their hands entwined. Although her poisoner was handled but for a short trial, her chest still ached. Surely others at court, like the Duke of Osbourne, secretly shared the countess's hatred of her. 'Twas why she could never become queen.

KIERA AND DEVON both feigned cheer at the Nolans' Longnight charity auction that evening, but they left early. Then they made love with desperate passion until they collapsed into slumber. After a late breakfast, they handled state affairs until luncheon.

While they were finishing their Longnight trifle, Mia brought her a note from Mr. Leshane stating The Blonde Nymph would sail midmorning tomorrow. After reading it, she frowned and tapped the note against her chin. Seeing Bobbi board would be reassuring.

Devon leaned toward her. "What is it?"

Kiera sighed. The ship sailed the same time as her next nightmara ride. "I must rearrange my nightmara ride tomorrow. Bobbi sails then, and we should watch to make sure she boards."

Devon smiled at her. "I'm sure Moonbud shan't mind rearranging."

She sighed again. Hopefully so, and hopefully, the nightmara queen-heir wouldn't read why when she asked. "I'll visit her straight after luncheon."

Her guards accompanying her, Kiera strode down to the nightmara stables, but the mara man at the door chuckled and said Moonbud was unavailable. Yet since she must see Bobbi leave tomorrow, she remained until the nightmara queen-heir could see her.

Moonbud met her at the nightmara stables an hour later. :*Sorry to keep you waiting, but I didn't expect you. Darkthorn and I went on a gallop alone. Finding time alone is difficult while staying here, and true mates need that.*:

Kiera blushed. Their *gallop* explained the mara man's chuckle, although doubtless Moonbud and Darkthorn had done more than gallop. "No, I'm sorry to disturb you." She paused. "What are true mates?"

Moonbud flicked her tail. :*Two aligned minds with the potential for deep and lasting love. We dominant mares often call ours once we reach maturity, since having them helps us be better and stronger rulers.*: She nickered. :*Although I didn't have to call far for mine.*:

Kiera almost sighed, her heart squeezing. Did humans have true mates, or just nightmara? If only Devon were hers. Although perhaps not, since she must return to the orphanage. She lifted her chin then smiled at Moonbud, burying all thoughts of Bobbi, Lady Morwynne, or leaving. "I'll be quick, so you can return to Darkthorn. I'm afraid I must rearrange tomorrow's ride. I've a pressing matter that can't wait."

Moonbud's taupe eyes bored into Kiera. :*I see.*:

Shoving against the powers pressing her mind, Kiera met Moonbud's gaze. The nightmara queen-heir would never negotiate with her if she read the truth. "The morning after tomorrow is the council meeting, but I could come the following morning."

Her nostrils flaring, Moonbud shook her head, and her powers withdrew. :*Your riding lessons are progressing well, so I believe we can skip this one.*:

Kiera nodded, her chest lightening. She'd expected Moonbud to protest more. She and Moonbud spoke for a bit then she headed back to the palace.

When she joined Devon in his study and told him what Moonbud had said, he grinned at her. "I told you Moonbud wouldn't mind. While you were gone, I asked our guards to arrange some horses that suit the docks. Even an unmarked carriage might attract attention there. On foot would be better than horses, but our guards wouldn't allow that."

So after breakfast the following morning, Kiera changed into the one orphanage dress buried in her wardrobe then donned an old cloak Mia had found yesterday. Then Devon joined her, dressed in the rough clothes and apprentice healer's torc he'd worn when visiting the orphanage in disguise, and they slipped down to the secret royal entrance where their guards waited with several rickety mares.

Once they mounted, Devon glanced at the guards. "Remain far enough behind that no one realizes we're together."

She sighed. That distance would also prevent the guards from seeing Bobbi. And 'twas best if even they didn't know about her. She shifted in her saddle as they took a circuitous route to the docks. Her mare's rough gait was nothing like riding Moonbud, but she controlled the mare with ease after all her lessons.

When they reached the alley near The Blonde Nymph, she and Devon halted in the shadow of a worn rowhouse with an unobstructed view of the gangway. Her stomach twisting, she soothed her mare as they watched the ship. She swallowed when Hawke finally arrived with Bobbi concealed in a dark cloak.

Devon leaned forward in his saddle and peered at Bobbi as she boarded the ship. "That's her?"

Kiera nodded. Doubtless Wren and Hawke had convinced the greedy woman that if people saw her, they'd prevent her from receiving the arachne's wealth. "The shape is right."

She and Devon watched in silence until The Blonde Nymph finally pulled out from the dock. She sighed again as they rode back to the palace. With Bobbi gone and after Lady Morwynne's trial tomorrow, Kiera could return her attention to her riding lessons and negotiating the Nightmara-Calatini Treaty. Her heart twisted. Then her time with Devon would end.

CHAPTER 53

While they ate luncheon after returning to the palace, Devon frowned at Kiera. She'd hardly said a word all morning, even quieter than after they'd confronted Lady Morwynne. Did Bobbi truly shame her that much? If so, she'd never believe he could love her and wish to marry her.

Yet somehow he must convince her that her parentage didn't matter and who she was did—he couldn't return to his lonely, overburdened life without her. Should he confess his love like Selena had insisted? After a moment, he sighed. No, mere words wouldn't convince Kiera. He must prove it with his actions instead. But how?

Supporting her like always during tomorrow's trial should help. Hopefully, the other councilors would vote Lady Morwynne guilty of treason without demur. Then he'd make Kiera's Longnight season the best she'd ever enjoyed. That should finally convince her his love was sincere. Then he could ask her to marry him again.

Yet perhaps he should wait until *after* Kiera had negotiated the Nightmara-Calatini Treaty to repeat his proposal. Only a true queen could so successfully charm court, start an education initiative, overcome her detractors, and renew a historic treaty. Plus, he'd have no reason other than love to ask her to marry him then. Surely she'd finally see that and accept his proposal.

He smiled at Kiera over his beetroot soup. But in the meantime, tonight's court event should cheer her. "Anticipating the Westons' caroling party tonight?"

Kiera beamed back at him. "I've always loved caroling, even though I'm only a passable singer." She sighed. "I hope the Westons allow Amaranth to join us this time. Her celestial voice is almost magical."

Devon chuckled. Yes, tonight's event helped. "I'm sure they shall. I doubt the Westons deny anything their adored granddaughters truly desire."

And when they arrived that evening, his speculation was proved correct. Lady Weston immediately embraced Kiera then flashed a grin. "Welcome, your majesties. Amaranth asked we tell Lady Kiera to find her at once—she's something to tell you."

Lord Weston chuckled and waved toward his young granddaughter bouncing and chattering. "She's over by Hawke and his wife telling them *all* about it."

Devon and Kiera smiled then he escorted her across the room. The little girl's delight would *definitely* cheer Kiera.

As soon as they arrived, Amaranth whirled and flung her arms about Kiera's skirt. "Guess what Grandma and Grandpa said, Mistress Kiera?" Once Kiera returned her embrace and shrugged, Amaranth continued, "They said I can sing a carol for *everyone* tonight. I'm singing 'The Lullay Carol'—and I'm accompanying myself on the keyharp."

Kiera beamed. "That's wonderful."

The little girl began to chatter about her upcoming performance. Devon and the others smiled and listened until Cassandra glided over and said, "Come along, Amaranth. You need to have some cider and calm your breath before you sing." She winked at Kiera and Wren then led her still bouncing sister away.

Devon chuckled. What amazing energy. Although the little girl would doubtless collapse after her carol was finished.

Kiera leaned toward Wren then lifted her sleeve and tapped her protection charm. "The person we discussed earlier has been unearthed and shall be handled shortly." When Wren inhaled, Kiera nodded. "But we can discuss that more later." She arched a brow. "I imagine you're relieved your houseguest is gone at last. Thanks for enduring her."

Wren sighed, faint shadows beneath her eyes. "I'm glad you decided how to handle her. Now we can enjoy our townhouse alone until the twins come."

Devon blinked. Twins? Hawke and Wren mustn't have told their families yet, otherwise the duchess would have planned another grandiose fete to celebrate. Then he coughed to disguise his laugh when Kiera murmured, "Enjoy, hmm?"

Wren blushed, but Devon and Hawke exchanged grins. If he and Kiera had their own townhouse, they'd probably enjoy it the same.

Kiera giggled then asked, "How's the Longnight season at the orphanage?"

Wren's blush faded, and she grinned. "Wonderful, although the orphans made us swear to not reveal anything. They want to surprise you when you visit in two days, in exchange for *your* surprise." She winked at Devon.

He smiled. Hopefully, he'd be enough. They should bring some gifts to make sure. The orphans could use those, regardless. He'd arrange it as *his* surprise for Kiera.

Her brow furrowing, Kiera glanced about the room. "Is Annalise here?"

Wren tilted her head. "I've not seen her."

Hawke shrugged. "Lady Annalise doesn't always attend the Westons' musical evenings." He flashed a crooked grin and nodded toward the seats. "Perhaps she heard that Lord Ravenstone and his mother were attending."

As Devon and Kiera glanced over, he suppressed a sigh.

The genial count was nearly frowning into his cider, his vibrant mother smiling beside him. Doubtless whatever was troubling Lord Ravenstone involved the Greysnowes—it always did.

Then Cassandra glided to the front and announced her sister was about to open the caroling, so Devon escorted Kiera to a seat, while Hawke and Wren sat beside them. He threaded his fingers through Kiera's as Amaranth began to sing. She was right—the little girl's celestial voice was almost magical.

DEVON WOKE LATE the following morning with Kiera sleeping entwined in his arms. His heart warming, he kissed her head but otherwise didn't move. Holding her was blissful. At some point, she stirred and woke, but she didn't attempt to rise either, so she must feel likewise.

But then his stomach rumbled, and hers answered equally loud.

Kiera smiled against his chest. "I suppose we should rise before our stomachs consume us."

He glanced at the clock on the mantel and sighed. Plus, they mustn't delay Lady Morwynne's trial. "And if we don't rise, we'll be late for the council meeting."

Kiera echoed his sigh, but they slipped from bed then dressed and devoured a hearty breakfast before hurrying to the council room. Their guards flanking the door, they strode inside.

As instructed, a strained Lord Morwynne occupied his mother's seat, while Lady Juliet sat beside him with the council room's communication mirror, the poisoned bottle of sparkling wine, a map of Ormas, her silver bowl, and the magical ingredients for her kin spell. The eleven remaining councilors muttered and eyed the outsiders, but they hushed as Devon and Kiera took their seats.

Holding Kiera's hand beneath the table to hearten her, Devon nodded at the councilors. Not surprising they all already realized something was amiss. "Morning. To start, we must address the absent Lady Morwynne."

As Lady Juliet chanted and gestured at the communication mirror, the glass glowed white then Lady Morwynne appeared with two royal guards behind her. The councilors glanced at each other then the mirror, and the silence grew as heavy as before a thunderstorm.

After a moment, Devon squeezed Kiera's hand and continued, "The countess has been confined to Morwynne House for attempting to poison Kiera."

While Lord Morwynne paled, the heavy silence stretched, and all the councilors except Aragon stiffened then eyed Lady Morwynne in the mirror askance. Aragon merely glared at the countess.

Lady Morwynne opened her mouth, but before she could speak, Kiera leaned forward and said, "If not for Devon's protection charm, we both would have been murdered."

As Lord Morwynne winced, the councilors stiffened further, and many of them glared at Lady Morwynne like Aragon.

The Duke of Osbourne turned to scrutinize Devon and Kiera then creaked, "King Sarastor must have seen Lady Morwynne's treason in the Mirror of Wisdom."

Kiera tensing beside him at the mention of the perilous mirror, Devon inclined his head. Thank the Goddess his father had risked using it. "Along with Kiera's appearance at the summer masquerade."

While Lady Morwynne scowled in the communication mirror, the other councilors shifted in their seats and exchanged glances.

Devon caressed Kiera's palm with his thumb until she relaxed then arched his brows at the royal witch. "Lady Juliet, could you please demonstrate how you unearthed Lady Morwynne's treason before the council?"

Lady Juliet nodded then performed her kin spell, explaining it to the councilors. When the glowing mist condensed above

Morwynne House on the map of Ormas, all the councilors in the council room scowled.

Devon eyed Lord Morwynne, who was white and tense at the evidence of his mother's treason. The poor count. "So only one of the Morwynnes could have attempted to poison Kiera. When we confronted them, 'twas clear young Lord Morwynne knew nothing about the attempt, but his mother confessed." He turned to the communication mirror and forced himself not to glare. "Any words in your defense?"

Lady Morwynne sniffed. "I only attempted to poison Kiera to protect Calatini from her ruinous education initiative, and with your protection charm, your majesty, you were never at risk."

Fire flaring through him, he suppressed a growl at Lady Morwynne's continued lack of remorse. The treasonous harpy. When Kiera squeezed his hand, he inhaled then slanted her an almost smile. Thank the Goddess she was here to calm him. He arched his brows at the councilors about the table. "Who votes Lady Morwynne is guilty of treason for attempting to poison Lady Kiera?"

All eleven councilors jerked nods and agreed, while Lady Morwynne scowled and her son winced.

As Kiera sighed, Devon caressed her palm. The councilors' immediate agreement proved they all accepted her as their queen. That should convince Kiera her parentage didn't matter.

The Duchess of Wildewall frowned. "A sentence of treason usually warrants death, but in this case..."

Devon and Kiera exchanged a glance, and he almost grimaced. A public execution of a councilor for poisoning the future queen *would* upset Calatini, especially the commoners who adored Kiera even more than court did.

Still pale, Lord Morwynne coughed then said, "Although Mother deserves death, I believe I've a better punishment—strip her powers and rank then imprison her at our country estate. Mother despises the place, and she'll have to suffer your victory the rest of her days."

Kiera frowned and leaned toward the young count. "You'd be responsible for imprisoning your mother, and she could live many more years."

Devon tapped his fingers on the table. Lord Morwynne's plan *might* be enough. "Could she escape and instigate more trouble?"

Lord Morwynne shrugged. "Lady Juliet could bind her to the estate and fetter her actions. 'Tis a common spell for the insane in the Tsarkan Empire."

The Duke of Oakmoor nodded. "So it is, and effective too. The Tsarkan emperor's first wife has been bound to their palace's original harem by that spell since she went mad after too much faedust and almost killed his favorite daughter eight years ago."

Devon almost smiled as Lady Morwynne eyed her son, her face pale and shriveled. Good, she was showing remorse at last. She rasped, "Arthur, how could you suggest that?"

Ignoring his mother in the mirror beside him, Lord Morwynne nodded at Devon and Kiera. "With Mother's expulsion from the council, I'd very much like to assume her position as the Minister of Health and Community, if you trust me, of course. *I* fully support Lady Kiera's education initiative and would be eager to help."

As Lady Morwynne whitened further, Devon arched a brow at Kiera. Dealing with the young count was as interesting as he'd suspected. And having the Minister of Health and Community's help should reduce the burden on Kiera. When she nodded, he glanced about the table. "Anyone have any objections?" Once the other councilors shook their heads, he nodded at Lord Morwynne. "We accept your punishment recommendation and appoint you to the council for the remainder of the current term."

Kiera smiled at the royal witch. "Lady Juliet, thanks for your assistance today. I believe we no longer require the former Lady Morwynne; you may deactivate the communication mirror."

Lady Juliet nodded and gestured toward the mirror, and the glass turned white then cleared to reflect the council room.

Devon beamed and squeezed Kiera's hand. Goddess, she was

the perfect queen, always gracious yet firm. He turned to Lord Islaye. "With the trial concluded, let's continue to other matters. Lord Islaye, I believe you promised us good news about the ore in Magehaven."

The tension in the council room eased as the studious count grinned. "And I have some. Miss Winston and Priest Griffith, an itinerant priest who's been helping since the explosion, have stabilized the ore during the past week, but they've not identified or fully counteracted it yet."

Devon smiled at Kiera. Priest Griffith must be the veiled witch's warrior priest. So her cryptic prophecy *was* coming true.

Kiera smiled back then leaned toward Lord Islaye. "Have any elves replied to our request for aid?"

Lord Islaye sighed. "Not yet."

Devon and Kiera exchanged another glance. According to the veiled witch, the Magehaven ore wouldn't be neutralized until a crippled elf lore master arrived. Hopefully soon. He turned back to the councilors and asked if anyone had other matters to discuss. When everyone shook their heads, he adjourned the meeting.

While Lady Juliet and the other councilors began leaving, the Duke of Osbourne leaned back and remained seated.

Aragon studied the elderly duke then clapped Devon's shoulder with a significant look, silently saying they'd talk later. When Devon nodded back, Aragon smiled at Kiera before following the other councilors out.

As Kiera swallowed, Devon eyed the Duke of Osbourne. What did the wily duke wish to discuss? He'd no upcoming events planned this time.

The duke folded his wrinkled hands before him. "My people tell me Lord and Lady Beza had an unwanted houseguest sail for Mist Isle yesterday."

His pulse quickening, Devon tensed as Kiera paled and gripped his hand. The duke had clearly unraveled their romantic tale about her parentage—what did he intend to do?

The Duke of Osbourne tilted his head. "Their guest resembled you in several decades, Lady Kiera."

Devon hid a smile when Kiera simply lifted her chin and drawled, "Did she? How remarkable."

The duke chuckled. "Not that it matters." As Devon and Kiera both blinked, he rose and swept Kiera a deep bow. "I again applaud your strategy. You're no more a lost princess than I'm a water elf, but you've prevailed against every obstacle. Reminds me of my late wife—she could out-strategize anyone, even me." He winked at Devon. "If I were still King Devon's age, I'd steal you away myself, but then Calatini would lose one of her greatest queens."

Devon grinned. Even more than the council's acceptance, the cagey duke's approbation proved Kiera's parentage didn't matter. He glanced at the blushing Kiera beside him. Surely she could see that now.

CHAPTER 54

*K*iera blushed at the Duke of Osbourne's compliment. He'd been scrutinizing her because he approved of her? How unexpected. She inhaled then murmured, "Thank you, your grace."

As the duke chuckled again and strolled from the council room, she twisted the Vireni betrothal ring. All this time, she'd assumed the councilors and the rest of court despised her common birth. And a few like Lady Morwynne did, but the rest of court like Hawke's family, the Westons, Lady Ducharme, and even the Duke of Osbourne had been welcoming. Her only major detractors remaining were the Greysnowes, and they didn't despise her for her birth but because they believed her a Ravenstone pawn.

She inhaled. Perhaps a poor orphanage matron *could* become queen after all. With Bobbi exiled, no one else at court should unearth her true parentage. And she'd succeeded as acting queen —she'd deftly navigated court, started an education initiative, and faced a magical crisis, kidnapper, extortioner, and poisoner. The only thing left was negotiating the Nightmara-Calatini Treaty, but 'twould be soon. And after over two months of night-mara rides, she understood the nightmara better than any queen before her, so she'd ensure Calatini fared well in the renewed treaty.

Devon chuckled and drew her upright. "Well, *that* was a surprise. Although the wily duke does love his strategy and secrets."

Kiera squeezed his arm as they left the council room. "Well, he *is* the Minister of Intelligence."

While they returned to the royal quarters, she glanced at Devon beneath her lashes. She could only become queen if he truly wanted to marry her. He'd initially proposed so she could negotiate with the nightmara, but considering how he'd acted since then, he now loved her as deeply as she loved him. So surely he'd soon confess his love and ask her to marry him in truth.

As they attended festive Longnight events over the following days, Devon continued treating her as lovingly as always—trusting her with important duties, providing thoughtful surprises, and holding her at night. Yet he never spoke of his love or renewed his proposal.

Then at her next nightmara ride, Kiera and Moonbud sailed over every jump without hesitation. Moonbud tossed her mane once Kiera dismounted and said, :*I believe you're comfortable jumping now. For your next ride, I'll construct a course to test your skills riding a horse.*:

Kiera grinned, her pulse quickening. She'd proved herself to Moonbud at last.

Moonbud craned toward her. :*Assuming you pass, which doubtless you shall, then we can negotiate the treaty at our following meeting.*:

Kiera swallowed but managed a bright smile. If Devon hadn't proposed by then, she'd have no reason to remain, so she'd return to the orphanage with her heart irrevocably shattered. But perhaps he would once he realized how little time they'd remaining.

So as she and Devon began luncheon before heading to the

orphanage, she flashed the same bright smile she'd given the nightmara queen-heir. "Moonbud intends to test my riding skills next time."

His spoon halfway to his mouth, Devon stilled. "So soon?"

Kiera swallowed and arched her brows. Didn't he want to ask her anything else—like a marriage proposal? "Not soon. I've been acting as your betrothed for nearly three months."

Devon set down his spoon without tasting it. "Odd. It doesn't feel that long."

She stared at him. What did he mean by that? When he said nothing further, her stomach twisted, but she forced another smile. "We'd best finish eating, so we're not late to the orphanage. The orphans *need* their surprise."

Devon returned her smile, and they both devoured their fish chowder, crusty rolls, and spiced cider in silence then left for the orphanage. When he handed her into the carriage, she blinked at the full bag on the backward seat and asked, "What's that?"

A grin hovering on his lips, Devon wrapped an arm about her shoulders as the carriage rumbled forward. "You'll see."

Kiera snuggled against him, her chest warming. Had he planned another surprise for the orphans? Goddess, he was wonderful. Hopefully, he'd ask her to marry him again soon.

When the carriage halted, Devon scooped up the bag and helped her alight then waved for their guards to remain behind.

Peter beamed at her then gave Devon a deep bow. "Afternoon, Mistress Kiera, your majesty. Everyone's waitin' for your surprise—the orphans been bouncin' about the dinin' hall the past hour. Miss Wren began a Longnight story to settle them.

Kiera chuckled. Not surprising, the orphans were often wild at Longnight time. After embracing Peter, she and Devon strode to the dining hall, which was festively decorated with paper snowflakes and evergreen garlands.

Wren glanced up, and her reading paused, but she recovered quick enough the orphans remained engrossed in her Longnight story. Meanwhile, Hawke eased over to them and winked. Then

Wren finished reading and waved toward them. "Look, Mistress Kiera is here with her surprise—King Devon here to meet you. And it appears he's a surprise of his own."

The orphans whirled to goggle at Devon, who smiled back. As one, the orphans swarmed them like a flock of excited sprites while chattering indistinct greetings.

Warmth filling her, Kiera beamed and embraced every orphan around her. And beside her, Devon was grinning while doing the same, although he shook hands with the older boys instead. He'd make a wonderful father one day.

After embracing Kiera, Janelle bounded over to Devon. "What's in the bag, your majesty?"

Kiera smiled when Devon winked at the girl and replied, "A surprise like Miss Wren said. But I *heard* you have a surprise for Mistress Kiera. How about we do that first?"

Janelle bobbed her head, then she and the other orphans dragged Kiera and Devon over to the white sheet hanging in the corner of the dining hall.

When the orphans yanked down the sheet, Kiera gasped and clasped her hands. This year's winter palace, the traditional display fashioned after the Winter Queen's home to hold Long-night gifts, was the best the orphanage had ever enjoyed, despite holding no gifts yet.

Not solemn for once, Sarya pointed at the ornate, six-foot ice sculpture with evergreen garlands at its base. "Miss Wren bought a winter palace made of magicked ice!"

Emma waved at the snowflake and icicle garlands on the wall behind the winter palace. "And it even has snowstrings." Then she waved at the gold light garlands above them. "And starlights."

The Bedsford twins bounced in place, and John said, "And there's enough space for the Winter Queen to bring everyone *two* gifts at least."

Grinning, Jacob interjected after his twin, "Miss Wren said they'll start appearing soon."

Kiera nodded, her throat constricting. In past years, the orphanage only had a trestle table covered with a white cloth and a few evergreen garlands. Bless Wren for purchasing all this. No doubt she'd purchased wonderful gifts too. "'Tis a lovely surprise. I can't wait to see it filled with gifts." She smiled at Devon. "Hopefully, the king's surprise equals your winter palace."

Devon chuckled. "Nothing so grand. Just some trinkets to enliven everyone's Longnight." He opened his bag and began handing the orphans small gifts wrapped in festive paper— white for the little girls, green for the little boys, and gold for the older children.

Kiera beamed as the orphans squealed and tore open their gifts. All the gifts contained a few pieces of hard candy and a small toy. The little girls received a cloth doll resembling the Winter Queen, the little boys received three wooden soldiers, and the older children received an illuminated deck of cards. She squeezed Devon's arm. Yes, definitely a wonderful father.

While the orphans began playing with their new toys, Wren drew Kiera out into the hall.

Kiera eyed her friend and frowned. Although smiling, Wren had faint shadows beneath her eyes, just like she had at the Westons' the other evening. So 'twasn't due to the late hour. "You look tired."

Wren rubbed her forehead. "Dratted pregnancy. I'm still plagued by nausea, and in the past week, I've begun suffering headaches. I suppose 'tis retribution for the ones Hawke got when bewitched by my glamour spell. But enough about that. Tell me about your poisoner like you promised."

Kiera grimaced yet explained about Lady Morwynne, her trial for treason, and being magically bound to her country estate. Then Kiera sighed and said, "To account for her sudden absence, I believe Lord Morwynne intends to tell everyone his mother went mad."

Wren snorted. "She did if she poisoned you for seeking to

improve the lives of the poor." When Kiera shrugged, Wren squeezed her hand. "I'm glad both she and Bobbi are handled. Now nothing stands between you and Devon marrying."

Kiera sighed, her heart squeezing. Only if he proposed in truth. "Our betrothal is fake, remember? I'll be returning here once the nightmara leave."

Wren hummed and tilted her head but only asked, "Shall we rejoin everyone?"

Kiera nodded, and they slipped back into the dining hall. The orphans were still engrossed with their toys.

When they joined him and Devon, Hawke wrapped an arm about Wren. "While the orphans are distracted, perhaps you should take a nap."

Wren caressed his face with a soft smile. "I love you, you coddler. But I'm fine."

Kiera swallowed, a pang darting through her. If only she could tell Devon she loved him so blithely. But she couldn't influence his decision to marry her, and if he didn't want her, having told him would make leaving so much harder.

As Hawke and Wren began to debate about her nap, Devon took Kiera's arm and murmured, "We should return to the palace. We've the Dabars' Longnight pastry feast to attend."

After visiting the kitchen to see Mary, Kiera and Devon strode from the orphanage and into his carriage. They sat beside each other like always, but he didn't take her hand or wrap an arm about her shoulders like he usually did. And he stared out the window without speaking.

She stiffened and studied him. Why was he acting so distant? Had seeing her at the orphanage reminded him that she was no true court lady and shouldn't become queen? Was *that* why he'd not confessed his love or renewed his proposal? Surely he would have by now if he believed her a worthy queen. Tears pricking her eyes, she began staring out the opposite window.

When the sprawling white palace came into sight, Devon murmured, "I suppose you'll return to the orphanage soon."

Kiera almost winced as she turned toward Devon, who was still staring out his window. He certainly wasn't renewing his proposal. Her ribs clenched. "Yes."

Devon stilled for a moment. Then he nodded. "I must send more money to the orphanage. Some of the orphans were too small for their winter garments." The carriage halted, and he helped her alight. "And their winter palace needs gifts."

She managed a smile, despite her aching chest. If only she could marry him, but he obviously didn't want that. "I'm sure Wren has some, but the orphans could use more. Thanks, Devon."

Devon shrugged as he escorted her upstairs to change. "'Tis nothing."

Once dressed in evening clothes, they left again for the Dabars' Longnight pastry feast. And although the food was both delectable and plentiful, Kiera had to force herself to smile and feign Longnight cheer. Devon appeared equally strained—he smiled often, but none reached his eyes. So as soon as dessert was served, they returned to the palace.

Back in his chambers, they sipped their spiced cider in silence then slipped into bed. She sighed as she nestled against him. Their betrothal would end soon, so she must enjoy his embrace while she still could.

FILLED with more Longnight festivities that Kiera attempted to enjoy, the days before her riding test passed swiftly. Devon stopped acting distant, but he still never spoke of love or marriage. So she clung to him at night, attempting to store memories she could cherish after they parted.

Bundled in a warm cloak and a heavy riding habit, Kiera met Annalise outside the palace on the morning of her riding test then frowned. Annalise had faint shadows beneath her eyes, and the heart-shaped firegem flickering at her throat accentuated her unusual pallor. Yet her tiredness couldn't be due to pregnancy like Wren's. "Are you feeling well?"

Annalise shrugged as they began toward the nightmara stables, the royal guards close behind. "A bit tired, thanks to the shorter days."

Kiera frowned. Did Annalise's powers tie her to the seasons like a nature witch? "Is that why you've not attended the evening Longnight festivities?"

Annalise nodded with a sigh. "After only lasting an hour at the Duchess of Childes's Longnight ball, I decided it best. Fortunately, chastened by King Devon's accusations of treason, my parents have let me, although Goddess knows how long their forbearance shall last."

Echoing Annalise's sigh, Kiera pursed her lips. Doubtless the ambitious Greysnowes wouldn't allow their daughter to miss court events for long. "Perhaps you should visit a healer."

Annalise grimaced as they reached the nightmara stables. "I would, but a magicless healer probably couldn't help, and a witch healer would realize I was a soul healer. I can't risk my parents discovering that."

Kiera winced. Especially if she was bound to someone her parents wouldn't accept. Poor Annalise.

Before she could comfort her friend, Leila opened the stable door with Nightrose behind her. She beamed at Kiera. "Ready?"

Kiera swallowed, her stomach fluttering. Goddess, let this go well. "Of course."

When they entered the paddock containing a series of jumps, she swallowed harder. The palomino stallion prancing between Moonbud and Darkthorn appeared almost wild. Intentional, no doubt. She inclined her head at Moonbud as they approached.

Moonbud echoed her nod. :*Ready to demonstrate your riding skills?*: When Kiera nodded again, Moonbud continued, :*Then mount and follow my instructions.*:

Once Annalise joined Darkthorn, Kiera mounted the restive stallion and gulped a bracing breath. She could do this. She calmed the stallion then arched her brows at Moonbud, who snorted and began her instructions.

Obeying the nightmara queen-heir, Kiera held the stallion to a steady walk then weaved him between serpentine pairs of poles. Her pulse quickening, she encouraged him to a trot and guided him over several low jumps in quick succession. Then to a canter and back through the poles. She slowed him to a walk around the paddock then spurred him to a punishing gallop. After several circuits, she urged him over the high jumps in the center. Grinning, she halted the heaving stallion before Moonbud. She'd done it! Without faltering too.

Moonbud bobbed her head. :*You may dismount.*: She chuckled. :*You performed even better than I'd expected. Perhaps you've some mara blood in you.*:

Kiera suppressed a wince as she slid to the ground. Not through Bobbi and some unknown Ormas merchant. "I doubt it. But I'd an excellent teacher."

Moonbud chuckled again. :*Flatterer. I'll see you in three days to negotiate the treaty.*:

Kiera's chest swelled then abruptly hollowed. She'd only three days left with Devon. She gritted a brilliant grin. "Until then."

As Darkthorn nuzzled Moonbud, Kiera and Annalise left the paddock with her guards. She sighed. How would Devon react when she told him about her successful riding test? Surely not with a proposal. If only he would.

CHAPTER 55

*D*evon paced about his chambers as he waited for Kiera to return from her riding test. Surely passing would help her see she was worthy of being queen, despite her parentage. But if it didn't, doubtless successfully negotiating the Nightmara-Calatini Treaty would. Goddess, let that finally be enough.

He sighed and clenched his hands behind his back. Because overcoming her detractors and earning the council's approbation hadn't convinced her. In the days since Lady Morwynne's trial, Kiera had appeared sober and strained. The only time she'd appeared truly happy had been at the orphanage, and afterward she'd agreed she'd return there soon. So his obstinate lady still didn't see she was meant to be queen.

Then Kiera's door sounded, and he burst into her chambers. "How did it go?"

Her riotous curls disheveled, Kiera shrugged with a weak smile as she undid several buttons at her throat. "Well enough. I performed everything Moonbud asked. We negotiate in three days."

Devon eyed her, his chest squeezing at her indifference. Passing hadn't heartened her at all. Perhaps honoring her triumph would. He beamed at her. "We must celebrate with sparkling wine at luncheon."

Kiera shrugged again without her usual delight at sparkling wine. "If you like. Although would you mind if we delayed that? I want to bathe after my strenuous ride."

His pulse quickening, he nodded. If only he could join her. But she was clearly too tired to make love. Perhaps her tiredness was also why she didn't appear excited. "Of course. Join me for luncheon in my chambers whenever you're ready." Then he strode out before he seduced her.

When Kiera joined him, Devon almost sighed. Although no longer disheveled, her smile was still weak. He forced a grin as he poured them flutes of sparkling wine. He toasted her. "To the only lady who could have gained Moonbud's trust."

Shifting in her chair, Kiera blushed and sipped her sparkling wine. "Nonsense. Any court lady could have done the same."

His jaw twitching, he set down his sparkling wine. *Why* couldn't she see how wonderful she was? "Now you're speaking nonsense. No other lady I know could have learned to ride in under three months while learning how to handle court and starting an education initiative."

Kiera leaned toward him, her navy eyes darkening. "Truly?"

Devon swallowed as tingling warmth flooded him. Goddess, she was tempting. If only he could draw her in his arms, confess his love, and renew his proposal. But she'd refuse him if she didn't believe she could be queen, and he couldn't risk that. He must wait until after she'd negotiated the treaty. He coughed. "Yes. We should eat before the food gets cold."

Kiera blinked then straightened with a tight smile. "I'm as ravenous as *two* starved manticores today."

He nodded, and they devoured their chestnut soup in silence. He might blurt his love or propose if he spoke before he'd settled himself. But when they began their crispy goose, he asked, "Have you decided who you'll bring as advisors to negotiate with Moonbud?"

Kiera hummed and tilted her head. "You, of course, and... Lady Ducharme, I think. She's a strong lady with influence, which the nightmara like. Plus, as Minister of Defense, she knows *precisely* how dangerous them moving from the Nightmara Plains would be. Moonbud shall read that from her mind and reconsider."

Devon beamed at her. Yet another instance she proved her worth as queen. "Clever." As she blushed, he arched a brow. "You could probably bring more advisors if you want them. Moonbud trusts you enough."

Kiera grimaced and cut her goose. "No, I'll keep to the traditional two. These negotiations are already irregular enough."

To encourage her, he chuckled and drawled, "Not as much as mine."

Kiera pursed her lips. "And we all know how well *that* went." She glanced at the clock on the mantel. "I'd best go. I must write Lady Ducharme and arrange other details for the nightmara negotiations before the Blackhams' Longnight games party tonight."

As she rose, Devon sighed. If only he could risk kissing her, but neither of them could spend the afternoon in bed with the nightmara negotiations so soon. But they could after tonight's party.

Yet while playing festive games that night, Kiera's bright smiles were as fake as the ones after she'd discovered Bobbi. And she didn't respond to his flirting. So afterward, he swept her to bed and made love to her with desperate passion to draw her closer. But in the morning, Kiera seemed as distant as before, or perhaps more so. She responded to his flirting with politeness, never initiated kisses, and rarely smiled.

When Kiera left for Elise's ladies' luncheon to celebrate the upcoming nightmara negotiations, Devon paced in his study. Kiera must be fretting over those negotiations—definitely not the Longnight season he'd wanted her to enjoy. He must do something to distract her. Perhaps another surprise. But what? Their evenings were already filled with Longnight festivities at court.

He hummed and halted. They *were* attending the traditional Longnight play tomorrow night. To enjoy some time alone, they'd not invited anyone to join them. But perhaps inviting friends would cheer her. So he wrote to Hawke and Wren then Lady Annalise. To ensure he'd company, he invited Aragon and Selena then Mel. Eight people would fill the royal box and prevent anyone else from intruding. Hopefully, Kiera would enjoy her surprise.

KIERA REMAINED distant the following day, almost as if she'd returned to the orphanage in her thoughts. His stomach tight after an almost silent dinner, Devon yanked on his evening clothes. Please let her surprise help. He couldn't bear to lose her. Once dressed, he strode into her chambers.

In a cream gown trimmed with bands of gilded evergreens and stars, Kiera frowned at her reflection in the cheval mirror. "Appropriate for the traditional Longnight play or too much?"

His blood heating, he wrapped his arms about her waist from behind. "'Tis perfect." He kissed her neck, inhaling her clean lavender scent. If only they could skip the play, but her surprise was waiting. "And gorgeous, as always. We should go before I'm tempted to remove it."

Kiera freed herself from his embrace with a cool smile. "Flatterer."

As he took her arm, Devon returned her smile despite his aching chest. Why did she keep acting distant? He tensed when he climbed beside her in the carriage and wrapped an arm about her shoulders. Would she pull away again? Yet she remained still, although she didn't speak. But neither did he. If he did, he'd either spoil her surprise or his future proposal.

When he escorted Kiera up to the royal box, she halted just inside the threshold. "Wren? What are you doing here?"

Turning around, Wren grinned and gestured to herself and Hawke. "Devon invited us. Didn't he tell you?"

Kiera blinked at him, her lips parting. "No, he said we were attending alone."

Devon squeezed her arm and drew her further inside, so their guards could stand along the back wall. "I thought you'd enjoy the surprise." He risked brushing a kiss against her lips. "We'll be alone plenty later."

Kiera blushed then caressed his jaw. "Thanks, Devon."

He smiled as she bustled over to Wren, and they began discussing the orphans' excitement over their gifts appearing on their winter palace. 'Twas good he'd invited his friends for company. But at least she appeared happy again. If only he could bring her as much joy as the orphanage did.

Aragon rose from his seat beside Selena, who was talking with Mel and a pale Lady Annalise. Joining Devon, he nodded toward Kiera and murmured, "Everything settled yet? Your excuse for your 'fake' betrothal shall be gone before long."

Devon almost winced, his gaze fixed on Kiera as Lady Annalise left Selena to join her. "I'm going to propose again as soon as Kiera negotiates the treaty. Then she'll have succeeded at everything as queen, and I'll have no other reason to ask but love."

Aragon frowned as Kiera and Lady Annalise chuckled at Hawke and Wren describing the Bedsford twins decorating the orphanage's winter palace with shells they'd found at the docks. "Are you certain 'tis wise to wait?"

Devon sighed, his chest squeezing. Kiera hadn't laughed like that since they'd visited the orphanage. "'Tis only another day." Thank the Goddess.

Rubbing her vast stomach, Selena waddled over to them. She appeared ready to give birth at any moment. "What are you two discussing? The play is about to start."

Devon and Aragon exchanged a glance. Doubtless Selena would scold again if she knew, and upsetting such a heavily pregnant lady *definitely* wasn't wise.

Aragon shrugged and replied, "This and that."

Devon eyed Selena. If she delivered in the royal box, court would gossip about it for years. "How are you feeling?"

Selena grimaced. "Eager to be done being pregnant."

Aragon rubbed her back with a tender smile. "We've only five weeks left."

Devon swallowed a laugh when Selena narrowed her eyes at Aragon and said, "*We*? Me, you mean." Before Aragon could do more than stutter, she shook her head. "Come, we should return to our seats."

Once they sat and Lady Annalise returned to her seat by Mel, Devon sat beside Kiera and draped an arm about her shoulders. His heart warmed when Kiera nestled into his embrace, unlike in the carriage earlier. Her surprise *had* helped.

As the curtains opened, Kiera kissed his cheek. "Thanks for inviting everyone tonight."

His cheek tingling, he forced himself to remain still rather than seizing her mouth. "Of course."

Kiera chuckled as the play's Lady Winter glided onstage and began her travels across Damensea. "Although to attend, Wren *did* need a nap this afternoon. I suspect Selena did too."

Devon swallowed and glanced at the pregnant ladies. Hopefully, the play wouldn't exhaust them. "Perhaps I shouldn't have invited them to an evening play."

As Lady Winter met the Goddess in disguise, Kiera smiled and patted his knee. "They'll be fine."

His body tightening at her touch, he captured her hand and kissed her palm. Then they turned their full attention to the stage. When the traditional Longnight play concluded with Lady Winter accepting the Goddess's offer and being reborn as the Winter Queen, he turned to Kiera, still nestled against him.

"What did you think of the play? 'Tis supposedly one of the finest in Ormas."

Kiera hummed and tilted her head. "Very nice, although 'twas odd seeing adults play the roles. And without any stumbles."

From the other side of Kiera, Wren laughed. "Most would say the reverse about the version we're accustomed to seeing." She hugged Kiera then allowed Hawke to draw her upright. "Visit the orphanage in the next week or two to see *our* usual version."

Her eyes flickering, Kiera flashed a brilliant smile. "I'll do that."

Devon tensed. Why did Wren's offer upset Kiera? As they waited for their friends to leave the royal box, he squeezed her shoulders. "I hope I may come too."

Kiera turned her brilliant smile on him as they began downstairs with their guards. "You may visit the orphanage any time you wish, assuming you've time. The orphans would adore seeing you again."

His jaw twitched, but he managed to return her smile. Why did she speak as if she'd not be involved with his visit? If she was already acting distant, tonight's surprise hadn't helped as much as he'd first believed. What else could he try? Perhaps keeping their lovemaking tender tonight would comfort her. He kissed her palm. "We'll pick a morning to visit after you finish negotiating the treaty."

CHAPTER 56

Kiera blinked at Devon as he handed her into the carriage. Why was he speaking as if they'd still be betrothed after the treaty was renewed? Perhaps because they couldn't end their fake betrothal until Moonbud and her night-mara delegation returned to the Nightmara Plains. She swallowed, her heart twisting. Could she manage to remain for however long that was?

Tears pricked her eyes as he wrapped an arm about her shoulders and brushed a kiss against her temple. Goddess, 'twas so hard not to beg him to marry her. But if he didn't believe she'd make a worthy queen, she must respect that—as king for years with generations of kings behind him, he must perceive something she didn't. Yet knowing their time together would end soon was crushing her.

She inhaled and suppressed her tears. Only focusing on their passion heartened her. No regrets or longing or sorrow could touch her then. Although they all flooded back once their passion cooled. She swallowed then drawled, "My mouth is lower, you know."

Devon chuckled. "Is it? Perhaps I should try again." He brushed kisses from her temple down her cheek until he reached the corner of her mouth. "There it is." He brushed his lips against hers.

Tingling at his tender kisses, Kiera whimpered and yanked on his dark-brown hair to pull him closer and deepen their kiss. She needed their fiery passion to consume them.

Yet Devon lifted his head. "I'm not letting you goad me tonight. We *are* going slowly first this time." He pulled her into his lap and kissed her temple again.

She sighed, her pulse still throbbing. From his firm grip, he'd not relent. But tender passion would consume them too—it just took longer.

Devon escorted her upstairs. When they reached the royal quarters, he swept her in his arms and laid her on his bed. His green eyes black, he brushed a kiss against her lips then began unlacing her gown. "You're the best Longnight gift I've ever unwrapped."

Kiera shivered with hunger and unraveled his cravat. "So are you." Too bad she couldn't keep him.

As they removed each other's clothes piece by piece, they caressed and kissed each other everywhere, and they both moaned with relief when they finally came together.

Afterward, still intertwined and body aglow, she sighed and nuzzled his neck. Definitely as consuming as fiery passion.

Devon stirred against her. "See, going slowly first is transcendent too. And I'm already fit for a repeat."

She purred as he began tenderly making love to her again. After that, they made love once more then slipped into slumber still nestled together.

AFTER THEIR LONG NIGHT, Kiera and Devon woke with barely enough time to bolt breakfast before meeting Moonbud. Then they bundled up to withstand the cold and headed outside. Her breath frosting in the air, Lady Ducharme greeted them beside the palace, and they strode across the palace grounds with the royal guards.

When they reached the nightmara stables, Kiera gulped a breath, and Devon squeezed her arm against his side. She smiled at him for his silent encouragement then knocked on the stable door.

The door flying open, Leila beamed at Kiera with Nightrose behind her. "Moonbud and her advisors await you in the paddock, Lady Kiera."

Kiera nodded her thanks, then she and the others headed through the stables and into the paddock. After waving the guards to remain behind like usual, she glanced at Lady Ducharme. "Walk beside me. Lady Moonbud must see Devon is no more than my advisor, despite being king."

Lady Ducharme nodded, then Kiera, Devon, and the baroness approached Moonbud, who stood in the center of the paddock again. Although today, Darkthorn and an older night-mara stood behind her, her advisors no doubt. When Kiera reached Moonbud, they exchanged greetings and introduced their advisors. Then they began walking together through the paddock with their advisors close behind.

Kiera almost smiled. She and Moonbud had been doing riding lessons for so long 'twas odd to walk beside her instead. The nightmara queen-heir felt much larger somehow. She straightened her shoulders then glanced at Moonbud. "Would you care to begin?"

Moonbud inclined her head. :*I must admit I was dismayed when I learned King Devon had no queen, but now I'm grateful for that. Since you weren't a proven queen, we spent time becoming acquainted, and that also provided us time to ponder the treaty. It hasn't changed much since Nightwind and Sarilee first negotiated it four hundred years ago.*:

Kiera nodded. And the treaty was overdue for a change or two. No king should be trapped like Devon had been. But the nightmara queen-heir should put forth her changes first. So Kiera only replied, "Go on."

Moonbud turned to follow the fence. :*One of my earlier concerns was poor communication. Initially, I suggested signing the treaty more often, but King Devon's thought that 'twould cause needless legislation is probably right. After meeting with you for months, I now believe that spending time becoming acquainted is the answer instead.*:

Kiera smiled. Then Calatini's queen and the nightmara queen or queen-heir could comfortably deal with each other, which would further strengthen the treaty. "How long do you want to extend the negotiation?"

Moonbud hummed, her midnight tail flicking. :*To what we did — three months meeting every three days.*:

Kiera tilted her head. Doable with an adjustment. "Very well, but the meetings should start in spring or early summer. 'Tis cold to be negotiating now." After Moonbud chuckled but nodded, she asked, "What else?"

Moonbud halted by the oak beside the fence. :*After you introduced us, the veiled witch and I developed magical traps to capture those with ill intent toward the nightmara and mara. I'd like the mara to bury the traps every three feet along the border of the plains to prevent poachers.*:

Kiera arched her brows. Such traps would make the plains near impregnable. She glanced back at Devon and Lady Ducharme and waved for them to speak. This change was beyond her purview to decide alone.

Devon eyed the nightmara queen-heir. "What shall happen to those you capture? And what if the traps go awry like the Magehaven ore?"

Moonbud sighed. :*Those captured remain in the traps until we release them, but we'll check the traps daily. Then we'll try the prisoners like we do now.*: She flicked her tail. :*As for going awry, the veiled witch said the traps shall burn out if the magic twists or too much passes through them.*:

Kiera and Devon glanced at Lady Ducharme, who said, "Those traps sound an excellent defense. Could we bury them along all of Calatini's border?"

Moonbud tossed her mane. :*The traps require nightmara powers to fuel them, so they aren't feasible outside the plains.*:

Kiera eyed Devon, who nodded. Since he agreed, she turned back to Moonbud. "Burying those traps along the plains should be fine. What else did you want to discuss?"

Moonbud resumed walking beside the fence. :*Nothing else. I've decided the split loyalty of the mara clans helps keep the nightmara and Calatini aligned.*:

Kiera swallowed, her stomach tensing. Time to broach her change. "I've a change to propose as well. I understand why the nightmara insist on negotiating with queens, but that only works if the king is married." She lifted her chin. "If I hadn't snuck into the summer masquerade, Devon would have been forced to enter a loveless marriage for the sake of your treaty."

Her ears flicking, Moonbud snorted. :*Regardless of any treaty, kings must wed to ensure the continuance of their line.*:

Kiera leaned toward Moonbud, twisting the Vireni betrothal ring. Please let the nightmara queen-heir listen. "Yes, but what if the queen unexpectedly died before a negotiation or the king was still a child? 'Twouldn't be fair to force the king to wed in either case."

Turning back toward the center of the paddock, Moonbud eyed Kiera. :*True enough. What do you suggest?*:

Kiera hummed, energy surging through her. Her change was all but accepted. "If Calatini has no queen, the nightmara negotiate with the king's betrothed as you did with me. If he has no betrothed, with the dowager queen. If there's no dowager, with the unwed king himself."

Moonbud nodded. :*Very well. Anything else?*:

Kiera glanced back at Devon to make sure he'd nothing to add. When he shook his head, she said, "No, 'tis everything." She bowed to Moonbud. "'Tis been a pleasure becoming acquainted. We'll have the renewed treaty for you to sign tomorrow."

Moonbud returned her bow. *:I've been glad to become acquainted with you as well. King Devon is fortunate to have found you.:*

Her chest aching, Kiera inclined her head in thanks. Too bad Devon didn't feel the same and hadn't proposed in truth. To prevent the nightmara queen-heir from reading that, she strengthened the barbed fence about her thoughts. Then she, Devon, and Lady Ducharme returned to the palace to meet with the waiting council.

Devon opened the council meeting by summarizing Moonbud's requests then asked Kiera to explain hers. She did, and the councilors goggled until Lady Ducharme confirmed it. Then the councilors offered their congratulations, and the meeting adjourned.

Afterward, she and Devon spent the day with scribes getting the renewed treaty written then changed into dressing gowns and shared a late dinner in the queen's chambers.

Once Mia and Simon had cleared the tea table, Devon toasted Kiera with his sparkling wine. "To the best negotiator Calatini ever had."

Blushing, she drifted over to the sofa. She wasn't the best. She waved her sparkling wine. "The most well-prepared one, at least."

Devon sighed and set down his sparkling wine untouched. His face strained, he sat beside her on the sofa and took her free hand. "We've never discussed past negotiating the treaty."

Kiera gripped her flute of sparkling wine and stared at him. Oh, Goddess. He was about to tell her when she should leave. Her heart stuttered. 'Twould shatter her. She must stop him. So she tossed aside her flute, which bounced on the plush carpet, then flung herself into his arms and seized his mouth in a ravenous kiss. When almost dizzy, she wrenched her lips free. "We can talk tomorrow."

Panting too, Devon began, "But..."

She captured his mouth again and buried her hands beneath his dressing gown. Hunger throbbing in her veins, she undulated against him. It might be the last time she could demonstrate her love. She stopped kissing him to murmur, "Tomorrow."

Devon rumbled then tossed her onto the bed and leapt atop her. Their mouths and hands wild, they soon shattered in explosive release. As they gasped for breath, she ran her hands along his back, and soon they were making love with fiery passion again. After that, he succumbed to slumber with her wrapped in his arms.

Tears burning her eyes, Kiera forced herself to resist sleep's siren call and slid from his embrace. Even though the nightmara were still here, she must go before he told her to leave tomorrow. Her heart pounding, she lit a small candle then signed the treaty and penned a quick farewell to Devon. After collecting her few keepsakes into a small bag, she yanked on her orphanage dress and old cloak then placed the signed treaty, farewell note, and Vireni betrothal ring on the bedside table.

She studied Devon for a long moment. Thank the Goddess he was too exhausted to wake. Doubtless she'd also collapse once she returned to the orphanage. She licked her lips. If only she could risk one last kiss, but *that* might wake him. Blinking back her tears, she whispered softer than a wraith's sigh, "I'll always love you, Devon."

Like when she'd visited the Mirror of Wisdom, the four guards flanking the door started and gripped their swords when she slipped from the queen's chambers. As her erstwhile guards began to follow, she waved them back. "I'm returning to the orphanage, so your services are no longer required."

The guards exchanged a glance, then Walker replied, "Nevertheless, we'll accompany you. The king would have our heads if we didn't."

Kiera sighed. If she argued with them, Devon might wake. "Fine, but you must return to the palace once I reach the orphanage." She glared at all four guards. "And *none* of you, or anyone else, are to wake Devon. Am I clear?"

The guards frowned but slowly nodded.

With the two guards close behind, Kiera strode back to the orphanage. Her eyes darting to scan the shadows, she shivered during the lengthy and freezing walk across Ormas. The streets seemed even more dangerous after living in the palace. 'Twas fortunate the stalwart guards had accompanied her. Yet at the orphanage, she thanked them then shooed them back toward the palace. A poor orphanage matron had no need for guards.

She skulked through the sleeping orphanage then crawled into bed and burrowed beneath her thin covers. Goddess, her bed was frigid, small, and lumpy—and would never hold Devon. Muffling her sobs in her pillow, she allowed her tears to burst free at last. Her pillow was sodden and her face raw when she drifted into a fretful sleep a few hours before dawn.

CHAPTER 57

When Devon woke the following morning, Kiera wasn't nestled against him like usual, yet he must renew his proposal before she distracted him again. So he glanced about her chambers to find her and frowned. Where was she?

Then his gaze fell on the papers on the bedside table, and his stomach lurched. What were those? He rolled over and seized them, and metal clinked on the floor. His breath froze. 'Twas the nightmara treaty with Kiera's signature and a note. Dear Goddess. He tossed the treaty on the bed and ripped open the note.

Devon—

With the nightmara treaty renewed, you no longer need me. But the orphans do, and I want to celebrate the rest of the Longnight season with them. (If Moonbud asks after me, use Longnight with them to explain my absence.) Thanks for everything you've done for my orphans and asking me to act as your betrothed. I'll never forget the time we spent together. I wish you good fortune and happiness.

Kiera

His chest burning, he crushed Kiera's note. No longer need her? He needed her like a triton needed the sea—he loved her, and his life was arid without her. He glanced at the floor by the bedside table. The clinking metal had been her betrothal ring. Of course. He bent and retrieved the ring then clenched it in his fist. His family's magical ring hadn't ensured a happy marriage this time.

Kiera had left him. Because she believed her parentage meant she couldn't become queen? No, after convincing the nightmara to permit negotiations with kings, she couldn't possibly still believe that. Especially given how she'd already triumphed over every obstacle at court. Only a true queen could succeed so well.

Devon slumped. So why had she left without even telling him? Had she thought he wouldn't care? Surely she couldn't believe that after he'd spent the past months demonstrating his love over and over again. If she was willing to ignore his obvious love, her reason must have been strong indeed.

His heart wrenched. From how she'd returned his kisses, he'd never doubted that she loved him as deeply as he loved her. But what if all she felt was lust? She was too honorable to agree to marry him in truth if she didn't love him. And 'twould explain why she'd averted his proposal last night and fled before he could try again.

Devon gulped a ragged breath. What was he to do now? Loving Kiera as he did, he couldn't wed anyone else. But as king, he must ensure succession since the council electing a new king could be chaotic. Perhaps appointing his successor would mitigate that—the council would officially need to elect his successor after his death, but Calatini should accept his appointed successor without complaint.

He sighed. Aragon or his future son would probably be best. Although not royalty, Aragon and his family were his closest relatives, and like the Vireni line, theirs had been part of Calatini since the founding. Plus, Hawke could assume the Childes duchy. Not that either Aragon or Hawke would like those changes.

He grimaced and rubbed his face. Or perhaps he should just ask Lady Juliet or the veiled witch or Moonbud for a spell to make him forget Kiera. But would he have a mind left after such a spell?

His snorted laugh echoing through Kiera's—no, the queen's—chambers, Devon thrust himself from bed, grabbed the treaty, and strode back to his chambers. He must take the treaty to Moonbud, so he could settle that at least. Then he could spend the rest of his lonely Longnight season secluded in his chambers, unless another crisis like the Magehaven ore explosion occurred.

He tossed the treaty on his bed with Kiera's note and ring concealed underneath then rang for Simon. When the valet arrived with breakfast for two, agony stabbed his stomach, but he said nothing about the extra food. Instead, he dressed then dismissed Simon and bolted a heaped plate without tasting it.

After slipping Kiera's note and ring into the pocket by his heart, Devon yanked on his warmest coat, collected the treaty, and left with his guards to meet Moonbud. As always, he buried his upset beneath a faint smile to prevent gossip. There'd be enough of that when court discovered Kiera had left.

However, his smile tightened when Leila opened the stable door with Nightrose behind her then narrowed her eyes and asked, "Where's Kiera?"

He arched his brows. He wasn't explaining to the mara woman that Kiera had left because she didn't return his love. His ribs squeezed, but he drawled, "Elsewhere. I've brought the treaty for Lady Moonbud."

Leila humphed then waved for him to enter. She undeniably still didn't like kings.

Devon strode into the paddock and waved his guards to remain by the nightmara stables. Although they doubtless knew Kiera had left, his discussion with the nightmara queen-heir should remain private.

When he joined her, Moonbud was nestled against Dark-thorn, but she nudged the nightmara stallion to leave. She eyed Devon as Darkthorn nuzzled her then trotted to the oak by the fence. :*Where's Kiera?*:

He swallowed but lifted his chin. Concealing the truth from the nightmara queen-heir was futile since she could read it from his thoughts. "Returned to the orphanage. With the treaty renewed, she decided I no longer needed her."

Moonbud jerked back with a snort. :*What?*:

Since he couldn't answer that, Devon only thrust the treaty toward her. "But Kiera signed the treaty before she left. Would you care to review it then sign too?"

Her powers pressing against his mind, Moonbud stamped her front hoof. :*Not until you explain about Kiera. What did you do?*:

Almost crushing the treaty, he shoved against the nightmara queen-heir's powers. How could Kiera leaving him be *his* fault? "I didn't *do* anything. Kiera chose to flee in the middle of the night without telling me." Proving she didn't love him as he loved her.

Moonbud sighed. :*Because you never did the one thing she needed to stay. Goddess, why are stallions so obtuse?*: She craned toward him. :*You never told her you loved her.*:

His stomach hardening, Devon set his jaw. She just would have fled sooner if he had. "I showed her I loved her every day. If she couldn't see that, what good would words have done?"

Moonbud flicked her tail. :*I suspect she saw your love but needed the words too.*:

He frowned and tapped the treaty against his leg. Why was the nightmara queen-heir hedging? Hadn't she read Kiera's thoughts during their nightmara rides? "You suspect?"

Her ears twitching, Moonbud shifted. :*For someone without magic, Kiera was remarkably skilled at resisting nightmara powers and shielding her mind. I never would have known she believed your betrothal was fake if you hadn't told me first. So I can only deduce her reasons from your memories. But I doubt I'm wrong.*:

Devon sighed. Since Moonbud was a powerful nightmara who'd read thousands of thoughts, doubtless her deductions were accurate. "So why would Kiera need me to confess my love in order to stay?" Because she'd pity him and decide lust and rapport were enough?

Moonbud tossed her mane. :*If you showed your love but never spoke of it, she probably assumed you didn't believe she could be your true queen. Why speak of love that must end?*:

He gaped at her, his head whirling. Kiera assumed he didn't believe in her? "But I always supported her and mentioned how wonderful she'd done after every triumph."

Moonbud hummed. :*Kiera could have assumed that was mere kindness. After all, you shared everything else with her, even the burden of being royalty. Why else wouldn't you share your obvious love as well—unless you didn't believe she could be queen?*:

Devon scowled at the nightmara queen-heir. Ridiculous. "I didn't tell Kiera because she wasn't ready to hear it." Not that she'd ever have been since she didn't return his love. "She'd have fled if I had."

Moonbud shook her head. :*Kiera loves you too much to flee unless she believed you didn't want her as your queen.*:

Weight compressed his chest. If only Moonbud was right, but she couldn't be. "If Kiera loved me, she'd not have left without telling me."

Moonbud snorted. :*Obtuse stallion. Kiera couldn't tell you **because** she loved you.*: When he blinked at her, she sighed. :*She couldn't have suspected you didn't confess your love because you feared she'd flee. And since you never spoke of your love, she'd have never spoken of hers. She'd have shown you—as you showed her.*:

Devon swallowed, his pulse surging. So Kiera's furtive flight *wasn't* because she didn't love him? "Kiera truly loves me?"

Moonbud snorted again. :*Of course she does. We called her for you.*:

He frowned. Called? What did that mean? "You what?"

Ducking her head, Moonbud coughed. :*We, er, called her. Through dreams like dominant mares call their own mates.*:

Devon froze, his heart twisting. Calling sounded like a love spell, so the nightmara's powers must be behind his and Kiera's instant and visceral attraction. "You say Kiera loves me, but how can our love be genuine if 'twas created by a spell?"

Moonbud straightened and glared at him. :*Calling is no love spell. We just use our power over dreams and the mind to bring together true mates—aligned minds with the potential for deep and lasting love. So your love is completely genuine.*:

His chest easing, he sighed. Thank the Goddess. "But if the nightmara called Kiera, how could she have fled at the masquerade and again this morning?"

Moonbud hummed. :*Calling another's mate is much more difficult than calling your own. All thirteen of Calatini's dominant mares, including Queen Nightsnow, joined in the call the day before I left the plains, and they continued calling until you told me you found her again.*:

Devon rubbed his jaw. So they'd started eight days before the summer masquerade. Yet even though the nightmara had been influencing them, he'd no extraordinarily vivid dreams then. Had Kiera? Regardless, the nightmara's call must have inspired her to sneak into the masquerade.

Moonbud flicked her tail. :*Also Kiera was harder for the dominant mares to reach since no nightmara had ever met her. So unlike you, she probably didn't recognize her love that night.*:

He almost grimaced. Which explained why she'd fled. "If the nightmara had already called Kiera, no wonder you acted shocked when I had no queen."

Moonbud blew a sigh. :*Yes, although the dominant mares had continued their call until I reached Ormas to be safe, we'd expected you'd be wed, or at least betrothed. Love between true mates often blossoms swiftly due to their intense rapport.*:

Devon nodded. Exactly like his had. Yet Kiera had denied

their love because she didn't trust he could truly love her or believe she could be queen.

Moonbud tilted her head. :*When you asked for our help finding Kiera, the dominant mares redoubled their call, but she still managed to resist their powers. Fortunately, you found her yourself at that wedding, so they could stop. Maintaining a call for so long, especially for others and over such distance, is draining.*:

His throat clenching, he sighed. The nightmara had merely brought them together and not influenced them since, so they couldn't have prevented Kiera's flight this morning. He arched his brows at Moonbud. "A lot of exertion to avoid negotiating with a king."

Moonbud shifted but met his gaze. :*We didn't expect it to be. But once you'd met your true mate, we knew you'd not settle for another, so we had to keep calling her. Since humans are obsessed with birth, the Vireni line ending might weaken Calatini, which 'twould leave us vulnerable.*:

Devon quirked a wry grin. "After all that exertion, shall Queen Nightsnow and the other dominant mares be upset the true mate they called changed the treaty so nightmara might negotiate with a king in the future?"

Moonbud nickered. :*Some shall be, but my changes shall placate them. Besides, Kiera's change was sensible.*:

He gestured with the wrinkled treaty. They must settle that, so he could convince Kiera to return and marry him. "Speaking of the treaty, are you ready to sign now?"

Moonbud leaned forward, her powers pressing his mind again. :*That depends on what you intend to do about Kiera.*:

Devon straightened and met the nightmara queen-heir's probing gaze. He'd nothing to hide. "Go after her like I should have done as soon as she left."

Moonbud relaxed and tossed her mane. :*Good. I'll sign then.*:

He grinned. Finally. He called for his guards to fetch ink from the nightmara stables. When they did, he unrolled the treaty and signed beneath Kiera's signature then laid it on the ground for Moonbud.

After reading over everything, Moonbud dipped her right hoof in the ink tray then pressed it against the treaty. The Night-mara-Calatini Treaty was renewed at last. Thank the Goddess.

His shoulders lightening, Devon collected the treaty while Moonbud wiped her hoof clean on the grass. "I'll have copies sent over soon." He smiled at the nightmara queen-heir. "Although the treaty is settled and you've been away from home much longer than expected, please remain to celebrate the rest of the Longnight season with us."

Tilting her head, Moonbud hummed. :*Thank you, King Devon, we shall. Although we may actually remain until the worst of the winter storms have passed. Traveling now is wretched.*:

He rubbed his chilled hands. Yes, it probably was. He nodded. "Of course. Kiera and I shall be glad to have you."

With a final nod, Devon strode from the paddock with his guards and returned to the palace. He tapped the signed treaty against his leg during the freezing walk. How could he convince Kiera to marry him? Since she'd fled because she assumed he didn't believe she could be queen, he first must persuade her he did. He'd start by confessing his love and begging her to marry him.

He set his jaw. He must prove she was the only lady he'd accept as his queen. Perhaps arranging their immediate wedding would help, even though they must pretend to still be betrothed at court until their public ceremony and her coronation. His pulse quickened. And arranging a bloodbinding like he'd wanted since they'd met would surely convince her. If they took precautions, they could manage the risks of no heirs and dying when the other did.

Back at the palace, Devon gave scribes the signed treaty then headed to his study. He must wait to see Kiera until he'd arranged everything, but that shouldn't take too long. Besides, Longnight was tomorrow, and what better day for a wedding than the festival of the Goddess celebrating new beginnings, hope, and love?

He tapped his fingers against his desk. Mel could officiate the wedding ceremony with Aragon, Hawke, Wren, and Selena acting as their witnesses. So he wrote asking them to meet at Hawke and Wren's townhouse for dinner to organize everything. Meeting there rather than the palace should keep his wedding plans secret.

The ceremony arranged, Devon hastened to the royal witch's wing with his guards. He must ask Lady Juliet to create marriage tokens for a bloodbinding that wouldn't activate their protection charms. His heart fluttering, he inhaled and touched Kiera's betrothal ring in his pocket. Then he must decide exactly how to confess his love to Kiera. Goddess, let him be ardent enough that she *finally* believed he needed her as his queen. He couldn't fail again.

CHAPTER 58

*H*er eyes swollen and throat sore, Kiera roused from her fretful sleep not long before noon. Except for the day she'd left the orphanage to stay at the palace and the morning after using the Mirror of Wisdom, this was the latest she'd slept in years, doubtless because no one knew she was here. A pang darted through her. 'Twas disquieting to be needed by no one.

She rubbed her raw face. Goddess, she was exhausted. Her dreams had all featured Devon—some had been fantasies where they'd spent their lives together, while others had been nightmares where he left her for his perfect lady. So even asleep, she'd cried most of the night.

Kiera sighed and fingered the protection charm on her left wrist. 'Twas her one keepsake, other than her lasting love for Devon, from her time acting as his queen. She should really figure out how to remove it. A three-stranded gold bracelet with powerful magic would attract attention in a poor orphanage.

She sighed again then forced herself to rise. Wallowing in her empty bed and brooding over Devon and her time acting as his queen wouldn't mend her shattered heart. Perhaps seeing the orphans would cheer her, and keeping busy should distract her as well. Shivering in her unheated room, she changed into an old orphanage dress. She tugged at the serviceable skirt, but the dress chafed after months of wearing arachne silk.

She set her jaw and clenched her hands to quit fidgeting. Staying at the palace had spoiled her. She'd almost forgotten this was her *true* life—serviceable dresses instead of elegant gowns, just enough food instead of feasts, loneliness instead of Devon.

Tears pricked her eyes again. Although Devon was the only one of those that mattered. She gulped a breath. Well, at least she was a simple orphanage matron again, rather than a lowborn queen bearing the weight of the entire kingdom and dealing with court.

Kiera slipped downstairs to join the orphans for luncheon, even though her stomach was leaden. When she entered the dining hall, she paused to study the orphans at the trestle tables, and her chest lightened a bit. However, too engrossed with devouring their food and chattering with friends, none of them noticed her in the doorway.

Yet Wren and Hawke did. Seated at the head table, they exchanged a glance, then Wren rose and almost waddled to the back while Hawke remained to mind the orphans. After embracing Kiera, she drew back, her frown deepening the faint shadows beneath her eyes. "Kiera, what are you doing here? And what happened? You look wretched."

Kiera sighed. She might cry when she explained, so they should talk in private. "I'll explain in the matron's study."

Wren nodded and gestured to Hawke that they were leaving.

When they entered the matron's study, now hers again, Kiera made herself take the chair behind the desk. 'Twould hint to Wren what had happened.

Her hazel eyes dark, Wren dragged a chair beside Kiera and lowered herself into it. "Explain, please."

Kiera managed a tremulous smile. Please let her not cry. "I negotiated the renewed treaty with Moonbud, so my purpose as acting queen was complete. 'Twas time for me to return here, where I truly belong."

Wren gaped at her. "What?"

Kiera shrugged to feign indifference, but her throat clenched, so she couldn't offer further explanations.

Her mouth snapping shut, Wren leaned forward. "Did Devon tell you to go?"

Kiera swallowed as weight compressed her chest. Thank the Goddess she'd fled before he could. She'd never have recovered from that. "Not yet, but when we visited the orphanage, he said I'd be returning soon."

Wren flushed, her hands fisting in her lap. "He what?"

Kiera blinked at her friend. Why was Wren so furious?

But before she could ask that, Mary bustled in with a luncheon tray. After setting the tray on the desk, she hugged Kiera. "Why are you tired again? You were glowin' the other day."

Kiera almost winced. Because then she'd still believed Devon wanted to marry her. "The Longnight season at court is even more hectic than the regular social season. Probably because court and the council usually adjourn after Harvestfete, so most have only celebrated Longnight at their country estates."

As Wren snorted, Mary fisted her hands on her hips. "That betrothed of yours should be cherishin' you better, king or no."

Kiera licked her lips. Somehow, she must explain their betrothal had ended without inspiring Mary to storm the palace. But not now—she hadn't the strength. After Longnight tomorrow, perhaps. "I'll have plenty of time to rest while I'm here. I'm back to celebrate Longnight with the orphans, and you and Peter, of course."

Mary beamed at her. "How sweet. When'll King Devon be joinin' us?"

As Wren's eyes narrowed, Kiera gritted a brilliant smile. She must get Mary to stop mentioning Devon before she cried.

"Unfortunately, I doubt he'll be able to. With me here, his duties at court shall consume his time."

Mary tsked. "Surely he could manage an hour or two." When Kiera shook her head, the plump cook sighed. "Well, I suppose you know royal affairs better than me. I'd best get back to cookin' the Longnight pastries for tomorrow. 'Tis good you're joinin' us."

As Mary bustled from the study, Kiera turned back to Wren with a wry smile. Her friend's flush had faded. Good. Pregnant ladies shouldn't get so upset.

Wren sighed as she began eating the fish stew and black bread. "If Devon never actually told you to go, why did you? You two love each other. Surely he wanted you to stay."

Her heart aching, Kiera took her own luncheon but only stirred her stew. Although Mary's food was always savory, she couldn't bear to eat. "I suspect he does. But he never spoke of love or marriage, so he mustn't believe I should be queen."

Wren halted with her spoon halfway to her mouth and glared. "You'd make an excellent queen."

Kiera almost smiled at her friend's vehement defense. Then she sighed. If only Devon had felt the same. "True, but whether I would doesn't matter. A poor orphanage matron birthed by a greedy whore can't become queen." If court ever discovered her true parentage, their acceptance would turn to revulsion, and they'd savage her. Perhaps Devon was right that she couldn't become queen.

Wren scowled. "Devon *said* he didn't care about your parentage or poor upbringing."

Kiera shrugged and forced herself to eat some fish stew. She needed to stay strong to manage the orphans. "I doubt he does for himself, but as king, Devon must wed for the good of Calatini. And only a true lady is good enough, no matter how much we love each other." When Wren began to reply, Kiera leaned forward and asked, "Could we discuss something else, please? Plans for Longnight, perhaps?"

Wren eyed Kiera but nodded.

Kiera relaxed back into her chair. Thankfully, Wren had agreed. Goddess knew how much longer she could discuss Devon without crying. "The usual tomorrow? Breakfast and gifts in the morning, followed by the Longnight feast at noon, and Longnight Vespers in the evening? With Longnight games and carols throughout the day?"

Wren nodded again as she finished her stew. "Yes. I wrapped the last of the gifts yesterday. But 'tis fortunate you're here. Managing sixty-one orphans at Longnight is demanding, especially when carrying twins."

Kiera frowned. Wren looked as tired as she herself probably did, and her friend hadn't spent the night crying. "Are headaches and nausea still plaguing you?"

Wren grimaced. "Unfortunately. And I tire easily too—I feel out of breath after the most ordinary tasks. 'Tis vexing."

Kiera shook her head. Wren was sure to make herself ill if she didn't take care. "You mustn't be resting enough."

Hawke drawled from the doorway, "That's what I keep telling her, but she never listens. Perhaps she'll heed you."

Wren wrinkled her nose at him. "Don't start, you coddler. I *don't* need a nap."

Kiera suppressed a snort. Wren would doubtless say that mid-yawn.

Hawke sighed but only said, "I sent the orphans to their afternoon lessons. Jace is teaching yours, so you can visit with Kiera. I'd better join mine before someone gets injured."

Once he left, Wren arched her brows at Kiera. "Care to tour the orphanage?"

Kiera hummed. She would, but Wren should rest, so they'd better remain in the study. "Maybe later. Tell me how the apprenticeship program is going instead."

She and Wren discussed that then reviewed the orphanage accounts. Her throat tightened at all Devon had contributed. His generosity went well beyond his initial promise. He was the kindest and most wonderful gentleman. If only she could have remained by his side forever.

While she was struggling to mention Devon's generosity, Peter strode into the study. "Letter, Miss Wren." He beamed at Kiera. "How's our future queen? Mary's right, you do look a bit peaked."

Her ribs tight, Kiera embraced the burly porter. Mary wouldn't be the only one upset when she explained about the fake betrothal. Hopefully, Peter wouldn't storm the palace with his wife. "I'll be fine after some decent sleep and Longnight cheer."

Peter squeezed her. "Longnight cheer the orphans'll provide aplenty. The decent sleep? Not likely." He winked then left.

Kiera and Wren exchanged a grin. No doubt he was right.

Then Wren opened her letter. As she read, her eyes slitted, and her cheeks flushed.

Kiera tensed. Pregnant ladies, especially exhausted ones, *definitely* shouldn't get so upset. "What is it?"

Wren crushed the note. "Hawke's brothers are visiting our townhouse for dinner. We must leave immediately to prepare. Could you read the Longnight story to the orphans after dinner? If we return in time, Hawke can lead some caroling."

Kiera arched her brows. Why would Hawke's brothers visiting upset Wren? Yet asking would only upset her further. "Have fun. Maybe you can take that nap on the ride home."

Wren humphed as she bustled from the study.

Gathering the book Wren had marked for tonight, Kiera joined the orphans for dinner. Unlike at luncheon, the orphans bounded over then dragged her to the winter palace, now overflowing with gifts.

The Bedsford twins chortled, then John pointed at the Longnight display. "I counted over one-hundred and fifty gifts. That's *over* two for everyone."

As his twin began counting again, Jacob grinned at Kiera. "Do you like the shells?"

She winked back. The scampish boy was as proud of their decorations as Wren had said. "They make the winter palace even more festive."

Roger tugged on her skirt, his wiry body vibrating. "Guess what? Mr. Hawke caught a deer in the royal forest for the feast tomorrow." He clapped. "*And* Mary said there might be *all* the starpeaches I could eat."

Janelle hugged Kiera. "And you're here to visit us for Longnight!"

Her chest warming, Kiera beamed at her orphans. Their care-free joy might mend her shattered heart—eventually. "I'm glad I'm here with all of you. Shall we eat before Mary scolds us for spoiling her fine dinner?"

The orphans thundered over to the trestle tables, and while they devoured their food, she managed to eat a full plate. After dinner, she read the Longnight story Wren had marked about a young couple sacrificing their most precious possessions to buy gifts for each other. Since Hawke would be much better at carol-ing, Kiera played Longnight charades with the orphans until Wren and Hawke returned. When they did, Hawke led caroling on his violin until midnight. Then Wren ordered the exhausted and overwrought children to bed. A perfect evening filled with Longnight cheer.

Kiera eyed Wren, who was almost beaming. Her dinner with Hawke's brothers must have gone well. "You seem calmer now."

Hawke chuckling beside her, Wren bobbed her head. "Every-thing is settled as it should be now."

Kiera blinked. What did that mean?

Wren grinned at her and took Hawke's arm. "We should go. We'll see you tomorrow as early as we can manage. The orphans shall be more eager than crazed imps to open their gifts."

Kiera chuckled and nodded. They always were.

Hawke grinned. "By the way, the Westons mentioned they're bringing Cassandra and Amaranth after breakfast to celebrate Longnight with the other orphans."

Kiera managed a smile. Wonderful, more people who'd assume she was still Devon's betrothed. Although seeing the Weston sisters would be nice. After saying good night, she retired to her frigid and empty bed then dropped into slumber filled with more dreams of Devon. Her body aching and sluggish, she woke to squealing orphans running down the hall shortly after dawn. Yet she dressed then joined them, Mary, and Peter in the dining hall.

Smiling at the rowdy orphans, she ordered them to eat breakfast before they could open their gifts. Then she gulped several cups of kahve to help wake her. Wren and Hawke arrived while she was forcing herself to eat some porridge. Once the Westons arrived with their granddaughters and extra gifts, Kiera smiled at the orphans. "You can start now."

The orphans, including Cassandra and Amaranth, tore open their gifts from the Westons then descended on the winter palace like a tribe of crazed imps, exactly like Wren had said.

The orphans had settled and begun playing with their gifts when Peter approached Kiera with a gleam in his eyes. "Our first-foot wants to speak with you in the library, Mistress Kiera."

Kiera arched her brows. Since Jane's sailor admirer had died at sea a decade ago, the orphanage hadn't had the traditional first Longnight visitor bearing gifts to bring good fortune for the year. Who could it be? Perhaps Annalise had learned she'd returned to the orphanage? "Thanks, Peter."

Her pulse quickening, she rose and slipped from the raucous dining hall to greet the first-foot in the library.

CHAPTER 59

A satchel of first-foot gifts slung over his shoulder, Devon paced about the orphanage's tiny library. Goddess, please let confessing everything convince Kiera to marry him. His mouth dried as he touched her betrothal ring in his pocket. If she refused him after that, he might have lost her forever. What would he do then?

To distract himself, he halted before the library's sole book-case in the far corner. 'Twas only three-quarters full, and the few books were clearly well-loved. The orphans needed more than these few worn books—he must send some soon. Perhaps Kiera could help select them.

"Devon?" Kiera's voice rang through the library. "What are you doing here?"

His pulse surged, and he whirled to face her. Flushed and eyes wide, she was hovering just inside the threshold as stiff as a secretive rainbow unicorn prepared to flee. He must soothe her, or she'd leave before he could propose. He flashed a bright grin and opened his satchel. "Acting as your first-foot. Happy Long-night, Kiera."

Licking her lips, Kiera gulped a breath then glided toward him. "Happy Longnight, Devon."

Tingling warmth flooded him when she reached him. If only he could draw her into his arms and kiss her. But if he did, his restraint might shatter, and he'd make love to her on the orphanage library's floor. Then she might flee before he could renew his proposal. So kisses must wait until *after* she'd agreed to marry him. He swallowed and handed her the traditional first-foot gifts in quick succession. First a jar of salt, then a bag of coal, then a flask of spiritwine, and finally a Longnight treat—a tin of orenge nut sweet biscuits. "May these bring you and the orphanage good fortune in the coming year."

Having set each gift on the table by the bookcase to receive the next, Kiera eyed him over the tin of sweet biscuits. "Thank you." She paused then asked, "Shouldn't you be celebrating Longnight at the palace?"

Devon shrugged as he closed the almost-empty satchel and placed it on the bookcase. He smiled at Kiera. "Even at court, Longnight morning is celebrated with family, and I've none at the palace. Since they're my closest relatives, I usually join Aragon and his family, but I'd rather celebrate Longnight with you."

Kiera blushed then paled and clutched the tin to her chest, her navy eyes shimmering with unshed tears. "'Twould have been better for you to join them."

His heart pounding, he extracted the tin from her grip and set it with the other first-foot gifts then grasped her hands and kissed her palms. Those kisses were safe enough. "No, my place is beside you, whether in a palace or a poor orphanage."

Blushing again, Kiera inhaled and swayed toward him, clearly burning to kiss him too.

Devon shuddered and glanced away as his body tightened. True kisses must wait. Using her captured hands, he drew her to a pair of wooden chairs. "Allow me to tell you a Longnight story."

Kiera sighed but sat beside him. "Very well."

He squeezed her hands, his stomach quivering. Please, please let this convince her that he loved her and she was meant to be his queen. "Once upon a time, not too long ago, a lonely king searched court high and low for his queen, despairing he'd ever find her. But the king was not without allies. One summer, the thirteen dominant mares of his kingdom's nightmara herds called his true mate, a lady whose mind perfectly aligned with his, to his side."

Kiera gasped, her hands spasming in his.

He smiled at her then pressed kisses against her palms again. Hopefully, 'twas only the nightmara's involvement that surprised her. "So when he met her at his summer masquerade, his instant and visceral attraction swiftly blossomed into steadfast love, as is often the case with true mates. He knew that evening he'd found his queen at last. Yet the lady was of common birth and didn't believe him when he proposed marriage. So he invented a purpose for her to accept his proposal, intending to woo her until she realized he loved her."

Kiera stiffened and gaped at him. "In-invented? But..."

Devon shook his head. "Shhh, I'm almost finished." And he must confess everything before he proposed again. After having proposed with half-truths before, only the whole truth might convince Kiera he wanted her as his queen. He smiled and squeezed her hands again. "So the king's love came to court and was the best queen the kingdom had ever seen—she charmed court, overcame every obstacle, completed the king's invented purpose, and so much more. Yet she still didn't believe a king could love a poor commoner or want her as his queen, and she fled court without a word one winter's evening. So on Longnight, the king chased after his love to beg her to marry him again."

Kiera gasped again, her mouth still agape.

His pulse quickening, he gulped a deep breath. "Whether this Longnight story is a romance or tragedy is up to you." A romance, please, Goddess.

Kiera blinked then blushed.

He flashed a warm smile. *Now* he could renew his proposal. He released her right hand and withdrew her betrothal ring from his pocket then held it before her. "My dearest Kiera, I love you as deeply as a triton loves the sea. I need you by my side forever, so I can share your burdens and your joys, just as you'll always share mine. Please, will you marry me?"

Kiera stared at him, her blush deepening. "I... I..." Then she stiffened and licked her lips. "You truly believe a poor orphanage matron birthed by a greedy whore can make a worthy queen?"

Devon winced and lowered the ring. Even after his heartfelt proposal, Kiera still assumed he didn't believe in her. "I have, from the moment you revealed your education goal at the summer masquerade. And everything you did while acting as queen only strengthened my conviction."

Kiera tilted her head. "If you believed I could be queen, why did you never confess your love or renew your proposal?"

His chest tightened as he clutched her betrothal ring. His silence had hurt her and made her doubt her worth. He held her gaze. "Because I was afraid you'd not believe me and flee back to the orphanage. And I couldn't bear to lose you. So I tried showing you my love instead."

Kiera swallowed but said nothing.

Devon set his jaw and kissed her left palm beneath where her betrothal ring should be. "Despite what my silence made you believe, your parentage and poor upbringing don't matter; who you are does. You're everything I ever wanted in a wife and a queen."

Kiera blushed, her breath quickening, but she still didn't speak.

He leaned forward. Please let this finally convince her. "When Lady Annalise asked me what kind of lady I desired, do you know what I said? Mature. Intelligent. Compassionate. Strong. I *never* mentioned parentage or wealth. You may ask her if you don't believe me."

Swaying toward him, Kiera licked her lips, but yet again remained silent.

His chest squeezing, Devon kept his eyes locked on hers. Perhaps elaborating would help. "And you, my dearest Kiera, are all those things, and I love you for that." He kissed her palm again. "The poor upbringing you're so ashamed of *made* you the lady I love. It sharpened your intelligence, fueled your compassion, and forged your strength. Plus, it provided you with insight into Calatini that none born to privilege could have—myself included. And 'tis why you'll be the best queen since Calator's wife Annalise. You may even surpass her."

Kiera choked a laugh. "Surely not."

He arched his brows. Why couldn't she see how wonderful she was? "No? Shall we examine what you've *already* accomplished in your first few months acting as queen? You started an education initiative that shall forever improve the lives of the poor. Then you convinced the matriarchal nightmara to accept negotiating with kings if necessary, so that no one must ever marry to preserve our indispensable treaty with them. Meanwhile, you charmed court despite your poor upbringing, helped solve a magical crisis, and overcame every obstacle, including an unexpected extortioner and a treasonous poisoner."

Her dark-blonde curls jerking, Kiera shook her head and sighed. "True, I've performed well so far, but can that last? Sometimes I've believed it possible, yet reflection has made me doubt it. Although court accepts me now, what if they discover my true parentage? Surely they'd despise me, and their revulsion could transfer to any children we might have. I can't taint the Vireni line so."

His hand fisting on her betrothal ring again, Devon gathered her in his arms and pulled her into his lap to hearten her. "No king or queen is ever without detractors. If you'd been born a lady, they'd find another reason. Yet if you're concerned court shall despise you if they unravel our romantic tale, we can have our people spread your true parentage. But I think 'twould serve no purpose. Those that support you shall continue to do so regardless of your parentage, and the few that don't shall continue to oppose you."

Kiera hummed and tilted her head.

Her clean lavender scent weaving around him, he risked brushing a kiss against her lips. If only he could do more. "Consider the Duke of Osbourne. He didn't care when he unearthed the truth." He squeezed her. "'Tis your natural warmth, perceptive wisdom, and gracious strength that have charmed court, and none of those involve your true parentage."

Blinking, Kiera swallowed. "Perhaps you're right..."

Energy lightening his chest, Devon risked another gentle kiss. He'd almost convinced her. "I can't lie and say our life together shall be effortless. Ruling a kingdom is a heavy burden, but we're stronger together than apart. Until I found you, my duties and loneliness often overwhelmed me. I love you and need you by my side. Dare I hope you feel the same?"

Kiera caressed his jaw, her eyes shimmering with tears again. "Goddess help me, I do. My heart shattered when I left. I doubt even the orphans could have ever fully mended it."

He kissed the palm touching his face, and his own heart fluttered. Surely she'd agree to marry him now. "Then come back to me." He smiled at her. "I shan't marry another, you know. I'd abdicate first."

Kiera blanched and jerked back in his embrace. "You can't. You've no heir. Calatini would be thrown into chaos if you did."

Devon almost chuckled. Her instant concern for Calatini proved yet again her worth as queen. "I don't intend to abdicate. I intend to rule with my true queen. You." He kissed her nose. "Only a true queen would consider her kingdom first."

Kiera blushed. "Nonsense. Anyone from Calatini would worry about the Vireni line ending. Your family has ruled our kingdom since the founding. No other kingdom or empire has ever enjoyed such dedicated and compassionate kings, especially not from the same family for a millennium."

He kissed her nose again. She was adorable to believe anyone would worry about that. "But only someone with a true sense of responsibility would be so horrified by my abdication. And *that*, more than anything else, has defined the Vireni kings and queens. Which is why you're the perfect addition." When she blushed harder, he smiled at her. "Kiera, you're the only lady I'll marry. There's no one else for me. Ever."

Her eyes widening, Kiera gaped at him without saying a word. Then she swallowed and licked her lips.

Devon shuddered as his body hardened beneath hers. Goddess, he should wait until she'd agreed to marry him, but he *must* truly kiss her now. Holding her like this, with her lush curves pressed against him, was irresistible. So her betrothal ring clenched in one hand, he pulled her against his chest and captured her mouth.

Kiera fisted her hands in his hair then purred and deepened their kiss.

Throbbing hunger flared through him, and he began unlacing her dress with his free hand to touch her skin. When he caressed her bare back, she undulated against him, and he froze. If they continued, they'd make love before she'd accepted his proposal. In an unlocked library where one of her beloved orphans could chance upon them, no less. Despite his painfully hard body, he forced himself to gentle their kiss and raise his head.

Her cheeks flushed and lips swollen, Kiera panted and blinked at him. So tempting.

Devon shuddered again but relaced her dress. He must restrain himself for them to settle their marriage. He managed a smile. "Since we can't call them like the nightmara do, humans rarely find their true mates. But we have. So we'll enjoy a consuming passion and deep, steadfast love, and those seldom touch anyone more than once a lifetime. 'Twould be a tragedy to deny our love." He inhaled then held her betrothal ring before her again. "Please, Kiera, my dearest love, will you marry me?"

Her flush fading, Kiera scrutinized him without speaking for a long moment.

His blood surged through his veins, but he forced himself to remain still. He'd confessed everything he could to convince her, and he mustn't rush her. Holding her gaze, he stopped breathing as he awaited her reply.

CHAPTER 60

*D*evon's heartfelt plea ringing through her more sweetly than a siren's song, Kiera scrutinized him and forced the passion throbbing through her to settle. Becoming queen wasn't a burden to accept lightly, no matter how much she loved the king. Or how much he loved her.

She almost sighed. Which he clearly did. Barely breathing and his green eyes black, he watched her like a djinn watched a master who'd sworn to free him. And he was right that 'twould be a tragedy to deny their love. Especially if they were true mates the nightmara had brought together. She suppressed a wry smile. The nightmara's involvement explained the vivid dreams she'd had and the peculiar shimmer the veiled witch had sensed.

Kiera studied the Vireni betrothal ring he held before her. He'd first given it to her because he'd always loved her and believed she could be his queen. She exhaled. Although she wouldn't be the best queen ever like he believed, she *would* be a good and dedicated one. And if court ever ostracized her, she and Devon would face it together, and hopefully, overcome it.

She returned her gaze to his face, which had paled during her lengthy reflections. Without him, her life would be empty, regardless of how many orphans she raised. And as he'd promised, he'd never marry and would bear the burden of ruling alone. 'Twould probably kill him, and Goddess knew who his heir would be. Such chaos would harm Calatini more than a poor orphanage matron becoming queen ever could.

Her heart fluttering, Kiera smiled and cradled his face in her hands. "Yes, Devon, I'll marry you."

Devon beamed and leapt upright, despite her sitting in his lap. Then he whooped and twirled her in his arms before capturing her lips in a ravenous kiss.

Threading her fingers through his dark-brown hair, she smiled against his mouth then deepened their kiss. His perfect and irresistible kisses were all hers now—forever.

Yet when she began to unravel his cravat, Devon raised his head and stepped back. "None of that now. The library isn't locked, you know."

A blush burning her cheeks, Kiera nodded. So one of the orphans could discover them, although 'twas unlikely, given they were playing with their gifts and would be until the Longnight feast.

Beaming again, Devon kissed her left palm then slid the Vireni betrothal ring back onto her middle finger. "I never told you, but according to family myth, this ring ensures a happy marriage. So you needn't worry about our lives together."

She hummed and eyed the magical ring. The heavy gold and teal alexandrite ring fit as well as when she'd removed it two days ago, unlike when she'd first received it. Surprising. "Why didn't it return to its original size?"

Devon coughed with a shrug. "The ring only does that when the current wearer dies."

Kiera blinked. He truly *had* never doubted she was meant to be his queen. "How many people know that?"

Devon shrugged again. "Not many. My family rarely discussed the ring, but Aragon and his family know—they're my closest relatives, after all."

She quirked a wry smile. Which meant Wren knew too. "No wonder Wren smiled when I admitted you'd given it to me."

Devon winced and rubbed his cheek. "She slapped me at dinner last night. Then promised to start the satiric play she'd sworn to write if I hurt you."

Kiera gaped at him. *Devon* visiting was why Wren had been so upset yesterday. But from her friend's beam after dinner, he must have revealed he intended to ask her to marry him again.

Devon grinned. "Although your fierce defender calmed once I explained my plans."

Her chest warming at Wren's defense, Kiera returned his grin then teased, "Should I be worried her pregnant fury coerced you into renewing your proposal?"

Devon chuckled and drew her into his arms. "No, I invited her to dinner because I needed her help with my plans."

She threaded her arms about his neck. To continue teasing him, she drawled, "So *that* was why your proposal was so eloquent. Wren wrote it for you."

His mouth twitching, Devon kissed her nose. "No, I needed witnesses for our wedding today."

Kiera gasped, her head whirling. *Today*? "Our what?"

Devon flashed an impish grin. "Wedding. I've everything arranged." He sighed. "Although nothing shall change at court until our public ceremony and your coronation. But those shall take months to arrange, and I can't wait that long to marry you." He nuzzled her. "Besides, you may change your mind if we wait."

She pursed her lips. Now that she'd agreed to marry him in truth, she'd never change her mind. "I'm not so fickle. But what if I'd refused you?"

Devon shuddered. "I'd hoped that planning our immediate wedding would convince you if my heartfelt proposal didn't." He swallowed. "And Longnight celebrates new beginnings, hope, and love—what better day to begin our new life together?"

Warmth flooding her, Kiera brushed a kiss against his lips.

Goddess, how she loved him. "Very well, my romantic king. What did you have arranged?"

Devon grinned and returned her kiss. "Mel shall officiate at Hawke and Wren's townhouse this afternoon. Aragon, Hawke, Wren, and Selena shall be our witnesses." He chuckled. "Aragon's parents and Wren's parents are attending too. Aragon said his mother would manage to anyway."

She smiled. That sounded almost perfect. She shook her head. "I want to celebrate Longnight with my orphans. Could we move the ceremony here?" She hesitated then continued, "Would Selena mind if I asked Annalise to be my second witness instead? And I'd like to invite Moonbud as well. Plus, we must invite the Westons since they're celebrating with us."

Devon kissed her nose. "I'm sure Selena would understand you preferring your closest friend at court. I should have realized you'd want to remain here. And invite whomever you wish."

Kiera hummed. How could they manage her final change? "I want Mary and Peter there too, but someone must mind the orphans."

Devon winked. "Two of our guards can manage that. Let's write everyone about the changes. The other two guards can deliver our notes."

She beamed at him. *Now* their wedding ceremony would be perfect. Once they penned their notes, she waved toward the door. "We should rejoin everyone. 'Tis almost time for the Longnight feast."

Devon grasped her hand with a warm smile. "Wait, I've a Longnight gift for you."

Kiera winced and worried her lip. He'd purchased a gift in addition to that heartfelt proposal? "I've nothing for you—perhaps you should save it until next year."

Devon drew her into his arms and kissed her. "Kiera, you've finally agreed to marry me. 'Tis the greatest gift I could have received this Longnight."

She blushed then caressed his face. Goddess, he was wonderful. "You romantic."

Devon released her to extract a package the size of a slim reference book from his satchel. "Desperately in love, more like."

Kiera beamed and accepted his gift then ripped off the festive, white and gold paper. Doubtless she resembled a crazed imp like her orphans had earlier today. Beneath it was a persimmon-wood box carved with intricate shells, pearls, and ocean waves. A perfect gift for an erstwhile mermaid. "Devon, 'tis beautiful."

Devon rumbled, "The true gift is inside. Open it."

Her heart surging, she opened the box, and inside was an ornate, gold dagger and two slim, gold bracelets of different sizes. She glanced at Devon with arched brows.

Devon smiled back. "I had Lady Juliet create our marriage tokens—they're a fourth strand for our protection charms. They'll fuse to the enchantment strand. The dagger is for a bloodbinding, if you're willing."

Kiera gaped at him. But then their life forces would be irrevocably bound, and they could only bear children together. "We can't. What if I'm barren? A king requires heirs. Or what if I die before our children are grown? You'll likely die too."

Devon shrugged. "As I said before, I shan't marry another, so if you can't bear children, I'll have no heirs, regardless. If we appoint a successor before we've children and a regent after, Calatini should be protected."

She hummed then nodded. That sounded reasonable. She peered at the delicate strands. Their names were engraved on the outside. Romantic again. "Shan't the bloodbinding activate our protection charms?"

Devon smiled. "Lady Juliet said not, as long as we remove our protection charms during the bloodbinding and only attach the marriage strands afterward. She even thought they might make her protection charms more powerful." He leaned toward her. "So, Kiera, shall you perform a bloodbinding with me?"

Tingling lightening her chest, Kiera closed the box and kissed him. "I'd like that—as long as we don't have to tell the council."

Devon flashed a wry grin. "I think 'twould be best if we leave that as a secret between us, our witnesses, and Lady Juliet. But none of them shall tell anyone. Our witnesses are our closest family and friends, and the royal witch is accustomed to keeping royal secrets."

She chuckled. True enough. "Shall we rejoin the others now?" Carrying their notes in one hand, she tucked the persimmon-wood box beneath her other arm then nodded at his first-foot gifts. "You should carry those."

Devon scooped up the gifts. "As you wish."

When they slipped inside the dining hall, most of the orphans ignored them because their gifts still engrossed them. But the adults all glanced at them, although the Westons merely smiled then turned back to their granddaughters.

While Devon set the first-foot gifts on a trestle table and took the notes from Kiera, Wren waddled over with Hawke close behind. She grinned at Kiera's betrothal ring and said, "I told you everything would be settled as it should be."

Kiera chuckled. "So you did." As two royal guards left with the notes, Kiera beamed at Mary and Peter, who'd joined them. "Devon and I are marrying at the orphanage this afternoon. The royal guards shall mind the orphans, so you can attend the ceremony."

Mary's squeal when she and Peter hugged Kiera did attract the attention of the Westons and orphans. The orphans soon returned to their gifts, but Lord and Lady Weston exchanged a glance then drifted over.

Once Mary and Peter released Kiera, Mary wiped tears from her eyes then said, "We should eat the Longnight feast while the food is fresh."

Kiera, Mary, Lady Weston, and Cassandra laid out the Longnight feast, while Devon, Hawke, Peter, and Lord Weston gathered the rowdy orphans. Everyone ordered Wren back to her seat when she kept attempting to carry things. Pregnant ladies, especially ones with shadows beneath their eyes, needed to rest.

After a prayer of thanks to the Goddess, the Winter Queen, and the Water King, Kiera and the others enjoyed the finest Longnight feast the orphanage had ever had. The dining hall rang with laughter and chatter, although the orphans groaned whenever the adult couples kissed.

Soon after the Longnight feast was nothing but scraps, Mel, Aragon, Selena, the duke, the duchess, and the Keyes swept in. The small gifts they brought made the orphans rowdy again, despite their stuffed bellies.

Then Kiera gaped when Annalise trudged inside, leaning on Moonbud. Although she'd invited the nightmara queen-heir, a horse-like magical creature inside an orphanage was odd. But even odder was Annalise—like the morning after the former Lady Morwynne's poisoning attempt, her normally radiant friend was as bloodless as a banshee and appeared about to collapse.

Kiera darted over and grasped Annalise's arm. "Are you ill again?"

Annalise managed a tremulous smile. "The shorter days, remember? Don't fret about me—'tis your wedding day."

Kiera sighed but nodded. Hopefully, Annalise was as fine as she claimed. She certainly didn't look it.

Devon strode over and captured Kiera's arm. "Everyone is here. Shall we start the wedding ceremony? I'm eager to make you my wife."

Her heart dancing, she caressed his jaw. No more than she was to make him her husband. But she arched a brow. "You're just worried I'll flee again."

Devon chuckled as he escorted her from the dining hall. "Perhaps."

With Moonbud and the other guests, the orphanage's tiny library was more crowded than the duchess's ballroom during a fete. While everyone managed to find a place, Devon showed her the trick to removing their protection charms. Then the wedding ceremony began.

Smiling into Devon's eyes and her pulse racing, the ceremony flew by for Kiera. Soon they were crowned with bound marriage garlands made of evergreens and spoke their vows, then Mel cut their palms, pressed them to their marriage strands, and bound them together.

Energy surging through her, she beamed at Devon, who grinned back. Although no witch, she could almost sense his life force intertwining with hers. As Mel announced them, she and Devon attached their marriage strands to their protection charms and slid the now four-stranded bracelets back onto their left wrists. Then Devon kissed her, and they and their witnesses signed the matrimony certificate.

Light bubbling in her chest, Kiera threaded her arm through his, and they began back to the dining hall. "Longnight games or carols when we rejoin the orphans?"

Devon grinned then kissed her palm beneath her ring. "A Longnight story, I think. After all, I know the perfect one about a lonely king wooing his true queen."

She smiled and caressed his jaw. After that romantic tale, she'd not be the only one who loved him—the orphanage girls would adore him forever. But the boys... "You'll need to add some sword fights to entertain the boys."

Devon chuckled as they sat at the head trestle table overlooking the orphans. "I'm not tainting our story. I'll tell a second about pirates to appease them."

Kiera drew his head down for another kiss, and groans from the orphans filled the dining hall. Laughing, she and Devon drew apart, and her heart warmed as he leaned toward the orphans and began, "Once upon a time..."

WANT MORE?

Sign up for my newsletter for a bonus epilogue about Kiera's first natalday as queen (which happens to be Devon's too) as well as other exclusive stories and book extras, new book announcements, giveaways, and more.

And order the next book The Secret Soulbond about Annalise and Dare today! Keep reading to learn more about the next book in the Calatini Tales.

LIKE THE NIGHTMARA AFFAIR?

Please consider writing a review. Reviews truly help spread the word about the titles you love.

THE SECRET SOULBOND

*I*n the Regency-inspired kingdom of Calatini, two powerful houses nurse a generations-old feud... while their heirs conceal their secret soulbond.

Lady Annalise Greysnowe is the most beautiful lady in Calatini but conceals her true self behind an ice-perfect mask. Her ambitious parents can't wait to marry her to the king or any wealthy lord that will improve their standing at court. Anyone except the one gentleman she truly desires—Dare, the genial Count of Ravenstone and her family's ancestral enemy.

Despite the feud, Dare only seeks peace with Annalise's family. As a nature witch, he knows that such strife simply harms everyone involved. Plus, he can't forget his intense attraction to Annalise. Something more than her otherworldly beauty calls to him—perhaps it's her love of animals, or her warm and radiant smile whenever she rides her beloved horse, or the hints of potent magic akin to his own.

For Annalise is a rare and coveted soul healer able to heal anything at the risk of forming an irrevocable soulbond. Yet when Dare is nearly killed, she must use her secret powers to heal him, forever binding herself to her family's enemy. Annalise and Dare agree to conceal their soulbond until they can convince her family to end the feud and accept their marriage. But her parents refuse to relent, and their forbidden love activates an ancient curse, so not even their powerful soulbond may be enough to keep them together...

THE SECRET SOULBOND is a Romeo and Juliet romance that sparkles with magic and ends with a heartwarming happily-ever-after. The Calatini Tales will spellbind any reader looking for lush fantasy romance.

*WANT MORE? Order **The Secret Soulbond** today!*

CALATINI TALES

The enchanting Calatini Tales includes...

The Spellbinding Courtship (Book 0.5)
The Enchanted Bird (Book 1)
The Nightmara Affair (Book 2)
The Secret Soulbond (Book 3)
The Goddess's Illusion (Book 4)
The Sun-Nymph Bride (Book 5)
The Beast Curse (Book 6)
The Lethe Elixir (Book 7)

ABOUT KATHERINE

A lifelong creator of her own bedtime stories, **Katherine Dotterer** writes cozy tales of fantasy romance inspired by Regency England. Born and raised in Maryland, she still lives there in an almost cottage surrounded by trees. When not writing, she enjoys reading anything she can find, singing in local choruses, hiking in nearby parks, watching the wildlife outside her windows, and cuddling with her cats. Visit her at Katherine-Dotterer.com to learn about her book releases, read her many book extras, and sign up for her newsletter.